GW00481186

When Good Men Do Nothing

By

Paul Grzegorzek

All that is necessary for evil to triumph is for good men to do nothing

- Edmund Burke

WEDNESDAY

1

GEMMA LOOKED up at the front of the building, nerves twisting her stomach.

For the third time since she got out of the taxi at the bottom of the road she resisted the urge to call her sister and make sure her daughter, Ruthie, was ok.

She was so out of the whole idea of dating. The very thought of dipping into someone else's life and seeing if there was something there that might work for you was uncomfortable.

And leaving her daughter behind to go out on this quest, play this grown up game of sexual attraction felt wrong, on the very edge of discomfort, but then ... an edgy grin tugged at the corners of her mouth.

She'd met David on the beach a few weeks before as she queued to buy Ruthie an ice cream. Out of the blue the handsome man in the queue beside her was striking up a conversation, actually talking, incredibly seeming interested in her and then insisting on paying for the ice cream despite her objections.   She'd been drawn to him immediately, his easy manner and charming smile cutting through the armour that she'd wrapped herself in ever since Ruthie's father had left her.

And then there was the little voice in her mind saying, "isn't this what paedophiles do, pick on some single mother and play on her insecurities and take advantage?" But despite that, despite the insecurities, she and David ended up chatting and laughing while Ruthie ran into the seafront playground and was mucking about happily with some other kids. He'd been so nice, so easy that soon a faint and irrational hope was springing up that maybe, just maybe, she might have met someone who might want her, stretch marks and all.

A few days later they'd run into each other on the street, and then again in the supermarket. This time she hadn't got Ruthie with her, so a coffee had seemed quite safe – and coffee had lasted an hour and ended up with an invitation to dinner. That wasn't so easy because of his work, her

4

need for a baby-sitter. But here she was three weeks later, standing outside his flat on Oriental Place, the sharp tang of the sea carried on the strong wind that whipped her long hair into tangles. She was another her, a Gemma from somewhere in her old past, scared and excited.

She climbed the steps to the communal front door and saw that it wasn't properly shut, the lock damaged.

I'd get that fixed, she thought to herself and then immediately banished the thought. It wasn't like her to make decisions so quickly, particularly not with men. Once bitten, twice shy had been her motto for the last four years. She climbed the stairwell to his flat, noting with approval that despite being shared by several people, the hallway was clean and tidy with freshly painted walls and thick carpets. The owners clearly cared about the building, which would be good if they moved...

She caught herself before she could finish the thought. She hadn't even slept with him yet, although tonight was the night that, well who knew what might happen? She hesitated at the door, one hand raised to knock, saw the time on her wrist watch. She was twenty minutes early, but , well, she was here now. Taking a deep breath, she almost knocked but stopped. Instead, Gemma smoothed her hair and pulled out her compact, checking her makeup in the tiny mirror. Large brown eyes stared back at her from under long lashes and as she smiled to check her teeth a lone dimple popped into view.

"You'll do", she said, tucking the compact away and then knocked on the door – the sound of knuckle on wood hollow, out of kilter with her heart beat.

A few moments later it opened to show a surprised looking David, wearing a white dressing gown with his dark hair still wet and plastered to his skull.

"Uh, hi, you're early!" he looked slightly panicked. "I only just got out of the shower. Come in, please".

He kissed her on the cheek and opened the door to let her into the flat.

"Wow!" She said as he led her along the hallway and into the lounge. His flat was perfect. Not a thing was out of place, and the furnishings were expensive looking. A black leather sofa and armchair sat on a pale carpet, while a glass and chrome dining table and chairs filled the area in front of the bay window. The walls were adorned with pictures of boats, a passion of David's as well as being his living.

"This is amazing," she said with a smile.

David looked down at the floor. Suddenly Gemma realised that he was as nervous as she was. "Thanks. I think of this as my haven against the madness of the world, you know..."

They stood there for a moment smiling at each other, then David shivered suddenly.

"I, uh, I need to get dry and change my clothes, have a seat".

Gemma moved towards the sofa but then the nerves caught up with her.

"Can I use your bathroom?" she asked.

"Of course, it's through here". He led her to a small but expensive looking bathroom and grabbed a towel before leaving her alone. She looked around with a smile, thinking about the contrast between this place and home, which was really her sister Lucy's house which she and Ruthie had been sharing for the last couple of years.

Not that she was ungrateful. It was so much better than being alone, but Lucy's house was getting on a bit and none of them had the money to get the necessary repairs done.

Gemma was about to head back out into the lounge when she heard a knock at the front door, loud and insistent. Curious to see who it was, she opened the door a crack but didn't go out, not wanting to announce her presence until she knew that David wouldn't mind.

She caught a glimpse of him hurrying out of the bedroom, still in his dressing gown with a frown on his face.

She waited impatiently as he opened the door, then cocked her head to one side as she heard a strange sound, followed quickly by another. It sounded like someone letting a tiny bit of air out of a balloon very quickly, and she was about to step out and investigate when David stumbled back into the lounge, the front of his white dressing gown now dark red.

She stood rooted to the spot, eyes wide as she saw her boyfriend fall backwards through his bedroom door and disappear from view. A tiny voice in her head was telling her she should run, or hide or lock the bathroom door and cower in the darkness, but instead she just stood there watching the nightmare unfold in front of her.

A few moments later a tall figure in a balaclava came into view from the hallway, a long pistol clenched in one fist as he followed David into the bedroom.

The rest of her brain finally caught up with the voice and suddenly her legs were her own again as she realised what was happening. Someone had shot David. Someone who was even now in the flat and would most likely kill her too if he knew she was here.

Before she could move the whispering sound came again, this time from the bedroom. Tears filled her eyes and blurred out the world, but she wiped them away as clarity struck.

Whatever the reason this man was here, whatever he'd done to David, if she didn't get out now then Ruthie would have to grow up without a mother.

The thought was so powerful that before she knew what she was doing Gemma was halfway across the lounge to the hallway and gaining speed rapidly, intent on nothing but getting out.

Blood marred the pale carpet just inside the door and Gemma stumbled as she saw it, letting out an involuntary sob.

She reached the half open door and threw it open, but rough hands grabbed her from behind, one wrapping around her middle while the other snaked over her shoulder and clamped itself firmly around her throat.

"Please," she whispered hoarsely, too scared to even scream, "I have a daughter".

Whatever reply her attacker might have made, the encroaching darkness blotted it out as the hand tightened around her throat and she slipped away into oblivion.

THURSDAY

RAIN SWEPT across the street and hammered the windscreen of the car as I forced the door open against the wind, soaking myself to the skin in seconds. Looking down the street I saw the tips of the waves being whipped into a frenzy by the storm and wondered when August had become such a miserable month.

Hunching my shoulders against the downpour I ran across the road to the door of an unassuming block of flats and flashed my badge at the miserable looking officer guarding the portal.

'Morning Sarge,' he said, rain dripping off the front of his helmet in a steady trickle that disappeared inside the front of his collar.

'Morning. Anyone else here yet?'

'Senior SOCO is upstairs with the DCI.'

I nodded and hurried inside, pausing in the hallway to shake the worst of the rain from my jacket, wanting to make a good impression. I hadn't met the new Detective Chief Inspector yet – he'd just transferred from North Downs Division – but rumour had it he was a stickler for both punctuality and neatness. A real old-school copper.

The flat I was looking for was on the third floor of the old Victorian mansion, converted into flats, like so many Brighton properties nowadays. Another officer, this one rather drier than his colleague downstairs, insisted on seeing my warrant card despite the fact that he knew me.

'Can't be too careful Sarge,' he said with an apologetic smile.

'I take it the DCI is inside?'

'Yes Sarge, he's been in there for about ten minutes. Keeps looking at his watch and muttering your name.'

'I...' I stopped as I caught the grin. 'Ha bloody ha. Go swap with your colleague downstairs, he's soaked through.'

The grin held for a moment, then slid off his face as he realised I wasn't joking. Muttering under his breath he clomped down the stairs.

Once he was gone I strapped on a pair of paper boots from the pile just inside the door, no doubt left there by SOCO. Taking a deep breath I put my game face on and went to see what the reaper had left for me.

WALKING INTO the flat, two things immediately struck me. The first was that there was no damage to the door. The second was the smell. Almost every murder I've ever been to has the same smell: blood, faeces and something beginning to rot.

The flat was well decorated, light and airy, with matching furniture throughout. The walls were pale cream with oil paintings spaced at regular intervals, mostly of boats and ships – ranging from speedboats to tea-cutters. Apart from the blood trail leading from the door into the lounge, the carpet matched the colour of the walls.

Treading along the edges to avoid planting my size tens in the evidence, I eased my way into the next room. Two men stood there, both in their fifties with dark hair, but there the resemblance ended.

Derek Clinton, the senior SOCO, was a tubby, cheerful man with a shock of dark hair that was currently plastered to his head, thanks to the rain outside. His permanently red face broke into a grin when he saw me and he waved me over.

'Ah, Rob! I wondered when you'd get here. Have you met DCI Burke yet?'

'No, I haven't had the pleasure.'

Burke was a cadaverous looking man who stood a good three inches taller than my own six feet, his thinning hair combed severely over a well-developed bald patch. Everything about him shouted precision, from his perfectly tied Windsor knot to his expertly creased trousers.

I held out my hand for him to shake - which he did with a rigid smile.

'DCI Burke. And you are?'

'DS Rob Steele.'

'Ah yes, the firearms man. Well as you can see there's not a lot to go on yet.'

He gestured at the large bloody stain on the carpet which led into another room on the far side of the lounge.

'He's in there I take it?'

Burke nodded. 'Nothing's been touched. I've been told that you prefer it that way so that you can do your 'thing'.'

My 'thing', as he called it, is Firearms Positioning Forensics, or in layman's terms being able to tell things like the height and position of the shooter in a murder. It can be done painstakingly by using measuring devices and pieces of string, but I'm lucky enough to have a knack for it and I can do it pretty accurately by eye alone.

Pulling on a pair of gloves, I left the two men and pushed the door open, following the blood trail into a bedroom that reeked of bachelordom. The walls were painted a dark red, with the double bed decked out in black silk. I felt like I'd just walked into an Old Spice commercial.

Lying face down on the bed was the body of a man, his dressing gown soaked in blood. The smell was worse in here, strong enough to make me want to gag as I walked carefully across the room to where the victim lay. It didn't take a genius to work out that the bullet hole in the back of his head had been the one that had finished him off, but I peered closely at it just the same, noting the fine circle of powder burns surrounding the wound.

Looking around, I studied the bloodstains on the floor and wished that I could roll the body over to take a look at the front of his chest. Unfortunately that would have to wait until the poor bastard had been photographed and his final resting place marked out.

I followed the blood trail back out into the lounge, ignoring the enquiring looks the two men gave me as I passed them, nose almost to the carpet as I studied the stains carefully.

A final look at the hallway confirmed my suspicions and I finally turned back to the Burke and Clinton.

'Well?' Burke asked, 'what do you think?'

I shrugged. 'Professional hit sir. Looks like the victim answered the door to the killer. Without checking the front of the body I'd guess it was two rounds in the chest as soon as the door opened, neither of them fatal. The victim managed to get to the lounge and then into the bedroom, probably trying to reach the phone next to the bed, then the killer came in and put a round in the back of his head.'

Clinton nodded as if he'd reached the same conclusion but the DCI frowned.

'Surely someone would have heard the shots?'

I shook my head. 'No sir. Powder burns around the wound on the back of the head are light and in a very tight circle. The killer used a silencer.'

Burke stroked his chin thoughtfully. 'Are you sure?'

'About the silencer? Absolutely. The rest of it is conjecture, but I'll bet you any money you like the killer was a pro.'

Burke looked at me for a few moments more without speaking, then seemed to come to a decision.

'How do you feel about running things on the ground for me?'

I looked at him in surprise. 'Sir? Shouldn't this have a Detective Inspector on it at the very least?'

'Normally yes, but everyone I talk to assures me that where firearms are concerned you're the man to have. Not only that but I'll be assuming personal command. Having an Inspector in the middle will just slow things down, and if I do need one I've got someone from Special Branch waiting in the wings. Pick your two best detectives and bring them on-board; this takes priority over anything else you're working on.'

'But I've got cases that I can't just drop.'

'Not anymore you don't. I'll reassign them to another DS. I need you on this.'

'Can I ask why sir?'

'Not here, I'll tell you back at the Nick. Meet me in your office in half an hour.'

Without waiting for my acknowledgement he walked out, leaving me standing alone with the feeling that my day was about to get a whole lot worse.

4

JOHN STREET police station is like a bad advert for seventies architecture. It's made of brown and white interlocking facia that aged the second it was built - and the inside isn't much better.

I took the stairs two at a time, too preoccupied to do more than nod at people I passed. I was worried by what Burke had said back at the flat and was eager to get the bad news over and done with.

The office was buzzing with the usual morning activity, detectives sharing gossip and gripes over the faded brown dividers that kept their desks separate. Ignoring them all, I threaded my way through to my cramped office at the back of the room and sat in front of the computer.

I'd barely had time to open my emails when a shadow loomed over my desk and I looked up to see the grim face of my Detective Inspector, Hugh Wadey.

Rumour had it that Wadey had gone to a very exclusive Swiss clinic to have his sense of humour removed, and I can tell you now that the operation had been a complete success. I'd never met a more uninteresting or job-pissed officer and, after two years working with him, just seeing his narrow face was enough to put me on edge.

'Morning boss,' I said, pushing myself back from the desk and dredging up an expression of rapt attention.

'I hear you've met DCI Burke. Not happy that he's put you on this shooting, not happy at all. Your team have got more jobs than the other two sergeants put together and now we're going to be light two detectives as well. Don't think that just because you're working a murder that I'll give your jobs to the other sergeants. You'll be making sure that the rest of your team takes up the slack. Clear?'

'Maybe you should take that up with the DCI, sir. I was going to take Nat and Karl, if that's all right with you?'

Nat Statham and Karl Bentley were the best detectives in my team of five. They both had years of CID and intelligence experience and were easily better on their own than the other three detectives put together. Karl because he could talk his way through red tape better than a legion of solicitors and Nat because she had a memory that bordered on eidetic. But they were also sticklers for detail - and bloody hard workers to boot.

Wadey shook his head vigorously, adding to the patina of dandruff that already dotted his blue suit jacket.

'No, I need them here. Take any two of the others.'

'But the DCI said...'

'He doesn't run things around here, I do. And I say...'

I just managed to repress a grin as DCI Burke appeared behind Wadey with a look that told me he'd overheard the whole conversation.

'Actually, I think you'll find that I *do* run things around here, and you'll give the DS whatever and whoever he wants.'

Wadey's face went ashen, and he span to face the DCI.

'Uh, yes sir. I was just expressing my opinion about, uh, DS Steele's lack of work ethic.'

That was typical of Wadey. Not that he was trying to put me down in front of the DCI – that I expected – but that even after two years he still couldn't call me Rob.

Burke moved past Wadey and stared out of the small window behind me.

'If that's all, Inspector?'

Wadey was many things, but stupid wasn't one of them. Knowing that he'd been outmanoeuvred, he nodded stiffly and stalked back to his own office.

'Thanks for that Sir. I thought I was going to have a bit of trouble there.'

'Don't worry about it. I've known Hugh since he was a probationer and he was always a jobsworth.'

He turned to face me. 'I suppose you want to know why this job is so important?'

I nodded. 'Yes sir.'

He stood at parade rest as he spoke, instinctively making me sit up straighter.

'The man we found this morning is David Taverner. Other than that, we know almost nothing about him – except that he's of interest to MI6.'

It took a few moments for the information to sink in and me to respond. 'Is it normal procedure to let the police know?'

'I guess not, but they obviously want to find out who killed Taverner and why.'

I sat back in my chair as I tried to understand the implications. 'So we're looking at an espionage job then? Surely that would mean they investigate?'

'Normally yes, but, for whatever reason, they want this to be investigated like any other murder so they're happy for it to remain with us for now. The moment that changes they'll take on the investigation and shut us out. The only difference is that they're keeping it clear of the press. No big briefings, no operation names, no serials written about it. Nothing.'

'So we'll have to send them regular updates I suppose. I'd better let Nat and Karl know they're on this now.'

'Yes, do. And I'm having you reassigned to new offices for the duration too. I don't want Hugh poking his nose in every five minutes. This job is 'need to know' only, so I expect the three of you to exercise absolute discretion.'

'Of course sir. Anything else?'

'Just one thing - but you're not going to like it.'

'Surprise me.'

He cranked out his rigid smile again. 'You won't need to be updating MI6, they're sending someone down to assist with the investigation. You know, open any doors that might usually remain closed for us, that sort of thing.'

'And he's going to be working out of your office?' I asked hopefully.

'No, he'll be on the ground with you. He's been briefed that the investigation is yours until such time as it falls within their remit or we get a suspect.' He checked his watch and frowned. 'As soon as we find you some suitable offices I'll let you know. Until then get your team up to speed and do what you do best.'

'Sir.'

He nodded once and strode out, and for the second time that day his departure left me with a sinking feeling.

5

OUR NEW office turned out to be an airless, windowless room in the basement at John Street. It was in the old cells, which had been ripped out and refurbished a few years before at vast expense, then used for nothing but storage. The room consisted of three desks, each with its own computer and phone, and a small evidence fridge in one corner. The place was filled with the sharp chemical smell of paint and new carpet and you could probably have swung a cat but only if it was wearing a crash helmet. As far as workplaces went it, was singularly uninspiring - but at least it was several floors away from Wadey.

I started dragging desks around to make myself a spot in the corner where I could overlook the rest of the room. The door opened and Nat came in, her shoulder-length blonde hair flying free of its usual ponytail. She was wearing a dark trouser suit over a black top that showed off her curves and height, and she had a boundless energy that made lazy officers scurry for cover when they saw her coming.

'You want me boss?' she asked, pausing in the doorway.

'Always.'

'You wish! What's up?'

'I need to brief you and Karl. You're both with me on the shooting that came in this morning and I need to get you up to speed. Can you grab him and meet me back down here?'

She nodded and left, returning a few minutes later holding a large box and with Karl in tow. He was a slight, pale man with shaved brown hair and he looked around the office with poorly-concealed dislike.

'Don't tell me we're gonna be working in this shithole?' he asked, his Glasgow accent rolling the *R*'s to within an inch of their life.

'Okay, I won't. I *do*, however, need to brief the two of you, so close the door and sit down.'

They sat and I filled them in on everything I knew. Even stretching it as far as I could, we had precious little.

'Questions?' I asked when I'd finished.

Karl nodded. 'Yeah. Doesn't it smell a bit fishy to you?'

'The room or the job?'

'The job. MI6 have an interest in this guy, then he gets shot in what's clearly a professional job and they want us to investigate it. And the press have been frozen out too. It stinks.'

I sighed. I'd been thinking the same thing myself but as the DCI had put us on the case, I couldn't exactly refuse and throw it back to MI6.

'Maybe so, but we treat it like any other murder. There should already be PCSOs doing house to house nearby, probably describing it as a break-in. SOCO were gearing up when I left the scene. What we need to do is look into Taverner's private life and see what we can dig up. Nat, you get family. Get me everything back to his grandparents and second cousins twice removed. If any of them are into anything dodgy I want to know about it.'

She nodded and turned to her desk, opening the box she'd brought in and pulling out a massive pile of paperwork.

'Karl, I want you on work, friends and neighbours. Find out who he works for, who he has back to the flat, anything that helps us put together a picture of who he is.'

The small man threw a mocking salute and turned to his own computer, leaving me to write up what we had so far.

The phone on my desk rang and I managed to cover my start of surprise by coughing into my hand before I answered it. Someone, somewhere must have already transferred the number to this phone, which was far more organised than the usual Sussex policy of 'I'll get around to it at some point'.

'DS Steele.'

'Rob, it's Mandy from the front office. There's a man here from London, says you're expecting him.'

'Thanks. Can you show him into an interview room? I'll be right up.'

'The man from London' turned out to be six feet of well tanned gym muscle in a suit that would have cost me a month's wages. He had brown hair just a shade darker than my own, but where mine was only kept in check with half a ton of gel, his was neatly shaved on the sides and slightly longer on top.

As our eyes met, he gave a warm smile and held out a hand.

I shook it and noted the extra squeeze he gave.

'Hi, I'm...' I began, but he interrupted with an accent that was pure Old Etonian.

'DS Rob Steele. Thirty-four-years-old, eight years in the police, covering response in Brighton, then firearms, then CID. Before that you spent four years in the Princess of Wales' Royal Regiment, coming out with the rank of Sergeant.'

'You forgot my shoe size.'

The man glanced down at my feet. 'Nine. I'm Harvey Merrington, and I assume you know where I've come from.'

I nodded. 'Close, I'm a ten. Can I see some ID please?'

He nodded in return and reached inside his jacket, coming out with a slim black wallet that opened to show an ID card with a silver crown and crossed swords embossed opposite his picture.

I handed it back and showed him down to the new office, introducing him to Karl and Nat. He nodded curtly at them both and then took a chair at the desk furthest from the door.

'Karl, Natalie, a pleasure to meet you both.' he said as he sat.

Nat's head whipped round so fast I thought her neck would break.

'My name is Nat', she said in a level tone, her eyes glinting dangerously, 'and if you ever call me Natalie again you'll regret it.'

Merrington held his hands up in surrender, clearly shocked by the vehemence in her tone. I knew from experience that she hated anyone using her full name and I looked around the office while she cooled down in the uncomfortable silence.

In the few minutes I'd been gone, Nat had personalised the wall behind her desk and it was now covered in post-it notes and mugshots of local criminals, with rap sheets and dates of birth underneath. It was a treasure trove of local information that Nat would be able to regurgitate at need, wherever she was. Her incredible memory would retain all the information haphazardly plastered in front of her desk and more than once I'd used her as a walking, talking intelligence folder to identify bad guys on the street. I raised an eyebrow but said nothing at her impromptu redecoration as Merrington finally broke the awkward silence.

'What have you got so far?'

I shrugged. 'We've been on it for about half an hour so we've not exactly solved it yet. I was just going to put a call in to the major crime branch and get a HOLMES analyst put on the staff.'

Merrington shook his head. 'I'm sorry, but we can't afford for anyone else to have access to information on Taverner, particularly not one of your analysts. We need to keep this as low key as possible so we'll just have to do this the old-fashioned way, I'm afraid.'

I looked at him in disbelief. 'So you want us to solve a murder without using the computer system that's specifically been developed to help solve murders? Hold on while I get my deerstalker and pipe, this could be a long one.'

25

Merrington raised his hands. 'I don't make the rules, I just work to them. We had an MI6 agent killed in London last month and it's been decided that any publicity on this one would be very bad for us, so we're investigating under the radar. What can you tell me?'

I sighed and shrugged again. 'Not much. Three shots, all close range from a silenced pistol. No idea who the killer was, but it looks like a professional job.'

'Okay, what's happening on the ground?'

'SOCO are in the flat as we speak and we've got people out doing house-to-house enquiries. Next step is to see if there's any private CCTV in the area. Fancy coming for a drive?'

I wanted him with me like a hole in the head but I could tell from the looks the other two were giving him that if I left Merrington here there'd be blood on the walls by the time I got back. Like them, I felt as if he was peering over my shoulder despite the fact that he'd been nothing but pleasant so far. This was our patch and our investigation, and I just hoped that he'd prove a blessing rather than a curse.

He smiled. 'Sure, why not. I don't really know Brighton, so it'll be good to see what I'm up against.'

As we left the office Nat raised her eyebrows at me and I shrugged back. It was clear that she was as curious as I was to know what MI6's interest was in this case, and I hoped that a drive with Merrington might give me the answers I needed.

6

THE MAN glanced about in the early morning light, making sure that no one was watching him as he crossed the marina and headed towards a boat that was moored on its own at the end of the quay.

He'd made a special effort to blend in, browsing charity shops until he'd found the exact items he was looking for.

Now, wearing a battered but serviceable rainproof jacket and baggy trousers, he was indistinguishable from any of the early morning fishermen casting their lines for mackerel off the marina wall. The look was completed by a black woollen hat that he'd tugged down over his head almost as far as the top of the collar he'd flicked up. The last thing he wanted was local CCTV picking his face up once things started rolling. That would be very bad for business.

Shifting his rod bag and rucksack to a more comfortable position on his shoulder he nodded at another angler already returning from the wall.

'Too choppy,' the angler grunted as he passed, then disappeared into the rain without waiting for a reply.

Grinning to himself, he turned away from the marina wall and moved towards the boat, confident that even if someone somehow saw him through the pouring rain they would think he was going out on to the open sea to fish.

With a final glance around he clambered on to the deck and through the hatchway, sliding open the door with an ease borne of familiarity.

Once inside he pulled the hatch closed and turned on his torch. Holding it between his teeth, he gingerly placed his rucksack down, undid the zip and pulled out a lunchbox sized device.

Moving slowly and dextrously, he lifted one of the benches that lined the narrow hull and placed the device inside. Once it was secure, he removed its lid and played the beam of his torch over the items within.

It was a fine job – even if he said so himself. Four blocks of C4 explosive shaped to burn through the hull and sink the boat with a minimum of fuss – if you didn't count a thirty foot high fireball as fuss.

Wiggling his fingers to get the blood flowing, he slid his hand into the device and connected two of the wires to the batteries.

A green light began to blink slowly as he pulled out a pair of clippers and removed several pieces of coloured cotton, making sure to pick up each piece.

As a final touch, he crossed to another bench and lifted it, pulling out the two gas canisters he knew would be clipped there.

Huffing as he carried them the short distance he placed them next to the device, replacing the lid and scanning the bench for any sign of his brief occupancy. He was counting on the theory that someone would see the flare as the gas went up and that the police would accept the simplest explanation when they inevitably, but reluctantly, investigated.

That was one thing about the police in this country, he mused, as he made his way back out of the cabin. They almost always took the simplest answer as the right one, and the path of least resistance was the path of least paperwork.

Casting a final look around, he smiled to himself and began to sing quietly under his breath as he disappeared into the rain, already confident of a job well done.

7

'I DON'T suppose you want to tell me why you have an interest in Taverner?' I asked as we cruised slowly along Oriental Place, my attention torn between what little of the road I could see through the rain and the nearby walls as I searched for cameras. I threw a wave at the soaked officers huddling miserably by the door of Taverner's building, noting that there were several scenes of crime vans parked half on the pavement.

'Operational security, sorry. I know it's difficult, but there are things that I'm not authorised to talk about until such time as you find them out through your investigation.'

I stopped the car in the middle of the road and looked at him in astonishment.

'Run that by me again?'

He smiled apologetically.

'Robert, we need you to know as little as possible about this man's life. The more you know, the more chance there is of operational security being breached. I promise you that nothing relevant will be withheld, except where it breaches...'

'Operational security. I get it. I thought we were supposed to be working together on this? What's the point of us sharing with you if you can't share back. And it's Rob.'

A car behind me beeped and I pulled away with a wave in the mirror, trying not to get wound up by the fact that Merrington knew far more than he was letting on.

'Okay, Rob. Look at it this way. We're interested in Taverner for a reason I can't share. Whoever killed him could have done it for any number of reasons, including the reason that we're interested in him. If we start running around and investigating and it turns out not to be connected to us, then we blow the whole thing. You, however, would be expected to investigate a murder on your patch so, no matter the reason, you nosing around won't be out of place. If I tell you something that you wouldn't be able to find out through your investigation and you act on it, then you could alert the wrong people and again the whole thing is blown. I'm not deliberately being an arse; I'm just trying to keep this investigation as genuine as possible.'

He sounded sincere and what he was saying made sense, but I disliked being kept in the dark about anything and it was a battle to keep my annoyance in check.

'Okay, fine. You're beginning to make sense now. What can you tell me about Taverner?'

'He gambled, he drank a lot and he womanised. That much you could probably tell from his flat.'

'You've been there?'

He nodded. 'Before I came to the police station. I wanted to see the scene first-hand.'

'Anything else?'

Before he could answer my mobile rang and I fished it out of my pocket as I pulled over.

'Steele.'

'It's Karl, you free to speak?'

'Yeah, go ahead.'

'I've found something. Revenue and Customs have him listed as working at the marina, at a speedboat hire place called Distant Vistas. You want me to go check it out?'

I felt a surge of excitement out of proportion to the mundane news. But, since my promotion, I'd forgotten how much I missed actually investigating crimes.

'No, we're already out so we'll go. Keep going, that's bloody good work, mate.' I rang off.

'Getting somewhere?' Merrington asked.

'You could say that. We found out where he works. Well, worked. Unless they want to use him for bait I'd guess he's out of a job.'

'How did you find it?'

'Revenue and Customs. It normally takes a week or so to get anything from them, even if it's urgent. Fortunately for us Karl has the gift of the gab.'

'Even we have trouble with HMRC. I'm impressed.'

I shot him a look. 'Us county mounties can occasionally get things done you know. We do this for a living.'

He held his hands up in mock surrender. 'That's not what I meant, I'm just genuinely impressed. If this were the Met, we'd still be choosing the doughnuts and deciding who was in charge.'

'We don't have the budget for doughnuts anymore.'

Merrington laughed.

'So tell me about this Firearms Positioning Forensics that you're an expert in.'

'It's not terribly exciting. Have you heard of blood splatter analysis?'

He nodded. 'I think so. Isn't that where you can tell what happened at a scene by the way the blood has hit the walls and so forth?'

'That's the one. FPF came out of that originally. A Canadian named Alan MacArthur came up with the idea that if you could read what happened from blood patterns, then surely you could do more by looking at wounds themselves, as well as working out height, distance, weapon type etcetera without having to do it all in a lab.'

'And it works?'

I nodded. 'It does indeed. There are different schools as well, all descended from blood pattern analysis. The only one that's taken off over here though is FPF. Odd when you consider how little gun crime we get compared to knife crime.'

'So what made you do the course?'

'Believe it or not, I did a distance learning Forensics Degree when I was in the army.'

'Must have been bloody long distance.'

'It was. I knew that I wanted to join the police when I came out, so I thought it might help. It didn't at first, but when I got into CID, suddenly I was closing more cases than anyone else based on knowing exactly what to look for forensically. Couple that with being a bit of a gun-geek and voilà, you have the perfect candidate for FPF.'

'Gun geek?'

'Yeah. When I was in the infantry I had a particular knack for tracing incoming fire. Always knew where it was coming from by the rounds that landed near us and the angle of the holes. Didn't think it was anything special until someone pointed it out. The more I practised it, the better I got and then my Captain gave me the nudge about the Forensics degree and I gave it a go.'

'Do you get many jobs?'

'Not down here, no, but as there are only eight of us in the country with the training, we get borrowed fairly regularly by other forces. It's normally a bit of a jolly if you don't mind looking at gunshot wounds.'

'A jolly?'

'Yeah, out of force overtime. I've been loaned out to nineteen of the forty three police forces so far. Best bit is you get paid twenty four hours a day outside of your home force.'

'But surely you don't do it for the money?'

I suddenly felt like I was having a job interview, but I was too pleased to have someone actually interested in FPF to care.

'No, I do it because I love it. I feel like I can walk into a scene and relive what happened. Not always, mind, but enough that it's helped to get some pretty good collars.'

I turned left on to the King's Road, wind buffeting the car as rain lashed down and turned the world into a formless gray vista that sped past outside the window.

Merrington seemed satisfied with my answers, and we drove the rest of the way in comfortable silence. A few minutes later I pulled into the marina, heading past the pubs and shops towards the residential area and on through to the quays, where I parked.

Leaving the car with the logbook in the window to prevent getting a ticket, we hurried through the rain towards the office complex where 'Distant Vistas' was displayed on a grubby plastic sign along with half a dozen other names.

Exchanging a glance, Merrington and I hurried in and stood dripping in a drab hallway with two doors in front of us and a set of stairs off to the right.

The door on the left was marked up as an estate agent, a few tattered brochures sitting forlornly in a plastic holder outside. The door on the right, however, had the sign we were looking for in purple and gold. I stepped forward and rapped on the door with a knuckle, stepping back again quickly as the door swung open to reveal a scene of utter devastation.

The office had been turned over, and not by someone looking to be discreet. The two filing cabinets had been tipped over and the drawers pulled out – spilling their contents across the floor. The desk at the far end of the room had been overturned. A computer tower sat on the floor nearby, the case torn open to reveal its guts. It looked like the hard drive was missing but. as I moved inside to get a closer look, something else made me pause.

Sticking out from behind the desk was a man's head, covered in blood, eyes staring accusingly at me as if I'd disturbed him in the middle of something. Two small holes in his forehead told me not to bother checking for a pulse.

Motioning for Merrington to stay where he was I pulled out my radio.

'Comms from CP291.' My voice shook slightly. Despite having seen dozens of dead bodies, I'd never before stumbled into a murder scene and suddenly I felt like my nice simple murder was spiralling out of control.

'291 go ahead,' came the prompt reply.

I drew a breath to speak but Merrington stepped forward and put his hand on my arm, shaking his head.

'Rob, we can't put this out over the radio. Phone your DCI by all means, but we have to keep this under wraps until we find out what was taken. I don't want anyone getting wind of this.'

I sized him up for a long moment, my copper's instinct warring with his orders to be discreet. Orders eventually won.

'291, stand down.'

'Roger.'

I tucked the radio back into its holder. 'Okay, we do it your way, but on one condition.'

'What's that?'

'You cut the bullshit and tell me exactly what's going on.'

8

BILLY COLLINS looked around nervously, one hand twiddling with his greasy blond hair while the other rested on the handle of the knife hidden inside his jacket. He didn't like meeting people in public, particularly not for jobs like this, but this time he didn't have a choice.

The man he was meeting was only reliable in one regard; as long as you were paying him, he'd do what you wanted. But you'd better make damn sure that you didn't let him know anything you didn't want the rest of the city to know in minutes.

Looking out from the underground car park tucked away at the bottom of Little Preston Street, Billy knew there were far more public places they could have met, but it still didn't mean he had to like it.

A car drove past and Billy did his best to look casual, leaning against the wall and lighting a fag before returning a hand to the knife, just in case.

The driver ignored him, too intent on arguing with the man in the passenger seat, and Billy relaxed slightly. This whole business was making him jumpy and he laughed at himself for being so nervous, but all the while his eyes were scanning the street, waiting for London Dave to turn up.

A few minutes later he was rewarded by the sight of his contact, a grubby looking man in his mid thirties with a week-long beard, a thatch of dirty salt and pepper hair and a nervous tic that made him nod in time with his walk. He was wearing a shabby blue jacket with more holes than fabric and something bulky hidden under it.

Waving him over, Billy retreated into the darkness of the car park and waited impatiently while Dave nodded his way across the road, head slightly twisted to one side as he checked for traffic.

'Got what you need,' Dave said without preamble, 'you got my money?'

Billy looked around one last time to make sure that no one was watching.

''Course I have. Need to see the goods first though.'

Dave shrugged and pulled a bulging carrier bag out from inside his jacket, passing it to Billy.

Pulling it open, Billy checked the contents carefully.

'This phone work?' he asked Dave in return.

'And this uniform is proper?'

'Yeah, nicked it from where one of the security guards lives. It was hanging out on the line in the back garden so I swiped it. Told you you'd come to the right man.'

Despite his shambling appearance, London Dave was one of the best burglars in Brighton. Getting into a back garden and stealing clothes would have been child's play for him.

'Sure. I'll believe that when it works. Told you I needed a pass as well.'

Giving Billy a sly look, Dave reached under his jacket and produced a plastic pass with a magnetic strip.

'Went to a lot of trouble to get this, it's gonna cost you extra.'

Billy's hand whipped out of his coat, knife glinting as it sped across the gap between the two men to rest against Dave's throat.

'Don't be taking the piss Dave. We agreed on five hundred, and five hundred's what you'll get.' He pressed the knife into the other man's neck and a thin line of crimson appeared.

'Okay, okay! Can't blame a man for trying, can you?' Dave wheedled, eyes almost crossing as he tried to look at the blade without moving his head.

'I'm not blaming yer, just saying is all.'

'Fine, here's the pass.' He handed it over and Billy stepped back, the knife vanishing as quickly as it had appeared.

Holding one hand under his nose to ward against Dave's sour smell, Billy handed over a bundle of notes which went straight into the burglar's waistband.

'Thanks Billy, you're a sport.'

'Whatever. You say anything to anyone and I'll cut your tongue out, right?'

London Dave nodded and shambled off faster than Billy would have thought possible, twisting around to look back every few feet.

Waiting until he was out of sight, Billy hefted the bag and crossed the road to his car, hiding the uniform and the pass under his seat. It wouldn't help much if he got stopped, but he was confident that he could make it back to his boss without anyone being any the wiser, and then they'd be a huge step closer to finalising the plan.

9

IT TURNED out that Merrington was right – at least as far as the DCI was concerned. Burke was the third person on scene after a response car and he immediately took us aside for a full briefing of what we'd found, while the two uniformed officers guarded the door to the office.

'Well?' he asked impatiently. 'Any ideas why my city is turning into something out of a bloody nightmare?'

I pointed at Merrington. 'Maybe you should ask him sir. I just work out how they got killed.'

'And?'

'He was shot sir.'

'And I'm sure it took all of your considerable experience to work that out. Have you done your 'thing' yet?'

'No sir. Not until SOCO clear it. The last thing I want is Derek Clinton upset with me.'

'You should worry less about him and more about me. Get in there and see what you can find out.'

It didn't take a genius to figure out that he was annoyed, although i suspected it had more to do with two bodies turning up the same day and far less to do with me not having entered the room and poked around.

Leaving Merrington with Burke, I stepped between the uniforms and closed the door carefully behind me, not wanting to be disturbed as I surveyed the room.

Moving carefully across the paper-littered floor I crouched by the body, trying hard not to look at the expression of surprise on his face.

For a moment I wondered what the last thing to go through his mind as he died was, then shuddered as I realised that it was a piece of lead. One minute, walking, talking and breathing, the next lying on the floor with two holes too many in your face. Not a nice way to go.

Unlike the first murder, this man had been shot twice in the head, the wounds so close together that they formed a figure 8 – one hole overlapping the other.

From the size of the wounds, the pistol used was a 9mm. Probably silenced, as the rounds hadn't had enough force to exit the skull. Either that or the shooter was standing by the door when he fired, but that was unlikely unless the man was an Olympic pistol pro.

Rooting through my pocket, I came up with a tape measure and pinned it into the floor next to the dead man's feet. I then stretched it out to his full five feet and nine inches, muttering to myself while I did calculations in my head.

I didn't usually bother with tapes and string and all the extraneous gubbins that surrounds my trade but, as this killing was undoubtedly linked to Taverner's, I wanted to make sure that I had everything covered.

Moving over to the upturned desk I measured that as well, then the height of each chair from floor to the seat. Frowning, I did the sums in my head as I stood in the centre of the room and raised my fingers like a pistol, pointing them at where the desk would have been.

Without turning the place upside down I would never find casings from the fired weapon but I was fairly certain that I had all I needed for Burke.

I left the room to find both Burke and Merrington waiting patiently.

The DCI raised his eyebrows. 'Well?'

'It looks as though both killer and victim were sitting down on either side of the desk. The shots entered at a slight upward angle, showing that the shooter's hand was slightly below the target area. There are no detectable powder burns around the wounds but also no exit wounds, so I believe that it was done from at least two feet away with a silenced 9mm pistol. Two shots between the eyes and none in the torso, which further leads me to believe that they were sitting down. Torso would have been a trickier shot, especially if the target had his arms folded.'

Merrington raised a hand.

'We're not in school, Merrington.' Burke said, exasperatedly.

'What makes you think they were arguing?'

'Well the biggest clue is that one of them is dead' I replied.

He shook his head.

'No, I mean how do you know it was an argument rather than a planned hit?'

'He was shot twice between the eyes. How many people do you know that will go for two headshots rather than putting at least one in the body first? And if it was supposed to be a hit, why not take him at the door or on the way back to the desk after the door was answered? No, I think it was an argument. And, I think that the bullets we find in him will match the ones in Taverner. Seems a little too coincidental to be otherwise.'

Burke nodded thoughtfully. 'And we're still no closer to having a motive?'

'Nothing's come up yet sir, but it's still early.'

'Well, keep me updated. The moment anything comes to light I want to know about it. I need to go and explain to the Chief Superintendent why bodies are beginning to pile up in his City.'

I nodded as he left, passing Derek Clinton, the senior SOCO, who was on his way in.

'You don't give a man much time, do you?' he said, without preamble. 'Do you have any idea how stretched we are at the moment? I'm struggling to cover one murder scene, let alone two!'

'Sorry Derek. I'll send an email to all the bad guys and ask them to lay off for a few days, shall I?'

'If you would. I've left my entire team at the last one and I've had to call down everyone in East and North Downs to help here. Ops 1 is going mad with unanswered SOCO calls, but I think a double murder takes priority. Not that he knows what's going on. This is all so hush hush, the SOCOs on their way down don't even know what they're coming to. What have you got?'

I told him what I'd surmised and he nodded thoughtfully.

'Okay. I'll work on the assumption that you're right until I find something that doesn't fit. There'd better not be a third one though, Rob. We won't have the staff to deal with it.'

'Don't worry, we'll have him in custody by tea-time.'

He chuckled as he eased himself between the two officers and entered the room. Turning to Merrington, I caught him chewing his lip until he saw me watching.

'I think it's time for our little chat,' I said, heading back out into the rain, 'and I think I know the perfect place. You'll feel right at home.'

10

STRETCHING OUT on the unfamiliar bed, Gemma wondered for a moment where she was – then the memories came flooding back. Fear lanced into her gut, making her gasp out loud as tears broke free and soaked into the filthy pillowcase. She'd been in the bedroom when David had answered the door, hoping that it wasn't someone who would drag him away from the night that was making her feel like a sixteen-year-old in love for the first time. When he came stumbling back into the room it had made her jump. She'd turned to tell him off, but the blood smeared all over his chest had shrivelled the words and turned them into a scream that she couldn't get out, no matter how hard she had tried. Then, before she'd time to think, the man had come into the room, long hair poking out from under the balaclava making him look like some kind of strange animal. She'd seen the pistol and watched him – unable to move – as he crossed the room and placed it against David's head and pulled the trigger.

She'd said something to him then – she couldn't remember what – but instead of shooting her he'd grabbed her by the hair and smashed her in the face with the butt of his gun. She'd woken here, in this tiny room, with nothing but a bed with filthy covers that stank of urine and blood.

Stretching out her wrists she felt the rough edges of a rope digging into them, almost tight enough to cut off the circulation. Stifling a moan, she tried to roll so that she could see more than the wall, but her feet were tied to something solid – a block of wood maybe. Left no other choice, she opened her mouth and let out a long scream, loud enough to wake the dead. She had no idea where she was, but she prayed that someone would hear her.

Within seconds the door crashed open and heavy footsteps swiftly crossed the room, the boards creaking as the owner stopped abruptly and leaned over her, his shadow accompanied by the smell of tobacco and chip oil. Rough hands grabbed her face, fingers digging painfully into the hinge of her jaw to force her mouth open. Helpless, she could only moan in terror as a filthy dirt-encrusted rag was shoved into her mouth until it made her gag.

'Shhh,' the figure said finally, then the shadow retreated, the footsteps creaking away again and the door was slammed shut, once more leaving Gemma alone in the dark.

11

MERRINGTON LOOKED around the interior of the McDonald's at the marina, a cup of coffee cooling next to my Big Mac and fries. His distaste was almost palpable.

'I thought you said I'd feel right at home! I haven't been into a McDonald's since I was a student.'

'I lied. I do that.' I paused as a woman herded three screaming children past our table. 'I thought that as this is so sensitive, you'd want to be somewhere we couldn't be overheard.' I waved a hand at the lunchtime din that surrounded us. 'So talk.'

My phone rang and I cursed silently as Merrington paused with his mouth open. The display flashed Lucy H and I pressed the cancel button before tucking it away again. Lucy was an old school friend I'd bumped into in the supermarket a couple of weeks ago. After swapping numbers we'd promised to keep in touch. I'd apologise later but right now I needed Merrington to talk.

'Sorry. You were about to say?'

Merrington sighed as he fiddled with his cup.

'You know I could lose my job for telling you why we're interested.'

'Right now I'm afraid I don't care. I've got bodies piling up and someone needs to tell me what's going on. You seem to be the best candidate.'

He sipped at his coffee and grimaced as he burnt his tongue.

'Taverner had links to some fairly interesting groups,' he began, 'and he had access to a boat. We think he was bringing people into the country illegally.'

'Couldn't Immigration have dealt with that?'

He shook his head. 'We're not talking about asylum seekers here. I can't say more, but trust me when I say that these are bad people.'

'Well, shouldn't Special Branch be involved then?'

'Telling Special Branch anything is a sure-fire way to make sure subtlety goes out of the window, I'm afraid. Anyway, Taverner has gambling debts, big ones, which is probably why he's been shipping people in under the radar. What we need to figure out is whether he was killed because of those debts, or because of someone he brought in.'

I sat back as I digested the information, inadvertently glancing at a picture of a burger that supposedly bore a likeness to the squidgy mess in front of me. Pushing it around its cardboard tray, I tried to work out how much of what he was telling me was true.

'So where does the second guy come in?'

'His name is Reggie Brown; he's the owner of Distant Vistas. Other than what's on his tax returns, we know next to nothing about him but, unless they were gambling buddies, it's likely their deaths were related to their 'work'.'

'Well I guess that's our next step then.' Pulling out my phone, I called Karl and told him to bring up everything he could find on Reggie Brown, giving him a guesstimated date of birth of 1950. He promised to get back to me as soon as he had anything and, after hanging up, I turned back to Merrington.

'Anything else useful you want to share before we go back to civilisation?'

'Not that I can think of.'

'Right then, let's get to it.'

'Where are we going now?'

'To get a warrant to search their boat, see if they left anything interesting there. I assume you use warrants in MI6?'

He smiled and shrugged. 'Sort of. I can probably make it easier for you though.'

Pulling out his phone, he made a call as we got up and left McDonald's.

'Roger? Hi, it's Harvey Merrington. Yes, fine thanks. Look, I need to search a property in Brighton Marina, it's a boat, shed or similar and any boats pertaining to it... Yeah, great. Maritime Act? Perfect. Okay, I'll sign it when I get back. Thanks.'

He grinned at me as he tucked his phone away. 'Well that's that sorted. I've just been granted authority under the Maritime Act allowing me to search any craft or vessel, or housing for said craft or vessel. Shall we?'

I looked at him in shock. 'You can do that?'

He nodded. 'We have access to any laws or powers granted to any police force or agency in the UK. It's just a matter of justification and being put on the right list. It'll stand up in a court of law if that's what you're worried about?'

I hadn't been, but it was good to know anyway.

'Okay, let's ask around and see where they park their boats then.'

'Moor.'

'Sorry?'

'You moor a boat, not park it.'

'Does it make a difference to where it'll be?'

'No, I just hate to hear people butchering the English language.'

'You think I'm butchering it, just wait until you go to Whitehawk.'

'That's the estate above the marina. Is it that bad?'

'You have no idea.'

12

AFTER A few false starts we found ourselves standing next to a boat with the company name painted on the side. It was about thirty feet long with a raised platform for the person steering and a hatch in the middle of the deck that led below. I was about to leap onboard when Merrington put a restraining hand on my arm and drew a Glock 17.

'Just in case.'

I shook my head. 'No *Harvey*, I'm sorry but there are rules and regs. You can't just go running around with a bloody pistol!'

'I can and I will. I'm licensed to carry and use it if necessary, and after what we've seen today I'm not taking any chances. You coming?'

He leapt lightly on to the deck and moved straight towards the hatch with his pistol out in front of him. After a moment's hesitation I followed him. I didn't like the fact that he was armed, but what I didn't like more was the fact that I hadn't spotted it under his jacket. I must have been getting soft.

He moved down the steps slowly, trying to see into the darkness below. Reaching into my pocket I pulled out my torch and passed it to him, careful to stay well into his peripheral vision so that I didn't startle him into firing accidentally. Bad enough that he was armed, without having to explain to my bosses why he'd sunk a boat by shooting it. He flicked the torch on and moved quickly, jumping the last few steps to land in what appeared to be one big hold that stretched the entire length of the boat. There were benches lining the sides with lockers underneath but, other than that, it was surprisingly tidy.

'Clear?' I asked, hovering on the steps.

'Clear,' Merrington replied, tucking the pistol back into its holster, where I was pleased to see that it didn't show under the tailored jacket. Maybe I wasn't getting soft after all.

'How about we take a side each and meet in the middle?' I said as I descended the last few steps into the dingy space.

'Fine by me. I'll take starboard.'

'What's that in normal speak?'

'Right.'

'Great, I'll take the left then.'

I moved to the rear and began lifting the benches to get at the lockers underneath. Most of them contained wet weather gear and fishing equipment, but one of them was completely empty except for a series of clips that jutted out from the back of the container as if something had been held there. While the others had smelled of brine and mildew, this one smelled metallic and clean.

'You got anything?' I asked, turning to look at him just as he opened the final container on his side.

'No, you?' he asked, and I shook my head as I flipped up the final bench, only to freeze, nothing but my eyeballs moving as they swivelled towards him.

'Merrington, I want you to walk very slowly towards the steps, then go up them and get off the boat. I'll be right behind you.'

'Why, what have you got?' he asked, moving towards me.

'Did you not hear me?' I demanded angrily. 'Get off the fucking boat!'

Ignoring the warning, he peered over my shoulder.

'Shit,' he breathed, backing away slowly.

At first glance, all we were looking at was a box full of wires with Plasticine in it attached to a couple of gas containers.

'Do you know what that is?' Merrington said quietly.

I knew very well what it was. I'd spent three years in Afghanistan as part of a protection team for a squad of bomb disposal engineers, and you don't spend that much time around homemade explosives without picking up a thing or two.

'I'd say that it's about eight pounds of C4 attached to a mobile phone detonator. Can't see a tilt switch and we know there isn't a light sensor or we'd be vaporised by now, but I'm sure there'll be some kind of anti-tamper device. I've had experience with these things, so do me a favour and get off the boat before it goes off.'

'What's going to happen when you drop that lid?' he asked, climbing the stairs slowly.

'I don't know. But I don't intend to hang around and find out. Get off the boat and call down when you're on the dock. Then I'll drop the lid and follow you.'

He nodded and disappeared into the murky daylight above while I sweated in the darkness below. My vision swam and I realised I was starting to hyperventilate and slowed my breathing as much as I could, unable to take my eyes off the device. One of the engineers I'd been protecting all those years ago, a Welshman imaginatively nicknamed Taff, had told me something about checking for tamper lines. It involved using a torch and a very fine metal rod and right now I had neither.

'I'm clear.' Merrington's voice floated down through the hatch.

'Then run!' I shouted, easing the lid down before clambering up the steps and on to the deck as fast as I could.

Merrington was already on his toes as I leapt off the boat and sprinted for the nearest structure, a concrete admissions box that guarded the barrier leading to the quay. I reached it in record time, passing Merrington with head down and arms pumping. I smiled in relief as he stopped next to me, hands on his knees as he sucked in several deep breaths.

'You okay?' I asked, seeing him nod in return. I couldn't remember the last time that I'd been truly scared – that bone deep terror that made your limbs turn to jelly and your heart feel like it was bursting out of your chest – but this was definitely one of those times. My hands were still trembling as they fumbled for my radio.

'Well that was too close,' I said when I trusted myself to speak.

Merrington nodded again and opened his mouth to reply when a dull *whump* made the concrete under our feet tremble. The boat seemed to expand outwards on a ball of flame and I could only stare in shock as the boat tore itself to pieces in front of us.

As the steering deck was thrown into the sky, the shockwave hit us, hurling me backwards to smash into the concrete wall of the box with a jarring thud that felt like it broke several ribs. Merrington cartwheeled past me, limbs flopping like a ragdoll's as he tried to control his spin, then my head crunched into the concrete and everything slipped

away into darkness.

13

THE BOMBER threw his binoculars into the footwell and pulled out into the morning traffic, steering carefully around the cars that had stopped in the road as their drivers lined the wall that overlooked the marina. Even up here, the blast had rattled windows — testament to the amount of explosive that he'd placed on the boat. Always a careful man, he had set the explosives on a timer then moved away to a safe distance to watch and make sure that no one interfered with the bomb.

Had he not been disturbed by that damn traffic warden, he would have been able to reach the radio switch and detonate the device as the two cops boarded the boat, but the officious little man in the green coat had been too busy leaning into the window and haranguing him for remaining in a parking bay for too long. He hadn't dared press the small button in front of him in case the man made the connection and identified him later.

Instead, he'd had to promise the man that he would move and then wait until the warden had stopped staring at him. Three seconds after he'd pressed the button a fireball had lit the underside of the clouds and turned them a bright, vivid orange for a moment before the sound hit and the ground rumbled.

Satisfied that his work was complete, he headed back into town, keeping his face neutral as cars with blue lights erupted from side streets like ants from a kicked nest and screamed towards the marina.

Parking up on a quiet street on the far side of the city centre, he got out and walked around the block twice to make sure that he wasn't being followed before slipping down the damp stairs to a basement flat and letting himself in. Once inside, he threw his coat on the sofa and moved through to the cramped kitchen, rooting around in the fridge until he found a can of Coke. Cracking it open, he took a few swigs before holding up his phone to check the signal and dialled a number from memory.

'Yes?' The voice on the other end was muffled.

'Boss, it's me. Job done.'

'Anyone hurt?'

'Just a couple of cops. Nothing to worry about.'

'Good. Stay out of sight. I'll call you when I need you again.'

The bomber hung up without replying and grinned as he heard the faint sound of sirens, basking in the satisfaction of a job well done.

14

SWEAT ROLLED down my forehead from under my helmet but I didn't dare lift a hand from my rifle to wipe it away. Four hours we'd been stuck in this damn hole, four hours being sniped at while Taff and Burrows tried to disarm the IED that had led us out here in the first place. Another burst of fire came in, rounds puffing up dust a few inches away from my head. Ducking back, I threw a hand signal to the fire team indicating the location of the shooter. Seconds later we popped up in perfect synchronisation and let off three rounds each into the stand of scrubby bushes. Leaves shredded and twigs burst apart as our bullets tore through the cover but the shooter had already moved on, finding another position to rain death down on our small group.

'Any chance we can get this done, Taff?' I shouted over my shoulder.

'If you want to swap, boyo, you come and take the top off this mortar shell without blowing us all to kingdom come!' Taff shouted back in his lilting Welsh accent. 'If not, bloody shut up and let me get on with it.'

I took the hint and returned my attention to the roadside, eyes sweeping in arcs as I tried in vain to spot where the next attack would come from. There were eight of us guarding the two Ordnance Disposal men, all trying to stay under cover in a shallow depression that would barely hide a child. Just to make things even more interesting, Taff and Burrows were working on an improvised explosive made from an old mortar shell wrapped in Detcord, powerful enough to vaporise all of us should they make even the slightest mistake.

I heard the scream before the gunshot echoed from the nearby hills. Rolling on to my back, I raised my rifle and fired, the rounds punching through the Taliban fighter who had vaulted a low wall and shot Forbes, the man stationed there. As soon as he was down I crawled over to Forbes, heart in my mouth as I rolled him to check the injury. Glazed eyes stared up at me and the smell of blood and shit reaching my nostrils was enough to tell me how bad it was without having to see the gaping hole in his chest.

I reached for my radio to call for a med-evac, but before I could open my mouth more weapons boomed and the attack began in earnest, bullets raining down from the nearby hillsides and catching us in a deadly crossfire that began to chew my men to pieces.

The radio crackled and hissed as rounds tore into us. I could hear it bleeping from somewhere nearby, only I couldn't find it. My questing hand reached out for it only to jam itself painfully into a hard surface that shouldn't have been there.

Opening my eyes, I saw nothing but blurry shapes as my nose finally caught the scent of smoke and burning plastic and I felt a stab of panic. They must have hit us with a grenade, or maybe Taff and Burrows had failed to defuse the bomb in time. How many of my men were dead, or too injured to move or cry out for help?

All of a sudden, rough hands grabbed me, pulling me along the ground.....

15

SOUND CAME crashing in – people shouting, car alarms going off nearby, the crackling of flames from the destroyed boat. Turning my head, I found a man in fishing gear towering above me as he dragged me away from the quay. Pain lanced through my ribs as I took a breath to speak, emerging instead as a groan. The moment he heard me, he stopped dragging and lifted me into a sitting position.

'Can you walk?' He asked, his voice wavering in and out through the ringing in my ears.

'I think so.'

Each breath brought with it not only pain but also the oily taste of burning rubber and plastic, thick enough to make me want to gag. Thick greasy coils of black smoke curled up from the remains of the boat, fighting valiantly against the rain that still poured down. Struggling to my feet, I stood unsteadily for a moment before moving towards the prone form of Merrington lying a dozen feet away against a concrete stanchion. In the distance I could see running figures and flashing blue lights as I bent over the MI6 agent, pressing my fingers to his neck and breathing a sigh of relief when I found a pulse.

I almost fell over as I tried to move him, then gave up and folded into a sitting position. The fisherman was shouting at me to move, but I waved him away and pulled out my radio, finding the on button at the third attempt. The moment it came to life I heard units fighting with each other for air space but I held the talk button down until it beeped and then held it to my mouth.

'Charlie Papa 291, urgent.'

'291 go ahead.'

'Yeah, 291, I've just been blown up and I've got an unconscious casualty with me. Can I have an ambulance to the East Quay at the marina please?'

There was a moment of silence that gave me time to realise how odd my last transmission must have sounded. Then: '291, ambulance and fire are already en-route. Are you injured?'

'I'm not sure. I think I've got a few broken ribs but other than that and an almighty headache I'm fine.'

'Roger that. There are units already at the marina making for your location.'

I dropped the radio back into its holder and sagged back against the stanchion. Merrington had blood trickling from his ears and nose and, as I wiped a grubby hand across my own face, it came away sticky and red. A noise from my left made me look up to see three uniformed officers and a PCSO racing towards where we lay. I raised a hand and waved, then pulled it down again when I realised that there probably weren't that many people lying bleeding in front of them and they'd most likely work out where they were going without my help.

As the first officer reached us she froze for a second, the look of shock on her face worrying enough that I instinctively batted it off with a joke.

'Has my makeup smudged?' I asked weakly.

'No Sarge, but you've got splinters all over your face.' She crouched down next to Merrington and felt for a pulse as she spoke. The other officers arrived and helped me carefully to my feet once I'd assured them that I could walk. We hadn't even made it off the quay when the first ambulance arrived, nudging its way through the gathering crowd with judicious use of sirens and swearing from the driver.

'Leave me, get that crowd back so the ambulance can get through,' I ordered the men assisting me, and after leaving me leaning against a wall they went to comply, forcing the crowd aside so that the paramedics could reach Merrington.

The next few minutes passed in a daze as shock began to set in, so I slid to the ground, closed my eyes and let the world flow past me. Although I'd come perilously close at times I'd never been blown up before, and I have to say I didn't like the experience – it ranked just above opera and holidays in Belgium. Every part of me was starting to hurt – I felt dizzy and sick. The only mercy was that I hadn't crapped myself. I don't think I would have been able to live it down if that had happened. I came out of my reverie as two paramedics hurried past with Merrington on a trolley, an oxygen mask strapped to his pale and bloodied face. Forcing myself up, I stumbled after them and slid into the back just as one of them tried to close the doors.

'You okay mate?' the medic in the rear asked, 'only we've got to get this bloke up to A&E sharpish, you'll have to wait for another ambulance.'

I shook my head. 'Don't worry I'll book myself in when I get there. I need to go up with him.'

'You know him then? Have you got a name for him?'

He closed the doors and banged on the inside, prompting the driver to pull away with the sirens blaring once again.

'Yeah, his name's Harvey Merrington. He works with me.'

'Oh really, and what do you do then?'

'I'm CID.'

'Oh. Hard to tell under the dirt, sorry. You okay?'

He kept checking Merrington's vital signs as we spoke, barely glancing my way.

'Everything hurts, and apparently I've got splinters in my face, but it's kind of hard to see from here.'

The medic, whose name tag introduced him as Darren, leaned over and lifted my chin. 'They look like fibreglass. Lucky you didn't lose an eye.'

'Wow, I feel better already. What's wrong with him?' I nodded towards Merrington.

'He's got a big old lump on the back of his head, probably got knocked over by the blast. What happened, if you don't mind me asking?'

'Cooking accident.'

He gave me a funny look as the ambulance pulled into the car park of the Royal Sussex County Hospital, only a few streets away from the marina. The driver opened the rear door and they wheeled Merrington out and straight into the resuscitation area.

I followed, ignoring the strange looks people were throwing my way. I was more worried about Merrington than I was my own injuries. We may have only just met but we were working on the same side and you always came second when a colleague got hurt. Nurses in blue scrubs and a doctor in dark green hurried over as soon as they had him placed in a bay, while a grey scrubbed healthcare assistant tried to usher me out.

'I don't think so.' I flashed my badge, almost shoving it up his nose to get my point across. He nodded and stepped back, letting me into the cubicle. The doctor – a man in his early forties with a widow's peak and the physique of a rugby player – looked over at me.

'What happened?'

I relayed the events surrounding the blast and seeing Merrington hurled past me, without revealing what had caused it. I wanted to keep that under wraps until I had a handle on what was going on and I knew from experience that nurses gossiped like fishwives. I half-smiled when I saw a nurse begin to cut away Merrington's horribly expensive suit, but then I suddenly remembered something.

'Uh, excuse me a moment,' I said, moving the nurse out of the way and reaching under Merrington's jacket to retrieve his Glock.

There was no way of doing it subtly, so I pulled out my badge with my other hand and waved it around before anyone could start screaming. There were a few wild-eyed looks, but everyone in the room seemed to take it in their stride as I tucked the pistol into my waistband. That done, I stepped back and let them get on with their work while I tried to figure out who had just tried to kill us and why.

16

HALF AN hour later I had a cubicle of my own in the minor injuries department, where a short Filipino nurse called Daniel pulled pieces of fibreglass out of my face with a pair of tweezers. I was acutely aware of the pistol's solid weight resting against my back – the feeling at once comfortingly familiar and worryingly illegal. I'd spent several years in the army and also a few years in the armed police – which had eventually led to the firearms positioning – but I'd been a long time unarmed and, despite my previous training, my supervision would undoubtedly fire me if they knew I was carrying. Burke had arrived and was pacing the waiting room while I had my face plucked and, by rights, I should have turned the weapon over to him. But I wasn't sure how he would take Merrington being armed and some obscure sense of loyalty to the man who had saved my life kept my mouth shut.

'There you go, all done.' Daniel stood back to admire his handiwork.

'Should I worry about infection?' I asked as I stood wearily.

'No, you should be fine, but keep the wounds clean and if the skin around them goes dark red, come straight back.'

'Will do. Thanks.'

He smiled as I walked back out into the waiting room, catching the DCI mid-turn.

'You okay?' He asked gruffly, but with a hint of genuine concern.

I nodded, then wished I hadn't as my brain wobbled inside my skull.

'Just about. I assume you want to know what happened?'

'It would be nice. I'll give you a lift back to the Nick. You can fill me in on the way.'

'What about Merrington?'

'He's awake and alert. No serious damage, just a nasty concussion. Lucky really.'

'Is he coming with us?'

'No, they want to keep him in for observations. He'll be out in a couple of hours with any luck. He's already been on the phone to his superiors.'

As we talked he guided me out through the main A&E entrance where my peppered face drew a few glances. I'd refused to have a dressing, not wanting to look like a reject from a plastic surgeon's table, and I guess it didn't look too pretty.

'Any idea what he said?'

The DCI shook his head. 'Other than that we're not to tell anyone about what actually happened on the boat, he's said nothing. I don't like it.'

'Being there when it happened wasn't much fun either.'

'I'll bet. My worry is that this is some kind of terrorist attack, or at least the prelude to one, so don't be shy on the details.'

The drive back to John Street only took five minutes, which was more than enough time for me to tell the DCI everything I knew – twice. He shook his head as I mentioned the device.

'This is far more than we bargained for when we agreed to work with Six. I think we need to do a full review and get Special Branch involved at the very least.'

'I don't think Merrington'll like that sir.'

'I don't give a damn what he likes. MI6 doesn't run this police force! I nearly lost a good officer today and I'm not going to let that happen again.'

I was about to make a quip about the "good officer" remark, but I saw him looking at me so I kept my lips firmly pressed together.

'Did you get a good look at the device?'

I nodded. 'Only a few seconds, but it was enough. Professional job – looked like Semtex. All the wires were the same colour, which means they used coloured tags when they built it and then cut them off. Stops you from having a red wire / blue wire moment when you're disarming it. I assume that even if you get Special Branch in, I'll still be on the case?'

He threw me a look. 'You sure? I thought that you wanted to get back to your usual work.'

'I take being blown up rather personally sir. I'd like to stay on-board if possible.'

He shrugged. 'I don't see why not. You seem to have a good working relationship with Merrington. Now get this morning written up and take the rest of the day off, you look like hell.'

Checking my watch as he parked up, I was surprised to see that it was only just after three. So much had happened since I'd first entered Taverner's flat that morning that it felt like a different week. As we entered the back door we went our separate ways – Burke off

to do whatever it was that senior officers did when they weren't giving orders and me to my

new office to try and write up what I could only describe as a pooch-screw of a day.

I walked in to find Nat furiously typing. She looked up as I came in and did a double take

when she saw my injured face.

'What the bloody hell have you done?'

'Had a fight with some angry fibreglass. It looks worse than it is. I thought you'd be out

at the marina with the latest body.'

She shrugged as she stood and moved over to the kettle. 'Karl is. We decided one of us

should stay here and keep working on the first one. What really happened?'

I hesitated for a moment, wanting to tell her the truth but hesitant to say anything that

might get me in trouble later if Six really were trying to keep a lid on it.

'A boat exploded, not sure why.' The lie stuck in my throat but I forced it out. I knew

that Nat would keep her mouth shut if I told her the truth which made lying to her worse,

but until I had a handle on what was going on, I decided to play along with Merrington's

request.

She raised a doubting eyebrow but didn't push it. 'It says a gas explosion on the news.'

'What?'

'BBC website. It says that officers were responding to a smell of gas and were

investigating when the boat exploded. Apparently they think it was the cooker in the galley.' She pulled up the article and I read it while she made tea. I have to admit I was impressed. Not only was it a feasible story, it was up less than two hours after the blast. MI6 clearly had a box of assorted explanations that they used in emergencies. No doubt they'd used channels of their own to make sure that the BBC reported the story first.

'I don't remember any calls about gas, Rob.'

I turned to Nat to be presented with a cup of tea and a suspiciously innocent smile.

'That's probably because someone approached the officers concerned and told them in person.'

'Of course. How very convenient.'

'Isn't it just?'

She smiled and shrugged, then ushered me out of the way so that she could sit back at her terminal.

'Aren't you supposed to be doing some work?' she asked over her shoulder.

'Probably. Any progress on Taverner?' I asked, changing the subject.

'Only one thing. There's some intelligence from about two weeks ago saying that someone called Tav owed a lot of money to a loan shark who's been making threats against him. The description we have fits what you've told me of Taverner.'

I felt the buzz hit me like a hot cup of coffee after a long shift. 'What's the loan shark's name?'

'MacBride. Doesn't give any first names, and there are eleven MacBrides on the system.'

I felt a grin tugging at the corners of my mouth.

'There's only one MacBride in Brighton that loans money. Danny. He specialises in loaning to heavy gamblers and then making them run drugs for him when they can't pay.'

Nat's fingers were already flying across her keyboard. 'Danny MacBride, born Glasgow 11/7/69. Previous convictions for armed robbery, GBH, attempted murder, possession of heroin with intent to supply, criminal damage. No further action on a dozen other cases – mostly assaults and handling stolen goods. No current address for him though.'

My grin spread further. 'It just so happens that I've got a live job running. MacBride's the lead suspect. It's not ready for arrest yet but it's a perfect excuse to bring him in if this does lead back to him.'

'What sort of job?'

'Extortion – small local business. Uniform took the statement and reckon the description matches MacBride. I need to get some more detail but once I've done that we can nick him at our leisure.'

'We need to find him first, Rob.'

'And where do we go when we need to find someone?'

Nat shrugged. 'Thomson Local?'

'No, Justin Evans.'

'Who?'

'Nat, you may be one of my best detectives but you've still got a lot to learn. Grab your coat, you've pulled.'

"Like you could handle me", she challenged me as we left the office.

Ignoring the quip, I smiled to myself. Finally I had a lead that I could follow up without being blown up or having MI6 frowning at me. The feeling was the closest to happy I'd been in a very long time.

17

'I STILL don't get it.' Leon Watson scratched his head, confused. Danny MacBride stood and crossed the room, placing a hand on the big man's shoulder.

'It's very simple,' he said slowly, 'you get to play dress-up.'

Watson stood suddenly, hands balled into fists.

'I ain't wearing no dress!' he shouted, then stopped, puzzled, as MacBride and Collins both began to laugh.

'Don't you laugh at me!' Watson warned, taking a threatening step forward.

Danny MacBride's face changed suddenly, the laughter dying as his lips peeled back from his teeth. Before Watson could take another step, MacBride grabbed him by the throat and squeezed so hard that the tattoos on MacBride's hands writhed as skin stretched over sinew and bone with a cracking sound. Watson grunted, one hand coming up to grab MacBride's wrist, but the look in the other man's eye stopped him before he made contact.

He began to struggle for breath, his eyes bulging and his face turning red, but still he didn't try to force his boss to let go. He knew from experience that if he tried to fight back, MacBride wouldn't stop squeezing until Leon was unconscious on the floor, and then the other men would take turns kicking him. He'd seen it before. Hell, he'd helped before.

The world had started to go dark when MacBride suddenly released Watson, letting him slump backwards on to the filthy sofa in the squat they worked from during the day. Massaging his neck, Leon looked up at MacBride, who was standing over him with an expectant look on his face.

'Sorry boss,' Leon croaked, still feeling his throat.

MacBride's smile came back out like the sun from behind the clouds. 'Course you are! Otherwise I wouldn't have you working for me, would I? You'd be dead and Billy here would be lugging you down the stairs and dumping you in the rubbish outside.'

Watson nodded. 'Yeah, I suppose. I just don't like being laughed at is all.'

MacBride shrugged. 'Who does? So, back to the plan then. You get to dress up as a security guard. Thought you might find it fun.'

Watson looked up and nodded, trying hard not to show his fear of the smaller man with the mad eyes. 'Uh yeah, great. But why am I doing it again?'

'Because we're robbing a bank, Leon.'

'What sort of bank?'

'What sort of bank Leon? The biggest bank in the world.'

18

JUSTIN EVANS was a cross between a garden gnome and something that you'd wipe off your shoe before you got in the car. He was small and seemingly inoffensive unless you were alone and female – then, suddenly, the claws came out and he became... unpleasant. Originally from somewhere in the Midlands, he'd decided over a decade ago, like so many other waifs and strays, that Brighton would be the ideal place to ply his trade. Although he'd finally stopped pawing women a few years before when both his arms had been broken in prison for being a rapist, he still preyed on lone females for their purses, normally with a knife in car parks late at night.

He would then spend his hard-earned cash on as much heroin as he could stuff in his cheeks, then wander back to whatever hostel had the pleasure of housing him that week and would inject as much of it as possible before someone bigger and uglier stole the rest from him. As a result, he had a score to settle with almost every criminal in Brighton. All it took was the right amount of pressure and he would sing like a canary.

During the day, he could usually be found sitting in Pavilion Gardens amidst the beautiful flower beds and carefully trimmed bushes, watching passing women as they in turn watched the scenery – marred only slightly by the greasy little figure in the blue parka with one hand down his trousers.

True to form, Evans was on his usual bench overlooking the gardens, close enough to the café that he could dart in and steal any tempting looking handbags but far enough away that no one noticed the smell. Holding a gloved finger to my lips to stop Nat from saying anything, I crept silently up behind the little man, holding my breath when I got close - to stop myself gagging at the reek of unwashed heroin user.

'Evans!' I growled suddenly, expecting him to jump and try to run. Instead, he turned faster than I would have thought possible, hand flashing into his pocket, emerging with a knife that he plunged towards my stomach. Without thinking, my hand shot out, grabbing his wrist and twisting sharply so that his hand moved clockwise, grinding the bones together and squeezing the nerve trapped by my fingers. He squealed, dropping the knife into my spare hand as he sank to his knees, arm extended and twisted into a painful lock.

Nat raised an eyebrow and murmured, 'That's not in the manual.'

I flashed her a quick grin and returned my attention to the filthy little man crouched in agony by my feet. 'Justin Evans, I'm arresting you for being in possession of a bladed article in a public place. Never mind trying to stab a police officer. You do not have to say anything, but if you do, it may help me forget that I saw your dirty little face this afternoon. Do you understand the caution?'

Evans was many things, including stupid, but a lifetime of brushes with the law let him see a chance when it presented itself. 'That's not my knife, guv! I put this jacket on this morning from the hallway, it must be someone else's.'

'And it wasn't your hand that just tried to stab me with it I suppose?' I let go and he rubbed at his sore wrist, straightening to his full five feet and two inches. 'However,' I continued, 'I might be persuaded to believe that, but I need to know a couple of things in return.'

Evans looked around to make sure no one was watching. Despite his regular use as a heroin piggy-bank, he knew that if anyone suspected he might be giving information to the police, he'd end up floating under the pier with a knife in his back.

'Go on, guv,' he said in a stage whisper.

Shaking my head, I wrapped the knife in my latex gloves and tucked it into my pocket. 'Danny MacBride.'

Evans was shaking his head before I'd even finished talking. 'Can't, guv. He'd kill me!'

I leaned in close and instantly regretted it as the smell of rotting cheese and worse hit my nostrils. Retreating rapidly and blinking away tears I growled, 'You don't have a choice. Not only will I nick you for carrying the knife but I'll make sure that I thank you for the useful information in a nice loud voice at the custody desk. How long do you think you'll last after that?'

Evans' face paled under the dirt. 'You wouldn't. We've always been right, you and me!'

'If by right you mean I haven't broken your fingers for attacking women, then yeah, we're right. But we'll be more right when you've told me what I need to know. Or would you prefer us to be wrong?'

He sighed and his shoulders slumped. He looked so pathetic that I almost felt sorry for him...almost. But I knew how rotten the heart that beat within his grimy chest was and I steeled myself against even a hint of compassion.

'Three...Two...' I began to count as I pulled out my cuffs.

'Okay, okay! What do you want to know?'

'Where's MacBride staying?'

'He works out of the squat on Steine Street opposite the pub. You know, the one that used to have the queer's head on the sign?'

'Number 2 – opposite the Three and Ten?'

He nodded so emphatically that his colony of nits and fleas began to jump around, prompting me to take a further step backwards.

'That's the one!'

'Okay, what's the setup?'

'Uh, he's got a couple of guys for muscle, both mates from back home. Oh, and Leon Watson.'

Watson was an old school bruiser with a PNC record longer than a queue at a dole office, and we'd bumped heads more than once over the years. Although he was in his fifties he still had a punch that had knocked out many an unaware PC.

'Right, so that's work. Where does he live?'

'I dunno guv. He don't talk about it.'

'Oh come on Justin. I'm sure you've tried to burgle him once or twice. If anyone knows where he lives it's you.'

'I swear guv, on me mam's life.'

'She's dead.'

'But if she *were* alive, I'd swear on her life!'

'Fine. Now I want you to piss off somewhere quiet and stop ruining the landscape for a few hours. Oh, and if I catch you with a knife again I'll cut your balls off. Clear?'

He nodded and scurried off. I turned to Nat who was looking at me with an unreadable expression.

'What?' I asked, heading back towards the Nick along paths lined with fragrant flowers and ornamental bushes. The fresh, clean smell was almost enough to get Evans' stink out of my nostrils.

'That was...unorthodox. I thought we weren't allowed to do things like that anymore?'

'We're not, which is exactly why the police are losing public confidence, losing prosecutions and generally looking like total arses. Used to be that the way you got into CID was by having a snout or two to throw you some info now and then – people like Evans. Now there's so much bloody red tape that you can't even piss without having to fill in a form. Tell me it didn't feel good to get out and get some info without having to fill in forms or ask Evans if we were considerate of his human fucking rights?'

Nat shook her head. 'I thought it was a bit much to be honest Rob. I know we got what we wanted, but you should have nicked him for the knife. Little pervert like that should be behind bars.'

'Why? We nick him for it and tomorrow he'll go into the YMCA kitchen and steal another one. If they won't put him away for stealing handbags, they sure as hell won't put him away for carrying a knife. You know last time he went in front of the judge for it, he said he used the knife for cutting through electric cables when he found stuff in skips? The judge let him off despite his previous. You tell me that makes sense.'

'It doesn't, but not nicking him doesn't make it any better, does it?'

'I disagree. I just saved the taxpayer over a grand. Think how much it costs to put him in court. Money saved, information gained, job done.'

'I don't think you're right, but I'm not going to argue with you. Where did you learn the move with the knife?'

I shrugged. 'Boy scouts.'

She laughed and suddenly the argument was over. 'So what do we do about MacBride?'

Glad to end the disagreement, I leapt at the chance to change the subject. 'Ah, now here's where the real police work begins. Have you done a surveillance course?'

'No, have you?'

'I spent eighteen months on surveillance when I came out of firearms.'

'Really! What made you give it up?'

'It wasn't conducive to family life.'

Nat winced. 'Sorry Rob, I should've guessed.'

'Nothing to apologise for, it's ancient history now.'

She shrugged and chewed her lip. I wanted to say something to make her feel better but I couldn't find it in myself. Just thinking about the days before my life had been torn apart was painful. I'd loved surveillance, and I'd been good at it too. But the long hours had taken their toll and Linda had insisted that if we were to have a family I had to give it up and find a department where the hours were more acceptable. Of course, I'd put her first and transferred to CID. It hadn't been much better but it was enough to make Linda happy. Back then that was all that mattered.

Taking a deep breath I shook my head to clear it and retreated into work as I'd been doing every day since they'd died. 'Just follow my lead, you're a quick study.'

'So what's the plan?'

'We find a vehicle, sit up on MacBride's place of work and follow him home when he comes out. Then we tap up our friend Merrington for some kind of warrant, and we go into the house and see what we can find.'

19

BEFORE I could follow through on my plan, I got a call from DCI Burke, who demanded that I get to his office immediately. He didn't say why but it didn't take a genius to realise that something big was happening.

Leaving Nat to head back to her desk I hurried up to see the DCI, finding him facing two other men across his desk. Mark Peters — a sergeant from CID who had gone to Special Branch a couple of years ago — I knew. He greeted me with a grin and a shrug that told me more than the phone conversation with Burke had. The other man I'd never met before. He was in his fifties with steely blue eyes and a grim expression that didn't change as I entered.

'Ah, Rob. Close the door.'

I complied, then stood with my back against the door, all the available chairs having been taken. Burke waved a hand at the other men in the room.

'DS Steele, this is DS Peters and DI Long from Special Branch. After today's shenanigans it's been decided that, no matter what MI6 want, we'll be running this as a proper murder investigation. Unfortunately for you, that means you've suddenly become a small cog in a big machine but I'm sure you'll adjust.'

I nodded, surprised at the sudden turnaround, but secretly pleased that I didn't have to make decisions way above my pay-grade anymore.

'I'll be running the investigation with DI Long as my second,' Burke continued. 'You'll be working the teams on the ground with DS Peters. More will be joining you as and when they're chosen. All the people for this are being handpicked. Someone seems intent on turning my city into a bloody mess and I want the best people stopping it from getting any worse. Any questions?'

I nodded. 'Do I get to keep Karl and Nat with me?'

'If you want them, yes. Liaise with Peters as he'll be running a team too. I want you to concentrate on the local side of things, leave the terrorism angle to Special Branch. I've told them everything you've told me so far, have you got anything to add?'

I shared what I'd learned from Justin Evans, omitting exactly how I'd uncovered the information. Burke nodded when I'd finished, clearly pleased with how things were progressing.

'Excellent. Surveillance are tied up with something they can't get out of until 1700, so if you can find this MacBride before then, we can hand him over as soon as they're done. We're having the first briefing at 1800, so I want you and yours on the fourth floor by ten to with everything you have.'

I nodded and took my cue to leave, followed by Mark Peters.

'Long time no see,' he said, pumping my hand.

'Yeah, how you been?' We'd never been particularly close, but Peters had a cheerful smile and an easy manner that made him pleasant company.

'Ah, you know. So what's all this shit about MI6?'

I filled him in on Merrington and he shook his head in sympathy.

'Rather you than me mate, sounds like a cock.'

I shrugged, unwilling to dismiss a man I'd almost died with.

'So what made them change their minds then? This morning it was all cloak-and-dagger, with MI6 telling us what to do. Now all of a sudden our bosses have grown their balls back and we're back in charge. What happened?'

He gave me a strange look, his eyes lingering on my face. 'You remember being blown up today, right?...'

'Kind of hard to forget.' Just thinking about it brought back memories of the terror I'd felt earlier.

'Well the powers that be decided that this job is too big for one bloke from London and three detectives in a shoe cupboard to deal with effectively. They've spent most of the day waiting for the OK from the Chief Constable and, as soon as he said yes, old man Burke got us on-board and all but shut Merrington out. He's advising now, nothing more.'

It made sense. I'd been wondering how one man could have enough power to tell my bosses what to do, even if he was from Six. Apparently he didn't, at least not anymore. I grinned as I thought of the look on his face when he found out he'd been gazumped.

'So what are you up to then?' I asked Peters as we reached the basement.

He shrugged. 'Looking at the terrorism angle. Apparently Merrington's got some information to share that we'll all get at the briefing. He's dragging his heels a bit but eventually he'll realise we're all working for the same team.'

'Well don't let me keep you; I've got some exciting surveillance work to do.'

He nodded, and left me to go and find Nat and take a crack at finding MacBride. What we were going to do with him when we found him I wasn't sure, but I was pleased that finally things were getting back to normal. Who knows, I thought as I headed back to the office, if I was careful I might even manage to avoid getting blown up again.

20

'COME ON Nat, we're off to save the world by sitting in a car for hours staring into space!' I boomed as I walked into the office, making her spill her tea.

'Where are we going?' she asked as she recovered, mopping at her keyboard with a file cover.

'As MI6 are now all but out of the picture, we get to be the sneaky ones and sit up on MacBride's place of work.'

'Great, I always wanted to be a spook!' she said, sarcastically.

'I'm sure you'll have a blast. Have you got something less... policey to wear?' I nodded at the trouser suit she was wearing.

She shrugged. 'I've got some running gear in my locker. Will that do?'

'Probably not but we haven't got time to go home and change. Get it on and meet me in the car park.'

We headed downstairs and I split off to my locker, changing into a pair of jeans and a hoody that I kept in there for emergencies. Then I made my way to the car park and got into the battered Ford Escort that we used for being discreet. As I waited for Nat, my phone beeped at me. The signal in the Nick was lousy and I was unsurprised to see that I had three missed calls. What *did* surprise me was that they were all from Lucy Hallett. She must have been far more keen on staying in touch than I'd realised and I promised myself I'd call her when I got home – if only to stop her from clogging up my message box.

I threw the hoody in the back seat and then sat in the car, drumming my fingers against the wheel as I waited for Nat. In less time than I'd expected, she came through the door and I blinked as I tried to find somewhere appropriate to rest my eyes. She was wearing a pair of skin-tight black leggings and a black lycra top that accentuated every curve. Already an attractive woman, it added a side to her that I'd never seen as I realised just how well toned she was. An officer walking the other way through the door almost slammed into it as he craned his neck to follow her as she moved towards the car. From the grin tugging at the corners of her mouth she knew the effect she was having. Pouring a metaphorical bucket of cold water over my brain, I leaned across and pushed her door open then started the engine. She slid into the seat with a smile and a few moments later we pulled out of the car park and headed the few roads over to Steine Street, which sat just off the Old Steine near the Palace Pier. The road itself was narrow, barely one lane. There were a couple of pubs and bars on it, as well as several near-derelict flats mixed in haphazardly with slightly more affluent housing. All the buildings were narrow but tall, giving the road a boxed-in feeling that was more than a little claustrophobic, despite one end opening out towards the sea.

I pulled the car up about a third of the way along, tucking it between two bins where it wouldn't stand out. Looking in the mirror, I saw that I had a perfect view of the front door.

'Can you see okay?' I asked Nat, who kept plucking at her running vest as if she could stop it from being almost indecently tight.

'Yeah, more or less. I wish I'd brought a hoody.'

'Do you want mine? It's on the back seat.'

She nodded and turned, reaching over to the back seat to grab the hoody. As she stretched, her t-shirt rode up to show a black tattoo, a tribal design that curled up over her left hip and disappeared around her back. I'd never seen it before and she'd never mentioned it, but before I could say anything she turned back and caught my eye as I stared.

'Eyes front, bucko.'

I did as I was told and, while she finished getting dressed, I called Karl and told him that I needed him to come and assist us by sitting at the Frank'N'Steine café on the Steine itself. That way we'd have all the exits covered and Karl wouldn't look particularly out of place in a suit.

We were there for almost two hours in the end, watching the steady flow of people going in and out of the old building before MacBride finally showed himself. His muscle came out first – a huge middle-aged man in a black leather jacket that strained across his shoulders, with greying hair and a face that only a mother could love.

'Leon Watson,' I said, identifying him to Nat.

'He looks like a nice man.'

'Not really. Got a punch like a mule's kick. He's a bit simple as well, but still very dangerous.'

She nodded. 'Born 13/6/1968 in Brighton, seven counts of GBH, four armed robbery and a string of minor assaults including one sexual back in the early eighties.'

I blinked at her. 'It scares me when you do that.'

She shrugged, nonchalantly. 'I had a quick look back at the Nick on MacBride's known associates.'

That was one of the things that made Nat such an effective officer. She had the ability to read something and regurgitate it – weeks or even months later. All it took was a brief glimpse and somehow the information just stayed in her head, waiting for the day that it might be of use.

'The one in Scouse finest is Billy Collins.'

I waved a finger towards the man limping out of the house behind Watson. He was a tall, skinny man in his late twenties with an overbite and greasy blond hair that hung down to the shoulders of his grey tracksuit top. A messy tattoo on his neck was supposed to commemorate the birth of his first daughter, but the tattooist had been drunk, illiterate or both and the result looked as if he'd been stabbed a few hundred times with a blue biro. Matching grey tracksuit bottoms and white Reebok classics finished off the look perfectly, despite the fact that the right trainer had a specially built up sole to compensate for a shotgun blast to the leg when he was seventeen. It made him walk with a gait that was half rolling seaman, half limp. Because of it, you could see him coming a mile off. Despite the handicap, rumour had it that Collins was MacBride's dirty job man, the one who dug the graves and sometimes even filled them. He had almost as many convictions as his boss, and although he'd never actually had a murder pinned on him, he'd been arrested for at least three that I was aware of.

Nat frowned for a moment. 'Been arrested four times for murder, three for GBH. None of them stuck but on the last two GBHs there was intimation that the witnesses had been scared off. Over twenty common assaults and ABHs, a few thefts and one arson. Oh, and one firearms offence when he was twenty-one.'

'What does he eat for breakfast?'

She shrugged again and grinned. 'If our intelligence was that good we wouldn't be sitting here waiting for them.'

MacBride himself came next, all chest and black-work tattoos that poked out of the sleeves of his bomber jacket and crawled over his hands. He was in his early forties with a few days worth of ginger stubble that matched his hair for length and colour. His face was set in a permanent scowl with eyes so wide and bulging that they looked like they were out on stalks. He looked exactly like what he was; a mean, evil bastard without a shred of compassion.

The three of them walked down the steps and began to turn towards the Steine, but then stopped as Leon held out a hand and pointed towards our car. Collins shrugged, seeming agitated and clearly not wanting to hang around, but MacBride nodded towards us and they began a slow amble in our direction.

'Shit.' Nat was watching them in the vanity mirror and I was using the rear-view, but if they walked up to us and peered in we'd still look out of place.

'Shouldn't you drive away?' she asked uncertainly.

I shook my head, worried. 'They'll spot us the moment we do. We need a reason to be here or we're made.'

Out of nowhere Nat grabbed me and pressed her lips against mine. I had little choice but to play along as I saw in the mirror that the three men were almost at the car.

As they walked past the window I caught MacBride looking in, then heard a burst of guttural laughter.

'Get a fucking room!' one of them shouted. Then they were past and walking towards the seafront end of the road.

As gently as I could, I pushed Nat away but she clung to the kiss, clearly enjoying herself far more than I was. When she finally pulled away she was red-faced and panting slightly, her eyes shining.

'That's your idea of a reason to be here?' I muttered, my face burning.

She shrugged, utterly unrepentant and I could see that she was taking an unhealthy amount of pleasure in my discomfort. 'It worked didn't it? Besides it's good for you to lose your composure once in a while.'

'It's just that, uh, Linda...'

I saw the realisation hit her like a brick to the face. She knew that I'd been alone since Linda had passed. Being reminded of her twice in one day was particularly painful, but I could see remorse in Nat's eyes as she saw the pain in mine. I tried to gather my scattered thoughts and find a way to ease the tension.

'Least said soonest mended, eh?' I said finally, pulling out my phone and calling Karl without looking at her. Keeping an eye on the three men, I held the phone to my ear and spoke over him as he answered. 'Karl, three x-rays heading south on Steine Street, turning right towards you. MacBride, Leon Watson and Billy Collins.' I described what they were

wearing and put Karl on speaker, handing the phone to Nat without looking her in the eyes.

'Grab that, he's on speaker,' I said, warning her in case she mentioned the kiss while Karl

could hear. She nodded sharply and took it while I started the car and pulled away, heading

the same direction the three men had gone.

'I've got them, they're moving across the Steine towards the bus stop.' Karl's voice

crackled tinnily over the speaker on the crap job phone I'd been graced with. 'A number 7

bus is pulling up, they're making for it.'

'Can you get on it without blowing out?'

'I reckon so. I'll call you back when I can.' The line went dead as I pulled an illegal right,

almost blindsiding a taxi in my haste to get on to the Steine.

'Steady Rob,' Nat half-yelled as the angry face of the taxi driver loomed inches away from

hers.

'Sorry.' Even concentrating on not getting us killed, I could see her looking at me out of

the corner of my eye.

'Look, Rob, about...'

I shook my head. 'Forget it, okay? Just one of those things.'

She shrugged and retreated, not wanting to push it. I didn't blame her. I knew I could be

an awkward bastard at the best of times and this certainly wasn't one of them. Silence filled the car with an almost physical presence until my phone rang again. Nat answered it hastily and put it straight on loudspeaker.

'It's Karl. They're on the bus, sitting upstairs. I'm at the back downstairs, I'll call you when they get off.'

'Thanks Karl, we'll be right behind you.' Throwing a conciliatory grin at Nat, I pulled into the bus lane and followed the number 7, catching it up at the Clock Tower. 'Now this is why I joined the job.'

'To drive a shit car through the middle of town?' Nat queried.

'Careful Nat, you're starting to sound like me. No, I meant proper detective work, watching criminals, finding out what they're up to.'

'Oh, yeah.' She sounded about as excited as if she'd just stepped in dog shit but I let it pass. Knowing Nat, by the end of the day she'd have forgotten that she'd ever upset me – a useful trick for someone who remembered everything.

Locking our recent incident firmly away at the back of my mind, I concentrated instead on keeping the bus in sight but not getting too close, feeling the old thrill of the chase. Hopefully MacBride was leading us straight to his home and from there to some answers for the murders that were stacking up all around us.

21

KARL WAITED until the three men got off the bus at the top of Davigdor Road and then followed, stopping halfway down the aisle to let a mother get her pram out. He stooped and took hold of the front, lifting it on to the pavement for her, receiving a grateful smile in return. When he looked up, MacBride and his men were halfway down Davigdor Road towards Windlesham Avenue, none of them showing any sign of having spotted or recognised him. That was the trouble with this sort of work, Karl mused as he followed at a discreet distance. Every time you went up to custody, numerous local criminals saw your face. And some of them had *very* good memories.

The three turned the corner and disappeared from view. Resisting the instinct to run to catch up, Karl instead picked up the pace a little, glancing at his watch as if running late. As Rob had once explained to him:

When you're following someone, the trick is to look natural. Nothing stands out more than someone who doesn't look like they should be there. If you're standing at a bus stop, tell yourself you're waiting for a bus and, more importantly, know why you're taking that bus. If you have to move fast, look at your watch and think about the meeting you're missing. It's all about body language, and the way we think changes that. If you feel out of place you'll look out of place, and anyone with half an ounce of awareness will pick that up.

'I'm going to be late to pick up my kids,' Karl muttered to himself, still looking at his watch as he turned the corner, 'and my wife'll give me hell.'

For one panicked moment, he couldn't see the men he was following, and his heart climbed into his mouth as he scanned the road ahead. Then he caught a flash of ginger hair turning a corner fifty yards ahead and he crossed the road, almost jogging to catch up. It was one thing trying to look natural but it was useless if you lost your target completely. He reached the next corner wishing he had someone else to help him. Following someone on your own was no easy task, and more Rob's forte than his.

'It cannae be helped,' he said quietly to himself as he saw MacBride walking along about thirty yards away, moving slowly now as if he was in no rush. Of Collins and Watson there was no sign, and he wondered briefly where they'd gone. Perhaps they lived in a flat nearby and MacBride was staying somewhere else. Putting them out of his mind, he stuck with the ringleader, knowing that MacBride was the main target. Pulling out his phone, he called Rob to update him.

"Rob, it's me. Yeah, we're on Windlesham Avenue, block of flats with a bird bath on the lawn, Worcester Court I think. Hang on, he's turning.'

He moved the phone from his ear as he hurried to catch up with his target. He was so intent on keeping MacBride in sight that he didn't notice two figures leap out of the bushes, one pushing him to the floor as the other brought a booted foot crashing down on Karl's head. Curling into a ball, Karl wrapped his arms around his head and tried to dodge the worst of the blows. Never a big man, Karl was still fast and he could hear grunts of exertion as the two men laboured to land kicks on his skull. The first blow had turned his vision blurry – it was as though he was staring at the world through a sheet of water – and try as he might he couldn't see well enough to block every attack.

After a few frantic blocks, another kick got through, the force grinding his head into the pavement. As his body went limp, Karl's last sight was a blurred boot descending from the heavens, turning the whole world to darkness.

22

TEN MINUTES later we were still sitting a few doors down from a block of flats on Windlesham Avenue in Hove. Karl had traced them this far but then his phone had gone dead. Figuring that he'd run out of battery, I decided to pull up and wait until he doubled back and found us. After a few minutes I tried calling him again. This time it rang through to answerphone without being picked up. By the time I got off the phone Nat had opened the glove compartment and extracted a can of Coke and a Mars bar.

'Where's mine?' I demanded.

She shrugged. 'I didn't get lunch.'

'You didn't get blown up either.'

'You want sympathy?'

'No, just a Mars bar.'

She grimaced and handed it over. I unwrapped it carefully and broke it in two, passing the smaller half back as a peace offering. She took it without a word and began to nibble at the chocolate on top.

'Do you want to hang on to the hoody until tomorrow?' I asked finally, having wracked my brain for anything clever or interesting that might defuse the tension and failing utterly.

'Uh, yeah, thanks.'

'Look...' We both spoke at once and then laughed nervously. I gestured for her to speak.

'I'm sorry Rob, it just seemed the right thing to do. I didn't want them to recognise you; I know you've nicked Watson before.'

I nodded. 'To be honest with you he probably would have if you hadn't acted so fast, it's just that after Linda...'

'I know. I realised that on the way over here. It's been a long time though Rob.' She stared at me intently, as if she could glean from my expression the answer that I couldn't put into words.

I paused for a moment. I've never been a great one for sharing, and even though I now had the perfect chance I couldn't quite take the final step. Pulling away from the kerb, I cruised along the road looking for anything that might tell me where MacBride had gone.

'Not long enough, apparently,' I finally replied, feeling the words hanging awkwardly in the air between us.

Nat turned away abruptly and looked out of the window. At first I thought she was ignoring me but then she stiffened and pointed down the road. I followed her finger and saw a small crowd gathered around something lying on the pavement in the mouth of an alleyway that had been hidden from our previous position.

'Rob,' she began, but I was already out of the car and running with barely time to switch the engine off, a cold lump in my stomach. I put on a burst of speed as I got closer, recognising the crumpled suit the figure lying on the pavement wore. Half a dozen people milled around and I forced my way through. A woman in her mid twenties was cradling his head, blood covering her hands. Ignoring the panic that threatened to engulf me I reached out and felt for a pulse.

'What happened?' I asked of the woman holding his head.

'Do you know him?' she replied, looking up at me.

'Yes, we're police officers. I need to know what happened.' I managed to keep my voice level.

'I found him lying on the pavement. I think someone attacked him – it doesn't look like he did it falling over. The wounds are on the top, back and sides.'

'Are you a nurse?' I asked, surprised at her calm authority and knowledge.

She shook her head. 'Paramedic. I've called for an ambulance, they should be here soon.'

'Thank you. How bad do you think it is?'

She looked down at the wounds – blood matted Karl's hair and soaked the ground beneath his head. 'I don't know. Scalp wounds bleed a lot anyway but that's not my main concern. He'll need a scan to make sure he's not got an internal bleed as well. It looks like he got hit pretty hard.'

I swore and stood as Nat arrived, having parked the Escort properly. Her face lost its colour when she saw Karl and she immediately went to her knees to check the wound. I left her in conversation with the paramedic and turned to the crowd waving my badge in the air for all to see.

'I'm Detective Sergeant Rob Steele,' I said loudly, 'and this man is one of my officers. Did anyone see what happened?' There was a lot of headshaking and muttering.

'Come on, someone must have seen *something*!' More heads were shaken as I saw the blue lights of an ambulance appear above their heads. It blipped its siren once as a warning to the crowd and pulled to a halt to disgorge two green-uniformed paramedics who rushed over and began checking Karl. I put my hand on Nat's shoulder.

'Can you go with him to the hospital? I need to stay here and find out what happened.'

She nodded and squeezed my hand. I dredged up a weak smile and turned back to the crowd, hoping vainly that someone would come forward with something, anything, that would help me discover who had tried to kill one of my officers.

Before I could start questioning the bystanders, Nat stood and tapped me on the arm, pointing to the driver of a Vauxhall Corsa that had pulled up behind the ambulance.

'That's Kelly Hardy, she's SV,' she said. The woman looked over as she got out of the Corsa and gave us the faintest of nods as my phone rang.

'Steele.'

'Sarge, it's Bob Miller from Surveillance. We've got units in location now, which building are we looking at?' I resisted the temptation to look up at the houses and flats surrounding us.

'I don't know, one of my officers was on them but he's been hurt. The last thing we heard from him was that they were approaching Worcester Court. It's those flats on the left with the bird bath on the lawn, then his phone went dead.'

'So they could have gone anywhere?' Bob asked.

'Yup. Until Karl wakes up I don't think we can do anything except plot up this location and hope. It's all we've got to go on.'

'Right-ho. Leave it to us then, you get your man sorted.'

'Thanks Bob. I'll update you if we hear anything new. Oh, and get on the radio and get a marked unit here, would you? I don't think there'll be much for them but if we don't show a presence it'll look sus.'

'You're the boss.' He sounded surly and I guessed he wasn't happy about uniform turning up in the middle of his stakeout but it couldn't be helped.

The paramedics had put an oxygen mask over Karl's face and were wheeling him into the ambulance with Nat following. I watched as the doors closed and then turned to the off-duty medic who had been helping Karl when I arrived.

'Thank you for what you did,' I said, pulling out my notebook, 'let me repay you by taking some details.'

'I prefer chocolates, but okay. I hope your friend's all right.'

I took her contact details and let her go. The rest of the crowd had disappeared at the sight of official police work. People love to stand and gawp after a crime, but try and get them to tell you what they saw and suddenly they vanish like mist. I was about to call Burke and explain what had happened when a marked police car turned the corner and pulled up in the space the ambulance had left. An officer in his late forties with a shock of greying hair and a drinker's ruddy complexion climbed out, the edge of his stab vest scraping the door where it stuck out over his paunch.

'Sergeant Steele, long time no see,' he said as he approached. 'Got a request for uniform to attend a possible GBH. Didn't expect to find CID here already. Normally you'd be trying to pass it off as a common assault.'

On any other day I would have laughed at the banter. 'Sorry Gary, not this one. You know Karl Bentley?' The officer nodded. 'It was him that was hurt. He's on his way to the RSCH now with Nat Statham.'

'Is she hurt too?' Gary Havers had a reputation as one of the laziest officers on Division, but I knew from past experience that the one thing guaranteed to make him pull out all the stops was another officer in need.

'No, she's fine but I wanted someone with him when he wakes up. Looks like he was smacked over the head with something heavy, although no one saw anything. I've got details from an off-duty paramedic who was here but everyone else buggered off. There's your scene.' I pointed to the pool of blood on the pavement, now tracked through with countless footprints.

'Bollocks. Did you never learn how to preserve a crime scene?'

'I was more interested in getting Karl into the ambulance and seeing if there were any witnesses.'

'So you'll be taking the lead on this?' he asked, his expression hopeful.

I shook my head. 'Normally yes, but I'm on another job. I need you to get to the bottom of this, Gary.'

He nodded and reached into his vehicle, coming out with a roll of blue and white police tape. 'Suppose I'd best get started then.'

I left him taping off the area, ignoring the SV officers as I walked past their car to my own. I deliberately hadn't told Gary about the job or the surveillance team, knowing that it would make him act differently. If MacBride and his people were watching, I wanted them to think that we had no idea where they were. And if, as I suspected, it was them who had attacked Karl, I promised myself that no other case, no matter how important, would stop them from getting the justice they so badly deserved.

23

I GOT up to the fourth floor just in time – filing into the large briefing room with about a dozen other officers. Burke was already there, sitting at the front with DI Long. Peters was off to one side, facing the assembled rows of blue chairs that filled the rest of the room. Merrington sat stiffly by the wall opposite the windows, his face waxy with pain. Burke nodded at me as I entered and gestured towards the front row. Relieved that I didn't have to sit at the top table, I moved to the front and sat next to the window. There was still no update from Nat about Karl and it was playing on my mind. I felt that I should have been at his side instead of here, despite the importance of this briefing.

I tried to get as comfortable as I could but my face was stinging and my ribs were beginning to hurt. Hopefully the briefing would be short and sweet.

Once everyone was assembled, Burke stood and cleared his throat.

'Ladies and gentlemen, welcome to the first briefing for Operation Sanguine.' He glanced at his watch. 'It's 1802 hours on Thursday 17th August, and for your information this briefing is being recorded on tape as per standard operating procedure. Can I ask everyone to introduce themselves by name and warrant number?'

Long introduced himself first, then Peters, then myself and all the other officers followed suit. When that was done Burke stepped forward again.

'Op Sanguine is the investigation into the murders of David Taverner and Reginald Brown. At 0725 hours or thereabouts this morning, Taverner's postman discovered his door open and saw blood in the hallway of Taverner's flat in Oriental Place. Luckily, he called us immediately instead of entering, and the first officer on scene discovered the body. It appears that Taverner was shot three times from close range with a handgun, but more on that from DS Steele in a moment.'

I felt eyes swivel my way. Firearms positioning was fairly new and therefore treated by most officers like bronze must have been by people used to using flint spears.

'At 1117 hours,' Burke continued, 'Taverner's boss, Reginald Brown, was discovered dead at his office in the Marina. He ran a company called Distant Vistas, specialising in sea tours around the area. He was discovered by DS Steele and Agent Merrington. He was also shot from close range, and again more from DS Steele shortly. His boat was then searched by the officers who found the body, leading to the discovery of an explosive device that destroyed the boat and injured both officers.'

Burke hesitated for a moment each time he said 'officers' and I guessed he was unsure how to refer to Merrington and not entirely comfortable with his newfound power over the Six agent.

'Although MI6 had initial control of the investigation with our staff as backup, it has now been decided to keep it in-house with Agent Merrington as an advisor. So far DS Steele and his team have been working on the case and he will now explain what they've found so far.'

He gestured to me and I stood with a barely suppressed groan, moving to the small lectern and leaning on it more than was perhaps professional, but far less than would have been truly comfortable.

'I'll start with Taverner,' I began, looking at the officers assembled in front of me. While I'd been on the move I'd been fine, but now I was in an overheated room with people expecting me to be direct and give them answers, it was all I could do to stay standing.

'From the wounds and the blood trail, Taverner opened the door for his killer. Two rounds were fired into his chest as soon as the door was opened, but neither was fatal. Taverner made it into the bedroom and was probably reaching for the phone when the killer shot him in the back of the head from point blank range. From the powder residue and the lack of calls from neighbours, we can deduce that a silencer was used.'

A man at the back who had introduced himself as DC Ross raised a hand.

'Yes?'

'Are you sure he used a silencer? They're hard to get hold of, harder than firearms themselves. Could he have used a pillow instead?'

'I'm certain that if he'd looked through the spy hole and seen a man standing there with a pillow in his hands, Taverner would have smelled a rat and not opened the door. Can I continue?' I hate it when people have a little bit of knowledge about something and then dredge it up without thinking about what they're saying. Ross had probably seen a film once where the killer silenced a pistol with a pillow and had just been waiting for the day when he could solve a murder with this little piece of cinematic genius. I let my gaze linger on him until he wilted and nodded.

'Thank you. Although I'm waiting for the victim's height and angle measurements on the wounds, I'm fairly certain our shooter was male and about 6'2.' So far no house-to-house has come back positive, and I've heard nothing about CCTV.' I looked at Burke who shook his head.

'Brown's killer appears to have shot him from across the desk, two nine millimetre rounds intersecting each other at the bottom and top edge respectively. It was done from close range with a silencer while both Brown and the killer were sitting down. And I expect the ballistics to match Taverner's, but that's pure conjecture at this stage. Brown's office was ransacked, but at the moment, it's unclear if anything was taken other than the hard drive from Brown's computer or if it was messed up to disguise the fact it was a hit, if that's what it was.'

I stopped for a moment as a dizzying wave of tiredness hit me. I clutched at the lectern for a moment and shook my head to clear it before continuing. 'Their boat also contained an explosive device linked to a pair of gas canisters, presumably designed to make it look enough like a gas explosion that the authorities wouldn't look too much further.'

An officer at the back raised his hand and kept it there until I acknowledged him. 'Yes?'

'Why would they bother to make it look like an accident if they shot the owner and the only other person with access to the boat?'

'That's a very good question, and one that I'm sure you'll help us answer in the next few days. From what I saw, the device was a professional job. The wires were all the same colour, so we can assume they used coloured tags or pieces of cotton wrapped around the wires while they were building the device, then removed them to ensure that disarming it would be a major issue if it was discovered.

'The last piece of information I have is that, apparently, a loan shark named Danny MacBride has been looking for a bloke called Tav who owed him a lot of money, and that he's been planning to take the money out of his hide. This is C21 intelligence, so it comes from a regular source and, as we know that Taverner liked to gamble, it fits. We located MacBride and two of his men earlier today and we've got an SV team searching for them as we speak in Hove. Any questions?'

Another officer raised a hand. 'Have we got enough to bring MacBride in?'

I shook my head. 'No, at this stage we're just working on intelligence, but I do happen to have a job running on the man at the moment.'

'Who hasn't?' Someone said from the back of the room and there was a wave of laughter.

'The job isn't ready for arrest yet but, when it is, we can use it to bring him in and search his flat if we need to. Anything else?'

Everyone shook their heads and I eased myself back into my seat as Burke stood again. 'And now I'll hand you over to Agent Merrington who will explain why MI6 have such an interest in this case.'

Merrington stood awkwardly and tried to stroll to the lectern with some sense of purpose. It might even have worked if he wasn't injured and wearing a suit that he'd been blown up in. Instead, the best he managed was an awkward shuffle that left him breathing hard as he forced a smile at the room.

'I'm Harvey Merrington, the MI6 liaison on this case. I'm sure I don't need to impress on you the absolute need for secrecy. What I'm about to tell you does NOT leave this room. You don't tell your wives, girlfriends, husbands, families, bosses, even the bloody Chief Constable if he should drop in for a cup of tea. Any operational security breach will be treated so seriously that you'll most likely end up in prison.'

The pain from his injuries had eliminated what little tact the man had left and I could hear angry muttering from behind me that stilled with his next words, replaced by a shocked silence.

'The reason we're interested in Taverner is that we think that he was actively involved in bringing terrorists into the country, and that these members are planning an attack, and soon. The trouble is, we're still not sure when or where, and we believe that this investigation may be critical to finding out.'

24

THE SILENCE lasted for all of about five seconds before every person in the room was clamouring for answers. Burke stepped in front of Merrington and raised his hands for quiet with limited success until DI Long stood and barked 'Quiet!'

Silence descended abruptly, allowing Burke to speak. 'We still don't know for sure that this is related, but we have to work on the possibility that it may be. I only found this out myself just before the briefing. We're speaking to the press in half an hour and we're only going to be revealing local leads, so do as Agent Merrington asked and keep your lips sealed. Some of you have been working all day so I'll keep this short. Those of you working nights, raise your hands.'

I glanced back to see five men and three women sticking hands in the air.

'Right. The next briefing is at 0700 hours. I want as much background detail as possible on friends and family of the victims. DS Steele and his team will take over from you in the morning. By the time he gets in, I want a list ready so that he can be out and at it straight after briefing. If you haven't been given an assignment yet, wait behind and we'll brief you individually. That's all.'

People stood and began to file out. I let the majority of them go first and was making my way towards the doors when Merrington appeared at my elbow.

'Thanks for earlier, Rob,' he said as he held the door open for me.

'Shouldn't I be thanking you?'

'Anyone would have done the same.'

109

'I doubt it. I've got something that belongs to you in my office.'

He shook his head. 'No you haven't' He pulled back his jacket revealing the butt of the Glock I'd locked in my desk earlier.

'How the bloody hell did you get that?' I hadn't been happy about having to hide his hardware in my desk drawer, but I was more than a little annoyed that he'd broken in to get it back.

'I have my ways. Look, I hope we didn't get off to too bad a start this morning?'

'Honestly?' I said. He nodded.

'I don't like the fact you've been sent down here, and I don't like the fact we've wasted the best part of a day running around in circles when you could have told us what you thought was going on from the start. As I'm sure you're aware, the first twenty four hours of any murder investigation are the most important, and we've lost most of that because of your cloak-and-dagger bollocks.'

He drew a breath to speak but I held my hand up.

'Don't take it personally. I just want to make sure we're clear. Now that we're running this investigation, I intend to do it properly, and I'm more than happy to keep you updated with what's going on and even get your help where it's needed, but if we're going to solve these murders, I need to know that you're on side and not running around in the background doing your own thing.' I could feel the day's frustration trying to pour out but I kept it carefully in check. It wasn't his fault that we were in this position, and the last thing I wanted to do was alienate him for following orders.

Merrington shrugged. 'Fair enough. You know that I didn't withhold the information for fun though, right? If I'd told you before it had been cleared I would have been for the chop.'

'I understand that but, whatever the motives, we've still lost precious time.'

He nodded in understanding and almost managed to hide the wince it brought on. I put a hand on his shoulder. 'Merrington, you look like shit. Go and get some sleep, huh?'

'I think I might do that.' he smiled weakly. 'See you in the morning?'

'Sure.'

Once he was gone, I turned and headed back into the briefing room. Burke and Long were briefing the night turn officers. Burke looked up when I came back in and I motioned that I wanted to speak to him in private. Leaving the briefing to Long, he strode over with a face like thunder.

'Whatever it is, make it quick. We've got a lot of catching up to do.'

'Long story short, sir. We found MacBride and two of his lads and Karl was following them in Hove. By the time we got there, someone had clubbed him over the head and he's in hospital. No witnesses, but my money is on MacBride spotting Karl and getting one of his lads to do the job.'

'How bad is he?' Burke said quickly.

I shrugged. 'Don't know sir, I'm off to the hospital to find out. Surveillance are keeping the area covered and uniform are dealing with the attack as a GBH.'

'Do you think it's wise to have them doing enquiries in the middle of a surveillance operation?' Burke queried.

'It'd look damn strange if we let one of ours get tagged and just ignored it.' I explained.

He grunted and ran a hand over his face. 'Fine. Keep me updated. If there's anything your man needs, let me know.'

'Yes sir.'

I headed off down the stairs, not bothering to wait for the painfully slow lift. My ribs jarred with each step and I realised that most of my frustration with the way the day had gone was probably just pain and tiredness. That and my worry over Karl. As I made my way to the hospital, I prayed that the prognosis was good and that he would be fine. If not, I dreaded the thought of phoning his wife and giving her the bad news.

25

TWO HOURS later I was soaking in the bath, a bottle of Paracetamol keeping me company as I tried to keep my damaged ribs under the cooling water. It had been a long, shitty day and, as depressing as the day was, it was infinitely better than being stuck at my desk trying to work out who had killed whom and why.

When I'd arrived at the hospital, I'd found that Nat had already called Karl's wife, Jeanette. Both women were sitting on opposite sides of his bed. He'd still been unconscious but the doctors were happy that he wasn't bleeding internally. It was small consolation as I watched his pale face for any signs of life, his hair shaved around the fresh stitches that criss-crossed his scalp. Nat had volunteered to stay for a while and I'd gratefully accepted. I knew that I should have been the one by his side when he awoke, but I was on my last legs. Had I stayed, I probably would have ended up in the bed next to Karl.

I twisted the tap with my foot – adding more hot water – my mind finding its way back to the investigation. It seemed to me that we had two distinct possibilities, two paths to go down. One was the gambling / loan shark route – where both Taverner and Brown were killed for bad debts. The other was the terrorism route – where whoever they'd brought into the country was cleaning up loose ends.

The bomb seemed to point towards the latter option. I seriously doubted that local criminals had the wherewithal to bomb anything but, at this early stage, we couldn't afford to dismiss any lead, however slight.

Grabbing a bottle of Dettol from the side of the bath, I rubbed some of the amber liquid on my face, shuddering and biting my lip as it worked its way into the wounds. It hurt like hell but, for a moment, it stopped me thinking about work. Usually I had a rule – never bring work home. Not that I had much else to occupy me, so evenings were usually spent running across the Downs or along the beach to clear my head and tire me out enough that I wouldn't dream.

I almost dropped the Dettol in the bath when the doorbell rang, its long sonorous chimes echoing along the hallway and through the open bathroom door. Sloshing water everywhere, I clambered out of the bath, muttering angrily to myself, and wrapped a towel around my waist before stomping to the front door and jerking it open without bothering to look through the spyhole.

26 .

STANDING ON my doorstep was my sister, Anna, a bottle of wine in one hand and a surprised expression on her face. 'What the hell happened to your face?'

'Uh, yeah, bad day.' I looked at her in confusion. 'What you doing here?'

'It's Thursday.' she said, exasperatedly.

'And?' I still had no clue what she was talking about.

'Pizza night?'

'Oh shit, I totally forgot. Come in.'

'If you're going to be like that I can leave.' she snapped, grumpily.

'Don't be stupid. It's been a hell of a day, that's all. It slipped my mind.'

'Hmph.' She swept past me and into the kitchen. Before I'd even closed the door I could hear her rooting around for a corkscrew.

'I'll get dressed, you get the menu,' I called as I shuffled back to the bathroom and towelled off.

A few minutes later, we were sitting in the lounge, me with a glass of juice, her with a glass of pink wine so sweet that just the smell of it set my teeth on edge. The TV was blaring in the corner, neatly removing the need for conversation as Anna studied the menu and I studied her. She was three years younger than me and far prettier – her hair a few shades closer to blonde than mine and cut short with a longer fringe. It made her look a little elfin, the image enhanced by the piercing blue eyes that we shared and the tiredness that pinched her face. She was the only family I had left. Our father had passed away the year before and the truth was I doted – although I'd never admit that to her face.

She looked up suddenly, catching my intent stare. 'Look at you, Mr moody! What's got you looking all thousand-yardy?'

I pointed at the TV where a local BBC reporter was standing at Brighton Marina in front of what was left of the boat I'd been on earlier in the day. See that boat?'

'Yeah.' She drew the word out and I guessed she had an inkling of what was coming next.

'I was on it a few minutes before it blew up. That's what happened to my face.'

'You're bloody kidding!' She sat up straighter.

'Really not. We've had two murders today as well, so you're lucky I'm even at home.'

She dropped the menu and turned towards me, hands reaching out and tilting my face up towards the light. 'You were lucky you didn't lose an eye. What happened?'

'I told you, the boat blew up.'

'A little more detail would be nice.' I spotted an annoyed glint in her eye.

'What else can I say? I was closer than I'd like when it blew up.'

She began to chew her lip, a habit I'd been trying to break her of for years. 'Rob, I don't like it when you get like this. Not with me.'

'Like what?' I knew what she meant but the pain was making me argumentative.

'Like a complete cock. I'm your sister, remember? I've known you for thirty one years and I know when you're not telling me something.'

I put down my glass and gently peeled her hands away from my face.

'I'm sorry Anna, I'm being a shit. I can't tell you much about today. It's all a bit hush-hush. Don't worry though, I won't be going near any more exploding boats in a hurry.'

'You'd better not. Right now you're the only man in my life and I don't want to have to buy another black hat. I've done that too often recently...' she trailed off, realising what she'd said and I seized the opportunity to change the subject.

'I'm the only man? Did Darren dump you? Why didn't you tell me?' I fired the questions at her, one after the other.

'You didn't bloody ask. And no, I dumped him. You know that woman I told you about that he works with?'

I nodded even though I had no idea what she was talking about.

'Well I found a text message from her on his phone, it was quite explicit.' Her eyes flashed with anger.

'So you dumped him?'

She nodded. 'Yeah, and he had the cheek to call *me* a fickle bitch!'

'Well you are.'

She flushed angrily, then laughed, the tension draining away.

'Yeah well, it's not like I was in it for marriage or anything, he was just a bit of a laugh, you know?'

I nodded. 'Yeah, but when are you going to stop going out with morons and find a decent man?'

She shrugged. 'About the same time you stop feeling sorry for yourself and enter the real world again.'

I gave her a warning look. 'Don't go there.'

She shifted back so that she could glare at me properly. 'Why not? I'm the only person you ever talk to outside of work and you never talk about her. *Them.* You can't spend the rest of your life hiding behind your work and not living your life!'

'It's worked pretty well so far.' I said stubbornly.

'Not from where I'm standing.'

'That's because you're sitting on a sofa.'

'Rob, don't! Stop deflecting.' I wondered when she'd swallowed a psychiatrist's pamphlet but let it pass. She had two little spots of colour in her cheeks, a sure sign of impending trouble.

'What do you want me to say?'

'It's not what I want you to say, it's what I want you to do. Linda and Molly died, and it was terrible, but it was *four years ago!* You can't be expected to spend the rest of your life in mourning. Linda would want...'

I cut her off with a sharp motion of my hand. 'Fuck it,' I muttered, trying to shut out the memories of my little baby girl in an incubator, tiny and weak after surviving the traumatic birth that had taken Linda from me, only for Molly to follow her mother two days later. I stood and stumbled into the hallway, leaning against the wall while I tried to swallow a lump in my throat the size of a golf ball.

Closing my eyes and emptying my mind, I ran back over the events of the day, building a wall between myself and the pain, pulling myself back from the dark hole that threatened to engulf me every time Anna and I had this conversation. The smell of cigarette smoke drifted out of the lounge and drew me back in to find Anna ordering pizza on the laptop with a Marlboro clenched between her teeth cowboy style. Picking the packet out of her bag, I took one and lit it, coughing once as I drew the heavy smoke down into my lungs.

'I thought you quit,' she said without looking up.

'Getting blown up makes you hanker for one.'

'Right. Must try that.'

'I don't recommend it.'

Ordering done, she slammed the laptop shut and we settled back on the sofa to watch TV, the silence far from comfortable, but about as close as it was likely to get until one of us finally backed down and apologised. If previous experience was anything to go by, I'd last about ten minutes before I finally gave in.

FRIDAY

27

THE NEXT morning I was in agony. I'd forced myself up just after 0500 and jogged along the seafront for an hour, my ribs protesting with every jarring step. Apart from an early morning angler and a few lonely, screaming gulls, I was alone and it felt good to be with my thoughts for a while. It wasn't the ten-mile run I was used to but it was enough to clear my head. Ten minutes before the 0700 briefing I eased my way into the office to find Nat already at her desk, diligently working.

'Anything?' I grunted as I sank into my chair.

'I'm fine thanks Boss,' Nat said archly, 'and no. not unless you count a list of friends and relatives of the deceased. Or deceaseds. Is that a word?'

'It's close enough. How's Karl?'

'He woke up at about 9 last night. Didn't see who hit him.'

'How's he feeling?'

'Sore but okay. They're going to keep him in until lunchtime and if nothing else is found, he'll be off home.'

'Thanks for staying with him. I would have done...' I trailed off.

'It's nothing. You were in no fit state. You don't look much better this morning.'

'Cheers. You ready for the briefing?'

She nodded and we made our way upstairs, joining the tired looking team from nights and a few other unknowns who were lounging around waiting for Burke. We passed the time making idle conversation, none of us wanting to broach the subject of the investigation until we knew exactly who was who and what they were supposed to know. Merrington's warning from the previous day still hung in the air like a bad smell, making everyone extremely cautious.

The man himself sat in the corner at the front, half turned so that he could watch everyone in the room. He gave me a nod, which I returned. My head snapped around as Burke strode in, flanked by Long on one side and Peters on the other, all with grim expressions on their faces.

Burke hit the lectern and turned while Peters and Long took chairs at the top table.

'Good morning team,' Burke began, his voice vibrant and his eyes gleaming. Say what you might about the man, he clearly loved a good murder, which made him the ideal man for the job, at least in my book. The more interested someone is, the better they'll investigate and the more stones they'll look under to find out what really happened.

We mumbled a collective good morning back and Burke glanced down at the sheaf of papers he held in front of him, then at his watch. 'It's 0702 hours on Friday 18th August. This is the second briefing for Op Sanguine, and is being recorded in accordance with policy. Can everyone please name themselves for the benefit of the tape.'

We went through the procedure, the same as yesterday until we hit the last three people – two men and a woman in smart clothes – who were sat in the third row back with a few chairs space on either side. Coppering is more like being in school than you might think and clearly no one wanted to sit next to the new kids.

They gave their names as Jane Thomas, Mark Stevens and Joe Hunt from the Home Office forensics department. This raised a few eyebrows, but it also explained why our own pathologists and Derek Clinton weren't here. MI6 still had some juice, if not as much as yesterday.

Burke coughed to get the room's attention back. 'I'd like to thank the night shift for an excellent job of work. We now have complete profiles on both men's families for DS Steele and his team to work on, as well as a list of friends and old business partners.'

He glanced down at his papers, then back up, waving a hand at the three Forensics officers. 'Our friends from the Home Office have joined us to assist, primarily to check the compounds used in the explosive. They'll be working with Derek Clinton and also with the pathology team. As for the terrorism angle, we've no real leads yet but we're following up on some intel out of Langley Green that may prove useful, we should have an update by midday. If any of you need to know about it, we'll call you personally and relay it.

'SV have had a team on MacBride since yesterday and, so far, nothing has come of it. They found him on the next street over from where one of our detectives was attacked. One of his men, Billy Collins, was spotted by the team when he went out to buy milk, if you'll believe it. You'll be pleased to know, however, that we woke up the Chief Constable at 5am to get him to sign an intrusive surveillance RIPA. As soon as MacBride goes out today, we'll have a team in his house placing audio and video devices.'

I blinked. Normally you'd to have almost enough to arrest someone for something very serious to get an Intrusive RIPA passed. Burke must have done some very fast, very effective talking and the man rose a few more notches in my estimation.

'Today is a day of action, people,' Burke continued, 'we need to find our killer, or killers, and bring them to justice. I will not have someone running amok with a firearm in my city. Are we clear?'

'Clear,' we mumbled. Burke nodded a dismissal and we filed out, all except Merrington and the Home Office folks.

'Rob, a word?' Burke called me back.

I turned and nodded. 'Yes sir?'

He looked at me critically for a moment. 'Are you okay after yesterday?'

'Yes sir, fine.'

'You don't look it. You know I nearly got killed once, got mistaken for a burglar by a farmer and got both barrels fired at me. I had bad dreams for weeks after, so I understand if you want to be excused. I'm sure we can cope without you if we have to.'

I was shaking my head before he'd finished the sentence. 'Thank you sir, but no. I'm fine, just a bit tired. My head's still in the game though, and if you took me off the case then all I'd do is think about it and drive myself nuts.'

The DCI smiled and clapped me on the shoulder. 'That's the spirit! Didn't think you'd want to back out but I needed to make sure. Oh, and before I forget, the system shows that you've got a case running with MacBride as the suspect.'

'Yes sir, it's an extortion job, small businesses being forced to pay for protection.'

'Well I want you to look into it when you get the chance. If these murders are related to MacBride, then I want to know everything I can about the man. How far along is the file?'

'I've got a statement that uniform took from a shopkeeper who didn't like being threatened, but that's about it. The only reason MacBride is a suspect is the description. I was going to go and see the shopkeeper but then the murders came in.'

'Do what you can. It may have nothing to do with it, but then again it might.'

I nodded and left, mentally kicking myself for not taking the chance to go home and bury my head under the pillow until I felt somewhere close to human.

28

I WAS halfway down the stairs when my mobile rang, the sound echoing off the drably painted plaster walls.

'Rob Steele,' I forced a cheerful tone despite my pounding head.

'Rob, it's Mandy from the front office. We've had some woman ringing for you about half a dozen times, something about her sister. She sounds really upset.'

'Okay, what's her name?'

'Lucy Hallett.'

'Really?' I said in surprise.

'You do know her then?'

'Yeah, we went to school together.' I suddenly remembered the missed calls and cursed. 'Thanks Mandy, I'll give her a call.'

I cut the call and pulled up Lucy's number. It rang twice before it was answered. 'Lucy? It's Rob Steele.'

'Oh Rob, thank God! I'm sorry to call you like this but I didn't know who to turn to.'

I could hear tears in her voice, raspy and choked where usually it was bright and vibrant.

'What's up?'

'It's my sister...Gemma...she's gone missing.' Lucy stumbled over the words.

'Have you called the police and reported it?'

'Yes, but they told me that she had to be missing for longer before they'd take a report.'

I sighed and looked at my watch. I really didn't have time for this. 'Look, Lucy, I...'

She burst into tears, sobbing uncontrollably. I closed my eyes for a second and let the storm of weeping pass before talking again. 'Okay, okay. When you called the police did you give them your address?'

'Yes, I did.'

'And did you get a reference number?'

'Yes, 1403 of yesterday's date.'

'Fine. I'm up to my neck in an investigation, but I promise you I'll have a look into your sister's disappearance. I'll be over when I can.'

'Oh, thank you Rob! You know I wouldn't have called if I didn't think it was serious.'

'I know. I'll be round as soon as I can, okay?'

I turned around and headed back up to the first floor, cutting through an office to get to the Intelligence Unit. Burke would skin me alive if he knew I was taking time out to do this, but the fear in Lucy's voice had made me think of how I'd feel if Anna went missing and I realised that I'd travel to the ends of the earth and back to find her. How could I say no to someone feeling like that if I had the power to help?

I never liked going into the Intelligence Unit. It was full of people working so hard that they ignored you until you coughed long and hard enough to bring up a lung, and then they only looked up long enough to hand it back. Today was no exception, the thirty-odd officers and staff beavering away to the sounds of furious typing from behind sad looking brown desk dividers covered in mugshots of Brighton's most wanted. I drifted through the almost silent chaos until I found Marcus Turner – an ex surveillance officer I'd known for years who had a wicked sense of humour that seemed to get darker the more his hair receded.

'Marcus, you got a moment?' I said, then waving my hand in front of his face.

He looked up from his terminal. 'Sorry? Oh, hi Rob. What do you need?'

'Who's on mispers nowadays?'

Marcus pointed towards a young officer in jeans and a black t-shirt at the far end of the room. 'Bernie. Be gentle with him, he's only been up here a week.'

'Thanks, you well?' I asked as I moved away.

'I'm here,' came the reply as he turned back to his screen.

I approached Bernie's desk and saw him watching me out of the corner of his eye. He looked young enough to be in school and had a certain hesitancy that so often accompanied new officers.

'Bernie?' I asked, giving him the chance to look up and pretend he hadn't been watching me approaching.

'Sergeant Steele.'

'So you're the lucky sod on mispers, huh?'

He nodded and tried to look happy about it. 'Yeah. Only seven in the last twenty-four hours.'

'Have you looked at serial 1403 of yesterday?'

'Gemma Hallett?' He asked without looking.

'That's the one. Can you bring up the serial?'

He nodded and his fingers flew over the keyboard, bringing up an incident log showing an entry in full 80's green screen splendour. Rather than strain my eyes and brain trying to sift through the all but indecipherable police jargon, I took a seat on the corner of the desk.

'Don't show me, tell me,' I said, wishing I'd bought another box of painkillers on the way in as the cuts to my face flared.

'Well Sarge, a woman called Lucy Hallett called in yesterday afternoon, reported her sister as missing. She got told to call back when she'd been missing for twenty-four hours. Anyway, apparently her sister Gemma went round to see her new boyfriend on Wednesday night and she hasn't been seen since. Lucy got left looking after Gemma's little girl, and apparently it's out of character for her to not be back when she says she will.'

I pulled the screen around further and began searching through the log, eyes scanning through the abbreviations to get the full picture. There wasn't much more in the log than Bernie had told me already but I hit print to get the address.

'Have you done all the relevant checks?'

He nodded. 'Yup. Checked with the hospital and run criminal intel, PNC and pretty much every other check I can think of. No trace anywhere that might be useful.'

'Great, thanks. You've saved me a hell of a lot of time.' I smiled at him.

The printer whirred noisily into life and spat out the log. I grabbed it and hurried out of the office, down the stairs and back to our little hovel in the basement. Nat was in there on her own, coat on and car keys in her hand.

'You busy?' I asked as I grabbed the bag that contained my cuffs, spray and baton.

'Er, no actually. I've made a couple of appointments, but I've got an hour or so to kill before the first one. I was just going to grab breakfast if you want some?'

I was so dosed on painkillers that just the thought of food was enough to make me feel ill. 'God no. I've got a favour to ask, actually. Can you put breakfast on hold for a bit while we go chat to someone about a misper?'

She raised an eyebrow. 'And you're looking into a misper instead of a murder because?'

I shrugged. 'Because I'm a muppet who can't say no to old friends. You coming?'

She sighed. 'Of course. Fill me in.'

'Great, as you've got keys you can drive.' I filled her in on the way to the car park, giving her as much detail as I could remember.

'Right,' I said to Nat as she slid into the driver's seat, 'we're going to...' I looked at the printout, 'Hollingdean Terrace. Don't feel the need to drive safely.'

She threw me a black look. 'After my close encounter with a taxi yesterday, we're going my speed or not at all,' she warned. I took the hint and shut up.

As we pulled out and headed across town, I hoped that I'd be able to wrap this up quickly and get on with the work I should have been doing before Burke found out that I'd gone AWOL. I probably should have known better.

29

LUCY HALLETT'S house was a small semi-detached property on Hollingdean Road within spitting distance of Ditchling Road, in a row that had originally been workers' housing back in the thirties. Now, however, the area was a good location for families, close to several schools and far enough off the beaten track that children still played in the streets, a rare sight in Brighton.

Although it didn't look much from the outside, I could see through the window that it was lovingly decorated and the furniture, while a little worn, was well cared for and just the right side of expensive. Lucy answered the door to us herself. She had dark rings under her eyes from lack of sleep and her hair and clothes were rumpled, quite at odds with the neat interior of the house. As soon as she saw me, she swung the door wide with a look that was equal parts relief and worry.

'Thanks Rob, I didn't want to bother you but I didn't know who else to turn to,' she said as she showed us into the kitchen and sat us at the table while she made a large pot of tea.

'How are you holding up?' I asked, watching her shaking hands fussing with the teapot.

She shrugged. 'I've been better. This is just so out of character for Gemma, but she's been different since she met her new man, and I think maybe he's got something to do with it.'

'New man?' I asked, not liking the sound of this.

'I don't even know his name, just that they met on the seafront. She can be so secretive when she wants to.'

'Okay, I think we'd better start at the beginning, don't you?' I said.

She nodded and concentrated on pouring the tea. I waited until she'd served us all and joined us at the table.

'I know you'll have answered all these questions before,' I said, opening my notebook, 'but I want to make sure I cover everything. The more I know, the more chance we have of finding your sister.'

She took a deep breath and drew herself up a little as if preparing herself mentally. 'Go on.'

'Tell me about when you last saw her.'

Lucy's eyes flicked up and to the right as she talked, a sign that she was accessing her memory rather than the creative side people used when lying. Not that I needed that small sign to tell me she was really worried – she looked ten years older than when we'd last met.

'It was about half six on Wednesday night when I waved her off in the taxi. She had a date over at her new bloke's place. They've been out a few times in the last month but she's been hurt badly before and she wanted to take it slow, so it was the first time they were going to...you know.'

I nodded and gestured for her to continue.

'Well, I was looking after her little girl, Ruth. She's only four.'

The same age Molly would have been if she'd lived. I shook my head to clear the thought. Nat noticed the hesitation and smoothly took over.

'Where is she now?' she asked.

'With my mum. She lives in Crawley and I thought a trip to Nana's would be better for her than sitting here asking when Mummy was coming home.' Lucy wiped the back of her hand across her face as her eyes welled up.

'She's never done anything like this before, will I ever see her again?' She wailed, tears suddenly flooding.

Nat moved around the table and gathered the crying woman up in her arms, giving me a look over the top of Lucy's head that said *'go easy.'* I nodded.

'I'm sorry,' Lucy said as she pulled a tissue from her sleeve and dabbed at her face, 'but this just isn't like her. She'd never leave it so long without calling. She just wouldn't!'

I took a sip of my tea and waited for her crying to slow. 'So she took a taxi?'

Lucy nodded and smiled gratefully up at Nat, who deftly slid back around to my side of the table. 'Yeah, she called a cab but I didn't catch the address she gave.'

'Any idea which firm?'

'Sorry, it was a private hire and it didn't have a number on the side.'

'Did she call you during the night?'

Lucy shook her head. 'No, but she said she wouldn't unless there was a problem. She'd even asked me to take Ruth to pre-school so that she didn't have to get up and run off in the morning if she stayed at his.'

'Did she say when she'd be back?' I probed.

'She said she'd pick Ruthie up, but I got a call from the school saying that she hadn't turned up. Then I called her phone but it just rang until it went to answer phone. That's when I called the police the first time.' She began to sob again and I busied myself with my tea until she'd recovered enough to answer my next question.

'Did she talk much about her new man?'

Lucy shrugged. 'A bit. Mostly about what they did together and how he made her feel. She's had some real bad luck with men, so meeting someone who treated her right was a big thing for her.'

'What sort of stuff did they do?'

'The usual sort of thing, you know. Went to the movies, had dinner out. Last weekend he took them both out to the Aquarium, Ruthie was talking about it all week.'

'Have you got any idea at all where he lives?'

'No, I'm sorry, I don't. She's really secretive about it for some reason.'

'Okay. Does she work?'

'No, she's a full time mum.'

'Any friends she might stay with or places she might hang out other than home?'

'Only Mum's place in Crawley, and she's not there.'

I hesitated for a moment before asking the next question. 'Uh, does she have a history of alcohol or drug abuse?'

'*Gemma?* Christ no. She rarely even has a glass of wine with dinner. She used to smoke weed when she was a teenager, but she hasn't for years.'

I nodded and closed my notebook.

'Whereabouts does Gemma live?' I asked with a sinking feeling that this wasn't as simple as I'd hoped it would be. I was beginning to worry about what might have happened to Gemma.

'Here. She moved in about a year ago after her last boyfriend left her paying off three credit cards' Lucy said. 'Did you want to take a look at her room?'

Sharing a concerned glance with Nat I nodded grimly. 'You know, I think that might be a good idea.'

30

GEMMA'S ROOM was as messy as the rest of the house was tidy – clothes and make-up scattered across the floor as if she was sixteen rather than thirty.

'It's not normally like this,' Lucy apologised from the door.

'That's fine,' I said, with a smile I hoped looked reassuring. 'If we find anything that might help to find her are you okay with us taking it? We'll return it after she's found.'

She nodded uncertainly. 'Like a diary or something?'

'Yeah, something like that.'

'Okay, if it helps find her, I guess.'

I pulled a pair of latex gloves from my pocket and wiggled my fingers into them before sifting through the debris in the hopes of finding something useful. Nat stood with Lucy by the door, distracting her with small talk so that she wouldn't realise that something was wrong. Nat and I knew each other well enough that she'd read my body language and instinctively done exactly what needed doing.

After a few minutes of checking I came up with something useful. Moving a piece of black fabric that probably stretched into a dress I found a silver photo frame. The photograph itself was of a pretty looking woman of about thirty with a definite resemblance to Lucy, hugging a little girl that had to be Ruth.

'Do you mind if I take this?' I asked.

'Sure. She'll want it back though.'

'I'm sure she will, I'll make sure it gets to her,' I promised.

The only other thing I found of use was a hairbrush with a smooth handle that might be good for fingerprints, as well as DNA from the strands of hair that clung to the bristles. I tried to find a tactful way of explaining why I wanted the brush, but Lucy's stricken expression told me that she'd already worked it out. Not that I thought the worst had happened but, if it had, I wanted to be able to identify her. I got her to sign for both items and hurried to the door, almost tripping over my own feet in my haste to get out and away from Lucy's sickeningly hopeful gaze.

'Please find her, Rob,' she begged as we left.

'I'll do my best, I promise,' I assured her, then gave her a quick hug and hurried down the steps towards the car.

As soon as we were far enough down the street I turned to Nat.

'Fuck, shit, fuck.'

'Eloquent.' she replied, deadpan.

'So how do I explain to Burke that I've just got myself involved in a proper misper while I'm supposed to be investigating a double murder?'

'You don't, you pass it to someone you trust and get them to keep you updated.'

I sighed and nodded. No matter how much I wanted to help Lucy, I knew that Nat was right and I just didn't have the time to investigate this myself. 'Okay, I'll see if someone can take it on.'

As we got back in the car my phone rang and I answered it to find the senior SOCO, Derek Clinton, on the line. Masking the start of guilt I felt at not being on the case I should have been on, I forced a cheery tone. 'Morning Derek, how can I help?'

'Morning Rob. Thought I'd update you on the forensics that have come back so far from Taverner's flat.'

'Go on, I'm listening.'

'We've got four sets of prints there that are worth anything. One set is the victim's, the second belongs to the other victim, Reggie Brown. Third set has one set on the door to the bedroom and another set on a CD that was on the floor and the fourth is a single thumb print. Both the last ones are unidentified.'

'Have you started running them through the database?'

'Just sent them off, but unless they're locals it could take days.'

I sighed. 'Well at least we've got something, I'll see if we can't narrow down the field a little bit for you with some good old detective work.'

'That'd be nice. Let me know if you find anything.'

'Will do.' I rang off and explained the gist of the conversation to Nat, who pursed her lips thoughtfully as she drove.

'So we need to come up with some names for Derek to run against the prints. Where do you want to start?'

I shrugged as we crawled through the Lewes Road traffic. 'By working through friends, family and colleagues. Hopefully nights came up with something that we can get our teeth into.'

'And if they haven't?'

'Then we've got a very long day of sitting at our desks making phone calls.'

'Great.' Nat grimaced slightly.

'Welcome to the wonderful world of being a detective.'

She smiled wryly. People thought that CID did all the exciting jobs, and while that *could* be the case, most of our time was spent at our desks, joining up the dots to get the whole picture before we so much as stepped out of the station. Although it was ultimately rewarding, we all had moments where we felt we should be out *doing* something, not staring at a computer for hour after hour.

Back at the Nick, we headed to the office where we discovered another detective, Eddie Brown, neck deep in paperwork at Karl's desk, a king-size frown on his round face. With his stocky frame, round head and shaven hair he looked a little like a teddy bear with the ears pulled off.

'Care to tell me why you're in here?' I asked with a matching frown.

Eddie glanced up and pulled a face. 'The DCI dropped me in as a replacement for Karl until he's back on his feet. So far I've got thirty pages of possibles for family, friends and anyone they used to work with. Well, I say *they*, most of it relates to Taverner. Seems like our Reggie was a very private individual.'

'Avoiding the taxman?' Nat asked.

Eddie shook his head. 'That's just it. If he was avoiding the taxman it would be easy. Instead he's registered with HMRC under four different names!'

That piqued my interest. 'That's a bit excessive. Any idea why?'

Eddie nodded towards Nat. 'I was hoping our girl-wonder here could tell us that.'

Nat had a head for facts and figures that had made her infamous on Division. She ran more cases than anyone else but also had a better detection rate. If anyone could make sense of all this, it was her.

'Let's have a look then,' Nat pushed Eddie's chair out of the way and slid her own in, then looked up at me. 'If you're not doing anything useful, you could make some tea.'

'I'm afraid I'm going to have to pass, I need to talk to someone about our missing lady.'

Nat nodded and turned to the paperwork. Eddie leaned over her shoulder and began to explain what he'd already figured out of the mess in front of them. Leaving them to it, I headed upstairs to the Intelligence Unit, hoping to convince Marcus to take on the job of finding the missing girl. All the while feeling like I was letting Gemma down by not dealing with it myself.

31

GEMMA'S FINGERS worked at the knots, her hands cramping almost to the point of uselessness as she twisted them to reach the rope. Crying with the pain, she kept going, determined to escape and get back to Ruthie no matter the cost. The gag sat hard against her tongue, the dry, acrid taste making her want to vomit. With no choice but to breathe through her nose, she could smell her own stink, strong enough that it brought the nausea to almost unbearable levels. She had no way of telling how long she'd been here, the room had no window and the only light came from the crack under the door.

As she picked at the knots, the rough weave of the rope bit into her wrists, and soon her hands were covered in blood from her lacerated skin. Taking a deep breath, she caught the rope with one hand and pulled hard, trying to slide her other hand through the blood-soaked binding. She screamed at she felt flesh tear, the sound muffled by the gag. The pain was unbearable, hot flashing agony that seared up and down her arm, but still she pulled. At last her hand came free.

Pulling the gag from her mouth, Gemma lay back, panting with the pain and effort. Steeling herself, she sat up and freed her other wrist, then undid the knots holding her feet to the end of the bed. For a moment she considered using the gag to bind her cuts but one look at the filth encrusted rag made her shudder. Putting something so dirty over an open wound was asking for an infection.

She giggled suddenly. Here she was, held captive against her will by a man who had killed her boyfriend, and she was worrying about her cuts getting infected. There was no mirth in the sound – she could hear the edge of madness in her own voice.

Shaking her head, she swung her feet to the floor and crept towards the door. Taking hold of the knob, she twisted it slowly and the door swung open to reveal a mouldy hallway, the smell of mildew strong enough to cut through her own stink. The floral wallpaper was peeling badly, and in places the plaster was crumbling. At the far end of the hallway she could see a door, wooden with glass panels in it, and through those panels faint sunlight shone.

Ignoring the other two doors, Gemma stumbled towards the light, but as she reached the end of the hallway the door suddenly swung open. Caught like a rabbit in the headlights, Gemma could only stare in horror as sunlight outlined the figure of a man, his face masked by shadows.

With a growl the man dropped the bag of shopping in his hand and reached out to grab her arms roughly. Gemma screamed and tried to turn but a fist caught her jaw, knocking her to the floor. Dazed, she felt the man grab her beneath her arms as he lifted her and manoeuvred her back down the hallway and into the room she had only recently escaped. As she lay helpless on the floor Gemma saw the man pull a pair of handcuffs from under the bed, and was powerless to stop him as he snapped one cuff around her wounded wrist and the other to the iron bed frame. Pain flared in her wrist and Gemma opened her mouth to scream, only to find the gag shoved firmly back in place.

Turning away from the bed, he left the room and, as he closed the door behind him, Gemma heard a phone ring, then his voice fading as he moved down the hallway.

'...the girl. Yes. I know, but we can use her, it'll be perfect... No, they've got no idea, they'll think it's an attack... Yes...'

The voice disappeared as another door slammed, leaving Gemma alone in the darkness once more with only her thoughts. Whoever they were, whatever they wanted, they were going to use her for something. But for what? Try as she might, she couldn't think of anything they might do that would get her out of this alive and as the realisation that she'd never see Ruthie again struck her, she dissolved into helpless tears.

32

LUCY HAD given me Gemma's mobile number and, as I perched on the edge of Marcus' desk, I listened to him ring it.

'It's still on and in signal,' he told me as he placed the receiver down, 'so it's either with her and she can't answer it, or it's been stolen.'

'Last time she was seen was Wednesday evening at 1830.' I informed him. 'We know she got into a cab, but we don't know which company or to where. Not a lot to go on, I'm afraid, but my gut is telling me that she's really missing, not just on a three-day bender.'

'Okay, leave it with me. Do me one favour though, huh?' Marcus looked directly at me.

'Sure, what?'

'Can you take the hairbrush up to SOCO and get them to take what they can from it? I don't want it sitting around on someone's desk for a week while we try and find her.'

'Sure. Thanks again.' I picked up the hairbrush, now firmly ensconced in its very own cardboard evidence box, and made my way up to the first floor and through the CID office. I saw Wadey glaring at me from his office but I pretended not to notice as I eased my way through the narrow door to the SOCO office and on into the labs at the back. Derek Clinton was already there, cup of tea in hand.

'See you started the party without me,' I said as I dropped the box on to a counter. 'In your own time.'

Derek swallowed a few times, washing down the remainder of his mouthful with a swig of tea. 'If you'd told me you were coming I would have made you a cup,' he said cheerfully, his red face veering sharply towards purple as he leaned over the hairbrush to take a look.

'Which scene is this from?' he asked, pulling on a pair of gloves and lifting the box to the central table – a solid steel affair with square edges and a large pull-down light.

'It's not. It's from a missing person that Marcus in DIU is looking into. It's a proper one as well, single mum missing for a couple of days. I know you've got a lot on, but is there any chance you can get prints and hair off it?'

The look he gave me would have sent a lesser man scurrying for cover. 'Do you have any idea how much work there is just from the two scenes we've got running? I've got hair samples, fingerprints, skin samples, clothing fibres, the list goes on. I've also got every SOCO from here to Hastings working on it, and I'm supposed to be updating the results as they come in. Does Burke know that you're doing this?'

I shook my head. 'No, that's why I've handed it over to Marcus. I know the misper's sister and she asked me to look into it. Please mate, I'll owe you a favour.'

He looked at me suspiciously. 'What kind of favour?'

'The kind that gets you out of trouble when you leave an entire bag of exhibits at a crime scene and it gets stolen,' I said, reminding him of the incident a few years back where I'd got him out of some very hot water by tracking down the missing bag and returning it before the powers that be found out.

Reddening even more, he finally nodded. 'Okay, but Burke'd better not find out.'

'Scout's honour.' I pointed at the brush. 'Do you think you'll get much?'

He shrugged. 'Depends how well the prints come up.'

As we talked, he carefully opened the box and lifted the brush out, then placed it on its back on the table. Placing his toolbox next to it, he pulled out a long brush and a pot of what looked like iron filings. Despite his bulk, Derek was surprisingly delicate when handling exhibits, and he barely breathed as he dipped the brush into the metal powder and flicked it lightly over the handle of the hairbrush. Picking it up between two fingers, he shook it gently, sprinkling the table with silver dust as the bits that weren't sticking to the print fell away. Making a pleased noise in his throat, he admired his handiwork, then took a piece of tape and pressed it over one of the marks before pulling it away smoothly, leaving a perfect print on the back of the tape. He pressed this on to a clear plastic plate and wrote in indecipherable SOCO script along one edge before cutting away the excess tape.

'That's one,' he said, putting it to one side and repeating the process until he had three good prints and two blurry ones.

'I'll just scan these in, won't take a minute.' He ambled over to a computer in the corner and passed the plates one by one over something that looked like a retinal scanner from a Sci-Fi film. Having done that, he clicked the mouse a few times and hammered at the keyboard with one finger until it eventually did what he wanted it to.

Finally, as he turned around, he was in time to catch me snaffling the last custard cream out of the packet as quietly as possible.

'You thieving bastard, put that back!'

'Put whaf ack?' I said indistinctly, having shoved the entire thing in my mouth as soon as I was discovered.

Derek sighed. 'You do someone a favour and they repay you by eating your lunch while your back's turned. Never trust a copper.'

'That was lunch? They must pay you less than I thought.'

'Don't even go there,' he said mournfully.

That's one thing I've discovered is the same the world over. Wherever you go, coppers and police staff will bemoan the fact that they're not paid enough. Mostly it's because they're right. What other job could you find where you get spat on, shot at, stabbed and generally hated by the public, yet still be the first person they call when they want help? And all for the grand starting sum of nineteen thousand measly quid a year. I sometimes wondered whether I should have listened to my dad and become a plumber. It might be a shit job but at least they get paid well, and when was the last time you heard of a plumber being spat at or stabbed?

Once the prints were logged on the computer, Derek picked up a pair of tweezers and held the brush up to the light. Ever so gently, he pulled several strands of hair free until he found one with a root still attached.

'Aha, got the bugger.' He held it up to the light. 'Beautiful. Dark brown with just a hint of red to it.'

I raised an eyebrow. 'Didn't realise you were a connoisseur.'

He shrugged, looking a little embarrassed. 'You have to take the small pleasures in life where you find them, and I like hair. You can tell a lot about a person by their hair you know.'

'Really?'

He nodded, clearly pleased to have someone to share his passion with. 'It's a complete chemical history of the body. With the right techniques, you can tell what people have been putting in their bodies, their toxicity levels, all sorts of things. It's like we're all walking around with these little signs that only a few can read, amazing...' He tailed off as he examined the strand closely.

Eventually he looked up. 'Okay Rob, leave this with me and I'll make sure it gets to the store. And remember that you owe me.'

'Thanks Derek. I owe you a pint.'

'And when would I have time to drink it?' he complained as I left, hurrying back down to the office. Hopefully Eddie and Nat had begun to make some sense of the reams of data that the night shift had left for us.

33

NAT AND Eddie had indeed come up with something in the twenty minutes I'd been away. When I walked through the door, Nat was smiling like a cat who'd not only got the cream, but had been in the bin and stolen the remains of last night's chicken as well.

'Go on,' I said, seeing that she was fit to burst.

'We were about to call you. Turns out that our man Reggie wasn't the shy and retiring type he appeared. His three aliases all have wanted markers on PNC for fraud – some credit card, a few cheques, that sort of thing. So I thought I'd run some more checks on the names, and it turns out that they're all real people who died.'

'That's some pretty fast work.' I was impressed.

'You haven't heard the best bit yet.' She was almost bouncing on her chair in excitement and I felt an answering smile cross my face.

'Hit me.'

'Two of the aliases are local, so were easy to check on our intelligence systems. But, one of them, Trevor Carver, was born in Liverpool. So I made a quick phone call to our liaison officer up there. And guess who Trevor Carver – the real one – used to knock about with when he was a lad?'

I suspected I knew where this was going but didn't want to spoil Nat's moment so I shrugged and gestured for her to tell me.

'Billy Collins.'

'MacBride's muscle?'

'Indeed. Trevor died of a heroin overdose when he was twenty-one. I guess Billy took his ID and sold it when he was short of cash.'

I crossed to where she'd scribbled frantic notes and lifted the piece of scrap paper to get a better look. 'That gives us two links between the victims and MacBride and his crew. Keep going with this and see what else you can find out on the aliases, I'm going to speak to the surveillance team and see if they've got anything interesting yet. Good job, both of you.'

The buzz was back, that first jolt of adrenaline that came from having pieces to try and put together. Find me any copper that doesn't get excited when they get a good lead and I promise you they're either dead or moments away from it. As I called the surveillance team leader, I felt like grinning and I waited impatiently for him to answer.

'Bob Miller.'

'Bob, Rob Steele. You still on MacBride?'

'Yeah, sadly. They've not moved from the flat since yesterday, except Collins going down the shop to get fags and beer after his ill advised milk run. Not the most exciting job I've ever been on.'

'Well, stick with it, something interesting's just come to light that might tie them in with the murders.' Something occurred to me. 'If they haven't left, does that mean...'

'Yeah,' Bob interrupted, 'we haven't been able to get in and install the technical equipment. We're hoping they'll leave sometime today.'

'Bugger. Thanks for the update.'

'Welcome.'

I threw the phone on the desk and looked over at Nat. 'They haven't left the flat so there's no cameras inside. I'm starting to think that we're on to something with them and not this amorphous terrorist threat that Merrington was talking about. I think I need to talk to the DCI.'

She nodded distractedly, still working through the pile of paper with Eddie, scribbling down notes on the margins of the pages to cross reference them.

'Keep me updated, okay?'

They both nodded without looking up and I felt a stab of jealousy to see them working so closely together. Eddie's crush on Nat had been a running joke in the office for years, but it had never bothered me before. I put it aside as I walked, and tried to work out if we had enough to bring Collins in for anything. I couldn't see that we had, but we certainly had enough to keep tabs on him until the forensics could come back from the murder scenes. That would have to do for now. If not, there was always the other job I had on MacBride. Whatever he was up to was sure to include Collins.

I came out of my musings when I reached Burke's door and rapped on the frame before walking in. The DCI was sitting behind his desk, idly squeezing a stress toy shaped like a grenade.

'You got a moment sir?' I asked as he looked up from his screen.

'Rob, yes, come in.'

I stood in front of the desk and relayed what Nat and Eddie had found, making sure that their part in it was clear. I've always hated supervision who took credit for their officers' work, and I tended to go out of my way to make sure that I didn't do it. Once I'd finished, Burke stood and walked to the window, gazing out over the back yard where seagulls swooped and dove above the parked police vehicles.

'Doesn't tie him to the murder though, does it?' he asked.

'No sir.' I assumed the question was rhetorical but I answered anyway. 'But it's the best lead we've got so far and it should be enough to keep the RIPA going.'

He nodded distractedly. 'I suppose so. We need to get on top of this, and fast. I don't feel like we're making enough progress, and the Chief Super is starting to breathe down my neck. It doesn't help that we spent the first day running around after Six when we should have been doing proper detective work.'

'No Sir.' He was still looking out of the window and I guessed that I was pretty much surplus to the conversation. He confirmed this when he turned to look at me and blinked for a second as if he'd forgotten I was there.

'Anyway, good work by your team. Get back to it and keep me updated.'

'Sir.'

'Oh, and how's DC Bentley?'

'Going to be discharged sometimes today, so I hear.'

'That's good.' Burke turned back to the window and I took it as my cue to leave.

I headed back downstairs with the intention of getting some proper work on the go – feeling as if I'd been to-ing and fro-ing all day without actually getting anything done – but stopped short when I found Merrington waiting for me outside the office.

'I thought you were off advising,' I said as I approached.

He shrugged, wincing as he did so, then smiled hesitantly. 'Seems like they're not too interested in what I have to say at the moment, so I thought I'd come see if I could lend a hand.'

I was about to tell him that I didn't have time to show him how to do real police work when it suddenly occurred to me that the man was being genuine. Left with nothing to do, he actually wanted to help the investigation rather than sit back and recuperate.

'Sure,' I said, holding the door open for him, 'I'll never turn down a willing volunteer. Welcome aboard.'

34

BILLY COLLINS stood beside the window, barely moving the curtain as he peered out and across the road.

'Rozzers are still out there,' he said over his shoulder, causing MacBride to grunt sourly from where he sat on the sofa a few feet away.

'They can't stay there forever,' MacBride said, changing the channel on the TV to find yet another daytime talk show hosted by a fake tan with big teeth. Throwing the remote on the table in disgust, he rose and looked out over Billy's shoulder.

'I told you the two snogging in the car were cops,' he said. 'We should never have come straight back here.'

Billy shrugged and smoothed back his long greasy hair with both hands, a nervous gesture that MacBride had seen him do a lot in the last twenty four hours.

'But I smacked that bloke in the suit before we got near the flat,' Billy whined, reliving the moment when he'd stepped out of the bushes and brained the small man with a piece of scaffold pole. 'And it can't be to do with *the job*. It's not like they're on to us. You know how careful everyone's been recently. Not a foot out of line.'

'If they aren't on to us, then why the fuck are there three cars sitting outside with fucking rozzers in them?' MacBride shouted, then took a deep breath and lowered his voice. 'Someone must have talked. I want you to find out who and deal with them.'

Billy looked at him in surprise. 'How am I supposed to do that while they're outside?'

'I don't care. Think of something, that's what I pay you for, isn't it? I need to get out and about, I've got things to do and people to see. Every hour I spend sitting in here is money lost, and money lost means customers going to the fucking Scousers instead. No offence.'

Billy glared at him but MacBride ignored the look. Even half asleep he'd tear the younger man apart and they both knew it.

'So what do you want to do?' Billy asked finally as they stepped away from the window.

MacBride shrugged and went back to the sofa, lighting a cigarette and balancing it on an already overflowing ashtray. 'The plan hasn't changed – we're still going to go ahead. We have to. Too many people are involved for us to back out now. Don't know about you, but I don't fancy ending up in a ditch with my throat cut. So that means you need to get out there, find out whose lips have been flapping and find out how much the pigs know.'

Billy nodded uncertainly. 'Sure boss, no problem.'

In one of the mercurial changes of mood that made him so terrifyingly unpredictable, MacBride grinned and clapped Billy on the back. 'That's my boy. Do whatever you have to do, but come up with something fast or we'll all be in the shit so deep we'll need snorkels. Oh, and microwave me another pizza while you're at it, I'm fucking starving.'

Billy hurried off to the kitchen, his mind whirring as he made and discarded plans until an idea hit him that was so brilliant there was no way it couldn't work. Throwing a pizza in the microwave, he twisted the dial and ran back to MacBride to give him the good news.

35

'SO TELL me exactly what I'm doing again,' Merrington said uncertainly as Nat shoved a pile of paperwork in front of him.

I'd cleared half my desk and now all four of us were sat in a space that would have been comfortable for two, trying to find anything that might give us a concrete lead. I was going through lists of the victims' families, their occupations and PNC records, while Nat and Eddie had the aliases and anything that might relate to them. We'd decided to break Merrington in gently, and he'd been given access to our intelligence system and a crash course in how to use it on my login. It would have been enough to get me fired if anyone had found out, but at this stage I was willing to take all the help I could get and I've never been averse to cutting a few corners for the sake of expediency.

'We need you to search for anything to do with the names that are on the papers, or any names that are similar. I know it's like trying to find the proverbial needle in the haystack, but we don't have a researcher so one of us has to do it.' Nat put a comforting hand on the Six agent's shoulder. 'But I promise that if you're really good, tomorrow we'll let you loose on the kettle.'

'I can hardly wait,' he muttered, already tapping away at the keyboard with his lip jammed between his teeth in concentration.

For the next hour or so we worked in relative silence, broken only by the rustling of paper and the tapping of computer keys, until suddenly Merrington sat up straight and pointed at his screen.

'I think I've found something,' he said excitedly, 'can one of you take a look and see if this makes sense?'

Swinging the screen, I scanned quickly through the intelligence log he'd been reading, my heart rate picking up when I saw it was about someone named Carver. A few lines later though, I shook my head and swung it back.

'Good spot, but no. Wrong PNC number.'

'Oh, sorry, should have seen that.'

I shrugged. 'I wouldn't beat yourself up about it, this intelligence system is about as straightforward as Central London at rush hour. Tea anyone?'

I was saved from kettle duty by the phone ringing, beating Nat to it by seconds.

'Steele.'

'Sarge, it's PCSO Tom Burnley.'

'Yes Tom, what can I do for you?'

'My team have been doing house to house enquiries around Oriental Place and we think we might have come up with something.'

'Go on.'

'Well there's a set of garages out the back of the victim's flat, and one of the owners has put a CCTV camera up. It's taken us a while but we've tracked the man down and seized the tape and there's something on it you should really see.'

'Are you in your office?' I asked, standing up.

'Yes.'

'Don't move. I'll be there in two minutes.' I dropped the phone in its cradle and moved towards the door.

'CCTV from the back of Taverner's,' I called over my shoulder as I left. I'd barely made it out of the room when the others caught up, following me up the stairs and along the corridor to the community policing office. Inside, Burnley was already waiting for us in front of their archaic VCR, the screen frozen on a grainy black and white image.

'Is this it?' I asked, trying to make out the details.

He nodded and rewound the tape, giving us a running commentary as he found the right place and hit play. 'This is the garages at the rear of David Taverner's flat,' he said, 'at 1900 hours on Wednesday evening.'

We watched, trying to make sense of the blurred shapes on the screen. Although CCTV in general has come on in leaps and bounds in the last ten years, most of the available systems at the lower end of the market are still of little use as anything other than a deterrent. As I watched, a dark blob moved on to the screen and stopped.

'Is that a car?' Nat asked.

'We think it's a van,' Burnley replied, 'but as you can see it's hard to tell.'

Someone got out of the vehicle, disappearing around behind it and out of sight towards the back of Taverner's flat in jerky time-lapse. I could just make out what might be a

159

staircase, and realised that while I'd been at the scene I hadn't bothered to look out the back as we knew the point of entry had been the front door.

'I need to forward it a bit,' Burnley said, speeding it up until the timer in the corner showed that it was 1911 hours. 'Here. Watch the staircase.'

As we watched, a dark figure appeared on the stairs carrying something large over its shoulder. It was almost impossible to make out clearly, but it looked like a large bag.

'So whoever it was took something from the flat?' I asked in confusion. 'And how did they get in the front door if they went up the rear stairs?'

Burnley interjected before anyone else could speak. 'If you'll allow me, I've spent a fair bit of time in that area and the fire escape stairs lead up to the landing on each floor. Whoever it was must have climbed up to the right floor and then gone in through the landing window.'

'Good work,' I said, already on the move with my phone out. 'That gives us a point of entry into the building and that might give us prints. Eddie, get that tape up to the technical unit and get the picture as clean as you can, then get a couple of working copies made. Nat, grab some keys. Go to the scene and find out if anything's missing from the flat. We need to know what they took and why. If we find that out, we may well have a motive and that brings us another step closer to finding the killer. Merrington, I need you with Nat. I'll stay here and see what else I can dig up that might help.'

They nodded and suddenly the room was a hive of activity as everyone began to hustle. All of a sudden, things were clicking into place and it was with no small sense of excitement that I hurried back to the office, hoping that before the day was out we'd have something

firm that would lead us to our killer.

36

'SORTED,' BILLY said with a grin. 'Marky and Trev C are turning up in half an hour. When they're here, we'll all go out and get in separate cars, then go off in different directions. We give them the slip, then meet up later.'

MacBride nodded. 'Sounds good, except one small flaw.'

'What's that?'

'Trusting two fucked-up skagheads! Marky and Trev fucking C? I wouldn't trust them to tie their own fucking shoelaces!' MacBride's glassy eyes bulged and a vein stood out on his forehead as he shouted. 'What the fuck were you thinking?'

Billy took an unconscious step back, hands raised in supplication. 'What choice did I have? No one else has got a car and could help.'

MacBride put his head in his hands. 'And what exactly did you offer them to help?'

'Not much, just a ten bag each.'

MacBride looked up, incredulous. 'A *ten bag* each? I take it back. You're a fucking genius! Wake Leon up and we'll go through the plan one last time before we split.'

Ten minutes later they were sat around the table, Leon still rubbing the sleep from his eyes. They'd been taking shifts watching the police watching them and the big man had been up most of the night.

'So I drive the van in and you're in the back with your friends,' Leon said, working through the plan bit by bit, 'and I get us through the gate with the pass and the paperwork.'

MacBride nodded. 'That's right. The van's hidden up already, the paperwork's in the glove compartment. All you have to do is drive the van in, show your pass and hand over the papers. They'll let you through the gate and into the loading dock.'

Leon thought this through for a minute. 'But won't they get suspicious when there's no writing on the side of the van? What if they realise it's not a real one?'

MacBride shook his head exasperatedly and explained it slowly and carefully once again.

'They use plain vans all the time to transport cash and I paid someone a small fortune to get our van put on the list. It'll all be perfectly normal until they open the back of the van and we all jump out and stick guns up their noses.'

'But what about the locks on the vault? Don't we need proper safe crackers?'

'No, Leon. We're not going to the vault. According to my man on the inside they've got a counting room on the second floor and on Saturday they'll have a couple of mil in there, with only unarmed security guards to look after it. All we need to do is grab one and force him to let us in and we're laughing.'

'Right. So what if that doesn't work?' Leon persisted.

'Then we've got half a ton of plastic explosive - and the others assure me they know how to use it. That's why they're coming along. That and the guns, of course.'

'Do you reckon we can trust 'em?' Billy asked suddenly. 'I don't like working with foreigners.'

'Hey, is that any way to talk about our business partners?'

'That's what they are, isn't it?'

MacBride nodded. 'Yeah, they are, but best we don't get in the habit of talking like that around them, eh? Wouldn't want you to make a slip and upset that big bastard they've got. And yes, I reckon we can trust them. This is about money, and where money's concerned you can't fault the commies. If they want their share then they'll muck in and do their part.'

Billy shook his head. 'I still don't trust 'em. What if we get the money and get away and they decide to take it off us?'

'Then that's where you come in. I want you tooled up and waiting at the farm. When we get out the back, if anything looks dodgy you start shooting and we'll join in, yeah?'

Billy nodded with an evil grin. 'Sure boss, no problem.'

A phone rang, startling them all. Billy hurriedly answered it. A few seconds later he put it down again and turned to his boss. 'They're both outside, Marky just down the road and Trev directly opposite. I'll take my car and head for the farm. Need to get my shotgun out.'

MacBride nodded. 'Right. Be careful both of you, and I'll see you later.'

All three men left, filing out one after the other as they mulled over their parts in the plan that, if successful, would make them all very wealthy men indeed.

37

TAVERNER'S FLAT looked like a naughty child with a pencil and excellent mathematics had been let loose. There were scrawls everywhere, with small cards here and there where something useful had been found.

Nat and Merrington stopped at the door and tied coverings on their shoes, then negotiated the hallway carefully. It was the first time Nat had been to the scene and she grimaced at the smell of old blood that still hung in the air. There were still two SOCOs working in the lounge, both on their hands and knees in full protective gear as they combed fibres from the carpet. The SOCOs looked up as they entered and one of them pointed imperiously to an area by the sofa, directing them to wait.

'Morning Yvonne,' Nat said, but the masked and paper-suited woman ignored her, so she stood tapping her foot impatiently while Yvonne finished the area she was checking, marking it with string so that she could find her place again.

Yvonne finally stepped carefully across the carpet, removing her mask to reveal a face that would have been pretty if not for her perpetual frown.

'Detective Statham, what can I do for you? I'm sure you can see that we're very busy.' She said without preamble.

'Yvonne. This is Agent Merrington from MI6.' Nat was hoping to impress her into some semblance of civility, but judging from the look on Yvonne's face, she'd failed miserably.

Yvonne Parker was famous on Division for her foul temper. More than one junior officer had been reduced to tears when their crime scene preservation skills had been torn apart by the woman now standing with her hands on her hips. On the plus side, Yvonne was one of the best SOCOs in the force, a redeeming quality that had stopped her from losing her job any number of times.

'And?' she asked, glancing pointedly at her watch.

'And we've discovered CCTV that shows someone entering and leaving the flat via the fire escape stairwell with what looked like a large bag over their shoulder. Does it look like anything is missing?'

Yvonne shrugged. 'I haven't had time to look. Help yourself, but stay away from that side of the room.' She waved her hand. 'I don't want you messing up the *work*.'

She stressed the word 'work' slightly, as if Nat didn't know what it was, then retied her facemask and returned to her piece of string. Merrington raised his eyebrow and Nat gestured for him to follow her into the bedroom. Once in, she shut the door and breathed a sigh of relief. Even having known Yvonne for years, she'd never managed to get her to mellow for a moment, and every encounter left her wanting to punch the woman in the face.

Refocusing, Nat began to look around the room for any obvious gaps where something was missing, then pointed to the far side of the room, glancing at the now bare mattress with a dark stain in the middle – the sheets having been carted off for forensic analysis.

'She's always been like that. I try not to let it bother me. If she was a police officer, I'd put her straight on a few things but as she's a civvy she can be as snappy as she likes. Do you want to start in that corner and I'll do this one? We'll meet by the bed.'

He grinned and opened his mouth but Nat gave him a level stare that froze the words in his mouth. He let out a sigh and nodded as she turned her back to him and started pulling open drawers.

'Can I ask you a question?' Merrington said as they worked.

Nat shrugged without looking away from her work. 'Sure.'

'How long have you worked with Rob?'

'Just over a year, why?'

'I was just wondering. He seems a bit, er...'

'Job pissed?'

'Well that's one way of putting it.'

She snorted. 'It's the only way of putting it. He's so obsessed with the job he can't see...' She tailed off and busied herself with the search. 'Anyway, why the interest in Rob?'

'Just asking, really.' The silence stretched uncomfortably until Merrington cleared his throat.

'So, uh, do you enjoy being a detective?'

Nat closed the door of the cupboard she'd been searching and turned to face him, hands on hips. 'You're very chatty all of a sudden. Yes, I do like being a detective. I get to fight the bad guys.'

'Have you ever considered changing careers?'

'Like what, *MI6*?' She stared at him disbelievingly.

He shrugged defensively. 'Why not? You get to *fight the bad guys*, as you put it, just on a much, much bigger scale.'

She laughed and shook her head. 'Nat Statham, super spy? I don't think so. I grew up in this city, and I think I'm doing enough by trying to keep it safe. I don't think my family would like me buggering about all over the world.'

'But your ability to remember things would be an asset. If I could remember half the things you do I'd be, well, I'd be twice the agent I am, probably.'

'Sorry Merrington. The only language I speak is English, and foreign food doesn't agree with me. I'll stick to putting rapists behind bars thank you very much.'

Merrington frowned but nodded and turned away, leaving Nat chuckling to herself and she carried on searching. She'd almost finished her side of the room when Merrington coughed to get her attention.

'What exactly are we looking for?' He asked.

'Spaces where something should be, like a bag or a case maybe, or patches that are clean of dust.'

'Like this one?' Merrington said.

She turned to see him standing on a chair to look on top of the wardrobe. He was pointing at an area directly in front of him and she waved him off the chair so she could climb up and take a proper look, grinning to herself as the Agent tried not to look at the parts she'd just elevated to eye level. Half the top was covered in thick dust, but the right side was completely clean.

'Good spot. So now we know that something's missing for sure. Doesn't help us know what, but maybe it gives us a motive.'

'But if Taverner was killed to get whatever was taken, why was Brown killed?' Merrington queried.

She shrugged. 'Who knows? Maybe something was taken from Brown's place as well?'

'Could be. The office was such a mess I doubt we'd ever be able to tell though.'

Nat got down from the chair. 'Anything you know that might help?'

'Sorry?'

'Your terrorist angle. Anything you know of that Taverner and Brown might have had that made them worth killing for?'

Merrington shrugged and looked her straight in the eye, as if willing her to believe that he was telling the truth. 'Honestly, I have no idea.'

She held his gaze for a moment then nodded. Even if he was lying, there was nothing to be gained by pushing it, and her gut told her that he was telling the truth. 'Fine. Let's get back to the Nick and throw some ideas around, see if we can make anything of this mess.'

'Aren't you going to tell your friend Yvonne about the window in the hallway?'

She shook her head. 'No, I've already got Eddie on that, he'll tell Derek and he can feed it down to our cheerful lady. One chat with her a day is about all I can stand.'

He nodded in understanding and they sidled out quietly to avoid disturbing Yvonne.

38

'WHAT HAVE we got then?' Nat asked. She had returned to the office with Merrington and we were all huddled around my desk with tea and a selection box of biscuits that she had unearthed from somewhere.

'So far we've got two bodies, both men who worked together, both killed in a professional manner with a silenced pistol. Then we've got this CCTV showing someone entering and leaving the stairwell at the rear of Taverner's property. Although we can't confirm that it's the killer, it's odd enough that it probably is, and if you couple that with the fact that the footage shows the person leaving with something, then that gives us a motive to work with. What have I missed?' I asked them both, wishing that Karl was here to put his tuppence worth in.

'The bomb on the boat,' Merrington replied, pointing to the slowly healing wounds on my face.

'How could I forget? So the killer put a bomb on the boat as well and we need to know why. My current theory is to remove any forensics that might be on the boat but it could just as easily have been a warning to someone else. Are we sure that no one else worked with the two victims?'

Nat nodded. 'As far as I can tell it was just the two of them, unless you managed to find something else while we were out. The business wasn't big enough to support more, at least not on the books. As for their more covert activities, I'm sure you could tell us more.' She looked at Merrington.

He shrugged. 'I only know what our intelligence says, and it's not confirmed. It may be nothing.'

'Well "maybe nothing" is better than nothing at all.' I said.

'Okay, but let's be clear. What I have to say doesn't leave this room, not even to Burke. If you can't agree to that and stick by it, I stop talking now.'

Nat and I shared a look and both nodded.

'Right,' Merrington began, 'as I'm sure you're aware, the country's under constant threat from terrorism. Thanks to our increased border awareness, it's getting harder and harder for said terrorists to get in through the ports, so they're turning to other means.'

'Such as hiring small boats to bring them over from mainland Europe,' I said, remembering our earlier conversation.

'Exactly. We had an anonymous tip that Taverner and Brown were bringing people in from France and that these people were part of another operation that we've been keeping an eye on in France and Spain for a few months now. Which is why we got involved instead of MI5. We already had a good idea of the main players and we wanted to retain control. So we were assembling a surveillance team to keep an eye on Taverner and Brown when Taverner turned up dead. We knew by then that both men had debts that could have got them killed, so we decided to tack on to your investigation rather than doing our own in tandem.'

'So you knew that Brown was in danger after Taverner was killed?'

He held up his hands. 'Hang on. Before you start throwing accusations about, we had someone check up on Brown after we found out about Taverner but they couldn't find him.'

I chewed that over for a moment, deciding it wasn't pertinent to our current investigation.

'I'm not accusing you, just trying to get the facts straight. So do you have anything else that might make you think the killings are terrorism related?'

Merrington shook his head. 'Nothing concrete, but if they were, then the boat being destroyed would make sense.'

I nodded. 'True, but I can think of a few reasons that it might have happened that don't relate to terrorism either.'

Nat leaned forwards. 'So where does that get us?'

'Nowhere fast,' I answered, trying to see all the pieces in my head and put them together into a picture that fit. 'So where do we go from here?'

'I could see if I can get some of the paperwork from Brown's office and see if there's anything useful there,' Nat offered.

I nodded. 'Good idea. Let's see if we can build up a picture of their business, see if anything stands out that we can use. You get on that, while I...'

My phone rang and I pulled it out to see that it was a private number, a must answer for any copper. While most people only pick up if they recognise the number, as police we're slaves to answering that unknown call as it's almost always work related.

'Steele.'

'Rob, it's Bob Miller. MacBride, Collins and Watson have just left the house and got into separate vehicles and we don't have the resources to cover all of them. Any chance you can grab a car and help out?'

'Of course. I can be with you in five minutes.'

'Two would be better. Currently we've got Collins heading into the town centre, so if you take him that'd make sense. Kelly's following at the moment, but Collins knows she's there and keeps trying to lose her.'

'I'm on my way,' I said, hanging up and hurrying out of the office without a backwards glance. My phone rang again. This time it was Marcus from DIU.

'Rob, we've got a hit on the phone from your missing woman.'

'I'm a bit busy, can it wait?'

'Not if you want to find her. We've been pinging the phone since you left the office with nothing happening, but suddenly it's on the move in the town centre. All of my staff are out on another job, so if you want us to follow this up I need you with me, and preferably someone else as well.'

'Shit. Give me a minute, I'll be up.' I turned and headed back into the office, almost banging into Merrington who had followed me out.

'Nat, grab a car and get hold of Bob Miller. They need you to help follow Collins. I haven't got time to explain now, something else has come up. Merrington, you're with me.'

Although the agent might disapprove of me ducking out on the murder, Marcus had said he needed someone else and Merrington was the only person I could think of in short order. Nat nodded and pulled her phone out without question.

As I ran up the stairs to the DIU office, I filled Merrington in. As soon as he saw me, Marcus grabbed a set of keys and threw them at me. He was already kitted up and ready to go as I introduced Merrington. Marcus raised his eyebrows but refrained from comment as they quickly shook hands.

We headed for the car park, as Marcus filled us in on what was happening. 'We got an urgent authority to find the phone,' he said as we hurried down the stairs, 'and after we rang it the first time it went dead, but in the last ten minutes someone has turned it back on. If your woman is in trouble we need to find whoever's got the phone before it gets turned off again.'

'Fair,' I said. 'But if Burke finds out then I'll be giving parking tickets in Whitehawk for the next fifteen years.'

'Best we come up with the goods then, eh?'

I nodded my agreement. Despite my protests, I wanted to find Gemma as badly as I wanted to catch the man who'd killed Taverner and Brown, maybe more. There was a good chance that Gemma was still alive, and I kept thinking of her little girl wondering when her mummy was coming home.

39

IT'S HARD to be discreet when you've got three blokes jammed into a small car driving slowly through town but I'd like to think that we made a good job of it. I drove with Marcus in the front and Merrington jammed in the back with a bag full of search kit as we cut back and forth across the town centre. Marcus had his phone glued to one ear while he threw directions at me, which I did my best to follow in the utter chaos that is Brighton's one-way system.

'Can you ring this number?' Marcus asked Merrington, passing him a scrap of paper. The agent nodded and tapped the number into his phone.

'Ringing,' he called after a few moments.

Marcus sat up straighter. 'We've got it, it's on the move south on West Street.'

I put my foot down and tore along Queens Road, almost taking off as I hit an amber light and flew across the junction on to West Street. There were two cars ahead of us – a silver Mercedes and a grubby looking green Kia.

'Keep talking,' I said, swerving to avoid a pedestrian who thought his right of way beat my sixty miles per hour.

'Six seconds to the next ping,' Marcus replied as the cars ahead hit the lights at the bottom of the road where it met the seafront.

Slowing down a little, I saw the Kia head left and the Merc head right.

'That narrows it down,' I said as Marcus pointed left.

I got to the junction just as the lights turned red but bulled my way through, raising an angry honk from an irate driver. Too busy to wave an apology, I pulled closer to the Kia so that Marcus could get the index. Staying about thirty yards behind, I saw only one person in the car. I couldn't see if they were male or female, catching only a glimpse of long blonde hair as the road curved.

'Got the index?' I asked, slowing to allow a car to pull out between us and the Kia, adding some cover.

Marcus nodded and made a phonecall to PNC, relaying the details and tapping his free hand against the dashboard impatiently while he waited for a result. My phone started ringing, but I was too busy trying to keep us hidden behind the car in front to answer it.

Reaching the roundabout by the pier, the Kia headed straight over and along the seafront road towards the Marina. I let another car get between us in case the driver was paranoid and thought a car full of burly men tailing him odd, then followed at a safe distance. We were almost at the bottom of Lower Rock Gardens by the time PNC got back to Marcus.

'Last keeper was a Sarah Milligan from Hounslow, with a new V5 issued,' he said with disgust. 'That helps.'

'Not really but we need to get it stopped. Can you answer my phone?'

'Let's concentrate on one job at a time, eh?' Marcus said. 'And besides, what would you say if it was Burke?'

'Good point. In which case could you put in a call and see if we can get uniform to stop the car?'

'Sure thing.' Marcus made another call, and I wondered what officers had done before they started issuing Job mobiles. Most cloak-and-dagger police work was done via phone, radios being too bulky and indiscreet. Pull a radio out in the street and everyone knows you're up to something, but walk down any street in the country and you'll see half a dozen people chatting into their mobiles.

As I followed the Kia, I tuned into what Marcus was saying. 'No sir. One occupant, shoulder length blonde hair but can't tell if it's male or female. Currently eastbound on Marine Parade just passing...Burlington Street. Yeah, great. Okay, give them my number, thanks Tony.'

'Well?' I asked as soon as he was off the phone.

'Just spoke to the Duty Inspector, he's sending a couple of cars our way. Should be with us in five to ten, so we need to keep on the driver til then.'

'Shouldn't be a prob... Shit!' I swore as the Kia swerved into the right-hand filter at a set of red lights while the car in front of me turned off left, leaving me no choice but to pull up next to the Kia.

I stopped about a foot further back than the other car but we were still close enough that I caught the driver glancing in his mirror, accidentally making eye contact.

We stared at each other for a moment before recognition hit.

The driver was Billy Collins – Danny MacBride's Scouse black bag man. The man Nat should have been helping surveillance follow. And from the way he put his foot down and tore through the red light it was a fair bet that he recognised me as well.

40

'THAT'S FUCKING torn it,' Marcus groaned as I put my foot down and followed, wishing that Sussex had got around to putting lights in their plain cars as I almost hit another vehicle. Marcus was already on the radio, calling up on the divisional channel now that the need for secrecy was over. In the background I could hear comms and other units responding, then a firearms unit cut across the chatter.

'Hotel Foxtrot three six, we're making from Peacehaven, ETA three minutes. Can I take talk-through with pursuing vehicle?'

I sighed with relief as I heard that. Although Divisional officers are excellent at what they do, Firearms officers are all pursuit trained and that can make the difference between a successful stop and a three-car pileup that is instantly classed as the police driver's fault. Marcus guided them towards us while I concentrated on driving as the Kia shot away like a cork out of a bottle along the A259, swerving in and out of the traffic in front of us.

Desperate not to lose him, I drove like a madman, leaning forwards to hunch myself over the wheel as if being closer to the front of the car would let me see obstacles that little bit faster. I lost count of the number of close calls we had, but I could feel Merrington behind me gripping the seat with both hands as I jinked and swerved as if I were piloting a Spitfire rather than driving a Fiesta.

Why Collins had Gemma's phone I didn't know, but I didn't have the time to be thinking about it as I poured all of my concentration into staying on the road and keeping us alive. We hit a roundabout and turned north towards Woodingdean, the smell of burning clutch filling the car as I pushed it hard.

'At least we can claim we were helping out with the murder investigation!' Merrington called cheerfully from where he clutched the back of my seat. He sounded suspiciously like he was having fun.

The Kia was pulling away, not having the weight of three people holding it back as we began to climb towards the traffic lights on the Falmer Road. A speed camera flashed as Collins doubled the speed limit, then almost rolled his car trying to avoid a cyclist struggling up the hill. Using the momentum of his skid, he slid into a junction on the other side of the road and accelerated out of sight between two rows of houses.

'Shit, he's in a residential area,' Marcus said unnecessarily, 'if he hits someone...'

I nodded and took the same turn at almost the same speed, throwing my passengers from side to side. An image had worked its way into my head that I couldn't shake; Gemma Hallett tied and gagged in the boot of the Kia, and nothing was going to stop me from catching up with Collins and getting her back.

'For fuck's sake Rob, slow down!' Marcus yelped as I went up the kerb and half on to the pavement to avoid an oncoming delivery truck.

Buildings flashed past, a mixture of bungalows and houses, all with their own driveways – each one a potential hazard that I trusted to my peripherals as I strained to keep the Kia in sight.

'Left...left into Batemans Road,' Marcus called out, half to me and half to the units he was directing via radio, impressing me with his local knowledge. As far as I was concerned this area was the bottom of Woodingdean and that was about as far as it went.

I took the corner more carefully than the last one and was rewarded with a glimpse of the Kia as it took another left further ahead.

'Shit.' I sped up again, forcing the protesting vehicle on.

Marcus pointed ahead. 'Don't take that left, take the next one. The road in there's a big circle with only one other way out. Take Holton Hill and you've got him.'

I did as instructed, glancing left as we passed the turning Collins had taken and seeing him turning right at the far end, exactly as Marcus had thought he would.

A grin tugged at the corners of my mouth as I imagined Collins' face when he tried to give us the slip and found us instead approaching him at warp speed. I could hear sirens in the background as I took the turning into Holton Hill and I knew that one way or another the chase would soon be over.

Collins clearly thought the same, however, as the moment I turned into the road and saw him halfway up, he jammed the brakes on and began to reverse so quickly that he bounced off several parked cars, tearing off wing-mirrors, leaving great scrapes along the paintwork.

Too full of adrenaline to do more than register the damage I'd probably get the blame for, I put my foot down for what I hoped would be the last time and bore down on the Kia. A few moments later we were nose-to-nose, my bumper kissing his as I tried to nudge him enough to make him lose control.

Collins jerked as the cars hit, looking back at me through the windscreen with a mixture of anger and terror that looked out of place on a face that I'd only ever seen plastered with arrogance, and I grinned at him and leaned even further over the wheel.

'Rob, Rob!' Marcus yelled at me, pointing over the top of the Kia to a marked Mercedes with blue lights flashing that now blocked the bottom of the road.

I'd been so wrapped up in Collins that I'd failed to see the lights, and a large part of me still wanted to run the little prick off the road. There's a lot to be said for being in a position where you can bully a bully, and Collins had had it coming for a long time. Blipping the throttle one last time, I slackened off and tapped the brakes, slowing enough that Collins could concentrate on looking behind him again.

When he did I saw his shoulders sag and the Kia finally slowed to a halt. But, instead of sitting there, the driver's door flew open and Collins made a dash for freedom, leaping over the bonnet of a car Starsky and Hutch style and sprinting back up the road past us.

Unfortunately for him, we'd been in the game for at least as long as he had and even as he stopped we were already piling out of the car and running towards him. Seeing us coming Collins turned and leapt up on to a garden wall, legs bunched to spring down the other side and make off.

Marcus and I jumped at the same moment, both hitting Collins with a combined weight of almost thirty stone. He squawked as my shoulder drove the breath from his lungs and Marcus swept his feet away, landing us all in a tangled heap on some poor bastard's lawn. The impact jarred my ribs, making me cry out in pain, and I almost let go of our quarry as he struggled to get away, arms and legs flailing at us frantically. He caught Marcus behind the ear with his heel and the Sergeant dropped like a stone, hands flying to his head as his eyes screwed themselves shut with the pain.

Pushing myself up to my knees, I grabbed hold of Collins' tracksuit top and slammed him back into the ground as hard as I could, hoping to knock the wind out of him enough that he'd stop fighting. Instead he reached up and dug his long, grimy fingernails into the back of my hand, hot agony flashing up my arm as he found the nerve between index finger and thumb. He wasn't, however, expecting the right cross that I thundered into his jaw. There are certain things that police just don't do anymore, and punching is usually one of them. The impact of my knuckles striking his chin travelled all the way up to my shoulder, but the pain was curiously absent as his eyes rolled up in his head and he slumped back to the ground, limbs flopping like a jellyfish in a rock pool.

'Fuck that hurt!' Marcus was back on his feet, hand firmly fastened to the back of his head.

'You okay?' I asked, switching my attention back to the unconscious Collins.

'Not really. Why is it every time I work with you I end up injured?' As he spoke, we rolled Collins on to his front and pulled his arms up behind him ready for cuffs, which came in the form of several uniforms from the other vehicle who wisely chose to use the gate instead of leaping the wall.

I was saved from answering as Collins came back to life, spitting and swearing as cuffs were applied and two uniform pulled him to his feet and began to search him.

'I ain't done nothing, yer fucked!' He spat in his lovable Scouse accent.

'Actually, I think you'll find you have,' I said in a matter-of-fact tone. 'I'm arresting you on suspicion of theft, and we'll move on to other offences after we've searched your car.

You do not have to say anything, but it may harm your defence if you do not mention, when questioned, something which you later rely on in court. Anything you do say may be given in evidence.'

He spat in answer, a gob of mucus just missing my shoes. Taking that as an understanding of the caution, I began rapping out orders.

'Right,' I looked at the officers holding Collins. 'Make sure he's got nothing on him, then hold him far enough away that he can see the car but can't interfere. Marcus, can I have you and Merrington searching the car with me?'

They nodded and we hurried to the Kia, my mind's eye still seeing Gemma huddled in the back. Hoping that I was right and she was still alive, I all but ripped the boot open. There was nothing but a few plastic bags and a tool kit.

'Shit!' I looked back at the officers holding Collins, who had a smug expression on his face. 'Has he got a phone on him?'

One of the officers, a hard-bitten twenty-year veteran named Steve, nodded.

'Yeah, Nokia touch screen jobby.' He held it up for inspection.

Without having to be asked Merrington rang Gemma's number again, all of us waiting expectantly for a moment before he shook his head, Collins' Nokia staying depressingly blank.

'It's still ringing, but I'm not hearing it, are you?'

I shook my head. 'Right, best we get searching.'

As I was already at the boot, I started there, throwing the bags out on to the ground after checking them, then pulling up the floor to expose the spare wheel and tools beneath. Several sweaty minutes later, Marcus and I both smelled of oil, stress and the remains of old Lucozade that had been lurking in one of the bags, and the rest of the car was almost done with no sign of the phone. Merrington was picking through the rubbish on the back seat with a grim look on his face.

I pulled Marcus to one side. 'It's got to be here somewhere, we were bloody following him all the way!'

He shrugged. 'Unless he ditched it?'

I shook my head. 'He can't have done, we were watching him pretty much the whole way. Still, it couldn't hurt to go back along...'

'Got it.' The call came from one of the officers searching the driver's seat, the tone one of almost savage glee.

Marcus and I both headed over, seeing the man holding up a mobile phone that vibrated as Merrington rang Gemma's number once more. Turning to the officers holding Collins, I gestured for them to move him so that he could see the find. The look on the Scouser's face was priceless.

'Well Mr Collins,' I said with a grin, 'I hate to say it, but it looks like you're fucked.'

41

BRIGHTON CUSTODY looks like a low budget version of the Starship Enterprise, with a raised bridge that the sergeants and custody staff sit behind, peering down on the mere mortals who bring their prisoners to be booked in.

Collins had clammed up the moment he saw the phone, his eyes showing his fear but his face hard as carved granite. He kept silent all the way to Hollingbury. Merrington had cadged a lift back to John Street to carry on with the murder investigation now that the action was over, leaving me to be assisted by a couple of uniforms.

The custody sergeant, James Gardiner, hurriedly stuffed the last piece of his lunch into his mouth, swallowing it without chewing as I led Collins to the desk.

'Morning Rob, circs?'

'This is Billy Collins, he's been arrested for theft and kidnapping.'

'Thanks. Mr Collins, I want you to listen carefully while the officer explains why you've been arrested.'

Collins stared sullenly at a point somewhere behind James' right shoulder while I outlined the basics of what we'd found without giving too much away, trying not to look at the swelling bruise forming on his jaw.

'Okay,' James said when I'd finished, 'do you understand why you've been arrested?'

Collins continued to stare into the middle distance like a catalogue model from *Criminal Monthly*.

'You have certain rights while you're here,' James continued, 'you have the right to have someone told that you're here, you have the right to free and independent legal advice and you have a right to consult a copy of the codes of practice. Do you want to do any of these things now?'

'We're holding calls at the moment,' I interrupted quickly. It was common practice to disallow contact in serious cases, to make sure that no coded messages were passed to someone who might be able to destroy evidence for the prisoner.

'Thought you might be. Do you want a solicitor Mr Collins?'

His stare didn't waver.

Looking around, I saw Steve Marshall, the officer who had cuffed and searched Collins, standing nearby. 'Steve, can you do me a favour and book him in? I need to sort out the paperwork.'

Steve grimaced but nodded and stepped forward, taking hold of Collins' cuffs while I gratefully slipped away to get on with the mountain of work that awaited me, starting with a phone call to Burke.

'Any particular reason you've been off gallivanting around Division chasing a misper?' he asked as soon as he heard my voice.

'It's hard to explain sir, but we've got Collins in custody which I think you'll agree is a positive.'

'There is that. I've read the log on the missing woman, any sign of her?'

'No sir, sadly not.'

'But you've got the phone?'

'Well, we've got *a* phone with her sim card in it. I called her sister on the way to custody and the phone itself isn't hers.'

'Has Collins given any indication of where she is?'

'No, the moment we found the phone he stopped talking. We need to do an urgent interview to find out where she is, and if she's still alive.'

'Do it. I'll get the Super to authorise it on the Custody Record, and I'll get people searching MacBride's place too. With any luck we'll turn something up linked to the murders and we can have them all in. Find that woman, Rob.'

'Sir.'

Hurrying back to the Custody Desk I broke with protocol, climbing the steps to stand next to James on the dizzying height of the bridge.

'I need an urgent interview without a solicitor,' I said without preamble.

'Reasons?' He knew me well enough to know that I wouldn't ask without good reason and already had the Custody Record open, fingers poised over the keyboard.

'We believe that he has vital information as to the location of a missing woman, and that if we wait for a solicitor it may be too late to help her. The DCI is getting a Superintendent to write an authority on the Custody Record as we speak.'

James nodded. 'Good enough for me. He was taken straight down to a cell to be searched and stripped. I assume you want all his clothing seized?'

I nodded. 'From the smell he's been wearing it all for a few days, so there's a fair chance that there might be something in it. Have you put him in a dry cell?'

He nodded again. 'Yeah, he's in twenty-eight. You want to take him straight down to interview?'

'Yeah. I'll let them take his clothes first though. I don't want to be dancing round a cell fighting with him in my best suit.'

'That's your best suit? You poor bastard.' James laughed.

'Thanks. Use your phone?'

He passed it over and I rang Nat, ordering her to drop everything and get straight to Custody.

'I'm almost there already,' she said, 'if you'd answered your phone while you were following Collins you would have realised I was only a few cars behind you. I spotted you at the bottom of West Street but lost you again when you went tearing off towards Woodingdean.'

'Sorry Nat. I was too busy trying to keep us on the road. See you in a sec.'

Thinking of all the work I still had to do before we had a proper interview, I started my Arrest Statement while I waited for Nat. True to her word she was sitting on the edge of the desk in the report writing room before I was a dozen lines in.

'Tell me all,' she said, eyes shining with excitement.

I gave her a rundown, leaving out my hairy driving. By the time I'd finished, a small frown was creasing her brow.

'What?' I asked, recognising the look.

'I just have to wonder. Why keep a phone with a missing woman's sim card under your car seat, and why keep it switched on? Especially if you're going to leave it on silent. It doesn't make sense.'

'Maybe because he's a moron? Who knows. He could have thrown it in there as a memento, or to check it for numbers later or something. We can cover that when we interview him properly.'

She nodded, unconvinced. 'I just don't want us missing a trick here.'

'Nor do I, but our priority has to be Gemma Hallett right now. We can go over this at our leisure once we've found her, dead or alive.'

A tap on the window made me look up. One of the Custody Assistants was beckoning me, prompting me to get up and stick my head out of the door. 'What?'

'It's your prisoner Sarge. He's refusing to come out of his cell.'

I swore under my breath and motioned for Nat to follow me, before heading into the bowels of the Custody Centre. With Gemma's life at stake, I couldn't afford for Collins to play the silent fool, but if he refused to talk there was nothing I could do.

Most people who enter Custody are desperate to put their side across, be they guilty or innocent, but Collins had played the game before and he played it well. Despite his possession of the sim card, without good forensic evidence he knew that we would struggle to tie him to anything. So his best bet was to sit back and say nothing until he got a solicitor who could work their twisted voodoo and get him back out on the streets where he didn't belong.

42

STEVE MARSHALL stood in the cell doorway, arms folded across his chest as he divided his attention between the pile of brown paper evidence bags next to him and the prisoner in the cell. When he saw me coming, his frown vanished, replaced by a look of relief.

'Glad you're here Sarge, here's your exhibits. I'll do a statement and then bugger off if that's okay with you. I've got too many other places to be.'

I nodded my thanks. 'Book them into the G83 on the way out and leave your statement on the custody record. Cheers.'

He picked up the bags and strode off as I leaned against the doorframe and squinted into the tiny cell.

'So I'm told you won't come out for interview,' I said to Collins, who sat on the low bench in a blue paper suit, his grubby feet poking out to display toenails black with dirt.

He stared past my shoulder while I glanced at the camera high up in the corner, glad that they hadn't got around to installing audio yet. 'Well I need you to listen to me carefully. This isn't a proper interview, it's an urgent one because we're looking for a woman and we think you may know where she is, or if she's even alive.'

He hawked and spat on the floor, then lay back and stared at the ceiling with his arms folded behind his head. I felt anger building in my gut and struggled to keep my tone level. Although the walls were thick here, any sound echoed along the corridors and the last thing I wanted was the cell occupants reporting what I might say if I lost my rag.

'Billy, what if it was your sister that was missing? How do you think you'd feel?'

Still nothing. Technically I was breaching PACE by talking to him in his cell like this, especially if he said something evidential, but with only Nat to hear me I could take the risk.

'Okay Collins, if you don't want to talk, fine. But when you get remanded in Lewes, I'll spread the word that you're a grass, and we'll see how long you last.'

It was an empty threat and he knew it, but it had worked on Evans and I was desperate. Instead of caving, however, Collins turned to me with a look of contempt.

'Why don't you come over here,' he said with sly smile, 'and suck my knob. Then maybe you'll get a little pillow talk.'

I crossed the cell in two strides, reaching out with both hands to grab hold of Collins before I saw the smile and reason reasserted itself. This was exactly what he wanted. If I lost it and threw him around, any chance of a successful case would be lost. And I'd have breached his human rights and be sitting in the cell next door. I stopped, my whole body quivering with anger.

'A woman's life might be at stake,' I hissed through gritted teeth, 'and if you've got a single fucking shred of decency left in you, you'll tell us what you know.'

'What I know?' He sat up as I stepped back. 'I'll tell you what I know. I know that sooner or later you'll have to let me go, 'cause you ain't got nothing on me. I'll be out of here before you get home, and then you'd better watch out. I'm not someone you wanna fuck with.'

I shook my head and deliberately turned my back on him, walking slowly back to the door to show him that I didn't feel threatened by him. It's all about psychology with people like

Collins — if I'd backed out or made a defensive reply he'd have thought he'd won, and I'd have a hell of a time with him when it came to interview. Instead I ushered Nat out of the doorway and swung the heavy cell door shut, throwing Collins the finger at the last second before the metal clanged against the frame.

'Fuck you too!' He yelled — his voice muffled.

'That went well,' I said to Nat as we hurried along the corridor towards the Writing Room.

'Yeah, you've got a real way with people.'

I shrugged. 'Doesn't help us find Gemma though, does it?'

'No.' Nat looked at me. 'Do you want me to see if I can find any other properties connected to Collins? Maybe we've got something on file.'

'Do it. I'll let Burke know what we've got, and then we'll regroup.'

She nodded and sat at the computer I'd been using while I called Burke and filled him in.

'So where does that leave us?' he asked when I'd finished.

'At a bit of a loss sir.' I leaned over Nat's shoulder and brought up the serial, leafing through the OIS log to see what was happening at MacBride's flat.

'A search team is already going through MacBride's place looking for Gemma's phone itself. No sign of Gemma, apparently, and there's nothing else that points to where she is. And MacBride and Watson gave Surveillance the slip. Nat's checking CIS for any other properties that Collins might be linked to.'

'Good, keep going. I'll head to MacBride's flat myself in case we find anything that links them to the shootings. Have you got everything you need?' Burke asked.

'Yes sir. And I'll let you know if I find anything.'

'Do that.'

Nat elbowed me in the leg as I put the phone down. 'I've got something.'

'What?'

She pointed to an entry on CIS – an intelligence report from about eighteen months before. It was sanitised, which meant we had no idea where it might have come from, and it told us that Collins had been keeping drugs in a rented lock-up on a farm at the back of Woodingdean.

'Good spot. Are there any other reports?'

She shook her head. 'This is the only one. Worth checking?'

I nodded, already on my way to the door. 'He took us into Woodingdean when we were chasing him, maybe he was on his way there. You can drive.'

I pulled my phone out to update Burke, then paused. If I told him, he'd insist on getting a warrant and then getting LST geared up, which would take hours. If Nat and I went on our own, we could sniff around first and see if anything was sus. If it was, we could pull back and call in the cavalry. Decision made, I called Eddie and dumped my paperwork on him. He took it in good humour, if you count a string of expletives longer than the Queen's

Speech as good humour, and then I hurried after Nat, eager to get to Woodingdean and

hopefully our missing woman.

43

'ARE YOU sure this is a good idea?' Nat asked as we bumped down a farm track that threw wet splatters of mud all over the car.

'It's probably not one of my better ones, but I think the end justifies the means if we find Gemma.'

I could see her looking at me out of the corner of her eye. 'You seem to be taking this quite personally.'

'Personally? No I'm not. I just hate the thought of Lucy waiting to hear about her sister, and that little girl waiting for her mother to come home. Even if the worst has happened, which it probably has, at least they'll have some closure when we find the body. It's important.'

Linda's face, white, cold and perfect as she lay on the mortuary table, a far cry from the screaming and blood of the birth that had torn her away from me.

My voice was rough when I found it again. 'Besides, we're just having a quick look. If we don't find anything, all we've lost is an hour.'

'Hmm. And my bloody job if we *do* find something without a warrant.' Nat grumbled.

'But you'll be in the dole queue with the satisfaction of a job well done.' I quipped.

'You might think shit rolls downhill but sometimes it fountains upwards too. I'll just say I was following lawful orders from you. I'll do my best to stop the crows pecking out your eyes when they hang you out to dry.'

Despite her joking tone she had a good point. But I was confident that I could wangle my way out of any trouble that might come from poking my nose in where it didn't lawfully belong.

The track ended in a yard with half a dozen converted stables, each one with a small barred window and a big steel door. No-one else was about, which I was grateful for when I stepped straight in a pile of horse dung and had to spend almost a minute scraping it off my shoe in a very undignified manner.

'Ah, the great outdoors. Give me a cup of tea and an Xbox any day.'

'Bloody philistine,' Nat responded, treading carefully. 'It's box number three.'

She pointed to the stable at the far end, indistinguishable from the others apart from the number 3 scrawled in white paint on the metal door. The bars over the window prevented me from placing my face up against the glass, but I pressed my cheeks to the bars and shaded my eyes with my hand to peer inside. 'Should have brought a bloody...'

'Torch?' Nat pressed one into my spare hand.

'Whatever would I do without you?' I flicked it on and pointed the beam through the window at an angle, seeing nothing but crates and boxes.

'Get demoted probably.' Nat responded.

'Probably. This is a waste of time, all I can see is boxes but they're blocking half the room. She could still be in there.' I banged on the door and listened carefully but heard nothing from inside.

'I can't hear anything.' I said.

'Well then, we need to come back with a warrant if we can get one on a single piece of intel.' Nat replied.

I sighed in frustration. Gemma could be lying a few feet away from us and we'd never know. Nat was right about the warrant. There was almost no chance that we'd get one to search property without enough intelligence to make it viable. Left with no other choice, we squelched back to the car and got in.

'At least it's stopped raining,' I said as we drove back along the track.

'My God, did you just say something positive?' Nat said in amazement.

'Me? Nah.'

Nat pulled to one side to let a red van pass, the two men in the front staring at us sullenly. The driver was a small man with classic Slavic cheekbones, but in contrast the passenger was a giant. His head was actually tilted sideways so that he could fit into the cab of the battered transit, and something in his eyes made me shiver when they locked on to mine for a brief moment.

Once they were past, Nat began to pull away but I put my hand on her arm. 'Did they seem odd to you?'

She shrugged. 'Not much is odd after working with you.'

'No, seriously. I don't like the look of them.'

She stopped the car and looked at me. 'What do you want to do, go back?'

I shrugged. 'Dunno, maybe.'

'Why?'

'Call it a hunch. They didn't look like right. Goliath looked at me like he wanted to kill me for a start.'

Nat's grinned. 'I'm game, what's the plan?'

Despite her instant agreement, I almost told her to drive on, but the feeling in my gut was so strong that it was almost a physical pain. On half a dozen occasions before, I'd had the same feeling and each time it had turned out to be right – once quite literally saving my life.

'Who says I have a plan? Let's just get in there and shove our noses in their business. It's what we get paid for, after all.' I grinned in return as she spun the car and headed back towards the farm.

As we approached the yard I saw the van standing empty, the rear doors open and blocking our view of box three. None of the other boxes were open and I felt a sudden prickling on the back of my neck as Nat pulled in.

'Can you see which...' I began.

'Three. I fucking hate it when you're right. What now?' She looked at me.

I took quick stock, realising that my fighting kit still sat in its bag under my desk. Nat didn't have hers either, so between us we had two radios, an investigator's notebook and some pretty foul language. It didn't seem like much compared to the giant I'd seen in the van.

'No harm in having a friendly chat I suppose,' I said, trying to sound more confident than I felt.

'You'll be the fucking death of me, Rob.' Nat shook her head.

'I hope not, I hate funerals.' The attempt at humour felt forced.

We got out as the rain began to fall again, bit spattering drops that hit like water bombs. I could feel my adrenaline pumping as we walked towards the van. Over the rain, I could hear the sound of someone shifting something interspersed with grunts as wood ground against wood from within the open door to box three. I looked at Nat and shrugged.

'Hello?' I called. Instantly all noise ceased.

Moving around to the back of the van, I saw that three long crates had already been placed inside, the scrape marks in the muck covering the floor showing that they were recent additions. Goliath came out carrying a fourth crate, this one square and almost as big as I was.

'Excuse me sir,' I began, but he moved past me without a word, placing the wooden box in the back of the van with its fellows before turning to face me. Up close he was an ugly son of a bitch, lips flattened and heavy brow jutting out over the rest of his features, casting them into shadow. He had an ugly scar running up the left side of his neck, the flesh fused and twisted as if from intense heat.

'Problem?' He asked in a thick accent, spitting out the word like a threat.

'I hope not,' I said with a smile, producing my badge. 'I'm Detective Sergeant Steele, this is Detective Constable Statham. We were wondering...'

The man moved with incredible speed for his size, a meaty fist coming out of nowhere and catapulting me from my feet as it crashed into my cheek. The world turned upside down and I found myself lying on the hard concrete with the wind knocked out of me. I gasped and writhed for a moment, desperately trying to get back to my feet but failing. I looked up and saw Nat hanging on to one of Goliath's arms, both of hers wrapped around a bicep bigger than my head as she tried to reach up for a choke hold.

He shook her off almost contemptuously and I finally surged to my feet, my shoulder slamming into a stomach that felt like stone. The force was enough to knock him backwards and he fell back into the van, striking his head on one of the crates with a sound like a mallet hitting wood. A noise from my left made me turn as the smaller man rushed out of the converted paddock box towards me, something glinting in his closed fist.

Before I could face him properly, Nat threw out a leg and tripped him, sending him flying into the side of the van with a crunch. She threw me a black look as I hauled her to her feet, just in time for Goliath to regain his own footing and punch me hard in the back, sending me sprawling on top of Nat as we both fell to the mucky ground. Rolling on to my back, I looked up with one foot raised to ward off my attacker, only to see something that made my blood run cold.

A pistol was now clutched in one huge fist, the barrel pointed directly towards my forehead as I lay helpless in front of him.

44

I'M NOT sure how long we stayed like that, my back pressed into Nat so hard that I could feel the buttons from her jacket digging into my ribs, my eyes never leaving the weapon that was about to end my life. I could feel the tension in her muscles, her body wanting to get up and fight but her brain keeping her down in the mud.

Suddenly the tableau was broken by the van roaring into life and the little man yelling something in a language I didn't recognise. As if waking from a dream, Goliath shook his head and reached out with his free hand to close the van doors, his eyes and the weapon pointed at me the whole time.

This is it, I thought, and strangely there was more sadness than fear, *this is where I find out what comes next. Please let it be oblivion.*

He stepped forwards, still keeping the pistol well out of my reach as he squinted down sight. I heard Nat's swift intake of breath from behind me, felt her tense even more as her hand found mine and squeezed. Then Goliath looked up as the sound of another engine washed over us, coming from further along the track. Snarling, he turned and ran to the van, jumping in the passenger side as it pulled away and shot off down the track.

Keeping hold of Nat's hand, I used my other to find my radio and hit the red button on top, sending out an ugly blatting noise that cut across all radio traffic.

'Charlie Papa 291, all eyes down for a red transit van, index Victor...' I paused as I tried to remember the rest of the number plate. Adrenaline doesn't help with memory recall, but I was saved by Nat who dredged the rest of it up from her formidable memory so that I could parrot it over the radio.

'..533, Tango Charlie X-ray. Two foreign males in the front, at least one of them armed with a pistol. Direction of travel is South along Farm Hill, Woodingdean, over.'

There was a moment of silence before comms responded. 'Confirm Victor 533, Tango Charlie X-ray and one of the men is armed, over?'

'Confirmed. And it's not a replica. Armed units only to approach.'

The radio went mad for the second time that day, units coming out of the woodwork to assist with the search. It never ceased to amaze me how no-one is available when an assault or a shoplifting comes over the radio, but as soon as a juicy job came in, particularly one that might hit the news, someone somewhere ripped the lid off the box and officers came tumbling out. Not that I was complaining, as I lay back and rested my head on Nat's stomach for a moment, our hands still welded together.

The engine turned out to be a white Toyota Hilux with what could only be the farmer sitting at the wheel. He pulled up next to us and stared out of the window for a moment before speaking.

'Can I help you with something?' he asked suspiciously.

I hauled myself out of the mud and helped Nat to her feet. 'Possibly. I'm Detective Sergeant Steele from Brighton police station. Do you own this place?'

He raised a doubtful eyebrow until I showed my badge. 'Uh...yes I do. I'm Frank Bell. Is there a problem?'

I pointed at the still-open box. 'Any idea who rents that?'

He shrugged. 'I'd have to check my paperwork, but I'm pretty sure it's a Liverpudlian bloke with an eighties mullet.'

'Do you have contracts?'

He looked down for a moment. When he looked up again, he took an awful lot of interest in my lapel.

'Uh, yeah, somewhere, but I've just moved offices and, well, you know...' I felt my hands begin to shake as the adrenaline left me in a rush and I tucked them behind my back. It may have made me look like an officious twat, but it was better than him thinking I was an alcoholic.

'What I know, Frank, is that two armed men just shifted a load of crates out of that store, and if you don't want to end up in a cell, then you'll be a bit more helpful.'

'Tactful,' Nat muttered from behind me.

Tactful or not, it worked. The farmer paled and turned the engine off, getting out of the vehicle and hurrying over to the door. 'Do you want to go inside?' he asked.

I grabbed him by the sleeve before he could enter and trample all over whatever evidence might be left. 'Don't. We don't know what's in there. I'm assuming that as you're the owner of the property you'll consent to it being searched?'

He nodded. 'Of course. Look, I had no idea, he told me he was using it for stuff he didn't have room for after a divorce.'

My phone vibrated in my pocket. I fished it out and answered it, already knowing who it was. 'Sir.'

'Do you mind telling me what the bloody hell you're doing calling up for another armed stop when you should be in custody preparing for an interview?' Burke shouted.

'We got a possible lead on where Gemma Hallett might be, and when we went to check it out, someone pulled a gun on us and nearly shot us before driving away with several large crates in their van. That's the abridged version sir, but that about sums it up. Oh, and I need a search team and firearms to my location.'

The silence on the other end of the line stretched out to uncomfortable proportions.

Finally, when he spoke Burke sounded like he'd given up on me, his voice flat as if he was struggling to keep his temper in check.

'Give me your location, wait for the search team and direct them as to what you're looking for. Then get to my office before I have to explain to the Chief Super why you're trying to turn Brighton into Downtown *fucking* LA.' Hearing Burke swear shocked me almost as much as having had a gun pointed at my head.

'Yes sir. We're at Little Hatch Farm, top of Farm Hill in Woodingdean. There's a set of paddock boxes that have been turned into storage and Collins rents Number 3, which is the one the armed men were taking crates out of.'

'Right, sit tight until they get to you.'

He rang off and I turned to look at Nat. 'I'm not sure if the shit has just rolled or fountained, but either way I seem to be covered in it. Are you okay?'

She nodded angrily. 'I'm fine, but I'd be better if that big bastard was lying face down in the mud! Fucking arsehole!'

'I'm sorry,' I said quietly. 'We shouldn't even have been here. It's my fault.'

She shook her head and looked up at me, eyes still hard. 'No, it's not your fault. You were right. They were up to no good. I knew when I joined the job that there might be days like this, you didn't force me to turn around.'

'No, but I would have done.'

'Don't spoil it Rob, I'm being magnanimous.'

'Sorry.'

We both laughed and I straightened as sirens began to bounce of the nearby hills.

Unsurprisingly, the first car on scene had an excited looking Merrington in it, along with Derek Clinton and Paul Banks, the Inspector in charge of LST – the unit that specialised in searching, warrants and public order.

'What have we got?' Banks asked before he'd finished getting out of the vehicle.

I relayed what had happened while the others listened with expressions that ranged from Clinton's outright shock to Merrington's excited nodding.

'Have you been inside yet?' Derek asked.

'No. Wanted to wait for you in case we disturbed anything. I think we need a firearms unit to make the place safe as well. I don't know what was in those crates but I'm going to play it safe and assume the worst.'

Banks nodded. 'I agree. I've got two vans gearing up now, by the time they get here we should have an ARV on scene and they can check it out. Burke wants you back in his office, Rob, and I wouldn't keep him waiting.'

'Right. Don't have too much fun without me, will you?'

Taking the keys from Nat, I made my way shakily to the car and we drove slowly back to the Nick, neither of us saying anything as we crawled along through heavy traffic interspersed with police vehicles looking for the van from the farm.

In the last two days I'd been blown up and almost shot, and I was almost looking forward to something as simple as a chewing out from a superior officer. After all, what was the worst he could do?

'I'VE A good mind to take your bloody warrant card off you and send you home!' Burke's face was purple and his right hand was squeezing his stress toy so hard I thought it might burst.

I tried to explain myself, 'I...'

'I'm still talking!' he shouted, spittle flying across the desk to land on the arm of my chair. I leaned away from him as the tirade continued.

'Never mind the fact that you disobeyed an order, you went out without your belt kit and nearly got yourself and DC Statham killed! I expected more from you, I really did.'

'So finding more armed men running around our city with links to the murders gets me a bollocking, does it?' I retorted, my frayed nerves finally snapping. 'And I didn't disobey an order. The last thing you said to me was *'find that girl, Rob,'* and that's *exactly* what I was trying to do! You want to shout at me for something, then fine, shout at me for going out without kit, but don't say I wasn't doing my job.'

I stabbed my finger into the top of his desk for emphasis, the words flying across the peeling varnish and hitting him hard enough that he sat back in shock. He probably couldn't remember the last time a lowly Sergeant had shouted at him − I'd most likely been in nappies when it had happened.

I sat back, folding my arms across my chest, prepared to continue fighting my corner. Burke stared at me for a long time before speaking, eyes searching my face as if looking for something.

Finally he shook his head. 'I don't know, Rob, I really don't. In the last couple of days you've shown some moments of real genius, and then you go and screw it all up. I'm not sure it's even your fault, but you seem to have a dangerous habit of being in the wrong place at the wrong time.'

'Always been the same sir.' The fight went out of me in a rush as I suddenly realised that Burke's anger came from concern for his officers, nothing more. 'I'm sorry I shouted, you were right. I should have done it properly and I take full responsibility for what happened.'

'If I was ten years younger I'd probably punch you in the face on principle for what you just said to me. You know you could have been an Inspector by now if you toed the party line a little more?' Burke said, his voice at its normal level.

I hadn't known that, but it didn't surprise me. My whole world had fallen apart four years ago and that tended to do funny things to your perspective on life.

'So what now?' I asked.

He looked at me with something approaching pity in his deep-set eyes. 'You're not leading the case anymore. I've given it to Riley.'

'Riley? The man's a desk monkey!' Riley was one of the other Detective Sergeants that worked under my DI, Hugh Wadey. He wasn't a bad copper per se, he just had no flair for the job and got things done by following the rules and hoping that nothing got too complicated.

Burke shrugged. 'I've got no choice. You'll still be working on the firearms angle. The results you asked for have come in, by the way. But we need someone a little more

210

orthodox to keep a lid on things. I appreciate that you were doing what you thought best, but this is a high profile case and I can't have us looking like cowboys. The public expects more from us than that. Deserves more.'

I couldn't argue with him on that score. To find Gemma I'd tried to cut a corner and it had backfired with almost fatal consequences.

'What about Gemma Hallett?' I asked.

'What about her? We've got units searching everywhere we can think of. We're doing all we can, but we need Collins to talk.'

'Right, well if I'm not interviewing anymore, maybe I can get to work on the other MacBride job, see if I can get something to bring him in with.'

'Do that.' Burke said, dropping the stress toy on to his desk and running his hands over his face resignedly.

I stood and left. Not wanting to return to the CID office, I headed down to our broom cupboard in the basement, where I found Nat sitting at her desk, staring into space with both hands wrapped around a steaming cup of tea.

'Hey,' I said as I squeezed into my seat and began leafing through the reports that someone had dumped on my desk.

'Hey.' She looked over at me. 'Go well with the boss?'

'Yeah. He wanted to give me a medal but I told him I'm allergic to praise, so he took me off lead and put me back on firearms forensics instead.'

She started to laugh and then stopped as she realised I was serious. 'Really?'

I nodded. 'Riley's got it.'

'Riley? But he's...' Nat spluttered.

'Shit. I know. I think Burke just needs a nice, pliable face on the investigation so that he doesn't get any grief from further up the chain. He doesn't like his officers being blown up and shot, apparently. It's bad for the day-to-day running of the Division.'

'So what are you going to do?'

'Me? I'm going to look at these reports, work out the results, then go home and get so pissed I can't remember my own name.'

'But you hardly ever drink.' Nat said, a note of concern in her voice.

'I think I'll class tonight as a special occasion.' I'd avoided alcohol as much as possible in the last four years – it brought out the worst in me.

'Sounds like a plan. I might join you.'

'Door's always open.' I said.

'I meant on my own,' she said, studiously looking at her screen.

'Oh, right. Of course, sorry.'

Nat sighed and shook her head. 'Can we go back to not being awkward please?'

I looked up at her, steam from the tea almost obscuring her face. 'Are we being awkward?'

'Aren't we?' she shot back.

'Pass. I'm a bloke, remember? We can't tell if things are strained, it takes up too much brain power.'

She finally cracked a smile. 'You know you're a complete idiot, right?'

'You wouldn't have me any other way. Look, I've got to get on with these reports but how about we go for a quick one after work?'

She nodded. 'I'd like that.'

For the next hour or so I buried myself in paperwork, reading list after list of measurements and angles, working it out in my head and scrawling notes in pencil on the pages themselves, then crossing half of them out and starting again.

Something wasn't quite right, didn't tally with what I'd seen at Taverner's flat, but my tired brain was refusing to function properly. Usually, with the measurements I'd been given, I could tell someone's height and the probable distance of the shot down to a couple of decimal places. But this time I couldn't seem to get it right, no matter how I did the sums.

I finally gave up when Nat plonked a cup of tea on the desk in front of me, blinking and shaking my head.

'Having fun?' she asked, trying to read my notes upside down.

'Not really. I'm missing a measurement somewhere, but I can't for the life of me work out which one it is. I'm too bloody tired and I keep seeing that big bastard pointing that gun at us.'

She nodded. 'Me too. Makes going home to an empty house a little bit nerve-wracking. Not that I'm implying... Oh for fuck's sake!'

I leaned back and bit my lip to keep from laughing. I knew I shouldn't, but I was tired enough that everything was starting to seem funny.

'What are you laughing at?' She screwed up a Post-it note and threw it at me, hitting me in the chest. Suddenly the missing measurement clicked.

I stood abruptly, almost running for the door. 'Nat, you're a bloody genius, I could kiss you. Come on.'

'Not again, that's how all the trouble started,' she muttered as she followed in my wake. 'Where the bloody hell are we going now?'

46

THE BRIGHTON Mortuary is, annoyingly, nowhere near either the police station or the hospital. Instead it sits, surrounded by trees and gardens, at the far end of the Lewes Road. Despite the pleasant surroundings, it's a place I hate visiting.

As Nat and I crunched up the gravel path to the door, the sun finally broke out from behind the clouds, hitting us with a sudden burst of light that had me squinting as I pressed the buzzer. The third time I pressed it, the door finally swung open to reveal a stumpy looking man in his late forties with a bristling moustache and a scowl that would have done Scrooge proud.

'What?' He demanded sullenly. 'I'm bloody busy.'

'Hello Ron, I need to see the shooting victims,' I said without preamble. I'd known Ron Bury for a long time and the one thing he hated more than anything else was prevarication. If I'd asked him how he was doing, he probably would have slammed the door in my face.

'Of course you do, because I just bloody put them away, didn't I?'

'Well you'll just have to bloody get them out again.'

He stomped away muttering to himself as I held the door open for Nat and followed her in. A second door led through to the business end of the mortuary and, as soon as Ron opened it, the unpleasantly familiar smell of decomposing flesh and strong disinfectant hit my nostrils.

'Eugh,' Nat snorted, holding her fingers to her nose.

Following Ron along the white-walled, green-floored corridors, we eventually made it to the storage area – a huge room with dozens of square metal doors in neat rows covering one wall. Ron muttered and fussed as he pulled on a pair of thick rubber gloves and opened one of the doors to reveal a sliding gurney with a white-sheeted body on it, rust-brown stains marking the otherwise pristine sheet at the head and chest.

'Taverner. Sign here.' Ron pulled a clipboard from the inside of the door and held it out. I took hold of the attached pen gingerly and signed my name and warrant number.

'I suppose you want gloves?' he asked.

I shook my head. 'Wonder of wonders, our budget has stretched to a bit of rubber.'

I pulled a pair out of my pocket, making a mental note to re-stock. In two days I'd gone through a week's worth of gloves and I didn't want to get caught short if the next few days were anything like the past couple of days. Once I was safely gloved, I reached into my inside pocket and took out a tiny tool that looked a little like a sliding rule welded on to a protractor with a compass at one end. I called it the Botherer, mainly due to the fact that I rarely bothered to use it. The name hadn't stuck and all of the seven other people who worked in my field called it by its real name – the FPFT, or Firearms Positioning Forensics Tool.

'Got a pen and paper handy?' I asked Nat, who produced her notebook and waved it at me.

'Great. Hang on to your lunch.' I pulled the sheet back to expose Taverner to the world. His eyes had turned milky – the sightless stare only slightly less disturbing than the deep purple colour of the bottom half of his body. I'd seen it before. After a while, all the blood finds its way to the half of a corpse closest to the floor, and a few years ago some wit had referred to it as Dead Man Trifle, ruining my favourite pudding forever.

The other disturbing thing was the exit wound from the round that had killed him. It had come out through his forehead, taking with it a chunk of skull about the size of an old fifty pence piece and allowing me to see the mess that had been Taverner's brain. Taking a few slow breaths, I pulled the sheet down further to reveal the smaller wounds in his chest.

Setting the slide on the FPFT, I placed it against the first bullet hole and slid the base plate so that it sat flat on his chest next to the wound. The plate was made of semi-rigid plastic so that it would conform to the contours of the body while keeping the shaft of the tool straight, and once it was settled, I twisted the slide so that it was at ninety degrees to the shaft and lowered it so that it touched the edge of the hole. I called the measurements out to Nat who obediently wrote it all down, then did the same with the second wound. Once that was done, I repeated the procedure with Reggie Brown, a task that was made far harder by the two wounds overlapping. Less than twenty minutes after first entering the mortuary, we stepped back into the sunlight, my head already busy with calculations and angles as we headed back to the car and drove off.

'Was that it?' Nat asked finally as we negotiated the busy Lewes Road on the way back to the Nick.

'Was what it?' I said, glancing at her briefly.

'Firearms Positioning. I thought you needed string and pieces of paper with holes in and torches and shit. I got all excited and all you did was take some measurements with your contraption and make me write.'

'It's not as complicated as you might think. All I need is height, distance – if possible – and as many angles as they can give me. I'm surprised that you haven't picked it up already, what with your mammoth nerd brain and all.'

'Mammoth nerd brain?'

'Yeah. You're the one who remembers everything that ever happened, aren't you? FPF should be a walk in the park.' I grinned.

She shook her head. 'I give up. I'll bet Roy Grace doesn't have to put up with idiots like you.'

'That's because he's a fictional character, and you are very much alive and kicking so you have to put up with me, warts and all. Besides, surely I'd be Roy Grace and you'd be what's his name? You know, the black dude.'

'Glen Branson.'

'That's the one. Does piss stinking cat lady count as a minority group?'

'Will you just leave it?'

'So, you think Firearms positioning is Dead Simple then?'

'You're so not funny.'

'Was Taverner Not Dead Enough?'

'Rob, stop.'

'I've got to; I can't remember any of his other books. Besides, as my old man used to say, you're Too Long Dead to waste life being an idiot. Ow!'

She raised her fist warningly. 'You'll get another one in a minute. Besides, that's not a book.'

'It was a good guess. Can you not punch me when I'm driving please?'

'Can you stop trying to be funny? It doesn't suit you.'

'No, I suppose it doesn't. Still, it stops me from thinking about... Shit!'

'You think about shit?'

I shook my head. 'No, I mean "shit I just thought of something".'

'Go on.' she said, her voice taking on a serious tone.

'If I'm right, the calculations add up to the shooter being over 6'2'.'

'How much over 6'2'?' Nat queried.

'I'm not sure.'

I could feel her staring at me. 'You're not sure? I thought you could pin it down to the nearest millimetre.'

'Normally I can. There's something about this one though, the measurements are, well, screwy.'

'Screwy how?'

'If I knew that I'd be able to work out the problem. So who do we know that fits the height parameters?'

'Collins is 6', right?' she asked.

'PNC says 6' exactly, I thought it might have been him at first but unless he managed to grow a couple of inches then he's not our man. Who else do we know that's tall and has access to weapons?'

'The van man?' she asked, catching on but still sounding sceptical.

'The van man,' I agreed. There couldn't be that many people over 6'2' charging around the city armed with a pistol. 'Collins has links to Taverner and Brown, the giant in the van links to Collins from the lockup. I'm not quite sure how this all fits together yet but I'll bet you that it does. All we need to do now is work out who the guy with the van is and where he's hiding, and I think we might have our killer.'

47

THE TWO men sat at a table inside the More Cafe on Trafalgar Street, one enjoying a black coffee while the other sipped at a tall glass of blond beer. The sky outside was overcast and threatening rain, but the air was hot and humid and neither man was enjoying the dark interior of the café despite the large open windows.

'So everything's in place?' MacBride asked finally, eyes flickering over the small park opposite as he watched a junkie trying to steal a handbag from a mother with a pram.

Yuri nodded. 'My men will meet you at the van tomorrow. Petr is leading them, everything from now on must go through him.'

MacBride leaned forwards just enough that the neckline of his tee-shirt exposed the black swastika tattoo on his chest.

'And you're *sure* the police won't twig?'

'*Twig?*'

'Yeah, twig. You know, catch on.'

'Ah. No, they will be too busy dealing with something else, this I promise you.'

'What kind of something else?'

Yuri shook his head. 'The less you know, the less you can tell if they capture you.'

MacBride snorted. 'This isn't fucking Chechnya! If they capture me they'll tickle me with feathers and offer me hot chocolate, not stick my head in a bucket and attach a car battery to my nuts!'

Yuri looked amused. 'You think they *don't* do that in this country?'

'Of course not. The whole justice system is run by pussies.'

'In my country, they do far worse than attaching batteries to your testicles. I would be very surprised if they don't do that here too, tucked away in some dark corner where no one can hear you scream.'

'Yeah, well, maybe...' He'd been about to say that maybe Yuri's people deserved it, but he remembered himself at the last minute and trailed off.

This foreigner unnerved him for some reason that he couldn't put his finger on, and Danny MacBride wasn't used to other people making him feel uncomfortable. He was usually the one scaring others, and to have the cold worm of fear working its way through his gut every time he looked at this man was getting on his nerves.

If the man hadn't come to him offering such a tempting prize, Danny would have sent him packing with a boot up his arse, but a couple of million, even split several ways, was not to be sneezed at.

'You were saying?' Yuri prompted.

'Maybe they do, but I've never heard of it. Not over here, anyway. So it's safe to tell me what you've got planned to keep the police busy.'

Yuri shrugged and a faint smile played across his lips. 'All I will tell you is that the police are being led around by the nose. They will be expecting a terrorist attack, so we'll give them one. When the time comes. all their resources will be in the wrong place and we will all be long gone before they realise they have been duped.'

'Come on, you must be able to tell me more than that. I thought we were partners?'

Yuri shook his head. 'I'm afraid I can't. The reason I wanted to talk to you face to face is a concern that someone may have talked. The police were sniffing around your man's lockup earlier.'

Danny sat up. 'Really?'

'Yes. You sound like this is troublesome. We have cleared out everything we had in storage so there should be no problem now, but I would like to know if your men have mentioned anything to someone they shouldn't have done.'

'I trust my men with my life.' He crossed his arms over his chest and glowered at the foreigner to cover his worry. He didn't dare tell him about the surveillance his flat had been under earlier or the man might call the whole thing off. Danny had borrowed too much money to get this thing off the ground to back out now; he had to go ahead no matter what.

'As I do mine.'

'Maybe they were looking for something else and it was just coincidence?'

'Maybe. Although I have little belief in coincidence.'

'What you believe in doesn't matter to me, sunshine,' MacBride said with a shrug, 'as long as we're all set for tomorrow. Look, I've got to get going, I don't like being out in public with... with what's happening tomorrow,' he finished lamely. He'd been about to say *with the police looking for me*. Probably not a good idea to mention that, he thought as he stood and dropped a note on the table to cover the drinks.

'So tomorrow then.'

'Tomorrow. Good luck, and I hope that the next time we meet that we will both be rich men.'

'Yeah, let's hope so.'

And if not, MacBride added in his head, *I'll make sure that the next time you see me it's because I'm plunging a knife into your guts for betraying me.*

For despite what he'd said to Billy he had a bad feeling about this job, or more precisely the people he found himself working with, and he suddenly wondered if he was going to make it out of this alive.

Pushing the thought out of his head, he walked out on to the street and mingled with the Friday afternoon shoppers, anxious to be away from town before someone spotted him and the police came looking for him again.

48

MY FIRST stop when we got back to the Nick was Burke's office. He was on the phone when I arrived and held up a hand for me to wait. I stood by the door impatiently, trying not to hear the conversation between him and his wife. I heard him say goodbye and before the phone was back in its cradle I was standing in front of the desk brandishing my notebook.

'Sir, I've done the sums and I think I might have found our shooter,' I said without preamble.

Burke sat back and folded his arms across his chest with a frown. 'Go on.'

'Well sir, from the angle of the wounds and the height of the victims, whoever fired has to be significantly taller than both Taverner and Brown. Over 6'2' in fact.'

'Neither of them were particularly tall, are you sure about the math?'

I nodded. 'We're looking at 6'2' to 6'7,' probably, allowing for a crooked arm.'

He looked at me in puzzlement. 'Crooked arm?'

I nodded. 'Yes sir. There are two different common firing positions, straight arm and crooked.' I demonstrated with his stapler, first holding it out with elbows locked and both hands wrapped around it, then with one elbow slightly bent.

'See how the barrel dips slightly when I hold it the second way? That gives us a two inch variation on height, three if they're over six and a half feet tall. It's all about the angles sir.

The only thing that confuses me is a slight dip I can't account for to one side, but with a little more work I'll have it sewn up for sure.'

He shook his head as he struggled to follow what I was saying. FPF was new enough that I got that a lot. 'And you can prove this in court can you?'

'I can prove it anywhere sir, but the field isn't old enough that courts are happy to accept it as expert witness testimony yet.'

'Then what you're telling me is useless?'

I shook my head. 'No sir. It gives us the beginnings of a profile on the shooter, and that narrows the field as we start getting suspects from other sources. Right now my money is on the man who almost shot myself and Statham earlier.'

'Well there's not a lot more we can do about it tonight.' Burke said. 'We've still got units out searching for the van, and Riley is about to interview Collins so with any luck we'll have something by morning.'

I bit my tongue, as I struggled not to bitch about my fellow sergeant. 'Anything else for me sir?'

He shook his head. 'No, just write everything you've done up.'

I nodded and left the office, collecting Nat from where she was waiting in the corridor.

'Well?' She asked as we headed back to the basement.

'He seems rather sceptical. I think it's all a bit too new-fangled for him.'

She snorted. 'Find me an officer who likes something new and untested and I'll buy you a pint.'

'How about you buy me the pint and I'll find you an officer later.'

'Deal. Have you got much left to do?'

'Once I've written this up, I've got to go and see a shopkeeper about an extortion job. Fancy helping?' I opened the door to the office and gestured Nat to go ahead of me.

She shook her head. 'Sorry, I'm up to my eyeballs in paperwork. I think I'll stay here, unless you really need me.'

'No, I think I can cope.' I sat behind my desk and cracked my knuckles before hunching over the keyboard.

The rest of my paperwork comprised my arrest statement from Collins' chase and writing several lines of neat but complicated sums on a form that I'd had to devise myself as Sussex hadn't even known about FPF until I'd done the course. One of the sums was still bothering me, tickling me with a hint of something that should have been obvious, but I was too distracted to do more than let my subconscious get on with it while I thought about other things.

Despite being off the case, I couldn't escape the gnawing worry that Gemma Hallett might be out there somewhere. I knew that instead of working on the extortion job, I should be out on the streets looking for her, but orders were orders, and I had the feeling that if I disobeyed too many more I'd find myself transferred to the arse end of nowhere looking for missing swans or the like. Half an hour later I waved Nat a goodbye that she barely acknowledged and made my way down to the car park, worry gnawing at me as I read the address off the case file and headed out in the hope that I might find something useful.

49

THE SHOP I was looking for was along Western Road, just a stone's throw from the border with Hove. The faded sign above the door proclaimed that it sold booze, sweets and tobacco, but once inside it was clear that the owner had branched out from his original inventory.

The walls were lined with shelves holding everything from groceries to glossy magazines, all massively overpriced.

Knowing the area as I did, the prices were probably as high as they were to make up for the losses he would suffer on a daily basis. Two large homeless hostels were situated nearby and the shop was on a direct route from their front doors into town.

The man behind the counter was in his early forties and Asian, with broad shoulders and a fierce expression that wasn't softened any by his thick moustache.

'Afternoon,' I said with a smile, 'I'm looking for Rakesh Patel.'

'I'm Rakesh,' he said with a frown. 'Who are you?'

I showed him my badge, holding it up so that he could read my name clearly. He looked at my face then squinted at the picture several times before he leaned back with a grunt.

'Is this about the man threatening me?'

'Yes it is. Is there somewhere we can talk privately?'

He nodded and picked up the phone, speaking into it in his native language. While I waited one of the local heroin users, Harvey Billingham, poked his head around the door then scarpered when he saw me.

Rakesh put the phone down and gave me a smile, the first gentle expression I'd seen from him.

'I should pay you to stand in the shop every day. He's one of the worst.'

'Don't worry; he's never out of prison for more than six months at a time.' Billingham was renowned for trying to score it big every so often, usually failing with spectacular consequences. The last time he'd tried to rob a bookmaker at knifepoint, only to be foiled by a group of boxers from a local club on a day out. According to their statements he had 'tripped' at least half a dozen times on the way from the door to the counter and back again. He'd almost cried with relief when the police turned up to arrest him.

A lad of about seventeen came out of a door at the back of the shop and slid behind the counter. Rakesh ruffled the boy's hair and led me through the still open door, then along a narrow corridor with boxes of stock piled from floor to ceiling.

It opened out into a very clean, well appointed kitchen where he sat at the table, indicating for me to pull out a chair and join him.

'How can I help?' he asked when I settled.

'I'm investigating what's been happening, but I've looked at your statement and I'm a little worried that there isn't enough information there. I appreciate that you've already told an officer what's been happening but could you go through it again for me?'

Rakesh sighed and shrugged. 'If I must. About three weeks ago a man came into the shop and told me that he could stop the troublemakers from coming in and stealing. I asked him how much it would cost and if he had a business card and he laughed at me. Then he told me that the area was getting more dangerous and that the people who didn't pay would find themselves in a lot of trouble. I chased him out of the shop, but then I came down the next morning and someone had poured petrol through the letterbox. There was an unlit match lying in the petrol. I'm not a stupid man - that was when I called the police.'

'And what did this man look like?'

'Well, he was white, and between twenty and forty years old.'

'Can you be a little more specific?' The poor description was one of the reasons MacBride hadn't been arrested for this yet. The officer who had taken the statement had matched the description up as a possible for MacBride, but I was hoping to get more. A firm description linking him to the threat would be enough.

Rakesh frowned, his face falling into familiar lines that didn't entirely fade when he looked up.

'It's difficult. He had tattoos on his arms.' That was what had led the original officer to link it to MacBride, but in my eyes it wasn't enough. I had no doubt that he was the man responsible but what you know and what you can prove in court are two very different things.

'What else?'

'He had very short hair.'

'What colour?'

'It was light hair.'

'Blonde, or slightly darker?' I had to be careful here. I didn't want to lead him to identify MacBride, the description had to be his and his alone. The best I could manage was gentle nudging.

'Ah, maybe darker than blonde.'

'Is there anything else?'

He shrugged. 'He looked strong. I'm sorry, there's nothing else.'

I nodded and closed my notebook. 'I understand. I'd very much like you to come back to the police station with me and look at some photographs to see if you can identify the man.'

Rakesh shook his head. 'But I have a shop to run. I have to do a stock take this afternoon so that I can order tomorrow.'

I felt my patience beginning to slip slightly.

'Let me be blunt Mr Patel. If this is the man I think it is, he's very dangerous. Do you and your family live above the shop?'

'Yes.' He nodded.

'Then I recommend that you take an hour out and come with me to help keep them safe. If you can positively identify the man, then you won't have to worry about him anymore.'

He sighed and ran a hand through his hair.

'Will it be quick?'

'As quick as I can make it.'

'Then let's go.'

Half an hour later, I pulled into a space out the front of the Nick and led Rakesh through to an interview room, seating him opposite me while I logged on to a computer and brought up the video witness program.

In the old days we had two different ways of identifying suspects. One was a line-up, with a number of people mixed in with the real suspect, all similar in appearance and safely ensconced behind one-way glass as the witness looked at them.

The other way was to show photographs, huge books with dozens of local suspects gracing the pages.

Now both were done using the Video Witness system, a clever program that took the age, height, weight, colour etc and brought up a list of photographs. You could also make sure that if you had a named suspect, then they would be included, all of the pictures anonymous to the witness but with full details available for the officers.

I keyed in the details I had, bringing up forty hits that included MacBride. Once I was on the right screen I turned the monitor towards Rakesh.

'I want you to look at the pictures. The man who threatened you may or may not be on this screen, or the following one. If you see him then point him out, but I want to make it clear that if you do make an identification, then you have to be sure as we will arrest the man you indicate.'

He nodded and began to scan the pictures. Some of them were people paid to have their image on the system, others bona fide troublemakers. He reached the end of the first page and shook his head, prompting me to bring up the second page.

It only took a few seconds for him to stab the flat screen with his finger.

'This man.'

I turned the monitor to see him pointing at MacBride.

'Are you sure?' I felt the excitement rising and fought to hide a grin.

He nodded. 'This is the man.'

I printed off a set of forms for him to sign, then promised to keep him updated as I ushered him into the reception area.

'Mandy, can you get this man a lift back home?' I called through the partition before racing back into the building and up to Burke's office.

The old man was still at his desk, bent almost double over a mound of paperwork.

He looked up as I knocked, waving me in.

'I've got a positive match on MacBride sir,' I said, waving the green file at him.

'For which crime?'

'The extortion job. The shopkeeper just identified him on video witness.'

He sat back and stared into space for a moment before focusing on me.

'What else have we got linking him to it?'

'Not much sir.' I flicked through the file. 'Nothing in fact. SOCO couldn't find anything when they attended the attempted arson so it's just the shopkeeper's word.'

'No CCTV?'

'None. His system's been on the blink for six months.'

Burke shrugged and looked back at his desk. 'Then don't arrest him yet. Leave it on the back burner and we'll use it if we have no other way to bring him in.'

'But what about the victim? I just promised him we'd arrest the man he identified.'

'And we will, but for now the murders take priority. If we go off half cocked with a sketchy job then we lose any element of surprise we might have if we can link MacBride to the murders.'

'But if we...' I stopped at the look on Burke's face. 'Yes sir, I'll just write it up and leave it in my tray.'

He nodded and went back to his work, leaving me to head downstairs with clenched teeth. Good with murders he might be, and I had no doubt that on one level he was right, but I wondered if Burke had forgotten the golden rule of policing; that we were there to serve the public, not ourselves.

50

THE PITCHER and Piano at the seafront end of East Street is a favourite bar of coppers and criminals alike. It's one of the few places in Brighton where they both rub shoulders without anyone drawing a baton or a knife. No-one was quite sure how it had ended up like that but, apart from the occasional instances where drunk coppers saw someone who was Wanted, it was a fairly peaceful co-existence that worked for both sides. Nat and I sat in a corner booth big enough for six, me drinking heavily watered Scotch and her drinking a pint of lager. Our suits, although still slightly muddy from our earlier encounter, were enough to mark us out as Job and, despite the bar being crowded, we were given a wide berth.

'Nothing like a nice quiet drink!' I shouted over the music and the general din.

'Yeah. You take me to all the best places. So do you think Burke will listen to you about Goliath?' She called back, moving a little closer so that she didn't have to shout full volume.

I shrugged. 'I hope so, but I'm not exactly flavour of the month after today. Speaking of which, I'm sorry I got you into that.'

'Don't. It's not like you dragged me into something against my will.' She swirled her pint.

I shook my head. 'No, that's exactly what I did.'

She moved closer and fixed me with an intense stare. 'But if we hadn't gone back we would never have known about those men and what they were keeping in that lock-up. Surely that has to be worth the risk?'

'Not really. I would never have been able to forgive myself if you'd been shot.'

She laughed but I could see that it was forced. 'I'm perfectly capable of making my own bad decisions you know. Besides, you wouldn't have had long to feel bad, he probably would have done you first.'

'Probably.' I looked away and took a slug of Scotch, trying to think of something cheerful to say.

'So,' I said finally, 'the big three zero in a few weeks then.'

She nodded and grinned. 'Yeah, I'm having one hell of a party, my sister is helping me organise it. You'll be there, right?'

'Free booze?'

'Of course.' She looked at me like I was mad.

'Then you don't need to ask.'

We both laughed, this time a little less forced. I felt genuine affection for Nat that went well beyond the usual work friendships you develop over time and our awkwardness of the last couple of days had begun to hurt, even though the awkwardness seemed to be mostly mine. It was good to just be out and having a laugh together.

'So what do you think of Merrington?' she asked, waving a passing waitress over and ordering two more drinks.

'His heart's in the right place but he seems a little out of his depth. I think there's an awful lot more that could be done to smooth out Sussex Police / MI6 co-operation.'

'Yeah, because we work together so often. Maybe you should apply to be the liaison officer,' Nat smirked.

'I can just see that working. Still, I think he might have had a point after all about the terrorism. Goliath and his little friend in the van didn't exactly strike me as locals.'

'No, and you have to wonder what they were storing in that lock-up. Do you think it might have been drugs?'

I shrugged. 'No idea. The last thing we need is more drugs on the streets of Brighton.'

'True.' She paused. 'Can I ask you something?'

The sudden change of tack smacked of something personal and I drew back a little. 'Sure, but I might not answer.'

'Why did you join the police?' Nat looked at me inquisitively.

It was a good question, and one I'd asked myself several times over the years. 'It seemed a logical choice when I came out of the army. I'd done my forensics degree thinking that I might become a Scenes of Crime Officer, but it wasn't enough adrenaline for me so I applied to join as a copper. The rest, as they say, is history.'

She nodded and took a sip of her drink. 'You know why I joined?'

'The pension?'

'Ha, no. I was working as a legal secretary at a criminal solicitor's. My mum got me the job there because the head honcho was a friend of hers from college. Anyway, we had a constant stream of lowlifes coming into the office and I used to sit in and take notes, listening to their excuses as to why they'd just happened to be caught standing over the victim, or that they'd just seen an open door and gone into the house to make sure everyone was okay, and had no idea how the jewellery ended up in their pocket. And one day something occurred to me.'

I'd known Nat for years and it had never occurred to me to ask what she'd done before. Somehow I couldn't imagine her working for a criminal solicitor, she was too, well, honest.

'What was that?'

She moved closer again and I could smell her perfume. Despite the day we'd had she smelled enticingly of musk with a hint of spice.

'It occurred to me that everyone knew they were guilty. I knew, the solicitor knew, the suspect knew, the police knew. And the police were the only ones actually trying to do something to prove it. The rest of us were just pretending that we believed their bullshit, and trying to find a loophole to prevent a prosecution. It wasn't about right or wrong, just who could outwit the other in court. I know that everyone deserves a fair trial and proper representation, but when it comes down to it, it's about who knows the law better and if a police officer failed to cross a 'T' or dot an 'I', then the whole thing would get thrown out. That's not justice, that's bureaucracy.'

'So that made you decide to join the police?'

She grimaced. 'That - and one of our clients nicked my bag while I was trying to help the little bastard.'

We both laughed.

'Well I hope you found the bugger and nicked hi...'

I stopped as I saw Nat staring fixedly over my shoulder at the door. Turning, I saw Danny MacBride walking through the door, Leon Watson looming behind him like a big, ugly shadow. A shiver ran down my spine and I wondered how one man could suddenly be turning up in almost every aspect of my life. The second I looked, MacBride made eye contact and a leer spread across his face. He swaggered over with Leon whispering into his ear, no doubt asking permission to break the unofficial truce and give me some grief.

'Not interrupting I hope?' MacBride asked when he got close enough.

'Of course you are Danny, what do you want?' I said abruptly.

'Just wondering why you were sat outside my gaff with your lady here the other day, that's all.'

I felt vulnerable sitting down while the two of them loomed over me but I couldn't show it. Instead I spread my arm along the back of the padded leather seat as I looked at him. 'Your gaff? Don't you live over in Hove? I haven't been there for weeks.'

'Don't play stupid, Detective. I mean on Steine Street. I believe you were rather... preoccupied at the time.' He grinned as if we were old friends sharing a joke, but the expression never reached his mad, staring eyes.

'Did you come in here to try and wind me up or are you going to piss off and get a drink?' I asked. I'd suddenly had enough of this. He was a potential suspect in two investigations I was – had been – involved in, and just to be seen talking to him in public could blow anything that made it to court.

240

'Now there's no need to be like that, Detective,' he said as Leon took a step closer, all glowering eyes and snarl.

Nat grabbed my arm. 'Rob, let's not do this here.'

I nodded and stood. 'You're right. The clientele in this place just took a nose-dive. Let's go have a drink where it doesn't smell so bad.'

MacBride tried to look injured but failed miserably. 'But we haven't finished our little chat!'

Leon stepped in front of his boss and went to put a hand on my chest. Before he could connect, I grabbed his wrist and twisted it into a lock so hard that he went pale and dropped to his knees, tendons bulging out under white skin as they stretched to popping point.

'Now that I've got your attention,' I said, keeping the lock firmly on, 'let's get a few things straight. Firstly, I've got no idea why you were wherever I chose to be the other day. Secondly, if either of you ever tries to touch me or mine again there'll be a proper reckoning. Clear?'

MacBride looked down at Leon's pale, sweating face and grinned as if enjoying his friend's pain. 'Of course Detective. Just wanted a friendly chat is all. Give my regards to Mr Collins when you see him next, eh?'

I nodded at Nat to move out from behind the table while I still had Leon on his knees. Warning or not, I knew that the man would probably try something as soon as I let go and I didn't want Nat catching a stray punch. As she reached MacBride she stared at him for a moment until he backed away – still grinning – arms spread as if bowing her out of the booth. She walked past and turned, watching my back for me as I spun Leon around by the wrist and toppled him back into the seat, giving myself a chance to back away safely.

As soon as I let go he was on his feet and moving towards me but his boss put a restraining hand on his chest to stop him.

'Not now,' he said loudly enough for us to hear, 'I'm sure the last thing you want is to end up in cells next to young Billy.'

If he thought I'd bite and say something, he was sadly mistaken, but as we left the bar I had to wonder how he already knew that we had his muscle in custody and, more importantly, how he knew that we were involved.

'Are you okay?' Nat asked, taking my arm as the adrenaline left me.

I shook my head. 'Not really. That was all a bit unnecessary, and it makes me wonder if that was an accidental meeting or not. Seems a bit convenient that they should just happen to come in half an hour after we arrive, on the same day I arrested Collins and start looking into another job he's involved in.'

'Well you know what the jungle drums are like around here. Someone in the bar probably recognised you and called him.'

'Probably. Ah fuck it, let's just find another bar and get shitfaced.'

'Is that a lawful order, Sarge?' she grinned.

'You know,' I said, putting an arm around her shoulders, 'I rather believe it is.'

51

THE DOOR rattled, making Yuri jump. He pulled a small Makarov pistol from his waistband and hurried into the hall, only to relax as Petr came through the door looking tired and angry.

'What happened?' he asked the big man.

'Cops. They came to speak to us at the farm. We got away with the crates though, and dumped the van before we delivered them. We used one of Andrei's friends' vans instead.'

'You weren't followed?' Yuri asked quickly.

Petr fixed him with a bleak stare. 'I'm not stupid Yuri.'

'No, of course not. But it's vital that we're not discovered.'

'You think I don't know that?' Petr said angrily.

As the big man walked past, Yuri saw matted blood in his tangled hair. 'You are hurt, my friend?'

Petr shrugged. 'Just a knock, nothing more.'

'Were there any problems with the deliveries?'

'No, none. The men were very pleased with their presents.'

Yuri allowed himself a small chuckle. 'I have no doubt that you will lead them successfully tomorrow, my friend.'

They entered the kitchen and Yuri poured them both coffee as they sat at the table.

'As long as the police haven't caught on,' Petr said, frowning at the thought. 'What if someone has talked?'

'Tell me exactly what happened.' Yuri ordered him.

Petr told the tale, leaving nothing out. When he'd finished, Yuri sat back with a smile. 'Don't worry, my friend, if they knew what was about to happen, they would have turned up with guns and many officers. I think that you were just in the wrong place at the wrong time. This will work, I promise you.'

Finally Petr nodded. 'I'm glad you trust me with this. I'll get it done, I swear.'

Yuri smiled with relief. The last thing he needed was the linchpin of his operation getting cold feet. 'Good, I knew I could rely on you. I must leave in the morning, but I will wait as long as I can. You know what to do.'

Petr nodded again. 'Everything is ready and the vehicle is parked nearby. When the time comes, the police will be so busy chasing their tails that they will never see us coming, that I promise.'

SATURDAY

52

I SLAPPED at my alarm clock, trying to shut off the insistent buzzing. As I cracked my eyes open, I realised I was curled up on my sofa and it was my phone that was making the noise. Stretching out, my foot hit something and I looked down to see Nat curled up on the floor, her work clothes crumpled and only half covered by the throw that usually sat on the sofa.

Despite my brave words the previous evening, I'd only managed one more whisky before I'd reached my limit, but Nat had gone at it like it was her last day on earth. I'd agreed to let her stay at mine so that I knew she'd be safe. She was half unconscious by the time we got a cab and the driver had given me a knowing wink as I'd eased her out of the car and dragged her up the steps to my front door. The phone went blessedly silent as I nudged Nat with my foot.

'Whassat?' she mumbled, rearing up with wild hair.

'It's morning.' The light was still on, the curtains drawn. From the little sky I could see above the top of the curtains, it was only just getting light outside.

'Oh shit, my head. Have you got any painkillers?' Nat sat up and put her hands to her face.

I nodded. Hearing her anguished plea made me glad I barely drank anymore. 'Yeah. I'll get you some.'

I rooted through the kitchen drawers until I found my stash of painkillers and then collected two pints of water before heading back into the lounge where Nat was sitting on the floor with her back against the sofa and her head in her hands. She squinted up at me as I delivered the chemical salvation.

'Uh, Rob, did we...'

'Get shitfaced and fall asleep in the front room?' I cut her off. 'You did, I only stayed down here so I didn't wake you.'

My phone rang again and I answered it, swallowing down a mouthful of water. 'Steele.'

'Rob, it's Mark Peters from Special Branch. Sorry to ring you so early, but a night-turn unit found the van and things are starting to get interesting. You might want to come in.'

'I thought I was off the case?'

'Not anymore. Merrington demanded that you get reassigned and Burke gave in last night.'

'Merrington? I'm surprised he's still got that much clout.'

'Me too. You must have made an impression for him to stick his neck out.'

'I guess. Where's the van?'

'Wild Park. Can you go straight there?'

'I left my car at the Nick last night.'

'Bollocks. Okay, I'll pick you up in ten minutes. You still live in the same place?' Peters asked.

'Yeah.'

'Okay, see you in ten.' Peters rang off.

I threw the phone on the sofa and stretched, wishing I had time for a run.

'I'm back on the case,' I told Nat, 'Merrington requested it.'

'Really? That's great news.' She gave me a feeble grin. 'If my head didn't hurt so much I'd even try and sound enthused.'

'Look, I need to get changed and jump in the shower, you're welcome to stay here until you feel well enough to move.'

She tried to stand but gave up after a few seconds, sagging back against the sofa. 'That might be a good idea. I promise I'll be gone by the time you get back.'

'No rush, you're on rest days today aren't you?'

She nodded. 'Yeah, I might get another few hours sleep.'

I left her curled up on the sofa and ran a cold shower, shivering my way through it but coming out the other side feeling vaguely more human. Hearing a car horn outside I threw on a pair of jeans and a t-shirt and hurried to the front door, opening it to see Peters sitting in a car blowing smoke through the open window.

'And when did they allow smoking in police vehicles?' I asked as I got in and he pulled away from the kerb.

'When they started getting me out of bed at 5am.' he replied, flicking the butt out of the window.

I looked at my watch for the first time since I'd woken up and saw that it was only half past five. 'Bloody hell. No wonder I feel tired.'

'Late one?' he asked with a sly grin.

'Later than I'd like.' I admitted, thinking back to the night before. Nat was the first woman to cross the threshold since Linda died – if you didn't count my sister – and it felt odd in a way that I couldn't place to be leaving her there on her own.

'Can't remember the last time I went out in town.' Peters said wistfully, bringing me back to the present.

'Serves you right for stealing all the overtime.' Back in the day he'd been famous for it, doing forty or fifty hours a month over the top of his rota. He never went out and he drove a poky little Renault. No-one was quite sure what he actually spent it on.

The sun was rising over the trees as we arrived, bathing the area in a golden light that made the park look peaceful – almost beautiful – belying the fact that it was across the road from one of the nastier places to live in the city. We turned on to the track that led to a café and the park proper, and as we turned a corner I could see the lights from two or three vehicles – one of them with its blue flashers still on.

Peters pulled up a few feet away from the vehicles and immediately a uniform loomed out of the semi-dark.

'I'm afraid this is....'

We both held our badges up and the officer produced a torch to check them. 'Thanks. SOCO's just turned up and the DCI's on his way.'

Peters raised an eyebrow at me but made no comment.

'Great,' I said, trying to sound enthusiastic, 'lead on.'

He led us towards the van, sitting half-hidden in some bushes to one side of the track. The rear doors were wide open and the tired looking form of Derek Clinton was suiting up behind it.

'They called you in as well, huh?' I said with a wave.

Derek looked up with a grimace. 'Yeah. As it's a firearms job they wanted me. Mrs Clinton wasn't exactly thrilled with a four-thirty wake-up call.'

'I'm sure you'll make it up to her. What have we got?'

'This chap here, what's your name?' He pointed at the officer who had stopped us.

'John.'

'John here found the van in the bushes. The doors were shut, so he opened them to make sure no-one was inside, but nothing else has been touched. I'm about to go in and check it out before the rest of my team arrive.'

'Well don't let us stop you. I always enjoy seeing a master at work.' I smiled.

'Master, my arse.' Derek replied, pulling on his gloves with a flourish.

'I'd rather not.'

He glared at me before turning his attention to clambering in the back of the van while we stood back and watched. Light blossomed as Derek turned on his head torch, panning it to and fro as he scoured the floor inch-by-inch with a visual inspection before he got down to the nitty-gritty of proper forensic work.

I heard another car turn off the road and head towards us, lights bumping up and down as it negotiated the rough track.

'Why am I here?' I asked Peters impatiently.

'Because you're a troublemaker who needs to earn his pay once in a while.'

'Thanks for the support.'

The car pulled up, disgorging the DCI, DI Long and, surprisingly, Merrington as well. The Six agent nodded and smiled when he saw me.

'Ah, DS Steele. You're looking well.'

'And you're a terrible liar. Any particular reason we've all been dragged out here so early?'

Burke, dressed in a pair of slacks and a check shirt, stepped forwards with a curt nod. 'Rob, a word?'

I nodded and followed him to the far side of the car. 'Sir?'

He hesitated for a moment as if trying to find the right words. 'As I'm sure you're aware by now, Merrington asked for you to be back on the investigation. As I'm sure you're also aware, if I didn't think you were capable, then I wouldn't have had you back. From what I've seen and heard, you're a damn good detective but I can't have you going haring off every time you get a sniff of something interesting. You're a supervisor and I need you to act like one. Understood?'

He held out his hand and I shook it. 'I understand Sir, thank you.'

I could have said plenty more, and nearly apologised again but managed not to. Least said, soonest mended.

'Right then, let's get to work, and see if this van of yours has got anything to do with the investigation, shall we?' Burke said.

I nodded and followed him back to the others, pleased to be back in the fold.

53

AN HOUR later, we returned to the Nick, having grown bored of waiting for Derek to turn up anything interesting. Merrington followed me back to my office while Burke and the two SB detectives disappeared off elsewhere with the understanding that we'd all meet up in the Command conference room on the second floor at 0800.

'Tea?' I asked Merrington as the kettle boiled.

'Please,' he said, sitting back in Nat's chair and idly pushing it in half-circles with his legs.

'So I understand you were the one who got me back on the case,' I said as I delivered his steaming brew. He nodded without speaking.

'Can I ask why?'

He shrugged. 'Honestly? You're bloody good at what you do and I like to think that we've worked well together over the last few days. I'm starting to know you and the way you work, and I think that if we're going to crack this case one way or the other, then you need to be part of that process.'

That was far more than the glib answer I'd been expecting. Although we seemed to get on well enough, I hadn't realised I'd made such an impact on the man. Maybe getting blown up together had formed a bond.

'Uh, well, thanks. I just wanted to say how grateful I am. Being taken off the case was horrible and I think I would have gone crazy if you hadn't stepped in and had me put back on it.'

He raised an eyebrow. 'You're welcome. It was nothing, really.' He was obviously as bad at sharing as I was and he looked at the desk as we both tried to find a manly way out of the conversation.

I cleared my throat noisily. 'Great. Now we're all back in love and everything, do you want to tell me what you know about the men in that van?'

He shrugged again. 'Not an awful lot, to be honest.'

'I was rather hoping you might have tapped into your Six databases and come up with something useful. Looks like we'll have to do this the old fashioned way and wait for SOCO to come up with the goods.'

Merrington looked at me. 'I've sent my lot what we've got, but haven't heard back yet. Apparently there's a massive backlog because they're working on...' he hesitated for a moment, '...other things. They'd probably place a higher priority on it if we had something else to link the van to the case.'

'Did Burke not tell you about the positioning data I gave him yesterday?'

'No. What did you get?' He sat forward.

I went over the whole thing with him piece-by-piece. To his credit, he got it much faster than most people do and actually began to get excited when I came to the crunch.

'So,' I finished, 'I rather suspect that the man with the van is our shooter. I just can't figure the connection between his mob and Collins.'

'Why don't we ask him?' Merrington said, an excited gleam in his eyes.

'Who, Collins?' I replied.

He nodded. 'Why not? He hasn't been interviewed yet, so let's go and do it.'

I thought back to Burke's earlier warning. 'I'm not sure that's such a good idea, at least not without checking in with the DCI first.'

'Where's your sense of adventure?'

'It's keeping my P45 firmly weighted down.'

'Fine, well ask Burke then.' He sat back and picked up his mug.

I dialled Burke's number and waited patiently while Merrington sipped his tea and watched me expectantly.

'Burke.' he tersely answered.

'Sir, it's Rob Steele. I understand that Collins hasn't been interviewed yet.'

'That's right, Riley's not in until nine.'

'Do you mind if Merrington and I do it? He seems to think that we might be able to find a connection between Collins and the men I saw in the van yesterday. I have to say I agree. It's worth a shot, at least.'

There was silence on the line as Burke thought about it for a moment, before replying. 'I don't suppose it would hurt, particularly if you manage to get something that finds us the missing woman. Get on it.'

I looked over at Merrington as I hung up. 'Done. You ever done a suspect interview before?'

He shook his head. 'Not the sort I can talk about. How difficult can it be?'

'If you haven't done one before, then you're in for a shock. It's not how television would have it. They don't admit to things and explain everything while raging at the unfairness of it all. And they never give up the goods due to the cunningness of the interviewers. The best we can hope for is to get something inadvertent and trip him up, but I guarantee the moment we do he'll start going "no comment". That's if we can even get him to talk in the first place.'

Merrington looked excited. 'Sounds like a challenge.'

'It is. Tell you what, you manage to get him to say something useful and I'll buy you a beer.'

'It's a deal,' he said as we left the office and headed upstairs to collect the file. 'What about his solicitor?'

I shrugged. 'Last I heard Collins didn't want one. I'm sure that'll change when he's sitting in a room with us, but until then we'll just play it by ear and see what we can dig up.'

54

WE MADE the journey in record time, the Saturday morning traffic only just starting to appear as we headed across town to Custody. The bridge area was all but deserted, with only one sergeant sitting on her own while two members of custody staff fussed around trying to look busy. This was the perfect time, the moment between all the Friday night morons being brought in and them being sober enough to interview. I knew the sergeant behind the desk but hadn't seen her for a while and I couldn't remember her name for the life of me.

'Morning,' I said cheerfully, getting a smile in return.

'Morning Rob. What brings you to my neck of the woods this early on a Saturday?'

'Billy Collins. We're here to interview.'

'This early? Let me just check his record.' She pored over the screen for a minute, making funny little humming noises.

'No, he still doesn't want a solicitor but I'd better check. If he doesn't change his mind, I'll have him brought out.'

'Great, thanks. We'll be in the first interview room.'

Usually before an interview I'd spend an hour or more writing out an interview plan – a list of questions that built from the basic and generic to those specifically about the offence, designed to lure the suspect in and trip them up. This time, however, Riley had done it all for me, using his penchant for tedious bureaucracy to design a flawless interview plan. He'd even arranged the file in perfect order for interview. It's a shame he was so bad at every other aspect of policing or he probably would have been a Superintendent by now.

I led Merrington into the cramped interview room, gesturing at a seat in the corner. 'You'd better sit there.'

He nodded and gestured at the huge tape machine that took up a good chunk of the available space. 'Fair enough. What the bloody hell is that?'

'A tape-machine. Three tapes, all stickered and marked up with evidence numbers.'

'Haven't you heard of digital media?' Merrington said with a smirk and shake of his head.

'Ha ha. It takes about thirty years for technology to filter through to the frontline. We're lucky we're not still using bloody gramophones.'

'That thing isn't far off it. So how does this work then?'

'You put the tapes in and press record.'

He rolled his eyes. 'Not that, I mean the interview.'

'He comes in, I do a spiel about who we are and his rights and then we start asking him questions. He gives us the run-around, and we try and get him to make mistakes.' I sat down at the table.

'Great. Our interviews are a little more aggressive than yours, I suspect, but I'll chip in where I can.'

'Fair enough.' Suddenly something occurred to me. 'One other thing, we both have to name ourselves on the tape. Is that going to be a problem for you?'

He nodded. 'I'm not giving an entire court and the whole criminal fraternity of Brighton my name and then telling them I work for MI6.'

'Well have you got something like a warrant or pay number?'

He nodded. '74318.'

'Well just call yourself Agent 74318 from MI6. I doubt anyone in court will ever have listened to an interview with someone of your lofty standing in it, so it'll do.'

The door opened and the Custody Sergeant stuck her head in. 'You ready?'

I nodded. 'Bring him in.'

She opened the door wider and ushered Collins in. He looked like he'd barely had any sleep and he smelled even worse than he had the day before. His long hair was lank and greasy and he had dark circles under his eyes that rather undermined his attempt at an arrogant leer.

'Sit there.' I pointed at the seat across the table from me, and he obediently sat.

'Do you want a drink before we start?'

'You got some vodka?' he said, grinning moronically.

'I'll take that as a no.' I was on familiar ground now. Interviewing was something I did on a regular basis — unlike being blown up and having guns pointed at me — and despite my tiredness it was nice to be back in something resembling control.

'You're about to be interviewed on tape. As you can see, the tapes are still sealed,' I pulled three at random from the tray next to me, 'and I'm now breaking those seals and placing the tapes in the machine. When we're ready, I'll press play on the machine and you'll hear a long beep. When that beep finishes, the tape will be recording and I'll start talking. Any questions before we start?'

He shook his head and I wondered what had made him decide to play along after his rigid silence of the day before.

'Right. Ready?' I looked at both men. They nodded and I pressed the record button, hoping that this wouldn't be yet another monumental waste of time while we still stood a chance – however slim – of getting something that might help us to find Gemma Hallett alive.

'IT'S 0715 hours on Saturday the 19th August, and we're in an interview room at Sussex House Custody Centre. I'm Detective Sergeant CS462 Steele, and this is...' I looked at Merrington expectantly.

'Agent 74318, MI6.' he supplied.

Collins twitched at that, his eyes flicking over to Merrington before coming back to rest on me, slightly wider than before as his leer began to collapse inward.

'Can you tell me your name and date of birth please?' I directed at him.

He hesitated for a moment, trying to decide whether or not to speak. With a final glance at Merrington, he mumbled 'Billy Collins, 12/7/74.'

'Thank you. Do you agree that there is no one else present in the room?'

He nodded.

'Out loud for the tape please.'

'Yeah, there's just us.'

'You do have the right to free and independent legal advice, which you've chosen not to take up at this time. Can I ask why?'

He shrugged. 'Don't need it yet.'

'That right is ongoing, and if at any time during the interview you feel the need to exercise it, the interview will be stopped until legal advice has been obtained for you.'

He nodded again.

'I'm going to caution you now Billy. You do not have to say anything, but it may harm your defence if you do not mention, when questioned, something which you later rely on in court. Anything you do say may be given in evidence. Do you understand the caution?'

He shrugged and looked away, pretending to be bored while his eyes moved like a pair of fireflies in a strong wind.

'What that means, Billy, is that I'm going to ask you a series of questions. You don't have to answer any of these questions, but if you don't and this goes to court, inference may be drawn from your lack of answer.'

'Can we just get on with it?' he asked, his Liverpool accent adding a drawn out H to his C's.

'Of course. You were arrested yesterday for kidnapping and theft. Tell me about the events that led up to your arrest.'

'I was driving along and you started chasing me. I didn't know who you were and I got scared thinking you were trying to rob me, so I drove away but you kept chasing me. If I'd known you were Gavvers I would have stopped, honest.' It was interesting that so many criminals thought that adding the word honest to the end of a sentence made it seem more plausible.

'My recollection of yesterday is slightly different but we'll cover that later. What happened then?' I asked.

'You smacked us in the face and bent us up, then started tearing me car apart. Then one of you's planted that phone and nicked me for kidnapping someone.'

'We planted it, did we?'

He nodded. 'That's right, I ain't never seen it before, and you won't get no prints off it either, I never touched it.'

He was right about the prints. The phone had a rough surface and SOCO hadn't been able to lift anything useful from it.

'When you say we planted the phone, I just want to be clear that we're talking about the same one here.' I pushed two photographs towards him.

'These are photographs of exhibit DK/01, a silver Nokia 3210 mobile phone, which was found in your car. Whose phone is it?'

'I dunno.'

'Have you ever seen this phone before?'

'Only yesterday when you found it.'

'When we found it?'

'Yeah, that's right.'

'I thought you said we planted it?'

He folded his arms. 'That's what I mean.'

'Finding and planting are two very different things, Mr Collins, I suggest you choose your words carefully. The sim card in this phone belongs to a woman named Gemma Hallett. Do you recognise the name?'

He shook his head emphatically. 'Nope.'

'Do you know where she is?' I persisted.

'No.'

'Gemma is missing, and she is believed to be either dead or being held against her will somewhere. Do you know anything about it?'

'No.'

'Was she in debt to your boss, maybe?'

He shrugged and leaned back. 'I don't have no boss.'

'Yes you do. His name is Danny MacBride. Loanshark, drug dealer. You know, the one who pays you money to break skulls.'

'You're talking out yer arse mate. I don't know no Danny.'

'So you didn't leave 2 Steine Street with him the day before yesterday, then get on a Number 7 bus with him across town?'

'What?' His eyes began to flicker again, moving between Merrington and me.

'You were on the bus with him Billy, I saw you. Remember the couple in the car?'

'That was you snogging!' He burst out, prompting Merrington to look at me with raised eyebrows.

Embarrassed I hastily continued. 'So you *were* there?'

'Uh...bollocks. I want a lawyer.'

I cursed under my breath. I'd known he was going to play that card eventually but I'd hoped to get a lot more out of him before he pulled it.

'Okay, the time is 0726 hours, I'm now switching the machine off.'

As soon as the tapes stopped turning I pulled them out and wrote on the labels, but looked up as Merrington moved in and sat down at the table.

'Bet you're wondering why MI6 are here, aren't you Billy?' He asked.

Collins shrugged. 'Don't care.'

Merrington leaned in towards him. 'But you should.'

'How's that?' Collins shuffled nervously.

'Because no matter what happens here with this investigation, I'm going to put you away for assisting in the commission of an act of terrorism. I reckon probably ten years for your part in it, maybe more.'

I nearly interrupted to warn Merrington that he was breaching PACE, but then I realised that, as he wasn't subject to it, I'd let him play this out.

Collins looked at me. 'What's he talking about?'

'Your lock-up, Billy.' I shook my head and busied myself with the tape labels again.

'What about my lock-up?' I could hear the panic in his voice now. Being arrested for kidnapping was nothing new for him – he was a dab hand at playing the Custody system. But the terrorism laws were new and draconian and even someone like him knew that the 'powers that be' could pretty much throw away the key so long as they thought you were a danger.

Merrington stood and leaned against the wall, inspecting his nails with studied disinterest. 'Doesn't matter, Billy. I know you won't talk.'

'Ah, go on! Tell us!' Collins was getting frantic.

'I really should wait until the good Detective Sergeant has found you a solicitor. Not that it'll help mind, as the terrorism offences don't allow for a solicitor to be present for interview.'

He was lying, but the only person in the room who didn't know that was quite obviously Billy.

'But I ain't no terrorist!' He wailed.

'I didn't say you were,' Merrington said, continuing to turn the screw, 'but you were involved in the commission of an offence, or at least you will be when they commit the offence.'

'Who?' As I glanced up, Collins' eyes told me that he already knew exactly who we were talking about and was just fighting for breathing space.

'The men who rented your lock-up from you Billy. We have reason to believe they may be terrorists. If they commit an act of terrorism and you were letting them store their gear in your lock-up, you'll be going down with them and the next time you breathe free air you'll be an old, old man.'

'I DON'T know what you're talking about.' Sweat was pouring down Collins' face and his eyes darted around the room as if looking for a way out. 'Besides, you can't prove nothing.'

'Oh yes we can.' Merrington leaned in close, his voice low and threatening. 'We've got enough evidence that you'll be an old man before you see daylight again. Unless, of course, you can give us something that proves you were helping us. Then maybe we'll forget all about it.'

Collins looked from Merrington to me, his eyes narrowing. 'How do I know I can trust you?'

Glancing up at the camera in the corner I weighed up the decision I'd been struggling with for the last few minutes. *Ah fuck it*, I thought finally, *in for a penny, in for a pound*. 'Billy, let me level with you.'

He turned to stare at me.

'I need to find that girl and I think you know something about her disappearance.' I held up a hand as he started to speak. 'But I also think that you know something that'll help us catch the suspect in a murder investigation. Your name is on the lease for that lockup, and my colleague here wasn't joking when he said they can put you away for being concerned with whatever it is they're up to. If you know something, tell us and we'll make sure the courts know you've co-operated.'

I sat back and watched him mulling it over, but I knew we had him.

Finally he looked up. 'Okay, how does this work? I ain't telling you nothing on tape.'

'That's fine. We need the information and I don't care if it's on tape or written on the back of a fag packet. Who are the guys from the lockup?'

'Some blokes that Danny knows.'

'How does he know them?' I pushed.

'I dunno, he just does. One of the fellers goes down the casino sometimes, maybe that's how they met.'

'What's his name?'

He shrugged. 'I dunno. Danny always calls him Useless, but not to his face.'

'What about the tall bloke, the one with the face like Jaws from the Bond films?'

'Petr. I know him all right.'

'Oh. How?'

'He's the one that comes to see us when he needs something. He paid the cash upfront for the lock-up too.'

'When he needs something? What sort of things?'

He shrugged again. 'Vehicles and stuff.'

Merrington interjected. 'Be more specific, Billy. Define *stuff*.'

'Just stuff! I dunno!' He was hiding something. Nervous sweat was pouring off him in stinking waves.

'Okay, we're done here.' I stood up. 'Lying wasn't part of the deal. Hope you like prison food, Billy, it's all you're going to be eating for a long time.'

I picked up the file and walked towards the door, holding it open for Merrington. He left without a backwards glance and I began to follow when Collins called out.

'Okay, okay! They rented a flat off Danny.'

We were back in the room in a flash. 'They're renting a flat off MacBride? Where?'

'I dunno, really! Danny knows though.'

'How many flats does Danny own?' I asked, wondering why our intelligence hadn't come up with any other addresses.

'He doesn't.' Collins explained. 'It belongs to a mate but Danny runs it all for him. You know, sorts the problem out if people don't pay their rent, that sort of thing.'

'Right.' I said. 'And this lock-up of yours. Any chance you had a nose around to look at what they were keeping in there?'

Collins shook his head vigorously. 'No way. They were proper snotty about that. Said that they took their privacy all serious and that there'd be grief if we got interested.'

'And you didn't think that was odd?' Merrington asked.

Collins turned to look at him. 'Course it was odd! But they're paying good money and Danny gets right shitty if we screw him around with money, so I left it be.'

'One last question.' I said. 'How long did they rent it for?'

Collins grinned. 'That's easy. I was supposed to be meeting Petr later to collect the keys. They only paid up until today.'

A cold shiver ran down my spine as Merrington and I exchanged a look. Whoever they were, it looked like we were running out of time to find out whatever they were up to. And we still had no clue as to the whereabouts of Gemma Hallett.

'What about the missing woman?' I asked.

Collins put his head in his hands and blew out a long breath. 'I found the phone. It was shit but I kept the sim card. You get a few days out of 'em before the owner cancels 'em. And I heard you can't track the sim card, just the phone.'

He had it the wrong way round but I didn't disabuse him of the notion. 'So you have no idea where she is? Where did you find the phone?'

He shrugged. 'Dunno, town centre somewhere.'

I moved forward until I was standing over him, forcing him to crane his neck to look up at me. 'I need you to be really specific, Billy. Tell me where you *found* the phone.' I had a feeling he was lying but I couldn't be sure and we were running out of time.

He stared up at me for a long moment before sighing and throwing up his hands. 'Fine, I took it off some lads the other day in exchange for their gear.'

'Who, and where did they get it from?'

'Er, London Mark and Big Dave. Dunno where they nicked it from.'

I knew both the names – two of the seemingly never-ending lowlife types that haunted the streets and back alleys of Brighton. If he was telling the truth, we needed to find the two men and we needed to do it fast. Leaving him in the room with Merrington, I went out and waved to a Custody Assistant to have Collins taken back to his cell.

Once that was done I collected Merrington and updated the interview with the Sergeant, leaving out the impromptu session at the end.

As we left the Custody Block to head back to the Nick, Merrington turned to me and pulled a face. 'I hate to say it Rob, but I think right now these men Collins was talking about take priority over your missing woman. If they're the people we've been looking for and they are planning something, we may only have hours to find them before something very bad happens.'

TWENTY MINUTES later we were running up the stairs in the Nick towards Burke's office. I'd tried ringing him but his mobile was unavailable and Merrington had spent the entire journey on the phone to MI6, speaking in some kind of code that I guessed was more a ward against electronic eavesdroppers than for my benefit.

We reached Burke's office side-by-side but as I raised a hand to knock, Merrington shoved it open and strode in purposefully. Burke was sat at his desk, mobile to his ear. He looked up angrily at the interruption, but something in our faces must have told him that something was very wrong.

'What?' he barked, hanging up the call immediately.

I stepped forwards before Merrington could speak. 'Collins talked sir – off the record. The men I saw at the lock-up have also rented a flat from MacBride. The keys are supposed to be collected today.'

Burke mulled it over. 'Any idea who or where they are?'

'Who. Not really. One of them is called Petr, the other we only have a nickname for. Where is unknown – MacBride is the only one who knows where the flat is. Next step is to bring him in.'

'Agreed. Merrington?' Burke looked at him.

The Six agent took a deep breath before speaking. 'I'm afraid this is where I take control. I've got a team coming down now from London and I'll need every resource you can spare, including every armed officer on duty that isn't in a critical post.'

Burke looked uncertain. 'How sure are you that they're planning something?'

'I've got no concrete evidence,' Merrington admitted, 'but if this group is the one we've been searching for, we know that they've been planning something in the UK for a while. Call it a hunch but I believe that something is about to happen and I need your help to make sure it doesn't. Do I have it?'

It wasn't the most convincing explanation but, to my surprise, Burke nodded, his mouth set in a grim line. 'You have it. I'll need it all in writing, of course.'

Merrington looked as surprised as I felt. 'Of course. First though, we need to find out where they are and bring them all in.'

Burke nodded again. 'How can we help?'

'I need Rob here as my second. He's had more hands on experience with this case than anyone else. Then I need to review all the forensic evidence we've got at both crime scenes and the van and see if there's anything there I can use to identify our men.'

'Of course,' Burke said. 'I assume you'll be working out of Rob's office?'

'For now. When my team gets here we'll need somewhere bigger though. A lot bigger.'

'I'll arrange something. I think I'd better call the Chief Constable.'

'Do that, but don't be surprised if his phone's engaged for a while. Oh, and I need you to get a team to bring MacBride in. But bring him here instead of Hollingbury, we don't have time to be chasing backwards and forwards across Brighton.'

Beckoning at me to follow, Merrington left Burke's office and we hurried down to my office where he pointed to the file. 'Show me all the forensic data.'

I spread the file out on the desk and found the list of prints and DNA taken from the crime scenes. 'Twelve sets of prints at the Distant Vistas office – two identified as Brown's and Taverner's, the rest unaccounted for.'

'What else?'

'Okay. We've got four sets of prints at Taverner's, only two sets unidentified.'

'Show me.' he ordered.

I pulled out a photocopy of the print. Merrington pulled his phone out and took a picture of it.

'I wish I'd known about this earlier,' he muttered as he fiddled with the phone, then held it to his ear before I could answer.

'Roger? It's Harv... Just sent you a print, I need it run through our database and Interpol, urgently... No, now... I don't care, something is going down today and this print might be the clincher that stops it...Great.' He rang off and grinned at me. 'The wonders of modern technology, eh?'

I suddenly felt out of my depth again as Merrington stole the show from under my nose, but to be honest I was glad he was here. Having him take charge meant that things would get done quickly – or so I hoped – and that could very well mean lives saved in this case.

Before I could respond, he snapped off another question. 'What else have we got?'

'The results aren't in from the van yet, but I can get hold of Derek and ask how it's going?' I said, standing up.

'Do that. I'll be here.'

Before I'd even left the office he was on the phone again. As I hurried up the stairs to the SOCO office I wondered if we were up to the task of finding these men before they could execute whatever plan they had in place. I bloody hoped so.

The SOCO office was unusually busy for a Saturday with three blue shirted officers all hammering away at keyboards.

'Anyone seen Derek?' I asked, and was rewarded with a finger pointed towards the lab.

Heading through, I found him still wearing his paper suit as he finished transferring the last one of several prints to a frame. He looked up. 'Ah, Rob. You're like my missus, turning up the moment the food's ready but far too busy to help cook.'

'This time I'm changing the menu, mate.' I filled him in on what had happened and his jowls drooped in shock as the news sank in.

'Shit. And you've got no idea when or where they're going to hit or what exactly they're going to do?'

I shook my head. 'None. To be honest, we don't even know if they are going to hit. We're just working on Merrington's hunch at the moment, but I'm inclined to think he's right. How many prints did you pick up from the van?'

'Three different sets on the inside, some good ones too.'

I nodded. 'I need you to run them as an urgent priority and I need copies straightaway.'

He nodded and hurried to the photocopier, placing the frames in one at a time as I impatiently snatched the results of the tray.

'Oh yeah, I almost forgot,' Derek said as we worked feverishly. 'I was going to tell you when I had confirmation but you running in here like this kind of threw me.'

'Tell me what?' I asked.

'Two things, really. The first is that we found some hair in the van, and, well, you know what I'm like with hair.'

'Come on mate, spit it out.'

'Well, as soon as I saw it, I thought to myself *where have I seen hair that colour before, brown with a hint of red?*, and then I remembered that hairbrush you brought in.'

I looked at him in surprise. 'Gemma Hallett's hairbrush?'

Derek nodded. 'Yeah. I know the cases aren't related, but I've sent the samples up to London on a priority run. If there's one thing I know, it's hair, and I'd bet my lunch the strands I found in the van belong to her.'

I was incredulous. 'Let me get this straight. You think Gemma Hallett was in that van?' No sooner had I begun to believe that the two investigations were separate than something came up to link them again and throw me into a flat spin. 'What the hell has she got to do with the shootings?'

He shrugged. 'Don't ask me, I just scrape clues off floors. You're the one who's supposed to put them all together.'

'Thanks. What's the second thing?'

'My wife's supposed to be going into town today. Do you think it'll be okay if I call her and tell her not to go just in case?' He looked at me plainitively.

I nodded. It was a complete breach of protocol, but I couldn't have him worrying about his wife when one phone call would keep her safe. 'Give her a call mate. Just don't tell her *why* she can't go in'

The last photocopy slid out of the machine. I grabbed it and ran.

'Thanks Derek, I owe you,' I called over my shoulder, not waiting to hear his reply.

Back at the office, Merrington repeated his phone magic, sending the pictures to his lab along with another phone call marking them all as urgent.

'You're not going to believe this,' I told Merrington when he'd finished doing that, 'but it looks like our missing woman was in the van at some point. If we find them, we could well find her as well.'

Merrington looked at me with something that looked suspiciously like sympathy. 'I doubt she's alive Rob, not with people like this and, even if she is, she'll probably be wishing she was dead.'

'Great, thanks for cheering me up.' I ran my hands over my face and up through my hair. 'Of course you realise that if she's linked to the van and the guys with the van are linked to Collins, then he's lying about the phone?'

Merrington nodded. 'That's a fair bet. He probably stole it whilst sniffing around their flat.'

'Christ. We need to re-interview him and this time do it properly.' I shook my head as I thought of the problems our impromptu chat would now cause. If I used information gained from an illegal interview, I breached PACE and we lost the case. It would be worth it if I thought he'd tell me where he really got the phone, but after this latest discovery I couldn't trust a word that came out of his mouth.

Merrington shook his head. 'Probably, but there's no time, we've got too much else on our plate.'

'So what do you want to do now?' I had my own ideas but Merrington was in charge.

'Now? Now we go looking for your friend MacBride, and if we can't find him we hope that the tech boys can do their job before your city turns into a bloodbath.'

58

WE SPENT the next ninety minutes driving around town visiting Macbride's known haunts. We'd put out an *eyes down* request on the radio, marking him as wanted for kidnapping, but so far no-one else had seen him either. His flat was a bust, as was the squat on Steine Street, and the last stop I could think of was Rakesh Patel's shop.

I double-parked on a nearby side street and we walked up the road towards the shop, battling against the tide of Saturday shoppers.

'You can tell this isn't London,' Merrington remarked as a large woman almost knocked him off his feet.

'Really?' I hoiked my thumb over my shoulder at the sea.

'No, I mean the people. Even at rush hour no-one likes to touch anyone else. Here it's all about barging through no matter what.'

'Welcome to bohemian Brighton – shop at your peril.'

The world turned green as we entered the darkness of the shop. Rakesh was behind the counter and, the moment he recognised me, he gave me a hopeful smile. 'You've arrested him?'

I shook my head. 'Not yet, we came here to see if you'd seen him this morning?'

'No.' He deflated slightly and I wished I had better news.

'Well if he turns up, I need you to call me immediately.' I passed him a business card and he tucked it under the phone.

'I will. Please catch him before he comes back.'

'We'll do our best Mr Patel.' We left and I let the flow of the crowd carry me back towards the car, too busy trying to work out where to go next to fight with the throng.

'Ideas?' Merrington asked as we reached the car.

'I'm thinking,' I replied, starting the engine but leaving it idling. 'We've done his flat, his workplace and the shop. There's nowhere else that springs to mind.'

'Well we can't just drive around town aimlessly, we don't have the time.'

'I know that! Just let me think a minute.' I drummed my fingers on the steering wheel. 'How long until your men get here from London?'

He glanced at his watch. 'Two hours maybe.'

'Right. Let me make a call.' I dialled Peters' number, continuing to beat a tattoo on the steering wheel as it rang. When he picked up I launched straight in. 'Peters, it's Rob. Listen, have you got someone that can go through all the intelligence we've got on MacBride? We need to find him sharpish and I don't want to spend all day driving around town in circles looking for him.'

'I thought you had a team working with you?' Peters replied.

'Nat's off today and Karl's still sick. I haven't seen his replacement yet today and I don't have his number. It shouldn't take more than about twenty minutes.'

Peters grunted. 'Okay, I'll call you back if we get anything.'

'Thanks.' I rang off and turned to Merrington with a shrug. 'Unless you can think of anything else that's about the best I can do. We could do with Nat, she only has to look at a piece of intelligence once and it lodges in her brain and sticks. She probably knows every house MacBride has lived in since he was twelve.'

He raised his eyebrows. 'That's useful.'

'Tell me about it, she's like a walking encyclopaedia of the criminal intel world.' I pulled out into the traffic, moving at a crawl as pedestrians crossed roads without looking. One particularly obnoxious man on a pushbike flipped me the finger as he cycled through a red light and almost into my bonnet, ringing his bell furiously as if it were my fault. 'I fucking hate Brighton on a Saturday.'

Merrington raised his eyebrows again but refrained from comment as I negotiated the traffic and headed back towards the Nick. As per usual, the local Council had decided that Saturday was the perfect day for men to be doing road repairs at the junction of Montpelier Road and Western Road. It was busy at the best of times, but today it was causing chaos as the road went down to one lane. We were only about five hundred yards from Rakesh's shop when my phone rang again. I threw it over to Merrington.

'Rob Steele's phone.' He answered. 'What? Where? Okay, hold on and we'll be right there.'

He dropped the phone into a pocket and looked at me. 'That was Patel. The man just came into his shop and threatened him again. He left about thirty seconds ago!'

'Shit.' Both lanes were rammed with traffic, and there was no way I'd be able to turn. Hitting the hazard lights, I jumped out and began to run back down the road, ignoring the honks of angry drivers as Merrington followed close on my heels.

'Which way did he go when he left?' I shouted over my shoulder as Merrington laboured to keep up.

'I didn't ask.' Merrington called back.

I tucked my head down and sprinted along the narrow gap between the two lanes, desperate to make ground and catch MacBride. The man was the key to the investigation and if he slipped through our fingers, the fallout could be disastrous. I glanced back to see Merrington falling behind, one hand clamped to his side where he'd taken the brunt of the blast from the boat. I put on another burst of speed, ignoring the pain from my own protesting ribs.

I reached the shop ahead of the Six agent and burst through the door to see Rakesh nursing a bloodied nose – several reddened tissues already on the desk in front of him.

'Where did he go?' I panted, leaning on the counter for support.

'Towards Hove,' Rakesh said through the wad of tissue he held to his face.

'What was he wearing?'

'A blue hooded top. He had the hood up.'

'And you're sure it was him?'

He pointed silently at his nose. 'Yes'

I nodded and ran back out, almost colliding with Merrington. His face was grey and he was almost doubled over.

'Use my phone, call Burke and get units out searching, he went towards Hove. Blue hoody, hood up. Should be easy to spot on a day like this.' I took off West without waiting for an answer, glad that I was in casual clothes instead of a suit. As I sprinted along Western Road I looked left and right down the side roads, determined to catch MacBride before he went to ground.

Suddenly everyone seemed to be wearing blue. Every flash turned my head, only to find it was an old man in a thick coat, a woman in a blue dress, a blue baseball cap. I ran past a Starbucks on my left on the corner of Lansdowne Place, scanning the tables as I passed, then on towards Palmeira Square.

The square consisted of a small park in the middle of a one-way system with a floral clock, the buildings around the outside a mixture of contemporary and Georgian with shops and pubs scattered here and there. As I reached the junction with Holland Road I looked up towards the old Hove Nick and was rewarded with the sight of a man in a dark blue hoody stepping over the low chain that surrounded the park.

I took a deep breath, and began to run towards the man. As I readied myself to tackle him, I prayed it was MacBride and not some poor sap just out for a walk in town. I reached the chain as he began to walk across the grass towards the clock itself, a raised bank of flowers angled so that it could be seen from a distance.

Suddenly he began to turn. I'd learned years before never to look at someone directly when chasing them, as some deep-buried survival instinct often alerts people if you fix your eyes on their back. True to my training I was looking past him, but still the man turned and I caught sight of a flash of short reddish brown hair under the hood as he broke into a sprint of his own.

'Stop, police!' I yelled now that the game was up. I didn't think for a second it would make him stop, but I hoped that when I caught him it would stop passers-by from stepping in and helping the wrong man. I could feel my breath hissing out of my lungs now as I chased MacBride. I knew that if I didn't catch him in the next thirty seconds, then my wind would be gone and I'd be forced to stop. Usually I could chase someone for miles but my injuries were already making each step agony. Putting on a final burst of speed, I closed the distance between us to a dozen yards, then closer, close enough to smell MacBride's stale sweat.

He reached the chain on the far side of the park and I saw him lengthen his stride to jump. I reached out and managed to brush his back with my fingertips, but not quite enough to grab him. Instead, as he jumped I pushed, sending him sprawling into the chain.

Falling, he went down on his face, hands only just catching his weight as I bundled on top of him. He fought like a wild thing, half twisting to smash an elbow into my throat. I tucked my chin just a moment too late, negating some of the force but enough got through that suddenly I couldn't get a breath.

I sat up gasping as my throat constricted, my oxygen depleted lungs going into spasm as they tried frantically to pull down air that wouldn't come. MacBride threw a second elbow, this one catching me in the solar plexus and, if he hadn't, then he probably would have escaped.

As it was, the shock of the blow opened my throat as it made my lungs expel what little air they had left. Then I was sucking it back in, huge lungfuls of air that gave me enough strength to smash my forearm into the back of his head, knocking his face against the ground. He howled in pain and tried to twist around but I clamped my legs around his, feet tucked under his knees to immobilise his legs. Another elbow flashed in towards my face but I blocked it, grabbing the proffered arm and twisting it into a lock hard enough that he screamed in pain. The sleeve of his hoody slipped back to display an arm covered in blackwork tattoos.

Using the locked arm to slam him into the ground again for good measure, I finally got control and twisted the lock. If he tried to struggle, his shoulder would pop out of its socket. Gasping for breath, I looked around and realised that we were lying in the road outside the park, several cars and a bus stopped nearby as the occupants watched in horrified fascination.

A crowd was beginning to gather and I made eye-contact with the man nearest me. 'I'm a police officer,' I panted, 'call 999 and get me some units here, please!'

He hesitated for a moment and then pulled out his phone. I returned my attention to my prisoner. 'Danny MacBride, I'm arresting you for attempted arson with intent to endanger life. You do not have to say anything, but it may harm your defence if you do not mention, when questioned, something which you later rely on in court. Anything you do say may be given in evidence. Do you understand?'

The man beneath me nodded. 'Just one thing,' he said, and the moment I heard the voice I knew what he was going to say. 'I get the caution, but I ain't MacBride.'

59

'KIERAN *BLOODY* Dacey.' I fumed as two uniformed officers led the now cuffed man towards their waiting car.

Merrington shrugged and looked up on me from the bench he'd slumped on the moment he'd arrived. 'Well you have to admit he looks like MacBride.'

'He fucking should, he's MacBride's nephew. The whole family's rotten, but it never occurred to me that Kieran would have gotten himself some tattoos just like his dear old uncle.'

'It's not your fault; you were just following a lead.'

I ran my hand over my face and sat next to him on the bench. 'I know, I know. And at least Mr Patel won't have to worry about his home being set on fire anymore but it means we're back to square one with MacBride.'

One of the officers taking details from those in the crowd who had stayed looked over. 'Did you just say MacBride?'

I looked up, the tone of voice giving me that faintest spark of hope. 'I did, why?'

'He got picked up about ten minutes ago in Whitehawk. I heard it over the radio.'

Merrington and I shared a look. I pulled out my car keys and threw them to the officer. 'I need your keys. You'll find a silver Ford Focus about half a mile towards town with its hazards on sitting in a traffic jam. Sorry.'

The officer rolled his eyes but handed me his keys, pointing to one of the three cars that had turned up to assist. Nodding my thanks I hurried over and got in, Merrington easing himself into the passenger side.

'We don't have a lot of time, Rob,' he said as I pulled out into the traffic.

I threw him a grin. 'Would you say it's urgent that we get to MacBride, matter of life and death maybe?'

He caught on and grinned back. 'Could be.'

I pressed the button on the panel next to the steering wheel and thumped the horn. Blue lights and sirens sprang to life and I put my foot down, tearing across Brighton at breakneck speed.

When we got to the Nick, we found two officers standing in the front office corridor by the open door to one of the witness interview rooms. MacBride was sitting cuffed on one of the scruffy blue chairs while he stared out of the window over the yard where all the marked vehicles parked.

The room was so small that when Merrington and I squeezed in it felt more than a little claustrophobic. MacBride continued to stare out of the window, refusing to acknowledge us.

Then he suddenly shifted, turning his piercing blue eyes on us and moving forwards to relieve the pressure of the cuffs on his wrists. 'Hello again Detective.'

I nodded at the officers who'd brought him in. 'Thanks lads, we'll take it from here. Just a quick Arrest Statement will do.'

'Can I have my cuffs back?' one of them asked plaintively.

'Later. I'll leave them with the sergeant in the Response Office.' They nodded and filed out, leaving us alone in the cramped space with our prisoner.

'You know it's a breach of my rights not to be taken to Custody, don't you?' MacBride continued, eyeing us both. His gaze finally settled on Merrington, obviously deciding that he was more important. 'Once a person has been arrested for an indictable offence, they need to be taken to a custody centre and dealt with according to PACE. I'm pretty sure you've fucked yourselves.'

'I had no idea you were a lawyer, Danny,' I said, sitting down opposite him and leaning back with a smirk that was meant to show that I didn't care despite the fact he was right.

'There's a lot you don't know.' he said with a knowing grin. 'I got nicked for kidnapping, and that means I get taken to Custody and read my rights. Either you sort it out or there's gonna be a shit storm that you'll be right in the middle of.'

'This isn't about kidnapping, Danny, not really anyway. That was just the easiest way to get you in lawfully.'

'Oh no? What *is* it about then?' he asked, pretending to be perplexed.

Merrington leaned in, clearing his throat to get MacBride's attention. 'It's about us throwing you in a big, dark hole and then losing the key. I need some information from you, and if I don't get it, I'm going to make sure that whatever happens to the men you've been helping will come down on you four-fold.'

MacBride looked at him impassively. 'Who the fuck do you think you are?'

'Agent Merrington, MI6.'

MacBride laughed scornfully. 'Yeah right. You got ID?'

'Not that I'm going to show you. Ask the Detective Sergeant here to confirm it.'

MacBride looked unimpressed. 'Like I'd believe anything *he* says. You bloody rozzers'll say anything you like if you think it'll get you a collar.'

'Not this time.' Merrington shot back. 'I understand that you've had dealings with some people recently and I need to know as much about them as possible. Your assistance now might well tip the balance when all this goes to court.'

'All what? I've got no idea what you're talking about.'

'How about a group of men renting a flat through you? Men who are using Billy Collins lock-up in Woodingdean.'

MacBride shrugged. 'Sorry mate, I've fingers in a lot of pies, you'll have to be a bit more specific than that.'

Merrington took a deep breath and shook his head. 'Don't try and play me, Danny. I can promise you that you'll regret it.'

'Promise me a blowjob and a fag afterwards and I'm all yours.' MacBride leered at Merrington, whose face flushed an angry red. I stepped in before he could lose his rag altogether.

'Danny, I don't think you realise just how much shit you're in right now. The people you're protecting could well be terrorists and we need to know where they are.'

MacBride curled a lip. 'What, coz they're commies they're terrorists? I thought you lot was supposed to be all politically correct.'

'No, not because they're... foreign,' I caught myself before I used his own phrase, 'but forgive me if I don't feel like sharing the in's and out's of our investigation with you. Just tell us where their bloody flat is.'

He shook his head. 'Nah, sorry mate. I'm a businessman, and I never let getting nicked interfere with good business. You take me up to the cells and see what you can make stick. Bet I see you down the pub the next day.'

'For Christ's sake Danny, sort your bloody priorities out! What does a few quid matter compared to the lives that might be saved if we're right?' I suddenly realised I was shouting and took a step back as a mocking smile spread across MacBride's face.

'Terrible sad when you don't get your own way, isn't it detective?'

'It's not my way I'm worried about you moron, it's... this is pointless.' I threw my hands in the air.

MacBride nodded. 'You're right, so if you two would like to go fuck yourselves...'

The next thing I knew Merrington was out of his chair and looming over MacBride with a raised fist.

Leaping forwards, I caught the punch before it could land and pulled Merrington away.

'A word outside?' I opened the door and pointed while MacBride watched us, his smile taking up half his face.

'What?' Merrington asked when I'd closed the door, his face red and his eyes still shining with anger.

'What the bloody hell has got into you? We don't go around beating people just because they don't tell us what we need to know.' I kept my voice as quiet as I could as we were only one door away from the public reception desk.

'Well maybe we bloody should! Anywhere else in the world and he'd be looking at us through a sheet of plastic and a bucketful of water right now if I had my way. Then he'd bloody talk.'

I shook my head in wonder. 'And we're the good guys?'

'Sometimes you have to commit a wrong to right a greater wrong,' he said as if he believed it.

'How are we any better than them if we're willing to hurt someone to get information? Surely that makes us the bad guys?'

'Does it?'

'Yes, I rather think it does. If he doesn't want to talk, that's his right.'

'And you're willing to balance the lives of all the people that could get killed out there on this one criminal's human rights?'

'I'm not happy about it, but there's only so much we can do. If he's not going to help us, we can't exactly bash him around until he says something...'

I stopped as I realised one of the front office staff was looking through their door to see us bickering like schoolboys. I glared at her and she hurriedly went back to work. 'Look, the bottom line is that I'm not going to let you hurt that man while he's in my care. If you want to beat him to a pulp, you'll have to take him back to your own bloody place.'

Merrington looked at me for a long moment then shrugged.

'Fair enough. Like you said, he's your prisoner and I shouldn't have lost my temper.'

I blinked at the sudden change.

'Right, well, thanks. We've got other lines of enquiry anyway, so I'm going to release him from custody. It's not like we can't find him again in a hurry.'

'What other lines of enquiry? We need to know where they're staying, you know that.'

'But we can't afford to waste time trying to crack him, we'll have to wait for the forensics to come back. What else do you suggest?'

Merrington shrugged. 'We throw him in a cell for a few hours and come back and see him later if nothing else pans out. We can't just let him go.'

'Fine, as long as you keep your hands off him.'

'Scouts honour.'

I opened the door again and we moved back inside. Once the door was shut MacBride grinned to show he'd heard the whole conversation.

'So you won't let him hurt me, eh? I suppose I should be grateful. If you're gonna put me in a cell, hurry up and fucking get it over with so I can go home.'

'One last chance to talk,' I offered, but he shook his head.

'Fuck yourself.'

'Fine.' I put a call through to the Response Office and we waited in silence for the officers to return.

When they arrived and I'd explained the circs in more detail, they hustled him away with poorly concealed annoyance while I hoped that I was right, and that my protection of a criminal's human rights hadn't prevented us from stopping the attack that we feared was imminent.

60

BEFORE WE could talk further, Merrington's phone rang. He hurried off to take the call in private, leaving me to head back down to the office on my own.

I sat behind my desk and placed my head on the wood for a moment, trying to pull my scattered thoughts together. The adrenaline from the run and the fight had drained out of me, leaving me so tired I could quite easily have curled up and slept in the corner.

I woke with a start as the door hit the wall, Merrington striding in with a smug smile on his face. I jerked upright and considered pretending I hadn't been asleep when I realised that I didn't particularly care.

'What are you so cheerful about?' I asked suspiciously.

'My chaps have come through, we've got an ID on one of the fingerprints from the van and, better yet, we know where he works.'

'Oh really, go on.' I shook the last vestiges of tiredness away, at least for the moment, and tried to concentrate on what he was saying as he held his phone up and read from the screen.

'Andrei Bazhenov, Russian national born in Kiev in 1972. Known links to several organisations, but he's a mercenary rather than a religious nut, so no reasons to expel him from the country or even watch him particularly hard. He's the terrorist version of a gofer, a fixer who stays out of sight and gets people whatever they need. He's not a nasty bastard per se, but he's got contacts all over the world. You want something, he's your man.'

'Is he one of the group you've been watching?'

Merrington shook his head and shrugged with exaggerated nonchalance.

'No, but that doesn't mean he's not linked to them. They probably just hired him on for transport and the like for the attack. Maybe.'

'Maybe.' I didn't like the uncertainty in his tone. What if we were wrong and they were in town for a different reason that had nothing to do with an all out attack? If we were barking up the wrong tree they could be getting away with murder while we were running around trying to save people that didn't need saving.

'He lives and works in Brighton,' Merrington continued, 'no current home address but he works at a catering suppliers based on North Road. I assume you know where that is?'

'Yeah, about two minutes walk from here. How do you want to play this?'

He shrugged. 'I've had an update from my guys and they're about twenty minutes away, but they'll still need to gear up and brief before deploying. Any idea how Burke is getting on with gathering up the ARVs?'

I shrugged back and threw him my phone. 'No idea. Knock yourself out.'

He caught it in his left hand and dialled Burke.

'No, it's Harvey Merrington. Yes. No, no, no joy there. What about the armed officers? Great, we'll be up there in five, no make it ten minutes.'

He threw the phone back.

'If I give you the address we're looking for can you bring up photographs and floor plans from your systems?'

'That depends on whether we've been there before. Give me the address.'

Several minutes of searching later, I had some Google Streetview pictures and an electronic line drawing of the building, but no floor plan.

'We've never had to raid it before so there's nothing on the system,' I explained as we hurried up to the fourth floor to where no less than a dozen armed officers waited.

'Fine, we'll do the briefing on the hoof.'

'You want to run the plan by me first, just in case it needs tweaking?' I asked as we cleared the stairs and moved towards the large briefing room.

He shrugged. 'We'll surround the building, close it down and start searching room by room. Quick and effective.'

I put a hand on his arm to stop him as he pulled the door open.

'And what if he's not there? We risk alerting them all that we're looking for them. I guarantee you that about thirty seconds after we go through the door, someone will be on the phone to the Argus and we'll be on the news about ten minutes after that.'

He frowned. 'Then what do you recommend?'

'How about we go in, just the two of us, and ask to talk to the manager in private? If Andrei's there, we get a team in to detain him, if he's not then we find out where he is and work the rest out from there.'

He mulled it over for a second before nodding.

'It sounds like a plan, let's do it your way. Just make sure you put a vest on, for Christ's sake.'

We moved through the door and into the briefing room to find two rows of officers sitting there waiting patiently, all wearing tactical vests with Glocks holstered at their waists and the occasional yellow flash of a taser here and there.

Burke, Long and Peters were already sat at the top table and, for once, I went to join them as Merrington headed straight for the lectern.

'Ladies and gentlemen,' he began as he spread the pictures out in front of him, 'I'm afraid this is a bit of a short notice briefing, but I make no apology for the fact. I'm not sure how much you've been told already?' He paused and looked at Burke, who shook his head.

'Ah, ok. I'll make this very brief, but I'm sure you'll understand that this is well above top secret and should not be talked about with anyone outside this room.'

He glanced around until he got enough nods, then he outlined the case so far. From where I was sat facing the armed officers, I could see their faces change from boredom to interest to outright worry as they realised just how serious a situation this might turn out to be.

'So,' Merrington summed up, 'the current plan is that myself and DS Steele will go in and speak to the manager and try and locate the target. If he isn't in the building, then we'll get a location from the manager; if he is, then we'll try and get him isolated and then call you in to detain him. I'll leave specifics to you as I'm not familiar with your tactics, but I've got maps of the area and pictures of the building here.'

He stepped forward and handed them to the nearest sergeant, who studied them before passing them on to the next officer.

'I need you to be ready in fifteen minutes.' As a rumble of protest passed through the officers, Merrington held up a hand.

'I'm sorry, I know it's short notice but we're working against a clock that we can't see and I don't want it to run out before we've brought these people down.'

The rest of the briefing was tactical, the firearms sergeant spreading the photographs on the floor while everyone gathered round.

The premises itself was a warehouse that was actually on Vine Street, a small side street off North Road in the centre of town. The warehouse was next to a pub called the Fountain Head, and it was agreed that one car with two officers would sit at either end of the street while the rest waited in a borrowed PSU van that would sit just around the corner until needed.

Once we were all set, Merrington and I cadged a lift in the van so that we could be sure everything was in position before we went in. I'd dug out my vest and now had it on under my clothes, making me look bulky but not too obvious.

Peters joined us in the cramped back of the van while Burke and Long remained behind to run things on the radio. The atmosphere in the van was tense.

One of the armed officers looked up at me as the van pulled up near the pub.

'Try not to get shot, huh?'

I nodded. 'I'll do my best. Try not to be late if we need you.'

He smiled and opened the door for me. 'Don't worry about us, we'll be right there.'

I could feel sweat trickling down my back under the vest as we walked along the road in the blazing sunshine, eyes already scanning the area in case this was their base of operations.

I doubted that it was, however, as a little bit of digging had shown it to be a legitimate company run by someone called Justin Smith, which was about as English a name as you could get.

The front of the red brick building was mostly taken up by huge doors large enough to fit a lorry through, which made sense for a catering suppliers. The doors were black painted wood with a smaller, human sized door in the middle with an entry system next to it.

The smaller door was ajar and Merrington slid his right hand under his jacket as we stepped through into sudden darkness, welcoming the cooler air as I tried to shift my sweaty vest into a more comfortable position.

We found ourselves in a brick paved yard with two vans parked up neatly next to a stack of crates, with a large loading bay door just behind them. On the other side of the yard was a small door with a white plastic sign saying *Reception*, and I pointed Merrington towards it.

He opened it cautiously to show a short corridor with a door to our left and a turn to our right that led out of sight.

Pushing the second door open, I went into a pleasant office with a small desk and several potted plants that took up most of the available space.

A woman in her late thirties sat behind the desk, glasses up on her head as she chattered to someone on the phone. The moment she saw me she ended the call and pulled her glasses down.

'Can I help you?'

'I hope so, I'm looking for the manager.'

'And you are?'

I showed her my badge. 'The police, but I need you to keep that quiet for now.'

Her eyes gleamed all of a sudden and it was only then that I noticed the crime novel sitting on her desk. No doubt by the time we found the manager she'd be on the phone to a friend telling them all about what was happening.

'Really quiet,' I repeated as she picked up the phone and made a call.

'Justin, it's Marie. There's someone here to see you, it's very important.' She looked up at me with a wink. 'I can't say, but you should get here now.'

'He'll be here in a minute, can I get you a cup of tea?' she asked as she put the phone down.

'No thanks.' I turned to Merrington and saw that he was half in the door with his back to me, eyes scanning the corridor in case our target happened to wander past.

A few uncomfortable minutes later the manager arrived, sweat staining his shirt under the arms. He had a red face that really didn't suit his carefully styled hair and a goatee that was beginning to turn grey.

'Hi, I'm Justin Smith. Who are you?' He asked without preamble.

Merrington stepped out into the corridor and I followed him, swinging the door shut on the PA as I showed Justin my badge.

'DS Steele. We need to talk to you urgently and in private about one of your staff.'

His eyes widened and he nodded, leading us along the corridor and around the corner to a second office.

This one was much larger than the last and the shelves were covered in fishing trophies and pictures of him winning various angling competitions.

There were only two chairs but none of us sat, Justin standing nervously by the desk and Merrington and I stopping as soon as the door was shut.

'How can I help?' He asked, and I noticed that his hands were shaking slightly.

Merrington spoke before I could. 'Andrei Bazhenov. Does he still work for you?'

The manager nodded. 'Yes, but he's not in today.'

I turned away and spoke quietly into my radio. 'All units, stand down, repeat stand down and await further instructions, target is not in the building.'

'What exactly does he do here?' Merrington asked as I turned back to the conversation.

'He's a delivery driver. Has he done something wrong?'

'We're not sure yet. Do you know where he lives?'

The manager shook his head. 'I'm sorry, he moved a couple of months ago and he hasn't given us the new address yet.'

'Has he borrowed a work van recently, or gone off his delivery route. Yesterday maybe?'

'Uh, I've got no idea,' Justin said uncertainly, 'but he always uses the same van so it shouldn't be hard to check.'

'Hard to check?'

'Yeah, we've been having a few problems with the staff using the vans when they shouldn't, so we had the vehicles Lojacked last month and we haven't told them. Give me five minutes and I can give you a print out of every location he's been to in the last week, if that'll help?'

I nodded with a smile spreading across my face. We'd needed a bit of luck, and this man and his paranoia had just provided what may very well be the straw that broke the camel's back and gave us the men we were looking for.

61

NAT WOKE to the sound of someone hammering at the door, an insistent banging that she decided to ignore until it went away. After the third round, it stopped and she sat up as she heard the letterbox flap swing. Rubbing a hand over her face she groaned and wondered what had made her think it was a good idea to make a sizeable dent in Brighton's beer stocks the night before.

'Bloody Rob Steele, that's what,' she muttered as she gathered her belongings together and smoothed the worst of the creases out of her trousers. Staggering into the kitchen she checked her phone for messages. Finding none, she put it on the counter while she poured and drank two pints of water then took four Ibuprofen from the packet Rob had left on the counter.

'Twenty-nine-years-old and I can't handle a hangover anymore,' she said mournfully as she headed towards the front door and let herself out. A second before it slammed shut, she remembered her phone on the kitchen worktop.

'Shit!' She cursed as the lock engaged with a solid sounding *clunk*. Rattling the door, Nat knew she'd never get back inside but with a murder case going on she *had* to have her phone. Leaving it behind just wasn't an option.

Looking around at the quiet street, she clambered up on to the railings beside the steps and leaned out over the basement flat, ignoring the twenty foot drop to the hard concrete below. Her fingertips grasped the window frame and she wiggled the wood but Rob had left the window lock on and it wouldn't budge.

'Fucking security conscious coppers,' she swore under her breath, and looked around once more to make sure that no one was within sight.

Satisfied that she was unobserved, Nat gripped the railings with both hands and kicked out, shattering the window with a smash that could probably be heard the next street over. Not waiting to see if the noise brought any sleepy neighbours to investigate, she swiftly undid the lock and lifted the window before clambering inside.

Back in the lounge, she shook broken glass from her top and hurried through to the kitchen, wondering how she was going to explain to Rob that she'd broken his window. The thought made her grin. Much as she liked Rob, sometimes he could be *far* too serious, and she loved the occasional moments where she could bring him back down to earth, make him seem a little more human. Hell, if she did it enough maybe one day he'd pull his head out of his arse and notice...

The sound of a key sliding into a lock made her freeze in the act of reaching for the door. It swung open to reveal a waifishly pretty blonde in jeans and a skimpy top letting herself in.

'Who the bloody hell are you?' Nat asked suspiciously.

'Er, who the hell are you?' the blonde said, looking at Nat in confusion, then in worry as she saw the broken window.

'I asked first. You've got about five seconds to tell me who you are and why you've got a key or you're in serious shit.'

The blonde stiffened, angry but uncowed. 'I'm Anna. This is my brother's flat.'

Nat was taken aback. 'Oh right. I work with Rob.'

Anna grinned suddenly. 'You're Nat, aren't you? Rob told me about you.'

'Nothing good I hope?' Something about the other woman appealed to Nat. Despite finding a stranger in her brother's home, she was far from worried or afraid and that said a lot.

Anna's grin widened as she relaxed. 'Uh, headstrong, stubborn, that sort of thing. He even used the word vituperative.'

'What the bloody hell does that mean?' Nat looked perplexed.

Anna shrugged. 'I've got no idea. Rob probably doesn't either. What happened to the window?'

Nat shrugged. 'Forgot my phone.'

'Oh. Don't police officers get in trouble for breaking into houses?' Anna grinned back.

'Not if their sergeant's sister puts in a good word, they don't.'

'It would be my pleasure. It's just nice to see another woman in the house.'

'Don't get your hopes up.' Nat replied. 'As you can see, I've been sleeping on the sofa.'

'You can wear his underwear for all I care – it's really none of my business. I'd say whatever you do, don't hurt him, but I think he's still so fucked up from Linda...' Anna tailed off.

'I never met her,' Nat said, suddenly uncomfortable with the way the conversation was going and eager to leave.

'She was a wonderful woman – I loved her like a sister.' Anna's eyes clouded for a moment but then she shook her head. 'Sorry. Way to scare someone off, I'm sorry.'

They both laughed as Nat moved back towards the door.

'If you speak to Rob later, can you tell him that I've lost my phone so I'm going into town to buy a new one?' Anna asked as Nat stepped outside.

'Did you want to call him? You can use my phone.' Nat held her mobile out and was rewarded with a brilliant smile.

'Thanks! You're a star.' Anna dialled Rob's number and held the phone to her ear for a few seconds before pulling it away and dialling again. A few moments later she handed it back. 'He keeps hanging it up.'

'I'll tell him you called round.' Nat said, putting the phone away. 'Did you want him to meet you if he gets a chance?'

Anna shook her head. 'No, it's fine. I'm supposed to be meeting with some friends later anyway, so just say hi. That'll worry him, the thought that we've been talking about him.'

'Do you think it will?'

Anna shrugged 'I doubt it, but I live in hope. Nice to meet you. See you again?'

Nat nodded and then pointed to the window. 'About that...'

Anna laughed. 'Don't worry, I'll get it boarded up but you owe me one.'

'Thanks.' With a final wave she headed on to the road and towards the bus stop, mentally kicking herself. Although she didn't particularly care about the window, she'd nearly made a fool of herself in front of Rob's sister and she hated to look stupid.

'Well done Nat,' she muttered to herself as she waited impatiently for the next bus, 'way to meet the family.'

62

WHEN WE got back to the Nick, I had a list of GPS co-ordinates that I desperately needed to feed into a computer mapping system. My phone had rung twice in the car on the way back – Nat both times – but I didn't have time to answer the call so I thumbed the red button.

We piled out of the van in the Nick's back yard and I hurried inside with Merrington and Peters while the other officers waited patiently outside, the sun gleaming off weapons and tactical helmets.

'How many co-ordinates are there?' Peters asked as we headed into my office and I sparked up the computer.

'About half a dozen that aren't delivery drops, he marked those in red,' I replied as I brought up the local mapping system. I began to feed the co-ordinates in, storing each location to look at when I was finished. My phone rang again and I was about to kill the call when I saw it was Burke. 'Sir?'

'News?' he barked.

I filled him in while Peters took over on the computer. 'We've got six unknown locations sir, all stops for about five minutes except the last one which was about thirty seconds. Then our man took the van back to the warehouse and clocked out.'

'And what are you planning on doing when you've got all the locations?' Burke asked.

'I don't know to be honest sir,' I replied. 'We haven't got that far yet. It all depends on where they are.'

'Keep me updated and don't do anything without letting me know, the Assistant Chief Constable is on his way over from Lewes.'

'Great. I'll let you know as soon as we have something.'

I cancelled the call and looked over at Merrington. 'Have you got any idea what we're supposed to do when we get a fix on those co-ordinates?'

He shrugged. 'I've got a theory, so I've got my people working on some intel.'

'Care to share?'

He shook his head. 'Not really.' He held up a hand as I drew a breath to launch into a tirade about co-operation. 'I'm not being deliberately secretive, but if I'm wrong I don't want to cloud your thinking. You've been right on the button so far and, if I'm wrong, I'm out of ideas so I'm relying on you.'

I let the breath out slowly and grinned. 'Wow. That was almost a compliment.'

'Got it,' Peters interrupted as the printer whirred into life. 'Six locations, five within central Brighton and one in Moulscoomb. Images printing now with maps.'

Paper began to shoot out of the printer and I grabbed it piece by piece, studying the images and the maps carefully.

'Okay. We've got one in Queens Park Road, one on Marine Parade, Cavendish Place, Victoria Road, Goodwood Way in Moulscoomb and the last stop, the short one, is in Buckingham Road up by the station.'

Looking at the overview map pinned to the wall of the office, I grabbed a pencil and drew a line connecting each address. 'Apart from the one in Moulscoomb, it's pretty much a circle around the city centre. Anyone else getting a bad feeling?'

Both of them nodded. I opened my mouth to speak again but Merrington's phone rang and I waited while he went outside to take the call. He reappeared a few moments later.

'Okay, cards on the table time,' he said with a grimace. 'Do you remember the attacks in Mumbai?'

I felt my stomach sink. 'Yeah. Lots of men armed with rifles and grenades attacking the city at random, mowing people down in the streets.'

'Exactly. That's what I've had my chaps working on. Turns out that the men had managed to get into the city a few weeks before and lay low in two- and three-man cells across the city. They had the weapons delivered last minute and then they went on a rampage at a pre-arranged time. Sound familiar?'

'Very. You think the people we're looking for are planning something similar?'

'I think there's a bloody good chance. Our intel has it that a group of Russian separatists have been planning something based on those attacks, led by a man named Yuri Petan. He's on every terrorist watch list in the western world and he's a slimy bastard. Just last year he slaughtered an entire village in Georgia, men, women, children. No one left alive. Nearly been caught a dozen times but always managed to slip away.'

'So he's here in Brighton?' I asked.

He shrugged. 'Maybe. I'd like to find out before the shooting starts.'

'But why Brighton?' Peters asked.

'Soft target,' I replied, picking all the maps up and leading the others up the stairs to Burke's office. 'You can't so much as fart in London nowadays without getting an armed surveillance unit attached to your arse, but Brighton's easy.'

Merrington nodded agreement. 'It's what I'd do. Popular, well known city on the coast. Easy to get into, no border controls here, no real counter-terrorist officers.'

Peters bristled but Merrington shook his head quickly. 'I'm not saying that you're not good at your jobs, but there are fewer than a hundred of you in the county while London has several thousand, plus all the agencies. You're an easy target.'

'But why England at all?' Peters persisted. 'What possible interest could a group of Russians have in attacking England?'

Merrington shrugged. 'Yuri is a gun for hire, with links to extremists all over the world. He might be planning it on the ground, but you can bet that whoever is pulling the strings is paying him in cold, hard cash.'

'So where does that leave us?' I asked.

'That leaves us with a difficult choice. We have no idea how many there are in each cell, or if we've definitely got them all. There may be some we haven't located or even something else that we've overlooked. The bottom line is that we're short on resources, even shorter on time and we have some very difficult decisions to make.'

As we filed into the DCI's office I couldn't help but agree, and I worried that whatever we did, someone would slip through the net and there would be carnage on the streets that we would be powerless to prevent.

'DO YOU believe in fate, Gemma?' The voice woke her with a start, her arms and legs cramping as they strained against the bindings.

'You should, because it believes in you.'

Gemma twisted as she tried to get a look at the speaker — the accent was thick, the words clipped.

She tried to speak but the gag was still in her mouth, soaking up all the spit and drying her mouth completely. A shadow loomed into view, and she shrank back in fear. She had no idea how long she'd been here, time had become a blur, broken only by the times when she'd had to relieve herself where she lay. The smell filled her nostrils now — urine and faeces overlaid with the stink of her own fear.

Rough fingers plucked the gag from her mouth, causing her to groan as her cracked tongue finally found room to work. A straw was placed between her lips and she sucked greedily, the water soothing the pain in her mouth and allowing her a small measure of relief.

'What do you want?' She whispered brokenly.

'It's not what I want, Gemma, it's what needs to happen.' the voice replied. 'Things have been set in motion that can't be undone, and now you're part of that plan.'

'I don't understand,' she whimpered, and the hand stroked gently at her brow.

'Your understanding isn't necessary. All you need to know is that you will play your part.' Drawing on strength she didn't know she possessed, she jerked away from the caressing hand.

'What if I won't?' She asked defiantly.

Gemma heard a chuckle. 'You have a daughter, do you not?'

'I...' Her newfound bravery fled at the thought of anyone harming Ruthie. 'Please, just let me go back to her!'

Tears trickled down her face as she closed her eyes and prayed for the torment to end, but the hand returned, grabbing her jaw in a vice-like grip.

'If you don't do what we ask then I will have no choice but to hurt little Ruthie. Isn't that what you call her? I don't want to, but believe me I will if you leave me no other choice,' the voice whispered. 'So when the time comes, you will do exactly as we say and maybe you'll be reunited with her. Do you understand?'

Terrified beyond speech, Gemma could only nod as the hand gave her jaw a final hard squeeze and let go. The shadow lifted as the man moved away, floorboards creaking under his weight until the door swung closed.

'OPTIONS PLEASE, gentlemen.' Burke's office was made even more crowded by Geoffrey Robinson, the Assistant Chief Constable. He sat on a chair at the side of the room, his epaulettes covered in what looked like gold-threaded scrambled egg. I'd only met him a couple of times, but all the scuttlebutt said that he was a fair, level-headed man.

'It's a question of resources sir, that and exact locations on the target premises.' I said quickly, before Merrington proposed closing off streets and kicking down doors.

'How do you mean?' Burke asked.

'Well sir, we can't be sure exactly which houses this Andrei stopped at, and we don't have time to do a door-to-door. Even if we could, we might end up knocking up the targets themselves and then we've got a bloodbath.'

Burke nodded in understanding. 'So what do you suggest?'

'Armed officers in plain vehicles on each of the streets, trying to pick up the targets as they leave. The targets need to get themselves from their houses to the city centre, if that's where they're going.'

'So you want to wait until they're in public before making armed challenges?' He sounded incredulous but there was method to my madness.

'Yes sir. It occurs to me that if we *are* dealing with terrorists, then not only can we not confirm the addresses, but it's extremely likely that they'll have the premises rigged to blow in case of discovery. '

He frowned as he thought it through. 'How many officers would you need?'

'A minimum of four per property,' I said. 'Preferably six so that we can have three two-man teams.'

The ACC looked over at Merrington. 'How about your men, how many have you got?'

The Six agent shrugged. 'A dozen men on their way, they should be here any moment.'

'What do you think of DS Steele's idea?'

Merrington pulled a face. 'It's not ideal, but I don't see what other choice we have. He's right about not knowing which houses they're in, and I understand that, even if we did, half the city is multi-occupancy so we'd be doing a door to door search with a high chance of being discovered before we found them. No, we need to do it his way.'

'Right then.' the ACC said. 'I'll call in some more officers from rest days, but they won't be here and ready for at least two hours. Can you cope with the numbers you've got until then?'

Merrington shrugged. 'We'll have to. It should be enough with my men as well. I'll find out where they are and then we'll do a final briefing on the fourth floor.'

The ACC nodded. 'We'll be there.'

We all stood and Merrington was on the phone before we'd left the office. As we headed back to the rear yard, I took the opportunity to give Nat a call.

She answered on the third ring. 'Hi Rob, how's your head?'

'Still attached.' I didn't have time for chit-chat so I forged ahead. 'I know it's your day off but is there any chance you can come in? Something big is brewing that I can't talk about on the phone and I'd be much happier if you were working on it with me.'

'I'm flattered.' I could hear laughter in her voice. 'I just got home, but I'll be in asap.'

I finished the call to see Merrington looking at me quizzically.

'Nat,' I said, 'so where are your troops?'

'In the back yard with your lot comparing cocks,' he replied as Peters opened the door.

True to his word, our firearms team were engaged in the politest Mexican standoff I'd ever seen with a group of men in black jumpsuits with tactical vests, helmets and a variety of weapons that were making our team blush. The newcomers were also, to a man, wearing full face balaclavas of thin black cotton with only a slit for their eyes.

'It's okay, they're with us,' Merrington said as he hurried over to where the sergeant stood toe to toe with one of the new arrivals.

'I thought they were sir, we were just chatting,' the man replied, stepping back.

I motioned the Firearms Sergeant over. 'We didn't have time to get introduced, I'm Rob Steele,' I said, holding out a hand to shake.

He took it and squeezed with an iron grip. 'Barry Fellows. So what's the skinny?'

'Not for the car park. Can you get your lot up to the fourth floor and we'll do a group briefing?'

He nodded.

'Oh, and best behaviour, the ACC's up there.'

He grinned his thanks at the warning and barked out a few orders. Within moments a stream of officers was heading for the back door.

I turned to look at Merrington. 'You ready to do this?'

He shrugged. 'Not really but we're not being left a lot of choice, are we?'

'Not really.' I replied.

As I left the car park I glanced up to see the windows of the Response Office lined with curious officers wondering what the hell was going on. And as I headed up the stairs to the final briefing, I realised that I was beginning to wonder the same thing.

65

MACBRIDE SHIFTED uncomfortably as the cuffs dug into his back. The officer next to him leaned over and looked at the metal bracelets.

'Too tight?' he asked amiably.

'Like you care,' MacBride replied, looking out of the window of the van as they approached the Custody Centre with its large green metal gate.

'We'll be there in a minute mate,' the officer said, seemingly unfazed by MacBride's rudeness, 'then we can have the cuffs off and get you a cuppa.'

'You can fuck your cuppa,' MacBride spat, starting to get annoyed by all the nicey-nicey bullshit. Back when he'd first started breaking heads, coppers had been real coppers, not these watered down, politically correct monkeys in uniforms. They'd been people worth running from, and worth calling 'sir' when they caught you or else be thrown in a cell over the weekend and left to rot in your own stink before they bothered to even talk to you.

Shaking his head in disgust, he wondered how things had slipped so much. Here they were offering him cups of tea and trying to make him feel at ease when, in the old days, his head would have been between his knees and a size ten would have been holding it there for swearing. Pathetic. A half decent criminal could run rings around the police nowadays, as his organisation proved. If they knew even half of what he was involved in, they'd have marked him down as the most wanted man in Brighton. Prostitution, drugs, robberies, money laundering, loan sharking, the works. Looking at the officer next to him, he grinned as he pictured the young man in the uniform lying on the ground in a pool of his own blood.

Once I get these cuffs off, he thought as the gate rolled slowly back and they headed up the ramp.

The car pulled up outside the loading bay and the driver peered into the gloom within. 'That's odd.'

'What?' His colleague asked as MacBride craned his neck to see.

'There's a black van in there with three guys in suits and a Custody Sergeant. Maybe someone died.'

He got out and walked around to open MacBride's door, holding him firmly so that he couldn't make a last minute bolt for freedom. As soon as they were outside, however, one of the men in suits came over with his partner trailing behind.

'Is that MacBride?' he asked the officer.

The officer looked uncertain. 'Uh, yeah. Who're you?'

The man pulled a slim black wallet from inside his jacket and flicked it open. 'MI6. Danny MacBride is now under arrest for assisting in the commission of an act of terrorism and he needs to come with us.'

MacBride felt a little quiver of fear as he looked at the plain black van. It was the sort of vehicle, he thought, that people got into and were never seen again.

'Nah, I'm with these lot,' he said, but the man ignored him and beckoned the Custody Sergeant forward.

'I'm afraid they've got all the relevant paperwork,' the Custody Sergeant agreed as he approached. 'It's unorthodox but it *is* legal.'

The officer shrugged and handed MacBride over to the nearest suit. 'I want my cuffs back though.'

The suit shrugged and produced a pair of cable ties, slipping them on to MacBride's wrists above the cuffs and tightening them. 'Help yourself.'

MacBride tried to squirm but the man in the suit grabbed his thumbs and twisted them almost to breaking point. Leaning in, the suit whispered in his ear. 'No fucking about mate, you're with the big boys now. Try playing up and I'll bury you.'

MacBride shivered as the voice worked its way through into the animal recesses of his brain. He'd been in the game for long enough to know when someone meant business and this man sounded like a killer.

'Yes Sir,' he whispered back, and as he was marched towards the van he reflected that maybe modern coppers weren't so bad after all.

66

'SO YOU'VE all got your teams and there shouldn't be any questions by the time I've finished. Once you've identified the targets, you are to work as two two-man fire-teams. Our targets may be armed and expecting to die today, so if you have the slightest inkling that they're going to pull something, take them down.'

I saw the ACC frown at Merrington's choice of words but he let it pass as the agent continued.

'The command team on the ground will be myself with Detective Sergeant Rob Steele as my liaison. DCI Burke will be back here with the Assistant Chief Constable.' That was a polite way of saying he was being kept out of the way.

'Now it's likely that they'll all deploy from their addresses within a few minutes of each other, so once it starts keep your eyes and ears open, and don't expect to be able to get through on the radio. Team leaders from my group will be provided with police radios so that we can remain in contact with the locals.'

He paused and looked around the room, making eye contact with each and every officer.

'Today is going to be tough, both mentally and physically. We're going up against a group of unknown number who have had months to plan this, and we're doing it with limited numbers and disjointed intelligence. I understand that you might not be comfortable with what you're being asked to do, but please remember that the people of this city are relying on you today to be the thin blue line that keeps them safe. Thank you.'

He sat next to me as the ACC stood.

'How was that?' the agent whispered. I wanted to ask him about the 'disjointed intelligence,' as he, the DCI and the ACC had closeted themselves in a room for almost half an hour while he told them far more than he could tell me. I'd stood outside waiting patiently while Merrington threw me the occasional apologetic look through the glass.

Once they'd come out, both the ACC and the DCI were fully committed to the operation and I wondered just what the MI6 agent had told them that he couldn't tell me.

'Pompous, but it got the point across,' I replied as the ACC began to speak, his sonorous tones filling the room.

'Ladies and gentlemen, we've got a job to do today so I'll keep this brief. I want to thank each and every one of you for what you're preparing to give today. For the fact that you are the silent minority who must perform dark deeds to keep the unknowing majority safe.

'As a part of your duties today you may be asked, and will be expected if necessary, to kill in defence of the people of this country, and know now that they will not thank you for it. Instead, you will be vilified by the public. They will call for your resignation, possibly even for your imprisonment, with only the few realising how much you put on the line when you pull that trigger.

'I want you to know that no matter what happens today, you have my thanks, and the thanks of every man and woman in this force for giving so much.'

He cleared his throat and wiped a hand across his face, and when he looked up again I saw the glittering of moisture in his eyes.

'There is a quote attributed to Edmund Burke, and it is one with which you may be familiar, but I believe it suits the moment. *'All that is needed for the triumph of evil is for good men to do nothing.'*

'Well let me tell you now that we are good men, and we will not stand by and do nothing while people threaten the safety of those we love! Evil will not triumph while we still draw breath. Good luck.'

He stepped back and, as one, we rose and clapped, the first standing ovation I've ever seen at a briefing and probably the last as well.

Even I felt a suspicious moistness at the corner of my eye which I hurriedly wiped away.

'Right, arseholes and elbows people, squad leaders grab your officers and come see me for deployment!' Fellows called, breaking the spell as the group began to move with a purpose.

'That's basically what I was trying to say,' Merrington said with a grin. 'The old bugger's a rabble-rouser when he wants to be, isn't he?'

'Yeah, he is that all right. Almost makes you believe we'll get this right, doesn't it?'

'Almost. You're with me; we're taking the address in Buckingham Road.'

'Right. Can I get Nat to join us when she arrives?'

He nodded. 'Of course. Come on, we'll take my car.'

'Your car? I didn't think you had one.'

'One of my team drove it down for me. It's nothing special but it'll do us in a pinch.'

'I can't wait to see this.'

He led me out to a black Mercedes C-class that sat in the rear yard like a tiger amongst pigeons.

It might not have been an Aston Martin, but it was certainly top of the line and had enough buttons on both sides of the dash that I was afraid to touch anything in case the roof peeled back and the passenger seat hurled me into space.

'Wow. This won't stand out much.'

'It probably won't, actually. That's why we're taking the one nearest to the station. It's not unusual to find expensive cars dumped near the train station. People who can afford them usually don't care if they get a ticket or not.'

I couldn't fault his logic but I still had reservations.

'We've got an old Escort we could use instead, you know. People who drive them don't normally give a shit about tickets either.'

He shook his head. 'This car may not be full of gadgets, but it *has* got a few and I think you'll like them.'

I slid into the passenger side and closed the door carefully, not wanting to damage the pristine car. The air conditioning was on and the moment I closed the door a blast of cold air washed over me, cooling the sweat that still trickled under my vest.

'Check this out,' Merrington said with a smile as he pressed a button and the large display in the centre requested a password.

Tapping something into the touch-screen keyboard, he brought up a menu with several different icons.

He hit one of them and the screen resolved into twelve different camera views, each moving in real-time in a dizzying kaleidoscope of images. It took me a moment to realise that they were cameras attached to the helmets of his men.

'You're fucking kidding me!'

His smile widened. 'No I'm not.'

He flicked a switch on the steering column. 'Two-four this is leader, test call.'

A voice came out of the stereo speakers, clearer than a police radio.

'Two-four check, loud and clear, over.'

'Camera check, pan left.'

One of the tiny screens moved to the left and he touched it with a finger, bringing it up so that it filled the entire screen.

'See why I wanted to take my car?'

'Uh, yeah. Optional extras are better in the Merc, clearly.'

'Clearly. Shall we?'

'Let's,' I replied, and we drove out at the head of a convoy that swiftly dispersed, travelling to their own locations as we moved into the final phase of the operation.

67

GEMMA BLINKED away tears as daylight hit her face for the first time in two days. The jacket she'd been given was huge, dwarfing her and coming down as far as the middle of her thighs. The man held her firmly by the arm, moving her along Buckingham Road towards an inconspicuous looking Renault Laguna. He wore a floppy sun hat and shades, and every time she tried to get a look at his face he would twist her arm painfully until she stopped looking.

He placed her in the passenger seat, belting her in carefully, and making sure to avoid touching her too much. Once she was secure he squeezed in behind the wheel and pulled away, negotiating the heavy traffic with stoic patience.

'You know what you have to do?' He asked for the fourth time as they pulled up at a red light.

She nodded distractedly, looking at her reflection in the wing mirror and wondering if even her sister would recognise her if she saw her now. Her face was smeared with dirt and tears, and despite being made to wash while the man watched over her, she could still smell her own faeces clinging to the remains of the slinky dress she'd worn for David. Thinking of him made the tears start all over again. Just a few short days ago she had been full of hope – thinking that she might finally have found the man that Ruthie would one day call Daddy. Now here she was being driven to what was most likely her death by a man who would kill her as easily as he might sneeze.

Looking out of the window, she wondered how the people passing by could be going about their lives, laughing and joking with each other when the world as they knew it was about to dissolve into blood and pain. The sky should be dark, Gemma thought, not cloudless and sunny. People should be running for their homes in fear instead of hurrying towards the city that would soon be filled with horror and the sound of gunfire. For a moment, she considered opening the door and screaming a warning, shouting at them to get clear, but she knew that they would just think she was crazy and laugh it off and, rather than saving them, she would be ending Ruthie's life instead.

The man drove past the Pavilion and on to Edward Street, heading up past the police station and further on towards Whitehawk. Gemma stared at the white and brown facia longingly, knowing that it wouldn't happen but still daring to hope that someone might see her looking and recognise her. Then it was gone, hidden behind the huge white bulk of the American Express building, and she could do nothing but face forwards until they finally pulled into the A&E car park at the Royal Sussex. The engine idled as he undid her seatbelt for her.

'You know what to do,' he said, leaning across and opening her door.

She looked at him in mute appeal but he shook his head. 'It's time. Don't make me force you.'

Holding back the tears, Gemma clambered unsteadily from the vehicle and shut the door, leaning on it for a moment to gather her strength. As soon as she moved off, the car roared away, not even waiting to make sure she entered the building. After all, what choice did she have?

Passing a row of ambulances, she made for the reception doors. Once inside, Gemma found herself at the back of a long queue, an old couple just in front of her leaning on each other for support like she'd hoped she and David one day might. Beyond them, a mother stood with a toddler in her arms and a baby in a buggy in front of her. Pushing past them all, Gemma cut in front of the man at the counter and rapped on the glass.

The receptionist looked up with a glare, taking in the tear-streaked face and long dirty coat and dismissing her as an NFA. 'There's a queue love, you'll need to wait at the back like everyone else has.'

Gemma shook her head and summoned up the courage to speak.

'I need the police,' she whispered, then repeated it louder.

The receptionist shook her head. 'This is a hospital, not a police station.' Her eyes narrowed as if remembering something and she looked to her right for a moment then back at Gemma.

Pulling a picture off the wall, she held it up and squinted at it. 'Here, you're not Gemma Hallett are you?'

Gemma squeezed her eyes shut as fresh tears fell and she nodded.

'Are you okay?' The woman asked, concerned now.

'No I'm not,' Gemma whispered, 'and I really need you to call the police now.'

And she opened her coat to display the vest they'd forced her into, rigged with enough explosive to bring the entire hospital crashing down around her.

68

HAVING PARKED on Buckingham Road – about twenty metres south of where the co-ordinates said the truck had stopped – I called Nat and told her to come straight to meet us. We were just on the bend where the road turned to meet up with Dyke Road and from where we sat we had a perfect view in every direction.

Nat joined us less than five minutes after I called her, slipping into the back seat with a sigh.

'Morning gentlemen. Care to tell me what's going on and why we're in such an obvious...oh.' She nodded at the display. 'Wow.'

I nodded. 'Yeah. I think their budget is slightly bigger than ours.'

'You don't say! So what's happening?'

I filled her in, watching her face drop as she realised the full impact of what was going on.

'Shouldn't we be getting the bloody army in or something?' she asked worriedly.

'Nice thought, but can you imagine the chaos if a load of armed soldiers suddenly rolled into town? No, this is the best shot we've got. At least we have *some* warning.'

'Great. My vest's back at the Nick.'

'No it's not. It's in the boot in your sports bag. Grab it and get it on.'

She climbed out and returned a moment later.

'No peeking,' she said as she slipped off her shirt and began strapping the vest on over her bra. This time I could see that her tattoo crawled not only over her hip but swooped back up from her waistline and across her stomach in a swirling black pattern. I caught Merrington glancing in the mirror and shook my head. He had the good grace to look embarrassed, but then I couldn't help looking either.

Nat glanced up and made eye contact with me. 'Enjoying the show?'

'I wasn't looking!' I protested.

'Sure.'

Desperate to change the subject, I remembered that she'd called me earlier. 'Did you need something this morning? You called twice.'

'Oh yeah, I forgot to tell you. Your sister stopped by and let herself in. She's lost her phone and she's going into town to buy a new one. She couldn't remember if you were working or not so she came around to see if you wanted to go with her. I lent her my phone to call you...

What?' she said, seeing my shocked expression.

'She's gone into town. *Today?*'

Nat's face dropped. 'Oh shit. Yes she has.'

'Did she say where she was going?' I asked, panic rising in my throat.

'No, sorry Rob. She just said she was going to get a new phone and then meet some friends. I think she was more interested in why I was there.'

'So am I,' Merrington muttered, but looked away when I glared at him.

'And I can't even *fucking* call her to tell her to get out of town!' I banged my fist against the glove compartment and the images on the screen flickered.

'Steady Rob,' Merrington chided me, earning himself another glare.

'Steady? My fucking sister is in town on the day we're expecting a bunch of terrorists to shoot the place up and you tell me to be *steady*?'

He shrugged and looked at me sympathetically.

'I understand how you feel but we've got a job to do, we can't just go running off.'

'Fucking watch me.' I lunged for the door handle suddenly but Merrington grabbed my arm in a surprisingly strong grip.

'I suggest, *Detective Sergeant* Steele,' he said in icy tones, 'that you sort your fucking priorities out. The best way you've got of keeping your sister alive is to stay here and do your bloody job. If that's too much for you to handle, then I'll happily relieve you of your duty and you can piss off into town to find your sister, but I seriously doubt that you'll have a job at the end of it and you may well be putting her in more danger by leaving your post. Your choice.'

The hardest thing I've ever done was letting go of that door handle. I sat back and took a deep breath, letting it out slowly as I tried to focus my scattered thoughts.

'You're right, but forgive me if I don't thank you for stopping me.'

'Forgiven. Look, I lost my brother to an IED in Afghanistan last year, while I was out there working from the same base. It took all I had not to grab a gun and go out hunting every last Taliban supporter I could find, so I really do understand. It's not easy, but those are the sacrifices that we make.'

I nodded, a little humbled by his admission but still terrified to my very core by the thought of anything happening to Anna. 'I'm sorry, I had no idea.'

He shrugged. 'Why would you, it's not like we've exactly had time to chew the fat in the last few days.'

'Yeah, well. Maybe you're not such a wanker for stopping me after all.' I forced a light tone that utterly failed to disguise the worry I was feeling.

'Oh, I can assure you I am. I'm just a wanker who's utterly dedicated to protecting my country, no matter the cost.'

'Fair enough. What was your brother doing out there?'

'He was EOD.'

'Emergency ordnance disposal? When I was out there I was looking after them. We were assigned to protect them while they dismantled the devices. Good lads.'

'Speaking of looking after people, I was wondering if you wanted a pistol, just in case.'

'I'm sorry, what?' I wasn't quite sure I'd heard him correctly.

He leaned across and opened the glove compartment to show me a Glock 9mm. 'I know you've used firearms before and this could get a little hairy. It's yours if you want it.'

'You're offering me a firearm that I'm not licensed to carry?' My eyes met Nat's in the mirror and she shook her head.

'Well, you might need it,' Merrington said defensively. 'Think of it as a peace offering.'

'There's nothing peaceful about me losing my bloody job for shooting someone.'

'Better you shoot them than they shoot you. Just remember it's there if you do end up needing it.'

'Uh, yeah, thanks.'

He closed the compartment and we settled back to wait. Merrington calmly, Nat looking at me with concern in her eyes and me with a rising sense of dread as I prayed that my sister would escape the coming storm unharmed.

69

My phone rang at the same time as Merrington's. Exchanging a worried glance, we both answered and I heard Burke's voice – heavy with worry – on the other end of the line. 'Rob, we've got a problem. Gemma Hallett has just turned up at Sussex County.'

I was surprised at his tone. 'Surely that's great news?'

'Not really, she's got a suicide vest strapped to her.'

'Say that again.' I couldn't keep the shock from my voice.

'You heard me. I need you to get over there and take charge, Division are having a bit of a panic. I've told them it's related to what we're working on but I can't risk giving them specifics.' Burke's tone brooked no argument.

'Understood. I'll get on it.'

'Good. Thanks Rob.' He rang off.

Merrington finished his call a few seconds after me and we shared another look.

'Gemma Hallett?' I asked and received a nod in return.

'What about her?' Nat asked from the back of the car.

'She's turned up at A&E with a suicide vest strapped to her, warning everyone that if they try to remove it then it'll blow, and that A&E is being watched and that if they try to evacuate then it'll be remotely detonated,' Merrington explained before I could answer. 'I think that takes precedence right now. The other team here will just have to cope on their own.'

'Isn't that what they'll be expecting though?' Nat asked. 'This has to be a diversion.'

'Maybe not.' Merrington answered. 'Maybe this is what they were planning all along. We don't know how many people we're looking for or what they were storing. This could be it.'

'Do you really think it is?' I said.

'Probably. If that vest blows, we'll have hundreds of casualties and nowhere to treat them.' He was already pulling away, the acceleration pushing me back in the seat as he took a corner at almost sixty miles an hour, running a Renault Laguna off the road as it struggled up the hill.

'Just remember you've got no blue lights on this thing,' I reminded Merrington as I clung to the edges of my seat with both hands.

'Blue lights are for pansies,' he muttered, scattering cars left and right as he pulled into the oncoming lane with his foot to the floor. Nat squawked and scrabbled for her seatbelt while I closed my eyes and held on for dear life.

The turning into North Road nearly killed us. The road was packed with slow moving cars queuing to get into a car park and what little space they left was covered with slower moving pedestrians. Merrington jammed his hand on the horn and slowed to a conservative fifty. But Brighton being Brighton, a few people refused to scatter and instead stood with their arms folded, confident that the moral high-ground would protect them from harm.

'Watch out!' I yelled, pointing at a man with Gok Wan spectacles and a belligerent expression who was walking up the road towards us with his arms outspread.

'Seen him,' Merrington called, spinning the wheel and clipping the man with his wing mirror as we tore past.

'Better we get there slow than dead,' Nat called from the back seat, but Merrington ignored her, cutting through the traffic with a skill that I could only wonder at as we screamed towards the hospital at Mach 3.

'What I can't figure out,' I said as we hit Grand Parade, 'is how Gemma comes into this in the first place. Did they just snatch her off the street at random?'

'Hopefully she'll be able to tell us,' Nat replied from somewhere near the rear foot well.

'Hopefully.'

'Can you let me concentrate, please?' Merrington complained, taking corners faster than I would have thought possible – let alone safe. We shut up and let him drive, but my mind was still working furiously at the problem as we approached the hospital.

By the time we passed the Bingo Hall we were bogged down in heavy traffic that not even the Stig could have hurried through, with enough flashing lights in the distance to make the reason for the snarl-up clear. Looking in the mirror, I saw a police motorcycle making its way slowly towards us. Opening my window I flagged him down with my badge and convinced him to give us a blue light escort through.

Even then it was slow going, but within a few minutes we were at the bottom of Bristol Gate and parked up next to a police car with its blues on blocking the road. Several response officers were taping the road off while a harried looking Inspector, Trevor Payne, stood arguing with a woman who was insisting she needed to make her x-ray appointment.

Seeing me getting out of the car, he left her arguing with his Sergeant and hurried over. 'Rob, good to see you. She's in the A&E reception area. Hospital security have moved everyone to the rear of level 5 but we can't risk evacuating in case they blow the vest.'

'Is anyone talking to her?' I asked, but he shook his head.

'Not at the moment. We've got her on camera and last I heard she was sitting just inside the main doors on her own.'

'How long until bomb disposal get here?' I asked.

He glanced at his watch. 'Another hour at least. They're fighting against traffic and coming from Aldershot.'

'Fine. I'll go up. This is Merrington, he's, er, in charge of the operation this is linked to.' They shook hands while Nat and I ducked under the cordon, placing our warrant card holders in pockets with the badge hanging out to identify ourselves.

Merrington hurried to catch up, leaving his car where it sat.

'How's your bomb disposal experience?' I asked him as we walked up the steep hill towards A&E.

'Limited.' he admitted. 'What exactly are we going to do here?'

'Talk to her,' I replied. 'Find out if she knows anything useful. I doubt they bothered blindfolding her when they brought her here – it would have looked too suspicious. If we can find out where they were holding her, it might give us something.'

'What about the threat that she's being watched?' Nat asked.

I shrugged. 'We won't know if it can be remote activated until we see the vest.'

'Great, so we're sticking our heads in the lion's mouth then.' He turned to Nat. 'You don't have to come with us if you don't want to.'

She glared daggers at him. 'Trying to protect the little lady? I don't think so. You can shove that chauvinistic bullshit right up your arse.'

Merrington's eyebrows hit his hairline. 'I didn't mean to offend.'

She sighed and shook her head. 'Sorry, I'm just scared shitless. How can you two sound so calm?'

I felt anything *but* calm. My stomach felt as if I was in a small boat on a choppy sea and my mouth was dry as a bone. 'Practice I suppose. If it helps, I'm bloody terrified too.'

'Not really. I was hoping for some rousing speech to tell me how safe we are and how it'll all be fine, actually.'

'We've had all the rousing speeches we're going to get for the day. Now it's down sheer, gut-wrenching terror and pissing ourselves.' I tried to smile at her.

'Thanks Rob, you're a rock.' she said with a mock salute.

'Pleasure.'

The banter would normally have diffused the tension but today it wasn't working. The closer I got to the A&E ramp, the more my stomach fluttered. I'd almost been undone by this group's handiwork once already this week and I had no wish to repeat the experience, but then I thought of Gemma with the vest strapped to her and my resolve hardened.

'Shall we?' I asked, and together the three of us moved up the ramp and into the deserted car park, heading towards the main doors and the woman who might well be the death of us all.

70

AS PETR returned to the flat he was almost run off the road by a Mercedes travelling at twice the speed limit, narrowly avoiding crashing into a parked car.

'Where are the police when you need them?' he muttered to himself as he pulled up outside the flat and got out, carefully glancing around to make sure he wasn't being observed. Seeing nothing out of place, he trotted down the stairs and into the empty flat.

Yuri had already left for Shoreham airport, expressing his sorrow at not being able to join them, but something about his words had rung false to Petr. Despite his respect for Yuri's talents, Petr had never particularly liked the man. There was something in his eyes – a weakness sometimes glimpsed – that made Petr wonder just how much he could be trusted.

Still, Petr mused, it gave him the chance for a greater share in the glory *and* the money, and this job would provide plenty of both. He went into the kitchen and moved the cooker away from the wall, lifting the scrap of lino that covered the floorboards. Underneath was a hidden cache that he had made himself, the floorboards coming up easily to show his cloth-wrapped AK-47. Pulling it out, he undid the bindings on the cloth, letting it fall away to reveal the deadly glint of the barrel.

Kissing the metal, Petr slammed in a full magazine and cocked it. Pushing his arm deep into the hole in the floor, he pulled out three old Soviet issue hand grenades, and finally his wickedly sharp machete.

The blade had taken the lives of more than a dozen people across the world and, every time he moved to a new country, Petr went through hell to ensure it was by his side. Now, as he strapped it once more, Petr hoped that the job they were about to undertake would give him the chance to use it. He'd never had the chance to kill an Englishman before, and he looked forward to hearing one scream.

71

FOR A place that was usually so busy the unaccustomed silence was eerie, broken only by the high shrill of a distant phone ringing.

Gemma sat alone in the middle of a row of seats just inside the main entrance, her face covered in smudged dirt overlaid with tears.

She didn't look up when we entered, just huddled there in an oversize coat that covered what was left of a slinky dress with a beige vest over the top.

'Gemma?' I asked softly, stopping a few feet away.

She finally looked up, eyes almost lost in the dark rings that surrounded them. I could smell her from here, and my heart immediately went out to this poor woman who had been caught up in something that by rights should have had nothing to do with her at all.

'Gemma, my name's Rob, I'm a police officer and a friend of Lucy's. I'm here to help.'

'Help?' The word came out half sob, half shout. 'How can you help me? I'm going to die!' She dissolved into tears again.

Crouching down, I made sure that my hands were in plain view in case I spooked her. Not only was she on the edge of panic but they might have rigged her with some kind of motion trigger too and I didn't want her running away and setting it off.

'Gemma, I spoke to Lucy yesterday. She's sent Ruthie up to stay with your mum for a few days so she doesn't know you're missing. By the time she gets back, you'll be back at home and all cleaned up, I promise you.'

It took a few moments for the words to sink in, but when they did a sickeningly hopeful light came into her eyes.

'She's okay?'

'She's fine.'

'But they said if I didn't do this then they'd kill her! They must know where she is!'

'Who did this Gemma?'

She shook her head. 'I don't know, I never saw him before. Please, make sure that Ruthie's safe!'

I glanced at Nat, who nodded and went outside. She'd make a call and before half an hour had passed Ruthie would be in protective custody.

'They've got no idea, I promise you. I need to ask though, why did they choose you?'

She shrugged and I winced, half expecting the vest to explode.

'I was at my boyfriend's place and they broke in and... and shot him!' Fresh tears started to fall. 'Then the man who did it hit me and when I woke I was tied up.'

I shared a look with Merrington as things started falling into place.

'Your boyfriend was David Taverner, wasn't he?'

She nodded.

'Okay, we can talk more about that later. Can you show me the vest you're wearing?'

She moved the coat back to show a desert webbing molle with wires and lumps of explosive identical to the ones from the boat.

This time, however, all the wires were green, and several LEDs flashed just below her chin, showing that we had just twelve minutes before the vest detonated. The sides of the vest were padlocked together through the heavy material and I could see wires running from the explosives to the locks.

'Now I need you to take the coat off and turn around so I can see the back of it as well.'

I still sounded much calmer than I felt. I was as close to pissing myself as I've ever come, but my concern for this poor woman was holding the fear back enough that I could still function.

Sweat rolled down my back and soaked into my already sopping waistband under the vest as she stood and removed the coat.

Glancing over at Merrington, I saw that his face had a waxy sheen and I could hear his breath coming in fast little gasps every time she moved.

Dropping the coat to the floor, she turned slowly as if she was a model on a catwalk, looking back over her shoulder at us.

Her legs were filthy and scratched, with deep red-looking marks where she'd been tied up.

The vest was almost completely bare on the back, the only thing on it a small mobile phone with a wire attached that ran up and over one shoulder before disappearing off towards the explosives on the front.

Merrington and I exchanged a worried glance. I'd hoped that they'd been lying about the ability to remote detonate it to prevent us from evacuating.

'Thanks Gemma, just stay there for a moment,' I said before leaning towards Merrington.

'Well?' I asked quietly.

He raised both eyebrows and shrugged. 'Well what?'

'What do we do now?'

'What can we do? We ask her some questions about where she was held and then we leave her until the bomb disposal units turn up.'

'And you think she's got that long, do you?'

'Not really, no, but what else can we do?'

'I'm not leaving her like this, I can't! We have to do something.'

'Like what, strip the wires with your teeth and hope she doesn't go boom?'

'I can hear you, you know,' Gemma said, turning to face us. 'I'm going to die, aren't I?'

I stood and faced her. 'No Gemma, you're not. I promise you I'll do everything I can to get you out safe. I'll be right back.'

Merrington followed me outside. 'I appreciate the sentiment, but what are you going to do that'll help?'

I ignored him, instead moving far enough away that I felt I was safe and pulling out my phone. Nat came over to talk to me but I waved her away as the number I'd dialled connected.

'Brighton comms'. The calm voice on the other end was a welcome sound.

'Comms, it's DS Steele. I need to be put through to the EOD unit on its way to the hospital as fast as you can.'

'Stand by.' The line crackled for a moment before ringing hollowly.

'Sergeant Davis'. The voice was gruff and I could hear sirens in the background.

'Sergeant Davis, it's DS Steele from Brighton. I've just looked at the vest and we've got less that twelve minutes before the timer hits zero. How long until you're here?'

'Fifteen at best speed, maybe longer. I'd advise you to get everyone you can clear'.

'Thanks, but that's not going to happen'. I rang off and dialled another number.

'Hello?' The accent on the other end was full of soft Welsh vowels.

'Taff? It's Rob Steele.'

'Fuck me! You're still alive then?'

'Yeah, look, I need your help. Did you ever defuse a suicide vest with a remote trigger operated by a mobile attached to the vest?'

'Yeah, once or twice.' Taff had been EOD attached to my unit in Afghanistan, and before he'd come to us he'd spent several years in Iraq. Although we rarely spoke we'd still kept in touch and there was no one else I trusted more when it came to explosives.

'Okay, how do I get the phone off without blowing the vest?'

'You're serious, aren't you?'

'Deadly.'

'Bugger. Is the phone battery wired to the explosives?'

'Looks like it, and there's a timer on the front too.'

'Right. Hang on a minute.' I could almost hear him thinking it through. 'Right. You can detach the battery from the phone and it shouldn't blow.'

'Shouldn't?'

'Yeah, shouldn't. Like you shouldn't be playing around with explosives in the first place.'

'I haven't got time to hang around, mate.'

'Right. Once the phone's away from the vest you should be okay, but watch out because if the bastard who wired it has got an ounce of sense, he'll have rigged a secondary trigger to blow when the phone moves.'

'Great. So how do I deal with that?'

'You should just be able to cut it. Do you reckon you'll be able to get hold of a scalpel or something similar?'

I glanced up at the building. 'I think I'll manage that.'

'Once you've got it, slide it up and under the phone. You'll feel resistance, and it's important that what you have is very sharp or it'll tug the wire and set the thing off. You sure you want to do this?' He asked.

'No. What about the timer?'

'Same as the phone, should be wired to the explosives. Check for a secondary but remove the phone first as any backup detonation will most likely rely on that. Where are you, anyway? I thought you were in the police now?'

'I am, I haven't got time to explain. Anything else I should know?'

'Only about ten years worth of explosives training. Other than that, nothing I can think of. Try not to die, huh?'

'Yeah, thanks. I'll call you later if I've still got my fingers.'

I turned the phone off before stuffing it back in my pocket.

I turned and headed back towards Gemma, passing Nat who had heard enough of the conversation to look worried.

'Rob?' she called. 'Where the bloody hell do you think you're going?'

I smiled at her sadly. 'I need to do this, Nat. I *can* do this.'

'Are you crazy?' she said.

I shrugged as Merrington moved up to flank Nat, arms folded and scowling.

'I've picked up a thing or two over the years. I've seen this done plenty of times, and even helped out on occasion.'

Merrington shook his head. 'You were infantry Rob, not EOD. If you get it wrong you'll bring the whole building down.'

'I don't have a choice. EOD won't be here until after the timer's wound down to zero and I don't see anybody else stepping up. If I don't get that vest disarmed then the whole place comes crashing down.'

Nat and Merrington shared a glance.

'What do you need us to do?' Nat asked.

'Get the other side of the cordon and get EOD up here the second they arrive.'

She shook her head. 'We're not leaving.'

I looked at Merrington for support but he just shrugged. 'We're a team, so we stand or fall together'.

I shook my head. 'I appreciate the sentiment but I don't have time for this. If we all die here, there's no one to stop the people who did this. The best thing you can do is get EOD up here, and for that I need you at the bottom of the hill, please?'

Fine.' Nat grabbed Merrington by the arm and dragged him towards Bristol Gate. 'Just be careful.'

As they moved away I turned and headed back towards Gemma, praying silently that I could defuse the bomb in the few minutes I had left.

PETR STOOD and folded his jacket, tucking it into his rucksack where it covered two of his three grenades. The third made a tennis ball sized lump in his pocket, but he preferred to have it close to hand just in case.

Pulling his boots on, he stamped his feet into them then tied the laces slowly, savouring the feel of the soft cloth and leather against his fingertips. It was always like this before a job, enjoying the simple things in life in case they were suddenly and abruptly taken away by a bullet or blade. Not that he expected that to happen today. No, the police would be far too busy with the girl.

Picking up the gleaming pieces of his AK-47, he slotted them back together and replaced the magazine before cocking the weapon with a satisfying *clunk*. Placing his phone to his ear, he prepared to make the call that would bring his men out of hiding and send them towards their target. It rang three times before it was picked up, Sergei's voice answering nervously.

'It is time,' Petr said, then hung up.

He didn't wait for a reply, knowing that Sergei would in turn call the others and soon the men would all be ready. Looking at his watch, he decided to give them five minutes to prepare and start making their way into town before he left. He toyed with his phone for a moment longer, wondering if he should make the final call now. His finger hovered over the button but at the last second he changed his mind, deciding to wait for as long as possible to give his men a chance. For when he set the device off, he knew, there really was no turning back.

SWEAT ROLLED down my face as I crouched next to Gemma, a borrowed scalpel in my hand. I couldn't tell which of us was shaking more, but every so often she would let out a whimper coupled with a shudder, forcing my heart into my mouth.

'Try and stay still, Gemma,' I said as the display hit four minutes.

She nodded, too frightened to speak as my questing fingers tried to tease the battery out of the phone. However, it had been well stuck in and I could see a few strands of glue trailing down the casing as I peered at it with Nat's torch clamped firmly between my teeth. If I stood any chance of removing the battery, I'd have to use the scalpel and hope it was sharp enough to cut through whatever glue they'd used.

'I need you to stay really still now. Try not to breathe,' I warned Gemma, easing the thin metal blade into the tiny gap between the casing and the battery.

It met resistance almost immediately and I gently moved it back and forth, putting as little pressure on it as possible. After a few moments, the tip of the blade moved suddenly and the battery started to shift. Taking the weight of the phone with my spare hand, I bent my head and peered up underneath, the torch beam reflecting off a tiny strand of metal wire that poked through the vest and attached itself to the bottom of the phone casing. Easing the scalpel up, I held my breath and sliced the wire, my eyes squeezing shut as I waited to be atomized.

A few seconds later I opened my eyes and looked at the phone resting in the palm of my hand. Placing it on the floor I turned my attention to the timer on the front of the vest.

It was an LED clock with three large wires coming out of it and disappearing behind the vest through the collar. I lifted it away from the vest slightly and saw that the other end of the tiny metal wire was connected to the back of it, disappearing through a small hole in the black plastic casing.

'Clever bastards', I muttered as I slid the tip of the scalpel into the hole and tried to pry open the cover.

'What?' Gemma asked as she tried to look at what I was doing right under her chin.

'They designed it so that anyone tampering with the timer would set off the secondary timer in the phone. We both owe a certain Welshman our lives', I replied as the cover came free.

'What does the timer say?' She asked quietly.

'Don't worry, we've got plenty of time', I lied as the timer began ticking away the final minute.

The back of the case came free, exposing a jumbled mess of wires. Ignoring them, I followed the thin metal strand to a small plastic connector hidden right at the back. Hardly daring to breathe, I gripped the connector with two fingers and pulled smoothly, feeling resistance before it slid out and the clock went dead.

'Oh thank fuck!' I breathed.

'What?' Gemma said, sounding panicked.

'We're alive.' I showed her the phone. 'They can't detonate it now.'

'What about the rest of it?' she asked shakily.

'I'm sorry, there might be other triggers I don't know about. Now that the timer and the phone are disconnected I don't dare try and do anything else. EOD will be here soon though, and they'll have you free in no time.'

'EOD?' she asked

'Sorry, jargon. Emergency Ordinance Disposal. Bomb squad. They're on their way. Will you be OK here for a minute while I see where they are?' She nodded and sat down carefully while I went looking for Merrington.

Merrington was leaning against a wall on the far side of the car park with a very worried looking Nat. The moment they saw me she strode over with Merrington trailing behind.

'I thought you were supposed to be waiting down by the cordon?' I said as they approached.

Merrington shrugged sheepishly. 'Couldn't leave you holding the can by yourself. Besides, your colleague here threatened to break my legs if I left.'

Nat smiled grimly. 'What's going on?'

I held up the scalpel and the phone. 'No remote detonation, and the timer is dead too. Get on the horn and tell them to start evacuating people, or better yet let's move her somewhere more secure. And see if you can get someone up here to stay with her.'

Nat nodded and began talking into her radio while Merrington and I leaned against the wall in the sunshine.

'So she's safe to talk to now?' he asked me.

I shrugged. 'She always was; she just wasn't safe to be near. You want to ask her some questions?'

'I do; I just didn't want to get blown up in the process.' He said with a brief smile.

I wiped my sweaty palms on my jeans. 'Neither did I. I don't want to be doing that again in a hurry.'

We moved back inside and Merrington crouched in front of Gemma. 'Gemma, my name's Harvey. Can I ask you a few questions about where they were keeping you?'

She nodded.

'Great. Do you know where it was?'

She nodded again. 'Near the station. I'm not sure of the name of the road though.'

'Can you tell me anything about the house itself?'

She shrugged. 'It wasn't a house, it was a flat. In the basement. I remember the man walking me up some stairs.'

'Can you tell us anything about him?' I interrupted. 'Anything at all?'

'He was tall, much taller than me.' she said.

'Do you remember anything about the outside of the flat?' Merrington asked.

'Uh, I only saw it for a second, but there was a big bush in the front garden with red flowers.'

Merrington clenched his fists. 'Fuck it!' He swore. 'That was two doors down from where we were sat!' Pulling out his phone, he ran out of the door into the car park as I put a careful hand on Gemma's shoulder.

'Thanks Gemma, you've been brilliant. We'll have you home in no time, okay? Before you know it you'll be back with Ruthie and Lucy.'

Two uniformed officers came through the front door hesitantly and I recognised one of them as Steve Marshall – the man who'd helped me with Collins' arrest.

'Steve, this is Gemma. She's a little upset but she's going to be fine.' I squeezed her arm and stood, leaving the other officer to approach while I took Steve to one side.

'I've deactivated the remote detonator,' I said, handing him the phone. 'It needs to be bagged for evidence. Can you wait with her until bomb disposal gets here?'

He nodded, looking nervously at Gemma. 'She's not about to blow up, is she?'

I shook my head. 'I don't think so. Do me a favour and get her a cup of tea and some food, she looks like she hasn't eaten in a week.'

'Will do. Christ, she's been through the wringer, hasn't she?'

'Looks that way. Keep her safe, yeah?'

He nodded again and I left, hurrying down the hill after Merrington and Nat. Now that we had an address, I hoped that we might be able to unravel the whole thing and stop whatever was about to happen before it truly started.

PETR CHECKED his watch and stood, pressing the green button on his phone and throwing it on the table as it connected. He wouldn't need it anymore, and it wouldn't matter if they found it after he had gone. Not that they'd have much of a chance, as the entire flat was rigged to explode as soon as anyone opened the door.

Sliding his rifle into the golf bag that he'd bought specially, he opened the door of the flat and took a deep breath before stepping out into the sunshine. *A beautiful day*, he thought as he climbed the steps on to the street, looking around as usual to make sure that no one was watching.

He turned towards town when something caught his attention. Both doors on a car a few houses down were opening and, as he tensed, he saw the top of a tactical helmet emerging, followed by a man in combat gear with no visible insignia. Swinging the golf bag off his shoulder he ducked between two cars as both men emerged, scrabbling out with rifles pointed at him over the open doors.

'On the ground, now!' one of them shouted through his balaclava. In response, Petr reached into the bag and found the trigger, putting a burst through the end of the bag and into the windscreen of their car. The sound echoed off the buildings, half-deafening him as bullets tore through glass and made both men duck back instinctively. Throwing the bag clear, he fired again, rounds smashing through the bonnet of the car and tracking up towards the man on the right of the car.

He dropped back while the other man fired a burst that slammed into the car behind him. Petr could hear screaming now, and the smell of cordite was thick in his nostrils as he dropped into a game that he knew well, all thought other than killing the men in front of him slipping away like smoke in the mist.

The second man had recovered now and put a burst through the front window of the car Petr was hiding behind, raining broken glass on him as the back window exploded outwards. Keeping his head low, he propped his AK-47 on the roof of the car and pulled the trigger, seeing rounds impact all over their car and on into the houses behind. They dropped back once more, shouting at each other as they ducked away from the storm of gunfire, and he grinned as he pulled the grenade out of his pocket.

The man on the left of the car tried to sprint across the road and come at him from the side but Petr saw the movement and let fly with the rest of the magazine, bullets pinging off the tarmac, forcing the man to scurry back into cover.

'You can't play my game!' Petr screamed, battle rage filling him, 'Die!'

Dropping his rifle to hang on its shoulder strap, he pulled the pin from the grenade and released the handle, counting to three before standing and hurling it over arm towards their car. Both men fired, but the rounds went wide. Petr tracked the grenade as it hit the kerb and bounced, coming to rest right at the feet of the man on the left of the car. The officer had time to look down, then back up again before it exploded, fire and shrapnel roaring up and enveloping him before he could even scream.

The force of the blast knocked Petr back, hands scrabbling for his rifle. As soon as he recovered it, he charged forwards to see the second man on his back, his hands clasped to his head and a smoking hole in his Kevlar vest where a piece of grenade shrapnel had torn through it. Seeing Petr coming, the man reached for his weapon but Petr was faster and his huge foot slammed down on the man's arm, cracking bones and making him scream.

'Please, no,' he begged, 'I have a family!'

Petr calmly reloaded his rifle and placed the still-hot barrel against the man's forehead. 'So?' he asked, pulling the trigger.

WE WERE almost at the clock tower when two of the cameras on Merrington's screen suddenly moved, the officers getting out of their car rapidly and pointing their weapons at a man that I recognised with a start.

'That's him, the one from Collins' lock-up.' I said, tapping the screen to make both of the pictures larger.

'Two-seven, two-eight, we're almost with you, do not challenge, repeat, do not challenge!' Merrington called out over his car radio, but I could see from the camera view that it was too late. I saw the large man duck down behind a car and then I saw gunfire a few seconds before a sound like Chinese firecrackers hit my ears.

'Fuck!' I yelled as Merrington put his foot down and ran a red light, hitting the back of a taxi and sending it spinning out of control.

'Nat, call it in!' I ordered, and she hurriedly complied.

We almost took off heading up Dyke Road as we cut through another red light, then Merrington nearly rolled the car as he took the turning into Buckingham Road at seventy. The scene that met us was one of devastation. Two cars were burning and several more were riddled with bullet holes. People were screaming in the background and even through the air conditioning I could smell charred plastic and cordite. Merrington slammed the brakes on just in time to avoid running over one of his tactical team lying in the road – his face a bloody mess under his helmet.

Flinging open his door the agent jumped out, pistol swinging wildly as he looked for the huge man.

'No sign,' he called, 'see if either of them are alive.'

'Stay here,' I warned Nat — who was still on the radio — then got out cautiously and hurried over to the man lying in the road. I didn't need to check for a pulse to know he was dead — his face was buried in the back of his skull and there was blood and brains scattered all over the place.

Moving around to the other side of the car I saw the second man, or what was left of him. His legs were blackened and scorched and almost all of his clothing had been burned away to reveal twisted and charred flesh. I knelt next to him, resisting the urge to throw up. Suddenly his eyes flicked open and he gasped through bloodied lips.

'Merrington, we've got a man alive here!' It was closer to a scream than a shout.

The agent appeared behind my shoulder and stared for a moment in horror at the bloody mess lying before me. 'Shit, Chris!'

I shook my head to clear it. I'd seen worse in Afghanistan, and this man needed us focused if he had any chance of surviving.

'I'll get Nat to call an ambulance,' I told Merrington, standing and starting to move back towards the car when I saw something that rooted me to the spot.

On the far side of the road, the huge man was creeping along behind the row of parked cars, AK-47 in hand and eyes on the Mercedes that sat with both doors still open and the engine running.

Grabbing Merrington, I hauled him around and pointed. The movement made our target turn, eyes widening as he saw us. Both he and Merrington lifted their weapons at the same time – the agent firing a fraction of a second faster. I saw the round hit the big man in the shoulder, throwing his aim off as the AK chattered and bullets tore through the air around me. Merrington jerked and crashed into me, sending us both to the ground.

'Are you okay?' I asked, pushing him to one side so that I could get up.

He didn't answer and, with rising dread, I turned him over to see blood soaking through his suit from the right side of his stomach. His eyes were closed and his face was pale. His chest was still rising and falling slowly, but he was barely alive.

'Nat,' I yelled, 'get that ambulance!'

I could hear sirens in the distance but I needed people here now. This whole thing was going from bad to worse and I could only wonder what was happening at the other locations if one terrorist could take out three of MI6's best.

I picked up Merrington's fallen pistol and slid it into the back of my jeans, then tore off my t-shirt and pressed it hard against Merrington's side as I did my best to staunch the flow of blood from the wound.

An engine roared nearby, and I dropped my t-shirt and stood as I recognised the sound of the Merc's supercharged engine. Peering over the top of the car I saw something that chilled my blood.

The huge man wasn't where he'd fallen. Instead he was in the driving seat of the Mercedes, one huge arm clamped firmly around Nat's throat while the other clung to the steering wheel as he reversed away. Running out into the road I raised the pistol, pointing it at his head through the glass.

His eyes locked on to mine as he reversed, but I couldn't bring myself to take the shot for fear that I might hit Nat. Lowering the weapon I stood for a moment, torn between getting the two injured men an ambulance and following Nat to try and keep her alive.

A few seconds later I was sprinting down the road, pistol in hand. Despite the gunfire, I saw people were peering out of windows and doors cautiously. Pointing at one of them with my free hand I screamed at him to call an ambulance, then put my head down and ran as hard as I could as the Mercedes turned the corner and disappeared out of sight.

PETR SQUEEZED his arm tighter as Nat twisted and struggled, clawing at his bicep with her nails.

'Stay still or die,' he warned, slicing his forearm across her throat so that she couldn't breathe.

Nat forced herself to relax, then twisted hard to her left and brought a hand up, stiffened fingers jabbing into Petr's throat. The move surprised him enough that she slipped free of his grip, throwing an elbow that caught him in the temple. He roared in anger and batted at her with his left hand but couldn't get enough leverage to do more than knock her backwards. She came on again, this time with fingers reaching for an eye socket while her other hand grabbed the steering wheel and tried to force the car off the road.

'Enough!' he shouted, reaching over his shoulder and grabbing a fistful of her hair.

She fought back but, even wounded, his strength was immense and he slammed her face into the headrest several times. Half-stunned, still she fought, her fingers dropping from his face to plunge into the bullet wound in his shoulder. He screamed as pain lanced through him, the car veering wildly into a row of parked cars, where it ground to a halt. Letting go of the wheel altogether, Petr twisted in his seat and used both hands to grab Nat by the throat, hauling her into the front of the car and squeezing as hard as he could.

She choked and gasped for a moment before going limp, her hands slipping away from his shoulder as she passed into unconsciousness. He pushed her away and she slid into a heap on the passenger seat, legs tangled around his rifle.

Taking the wheel again he reversed then spun the car a hundred and eighty degrees and turned to the right, heading up towards Seven Dials.

Looking around the car he'd stolen, he noticed the video screen. It only took him a few seconds to realise what he was looking at and he growled in anger as he saw an image of Sergei's body crumpled on a road, riddled with bullet holes. He could only hope that his friend had taken a few of the enemy with him before he died.

Looking at the other screens, he saw that the men with the cameras were still waiting patiently at the other locations, which meant that the rest of his men were alive and already on their way to the target. The bomb should have destroyed the hospital by now, and every police unit in the city should be tied-up looking for survivors and secondary devices, leaving him and his men free to complete their mission.

Glancing down at the pitiful form of the female cop, he was suddenly glad that he hadn't killed her. Even with one of his men down and a good chance that more police were waiting for them to hit the target, he had to try and complete his mission and a hostage with a gun to her head would be just the thing to prevent anyone trying to stop him.

I REACHED the end of the road as the Merc disappeared over the hill, heading north up Dyke Road. I ran in front of a taxi and waved my arms to flag it down, but even with my police vest on I must have looked a sight and the man swerved to avoid me, driving off at high speed.

The pistol probably didn't help, I realised, hurriedly tucking it into the back of my waistband. My radio was gone, and I cursed as I realised I had left my mobile in the Mercedes. I began to run towards town, intent on flagging down the first emergency vehicle I found, but suddenly a silver Mercedes with two men in balaclavas came tearing up the road and screeched to a halt, the window winding down as the man in the passenger seat got out.

'What happened?' the driver asked from behind his face covering.

'Your team are down – one dead, one injured. Merrington's been shot and he needs an ambulance. The target got away in Merrington's Merc and he's holding one of my detectives hostage.'

'Who's hurt?' a pained voice said from behind me and I looked round in surprise to see Merrington limping up the road towards us.

He held up the blood-soaked rag that had once been my t-shirt. 'Yours, I believe?'

'Keep it.' I was relieved to see him alive, but none of this was helping Nat. 'He took your car and he's got Nat.'

Merrington nodded towards the Merc. 'Get in. You two, do what you can for the casualty and then get the other cars to follow us when they can.'

One of the men ran to the boot and grabbed a large green rucksack while the other handed Merrington his rifle, a G36c with several custom mods, then they both sprinted in the direction of their downed colleague. We'd barely closed the doors when Merrington put his foot down and sped off north.

'I'm not sure where they went...' I began, but Merrington just shook his head and tapped the screen on the dashboard, identical to the one in the car we were chasing.

A few moments later it showed a map of Brighton with a red arrow that I presumed was Merrington's car, heading north along Dyke Road towards the bypass.

'Have all your cars got this kind of shit in them?' I asked.

He nodded. 'Mostly. It's amazing the amount of money the government is willing to spend to combat terrorism.'

'Fair enough.' I looked at the screen again. 'Bloody hell, he's on the A27 already!'

The red arrow was now travelling west at high speed. In response, Merrington put his foot down, the acceleration pressing me back into the seat as the turbo kicked in.

If you've never taken the Seven Dials roundabout at a hundred and twenty miles an hour, I don't recommend the experience. Somehow Merrington kept control of the car and soon we were tearing down the slip road and on to the A27 bypass where he really let the vehicle have its head. My eyes were glued to the needle on the speedo as it rose past one forty, then one sixty, then finally levelled out at about one hundred and ninety miles an hour.

Glancing up at the road, I saw the blurred images of cars flashing past us in what seemed like slow motion and hurriedly looked back at the dial as I felt my bowels loosen.

'Where does this road lead?' he asked, and I felt a fresh wave of fear as the realisation crashed home that he was driving this fast on a road he didn't know.

'Uh, Worthing, then on towards Portsmouth,' I answered, wondering if I had the stomach for a long chase at this speed. Then I thought about Nat, stuck in the car with that monster and anger bubbled up inside me, driving away the fear.

'Any ports or landing fields?' Merrington probed, never taking his eyes from the road.

'Yeah, Shoreham airport is a few miles down the road,' I replied as we did the entire Southwick tunnel in about three and a half seconds, dodging from lane to lane to avoid panicking drivers as we tore past, 'and Portsmouth has a naval base.'

He shook his head. 'He'll steer clear of anything military. Where's this airport?'

I pointed to the map on the screen. 'About two miles ahead, I think he's on the turning now.'

'Thanks. Hold on to your breakfast.'

'I haven't had breakfast.'

'Most important meal of the day,' he said absently as we went even faster. In less than thirty seconds we were at the turning that led down to Shoreham town, slowing to a relative crawl to take the corner without flipping the car.

'I think he's doubling back towards Brighton,' I said uncertainly, watching as the arrow on the display suddenly swung wildly.

'He's trying to throw us off the scent,' Merrington muttered, taking us up the ramp and back on to the A27 towards Brighton.

As we reached the top and pulled on to the three lane road he flicked his microphone on. 'All units, all units, this is leader. Do not, repeat *do not* follow my signal. Target vehicle is moving back towards Brighton along the bypass. Any units able to assist call up.'

There was silence from the comm system, then a single unit called up. 'Leader from two-five. We're the only unit that's had a ding, one target down. The others are still waiting in position. Confirm you want them to break away from overwatch?'

Merrington shook his head and growled under his breath.

'He's got Nat,' I said, my voice surprisingly level. I would have got on my knees and begged him to pull units away to help us, but after our earlier talk about Anna I knew what the answer would be and I couldn't blame him. If the men we were waiting for were going to attack the city centre, we needed to catch them before they could get into the main areas and wreak havoc. Pulling just one car away might be the difference between a successful operation and a bloodbath.

Merrington glanced my way for the barest second before gluing his eyes firmly to the road ahead.

'Sorry Rob.' He flicked the switch again. 'Two-five, that's a negative, all units to remain in place until contact is made.'

'Roger, leader.'

Despite the awesome speed the Six agent was getting from the car, we were still almost a mile behind our target when it turned off at Hollingbury and began to head back towards the city centre on the busy Lewes Road.

'Where the bloody hell is he going?' I wondered out loud.

'It's your city, you tell me.' Merrington replied.

'Okay, let's think logically. Prime targets would be the Pier – lots of people there on a day like this – the beach in general, the shopping centre and the Lanes. Or the Pavilion Gardens, or...' The list went on and on. I could think of a hundred places in the city that would be a devastating target for someone with an automatic weapon. The full scale of what might be about to happen hit me and I looked over to see the speedo needle resting just over eighty as we hit the Lewes Road and headed south. 'Can you go any faster?'

Merrington shook his head.

'Not here, too many cars.' As he spoke he swerved from lane to lane, weaving through the traffic like a rally driver. 'If we crash, we lose any chance of catching him.'

I nodded in understanding. The thought of losing Nat was too much to contemplate, so instead I concentrated on the arrow on the map.

'That's odd,' I said, pointing at it.

'Can't look,' Merrington said, eyes fixed on the road ahead. 'Tell me.'

'I could be wrong, but it looks like they're heading towards the police station. Oh shit, Nat's warrant card!' The full enormity of the situation hit me.

'What about it?'

'It's a proximity card. It opens every door in the entire bloody building!'

Forgetting his earlier warning, Merrington put his foot down and we screamed through the Saturday afternoon traffic, desperate to get to the Nick before it was too late and the terrorist with the automatic rifle made his way inside.

'IT'S HEADING up towards Queen's Park, he's not going for the Nick after all,' I directed, and Merrington shot past the police station and tore up the hill. 'We're getting closer.'

'We'd better bloody catch them soon; I can't keep this up forever.'

I looked over at his wide eyes and white face and for the first time realised how much strain the drive was putting on him. I'd been on blues runs before, heading through town at sixty miles per hour for perhaps three or four minutes, and that was challenging enough. Merrington had been driving twice and even three times that speed for about twenty minutes now and I could only imagine how hard he was struggling to stay focused.

'Can you reach your phone?' I asked.

'No, but it's in the left jacket pocket. Help yourself.' he replied.

I reached into the indicated pocket and, after a bit of careful manoeuvring, pulled out his phone and dialled Burke, getting a busy tone almost immediately.

Hanging up, I tried Peters instead and was rewarded with an answer on the third ring. 'Peters.'

'Peters, Rob Steele. We're in pursuit of an MI6 vehicle containing one of the men we're looking for. He's got Nat Statham held hostage. We're heading up towards Queen's Park and we need units to cut them off.'

He didn't waste time with pointless questions. 'Give me your exact location.'

I filled him in and then gave him the location of the car we were chasing as well.

'Right,' he said when I was done, 'leave it with me and I'll get units to you.'

He hung up and I dropped the phone into a pocket on the dash. 'Units are on their way.'

Merrington nodded and took a left, then an immediate right, then swerved left again through a stone arch and on to the road that ran around the edge of the park. 'Where now?'

'It's stopped!' I almost shouted. 'Two hundred yards as you follow the park around.'

He put his foot down once more and the park sped past. As we rounded the next corner, however, he had to slam the brakes on to avoid hitting the Mercedes we'd been chasing as it reversed away from a Tesco home delivery lorry blocking the road.

The driver of the Mercedes didn't slow, ramming into our front bumper with a bone-jarring crunch that threw me backwards into my seat. Before I could react, Merrington was out of the car, rifle up as he moved towards the driver's door of the other vehicle.

Struggling out of my seatbelt, I grabbed his Glock from my waistband and followed, no longer caring if I got in trouble for it. Nat's life was at stake and right now that was all that mattered. As I moved out and left I could smell the burning engine of the Merc, pushed almost to breaking point by our wild drive. The engine ticked rapidly – the noise reminiscent of a soundtrack drumbeat – making the whole thing seem eerily unreal as I approached the passenger door.

I could see someone in the driver's seat, head and shoulders just visible above the headrest. Something felt wrong but, before I could register what it was, the driver's door was flung open and a weapon roared, sending a flock of seagulls screaming into the air from the park.

Merrington dropped to one knee and let go a burst from his rifle, the bullets thudding home into something soft with heavy squelching sounds. Running to my side of the car I dropped to one knee to aim through the window. Almost immediately I realised that I needn't have bothered.

The driver was dead, having taken all three of Merrington's shots to the chest. But that wasn't what made my heart sink. The driver wasn't Goliath. And Nat was nowhere to be seen.

AS SOON as the car stopped Nat felt herself being hauled out like a piece of meat, still only half conscious from having the breath choked out of her. As her hands trailed through the footwell, her right one caught on something small and she grabbed it, recognising it as Rob's phone.

Her captor threw her over his injured shoulder, grunting with the pain as his blood soaked through her clothes. Picking up his rifle and rucksack, he carried her over to a nearby garage and hauled the door open, before shouting inside. A few moments later, the small man she'd seen driving the van in Woodingdean ran out, got into the car they'd just abandoned and drove off at speed.

Everything went green as they moved out of the sunlight and into the dim building, and Nat had to blink a few times to see properly. She considered trying to fight and escape while Goliath wasn't expecting it but, even injured, he'd proved that she was no match for him, so she clutched the phone behind his back and dialled Burke's number – hoping that they'd realise something was wrong and maybe trace the call.

'So you made it then?' a male voice came out of the darkness. It was an English voice and one that tugged at her memory, but in her current state she couldn't place it.

'What the fuck are you doing with her?' the voice continued as Goliath strode forward and threw her on the concrete floor hard enough to force the breath from her lungs. Gasping for breath, Nat managed to use the motion to hide the phone in her waistband. Just as she slipped it out of sight Goliath leaned over, grabbing her cuffs from her belt and slapping them around her wrists so tightly that she could almost feel her hands turning blue.

'Look, whoever you are, you need to let me go,' she began, but Goliath leaned over and casually kicked her in the head.

Nat cried aloud as the kick drove her skull painfully into the hard floor with a loud smacking sound, scattering her thoughts and filling her entire world with hot agony. She floated for a while, riding the waves of pain until they calmed enough for her to open her eyes, finding that she was now lying in the back of a large van – the interior a bright, painful white.

Goliath was standing just outside the van, a row of barely seen faces surrounding him as he spoke quickly and quietly in Russian. Nat knew enough to recognise the language, but spoken so quickly the words ran together and she couldn't even pick up the gist of the conversation.

'Any chance of speaking English?' the voice she'd heard earlier asked, and she strained her eyes to try and put a face to the voice in the dim light.

'I will speak English when you need to know what I'm saying,' Petr growled, then returned to speaking Russian.

The Englishman stepped forward, his face catching the light for a second. As his features flashed into sharp relief it was all Nat could do not to gasp out loud. The man was none other than Leon Watson – Danny MacBride's muscle. Wondering just what she'd got herself into, Nat prayed that her hidden phone was transmitting and that the cavalry was already on its way.

'SO THIS is the other man from the van?' Peters asked as I sat by the side of the road.

Within a few minutes of the shooting several armed units had arrived, followed shortly by Peters and several more Special Branch officers.

'Yeah,' I replied, 'they must have swapped out somewhere along the route, but where?'

Peters shrugged. 'You say you followed them on a tracker, is it advanced enough to tell you where it might have stopped for long enough to swap drivers?'

I straightened immediately. 'Why the hell didn't I think of that?'

I crossed to where firearms where quizzing Merrington.

'Can you track where it might have stopped for long enough for them to switch?'

He blinked for a moment. *'I can't, but it's all downloaded and recorded in real-time back at HQ. Let me make a call.'*

He pulled out his phone and started talking while I apologised to the officers I'd interrupted.

The man who'd been driving the car, one Andrei Bazhenov, was currently lying under a blue plastic sheet with two armed officers standing over him, weapons scanning the nearby streets. None of us knew how many friends the dead man had or where they might be, and tensions were running high.

As for me, I was almost beside myself with worry. Having seen firsthand what this lot did with kidnapped women, I had visions of Nat being strapped into a suicide vest and this time sent into the police station to blow the place up.

Not that I thought Nat would ever let them get that far, mind, but that thought was just as worrying. What if she fought so much they just killed her instead of whatever they had planned?

I heard my name being called and looked up, realising that I was pacing up and down like a caged animal as a crowd of curious onlookers began to form outside the cordon that firearms had set up, eager for a glimpse of something that would no doubt hit the news.

'Rob!' Merrington was already heading for the car.

'You've found it?' I asked, receiving a nod in return. 'Where?'

'Just around the corner from the police station, one of the side roads there next to an abandoned garage. I've already got two of my units en route.'

I didn't need telling twice and jumped in even as Merrington was pulling away, slowing only slightly as two officers lifted the tape to let the car slide under before he opened it up and we tore along the road as if someone's life depended on it.

I swear he didn't even look as he pulled out of the park and across Queens Park Road on to Carlton Hill, then down towards the police station, stopping only a minute or so after we'd got into the car.

'It's just around the corner,' he said as he checked the heads up display, 'and my lads are going to be at least another five minutes. Do you want to wait?'

I shook my head. 'No chance. If she's in there I want to get her back, and I want to do it sooner rather than later. Have you got a problem with that?'

'Not me. Just please don't get shot.'

'Likewise. Again, at any rate. So you think this abandoned garage is where they've gone?'

He nodded. 'My people think so. It's the only unaccounted for building in the street and it's right where they stopped. Add to that the fact that there have been no police calls concerning a man with a rifle and a hostage in a police vest and I think we're on to a winner.'

'Okay, so what's the plan?'

He looked at me with a shrug. 'I'm open to suggestions; this is your neck of the woods.'

'How about I get a look at the front door and work out the best way in?'

'Sounds good to me.'

I pulled off my vest and dropped it next to the car. It was a risk, but if I walked past with it on, I'd give the game away immediately. I moved around into the street on the far side from the garage, a rundown brick building with sagging blue wooden doors. The rest of the street was made up of a pair of cottages set well back from the road with massively overgrown gardens, while on my side there was a high wall that protected a Sports and Social Club from interlopers. At the far end was a footpath that led off and around the Social Club, and I used this to return to Merrington, running the last hundred yards as my patience began to wear thin with my worry for Nat.

'Doesn't look like there's anywhere else they could have gone without being seen,' I said when I got back, breathing heavily from the run. 'There's only one entrance at the front, no way around the side or back. It's a pair of wooden vehicle doors with a normal sized door inset on the right hand side. Couldn't get close enough to see the locks.'

I struggled back into my vest, wincing as the sweat-soaked inside chilled the bare flesh of my back.

'Okay, so we go in the front then. I'll go right, you go left and we'll see what we find,' Merrington said, checking the magazine on his rifle. 'You sure you're ready for this?'

I nodded. 'Don't have a lot of choice, do we? God only knows what they're doing to Nat.'

'No time like the present.' He grinned, but his eyes were a little wild around the edges and the grin was too manic to make me feel safe. Shrugging it off, I guessed that I probably didn't look quite normal after the day we'd had, and I swallowed my reservations and followed him around the corner, pistol gripped in palms that were as sweaty as my mouth was dry.

What we were doing was more than likely a sure-fire way to lose my job, but my concern for Nat was overriding any sense of caution I'd normally have. As we approached the doors I took a deep breath and let it out slowly, focusing myself on the task at hand. I needed to be together for this, any doubts or fears needed to be kept locked away where they wouldn't affect my ability to act without conscious thought or worry.

I'd done this before, long ago in my army days, and I knew that going into a potentially hostile situation with a head full of rubbish was more likely to get me killed than anything else. I'd seen it happen to too many other people, good people, and I didn't want to end up as a line of script on a wall somewhere.

Merrington moved swiftly across to the far side of the door and pressed his back against the wood, motioning at me to do the same on my side. As I pressed my back against the sun-warmed door, I realised that we'd be going in totally blind. It was so bright out here that anyone inside would have a massive advantage while our eyes adjusted, and for a moment I wondered if we *should* wait for Merrington's men to arrive before we went in.

If nothing else they'd have stun grenades, and they could make the difference between life and death. Before I could voice that thought, however, Merrington swung in, his foot connecting with the smaller door and caving it inwards with a loud cracking sound.

He moved in quick and low, moving to the right of the door as old reflexes took over and I followed in and left, finger already on the trigger and ready to fire.

Only to find the room empty.

There was a burnt oil smell to the air, mixed with diesel and something else that I couldn't quite place, but as my eyes slowly adjusted I saw nothing but a stripped workbench, a pair of old ramps and a lot of dust.

'Shit! Where the *fuck* are they?'

Merrington came out of his crouch slowly and peered into the corners as if he might find Nat hidden there, then turned to face me with a look of sorrow on his face.

'Sorry Rob. Wherever they're going, they've already left.'

'No, no, no.' I was shaking my head violently as I studied the marks in the dust. Two sets of wheel tracks, one in and one out, cut through the dust along with the treads from at least eight pairs of boots, maybe more.

'We're not far from the police station, would their CCTV cover this area?' Merrington asked hopefully.

'No, the Social Club will block the camera. Whoever chose this place chose it well.'

I headed back out into the sunlight, my head throbbing with anger and fear for Nat. I'd managed to save Gemma Hallett, only to lose someone close to me instead and now I was back at square one with no clue how to find her.

I slumped on the pavement, back against the bricks of the garage as the two units Merrington had called up arrived. Four MI6 men boiled out and started running towards me, but Merrington came out and waved them off, instructing them instead to secure the area for forensic analysis.

Once that was done he came over, his silhouette blocking the sun and making me squint as I looked up at him.

'So what now?' he asked, but I ignored him as something high up and behind him caught my eye. He followed my gaze. 'What?'

I pointed and scrambled to my feet, starting to run towards the back of the American Express building that blocked the end of the street.

'What is it?' Merrington called as he followed.

I pointed as I ran, indicating the camera I'd seen glinting high above, pointed directly towards the street. If anyone had come in or out of the road, the camera would have caught it, and that meant that the security office inside the American Express building would have the answers I needed to get Nat back alive.

81

LEON WIPED his palms on his trousers while he waited for the security guard to approach the van. This was the moment of truth and, despite the uniform, he knew this would be the hardest part. He knew he didn't have the sort of brain that could make things up on the fly, preferring to think things through at his own pace and come to a slow, safe conclusion. And if the guard asked too many questions, he knew he might panic. Just the thought made his heart beat faster as the bored looking guard finally reached the window and looked in.

'Pass please,' he said with a smile. Leon obediently handed it over, hoping the man wasn't sharp enough to spot where his photograph had been superimposed on top of the original one.

The guard looked at it for a long moment, then back up to compare it to Leon's face. Leon had to resist the urge to smile – a big, silly grin tugging at the corners of his mouth as his nerves almost got the better of him.

After what felt like a year, the guard handed back the pass. 'Thanks. You're a little early for the delivery but the guards are already waiting. Can I have your paperwork?'

Leon nodded, wrenching his right hand away from the pistol he had tucked down the side of his seat and using it to pass the required paperwork to the man.

The guard took it and scanned the pages carefully before nodding, scribbling on the bottom of the first page and handing it back. 'You know where you're going, yeah?'

Leon nodded and put the van in gear as the huge gate slid ponderously back and the guard waved him through. Driving down the ramp, he felt his nerves return as the building closed over his head and he drove them into the docking bay where four more guards waited, looking bored and grumpy.

Swinging it around in a circle, Leon backed the van towards the raised platform the guards stood on, wishing fervently that MacBride was with them. Since they'd met in prison, the man had been like a big brother to Leon, guiding him and giving him work.

Now MacBride had been arrested and dragged off to the cells, and Leon was on his own with the foreigners that his boss had brought in to help. Not that Leon was scared of them. There was only one man that scared him, and that man was currently sitting in a cell trusting in Leon to do his job and do it well. No, he wasn't scared — he was just worried that he might let MacBride down.

The back of the van bumped gently against the loading dock and Leon jumped out on to the concrete, walking slowly up the stairs to join the guard and trying hard to look natural. They were talking quietly amongst themselves when one of them looked over at him and laughed. Before Leon could stop himself, his hands clenched, fists half up and ready to fight. The one laughing froze, his eyes widening as Leon cleared the top of the stairs and looked down on the waiting men.

'Something funny?' Leon demanded, glowering.

'Uh, no, just making a joke mate.'

'If you laugh at me again...' Leon stopped and took a deep breath. He'd spent his life being laughed at for being slow, first in school and then prison when he got banged up for almost killing a teacher. It was the one thing guaranteed to make him lose his temper, and if he couldn't get it under control before the others were out of the van, he might ruin the whole operation. Then MacBride would be disappointed and that would be a *very* bad thing.

Taking another breath, Leon let it out slowly and forced a smile. 'Sorry, long day. I'll just get the back open.'

Holding the anger down inside, Leon put the key in the lock and turned, hearing it click open. The guards were standing behind him now, crowding around to help empty whatever was supposed to be in the van, and Leon allowed himself a little smirk as he thought of the looks on their faces when he lifted the shutter.

As it rolled up, he heard a gasp from behind him and he turned to see one of the guards bolt towards a red button on the wall. There was a soft *phut*, and the man dropped to the floor, arms and legs flopping like a ragdoll's as a red stain spread across his back.

The other guards dropped to the ground, hands shooting up as armed men boiled out of the van and surrounded them. Petr stepped out last, silenced pistol still smoking as he surveyed the men cowering in front of him.

'What's going on?' one of the guards asked, risking a few seconds of eye contact with Leon.

'This is a robbery!' Leon shouted back, wishing that he hadn't left his pistol in the cab so that he could look the part.

'Actually,' Petr said, placing the warm end of the silencer against Leon's temple, 'it isn't.'

82

THE AMERICAN Express building is a huge white monstrosity that sits about a hundred metres back from Edward Street behind its own plaza which, during a weekday, is strewn with harried looking staff smoking like laboratory beagles.

Today, however, the plaza was deserted and the mirrored windows only reflected myself and Merrington as we ran across the square and into the air conditioned reception area.

I'd never actually been inside before, and it took me a few seconds to get my bearings in the open area that was almost as large as the ground floor of the police station.

A row of turnstiles with a security desk sat directly in front of us, and as we approached a nervous looking security guard in a crisp white shirt had one hand on a phone while he tried to decide if we were a threat or not.

Despite my police badged vest, Merrington was clearly armed and in a blood covered suit and I'm amazed that sirens didn't start screaming out before we reached the desk.

I held up my warrant card and gave the man my best smile.

'I'm Detective Sergeant Steele from Brighton Police Station. I need to see your supervisor immediately,' I said without preamble.

The young man nodded and picked up the phone, speaking into it for a few seconds before hanging up.

'Something I need to worry about?' the guard asked me as we waited impatiently.

I shook my head. 'Not as far as I know, but I need to check your cameras out the back.'

Despite my best efforts to remain calm, I was pacing up and down again by the time a security supervisor arrived, grim faced with his belly straining at the buttons of his white shirt.

'I'm Colin Smith, can I see your warrant card please?' he asked immediately, then studied it carefully before handing it back.

'And yours please sir,' he said to Merrington, who handed over his slim black wallet.

Smith did a double take when he saw the ID inside, straightening slightly and sucking his gut in a little.

'This is serious then?' He eyed Merrington's rifle nervously.

I nodded. 'Very. Someone's kidnapped one of my officers and they stopped out the back near the Social Club. One of your cameras covers the area and I need to see the footage.'

'You'll understand if I phone to check you are who you say you are?'

'Do you have to? We might be running out of time here.'

Smith shook his head. 'I'm sorry sir, I don't have a choice. This will only take a moment.'

He picked up the phone and dialled three nines. 'What's your commanding officer's name?' he asked.

'DCI Burke.'

He nodded and spoke into the phone for almost a minute before thanking the person on the other end and putting the phone down.

'Sorry about that, but this place is more than a little sensitive. Letting armed men in without checking would have been more than my job was worth.'

'It would have been more than your life was worth if we weren't who we were claiming to be,' I said as we followed him through one of the gates and off to the left.

He shrugged. 'That's what we get paid for. Besides, I was pretty sure you were on the level or you would have come in shooting, not asking, but if I don't follow procedure then I'll be standing next door in the dole queue pretty sharpish.'

I couldn't fault the man's logic. He seemed like a no-nonsense, by the book kind of guy, and I wondered why he'd chosen to work somewhere like this rather than joining the police. That kind of attitude was exactly what I looked for in my detectives.

'Why is this place so sensitive?' I asked him as he led us down a narrow corridor and through several code-locked doors.

Smith stopped and looked at me in surprise.

'Do you not know? I thought all the officers knew how important this place is?'

I shook my head. 'Maybe the senior officers do. Enlighten me.'

'This building is the Amex headquarters for Europe and the Middle East. We also have a counting area and vault that holds... a lot of money. Not only that, but the servers here hold all data on every piece of Amex business and every customer."

'And you don't have armed guards?' I was incredulous.

Smith shrugged. 'Why do you think they sited it so close to the police station? If anything happens here they want an immediate response. They tried to get the building classed as American soil like an embassy so that we could have armed guards here, but the plans haven't been pushed through yet. Ah, here we are.'

Smith swiped his card and punched a combination into the keypad next to a solid looking metal door. It hissed open to reveal a room almost fifty feet across, one wall covered in CCTV monitors while two men sat at a long desk in front of them with four more monitors close at hand.

Looking up at the display, I wondered how they ever spotted anything in the kaleidoscopic montage on the wall. I'd seen some pretty advanced CCTV systems before, but this was something on an entirely different scale. It was a sea of constantly moving, changing images and just looking at it gave me a headache.

Smith waved a hand at the men who barely looked up at our entrance.

'From here we can look at sites in Africa, the Middle East, all over Europe,' he caught the look on my face, 'and, uh, the streets out the back.'

He gave instructions to one of the operators who obediently called up the correct camera and began to rewind the image on the screen.

'This isn't one we usually have up on the wall,' the operator said as he worked, 'it's low priority so we only physically check it twice a day during the camera patrols.'

'Of course it's all digital,' Smith interrupted smoothly, 'so we can do instant playback.'

The images were moving so fast that I could barely make out what was happening, but there was a flash of white on the screen for a moment, and then a few seconds later a flash of silver before the street was empty again.

The operator hit a button and the view returned to normal time, but from the clock on the screen it was showing an image from about ten minutes before we'd got there.

As we watched, Merrington's stolen car pulled up outside the garage. The big man who'd taken it got out, dragging Nat with him, and approached the garage. The door was opened and the man we'd caught ran out, getting straight in and driving away at speed while Nat was carried into the interior of the garage.

'So they *were* there,' I said, fists clenching and unclenching as I thought of Nat and what might be happening to her. Rounding on Merrington, I grabbed him by the lapel.

'What happened to your bloody terrorist attack? What are they up to?' I shouted, not caring that everyone was staring at me.

Merrington tried to prise my hand away but failed, instead resting his hand on top of mine.

'I don't know Rob. I thought they were going to try and attack the city centre. Maybe the hospital was all they intended and this is their getaway.'

'Then we've lost her?'

'I'm not sure, I think you should see this,' one of the operators interrupted, pointing to his screen.

I looked down and saw the screen split into four, each one showing part of Carlton Hill or John Street, just opposite the police station where the rear entrance to the Amex building was.

The operator nodded towards the screen.

'About a two minutes before you walked down the street without your vest, this happened.'

I watched as the garage doors swung open and a white van pulled out, a man closing the doors before he jumped into the back and pulled the shutters down.

The van then drove off, moving from one camera to another as it pulled around the corner and stopped at the back gate to the building we were in while a guard approached.

As soon as he saw what was happening, Smith burst into action, wrenching the door open and running from the room. Merrington and I had no choice but to follow him as I put the pieces together and realised what they'd been after all along.

83

MERRINGTON WAS already on the phone by the time we reached the end of the corridor, Smith fumbling with the lock in his haste to get the door open.

'Slow down mate, take a breath and get it right. Where are we going?' I asked him as he punched the code in for the second time.

'Loading dock,' he replied, pulling open the door.

'How far is it?' I asked.

He pointed to a steel security door at the far end of the corridor. 'Just through there.'

I grabbed him by the shoulder as he started to run again, swinging him around to face me. 'Stop for a minute and think about this. We're facing God only knows how many men and they're armed. If we go running out there like this then all we'll end up doing is becoming casualties.'

'But I've got men in the loading dock! I need to make sure they're okay.' He ducked out from under my restraining hand with surprising nimbleness for a man his size and began running down the corridor.

'Bollocks,' I muttered under my breath as I ran after him, Merrington at my heels.

'Smith, Smith! Wait a bloody minute.' I changed my mind about him being good copper material. He was running towards armed men with nothing but a radio and frown for protection and was more than likely going to get himself killed if I didn't do something to stop him.

By the time I caught up he was already hammering in the code. I slammed myself into the door and turned so that my back was pressed against it. 'Smith, stop. Don't make me arrest you.'

That got his attention. His eyes were like saucers – huge and round. His face was pale and he was panting heavily as sweat poured down his cheeks. The man's worst fears had just been realised and he wasn't handling it very well.

'Right, now you're listening, tell me what you're planning to do?'

He slumped against the wall, still breathing heavily.

'I just need to make sure my men are okay,' he said shortly.

'And you couldn't do that via CCTV?' I asked.

His eyes met mine and a flush spread across his cheeks. 'Uh...yeah. I'm sorry, I saw what was happening and I panicked. We have four men meeting each van that comes in and...'

'Okay, that's fine. I understand you're worried about your men, but if you go charging off you'll get us all killed, and maybe your men as well. How about you go back and check on CCTV, and then get some men to the front of the building to wait for the police to arrive?'

I looked at Merrington questioningly. He was still on the phone but he covered it with his hand and mouthed 'five minutes' at me.

'Right. In five minutes we'll have armed units crawling all over the place. Can you give me your radio and card so that I can stay in touch and get about?'

Smith frowned but nodded. 'You'll need my code. It's 43851. Swipe first.'

He handed over the card and radio, then hurried off back to the control room through the still-open door, closing it behind him with a clunk.

Merrington finished his call and tucked his phone away before hefting his rifle.

'Are you thinking what I am?' he asked.

'Do you think they're here for the cash or the servers Smith was talking about?'

'It has to be the servers. They hold every piece of information on every transaction and every customer that the company has, as well as all their financial data. If they go down then it will cause shockwaves that may well tear the financial world apart.' His voice was bitter. 'I should have known.'

'You *knew* about this place?' I asked, incredulous.

He nodded. 'It's a high risk target, but it's also a very well kept secret. There was nothing to suggest that the men we were after had any inkling about this place.'

'Just goes to show how wrong you can be, doesn't it?'

'None of which is helping us stop them or get Nat back. We can do recriminations later.'

There was a lot more I could have said but he was right. Nat was top priority, followed by stopping the terrorists from carrying out their plan. 'Okay, so we clear the loading dock first.'

Merrington nodded, then checked his rifle and took up a kneeling position facing the door. 'I'll go first and take the right, you go left again. Ready?'

I nodded and readied my own weapon.

'Great, let's go.'

My shaking hand nearly dropping the card, I swiped it through the reader and punched in the code. My mouth had dried out again and I had a sudden, urgent need to pee. Gripping the pistol in my right hand I used the other to crack the door an inch or so, ready to throw myself back into the corridor at the first hint of trouble.

Peering out through the gap I saw a slice of the loading bay, the rest blocked by the back of the van we'd seen on CCTV. Just behind the van were two security guards pressed face first against the wall with their hands on their heads while a third lay still in a pool of blood just feet away from an alarm point. It didn't take a genius to work out what had happened.

'Three guards, one dead and two against the wall,' I whispered to Merrington. 'Smith said there were four meeting the van.'

Motioning me into a crouch, Merrington put his eye to the crack above my head. After a moment, he moved back and drew me away from the door.

'There has to be someone watching them that we can't see, probably standing at the back of the van. Reckon you can make it across to the front of the van and round the other side without making a noise?'

I looked out again. 'Yeah, I think so.'

'Good. Here's what we'll do then. You move around to the front of the van and take up a position ready to fire. I'll move out across the dock and engage whoever it is they've got guarding the men out there. As soon as you hear me fire I want you to move in on the far side of the van.'

'Isn't that into your line of fire?' I asked.

He nodded tersely. 'It is, but if the firing hasn't stopped it'll be because I'm pinned down and I'll need you to take out the shooter from behind.'

I swallowed nervously. 'My God, we're really going to do this, aren't we?'

'Yes, we are. We don't have a lot of choice Rob. If we did, we'd be sitting in the CCTV room drinking tea and waiting for the cavalry.'

'What if there's more than one of them?' I asked.

'The plan stays the same. They won't be expecting an attack, so that gives us a chance.'

I sagged back against the wall, my heart beating so fast I thought it might jump out of my chest. It had been a long time since I'd been in anything resembling a fire-fight and it was something I never thought I'd be doing again.

Merrington surprised me by putting a hand on my shoulder and squeezing gently. 'You can do this Rob. You *need* to do this for Nat's sake.'

I pushed myself away from the wall and stood straight, sliding the magazine out of the pistol and checking the rounds. They sat there gleaming – each one a potential death that would be on my conscience for the rest of my life.

Looking through the door at the body of the guard, I knew that if I didn't do something now then God only knew how many more people would end up like that. Remembering the ACC's speech earlier, I realised that this was the moment. This was the second where if I did nothing, evil would triumph.

Flexing my fingers to stop my hands from shaking, I felt a calm settle over me. My mind was made up and we were going to do this. We had to. It was as if someone had flipped a switch in my head and buried all the misgivings. 'I'm ready, let's go.'

Merrington nodded and eased the door open, giving me just enough room to slip out into the room beyond. And, as I moved stealthily towards the front of the van, I silently prayed that nothing would go wrong.

84

I CROUCHED in the shadow of the van, smelling hot oil and old exhaust fumes as I waited, fingers flexing around the butt of the pistol. I felt like I'd been there for an hour, crouched close enough to the raised dock that I could hear the crunching of booted feet on the concrete, but glancing at my watch I realised that it had only been about a minute.

I resisted the urge to glance around the side of the van, knowing that if I did I could well get my head blown off. For the third time in a minute, I reached down with my left hand to make sure that the Amex radio was switched off. It wouldn't do to have Smith or one of his men call up at an inopportune moment, and tip off the man I was waiting to ambush. Keeping my breathing slow and steady, I began to count off the seconds.

I'd reached thirty-seven when I heard a scraping noise from the far side of the loading dock and a grunted question in a foreign language from a few feet away. My whole body was screaming at me to move – to do something – but I knew I couldn't deviate from the plan and kept my head firmly out of sight.

A few seconds later I was rewarded with the deafening boom of a firearm going off, followed quickly by the thud of a body hitting the ground and several men yelling in fear. Unable to hide any longer, I burst out from behind the van, pistol first, to see Merrington approaching in a crouch. Between us was the body of a man dressed in jeans and a t-shirt, a pistol still in his hand as his glassy eyes stared right at me.

A large red stain soaked the front of his t-shirt but I didn't bother to look closer. A wound like that stops you from needing to check for breathing or a pulse. Next to the corpse lay another man, wearing a security uniform. His hands were cuffed behind him and he lay face down, his head turned towards Merrington.

'You okay?' I asked the agent as he climbed on to the dock and nudged the body with his toe.

'Yes, he didn't get a chance to fire back. One down.' He bent over to examine the cuffs on the guard but I placed a hand on his shoulder.

'Hang on a minute.' I rolled the guard over and found myself looking into the eyes of Leon Watson.

'What the bloody hell are you doing here?' I asked in surprise.

'I never thought I'd be pleased to see a copper!' He said in response. 'Get me out of here and I'll tell you.'

I looked up at Merrington who was busily helping the Amex guards to their feet. None of them seemed injured but their faces were mute testament to their fear.

'Are you all okay?' I asked.

One of them nodded. 'We're fine, but they took Kevin.'

'How many were there and where did they go?' Merrington demanded.

'There were four of them led by a big bastard with long hair. They made Kevin take them to the server room. They've got a female copper with them as well.'

'How do we get there?' I asked, hurriedly.

The guard pointed to a door on the far side of the loading bay. 'Take that door, then the third door on the right. That'll take you to a set of stairs. Go right to the bottom and head straight along the corridor. The server room is at the end. You'll hear the fans before you see it.'

Merrington clapped the guard on the shoulder. 'Great, thanks. Rob, you coming?'

I picked up the dead terrorist's discarded pistol and handed it to the agent.

'What about Watson here?' I asked.

Merrington looked down at the prone felon. 'Let them take him back to the Control Room. He's cuffed after all.'

I shrugged and turned to the man who'd given us directions. 'Think you can do that?'

He nodded and, with the aid of his colleague, got Watson to his feet. As they marched him away he threw a look over his shoulder at me. 'I can help you, don't nick me, I was tricked!'

I nodded. 'Sure, they tricked you into driving a van dressed like a guard. I'll bear that in mind in interview.'

Merrington grabbed me by the arm and hauled me in the direction of the server room.

'Come on,' he said, grabbing the card off me and swiping it through the lock. He punched in the code and the door swung open to reveal a dim corridor. As he stepped into it, lights flickered on along its length, illuminating white plaster walls and matching plastic floor.

Several doors led off the corridor, but Merrington made straight for the third one on the right, pressing his ear against the wood and motioning for quiet. I stopped where I was, the squeaking of my trainers on the plastic floor dying away in tiny echoes. After a moment, he swiped the card and tapped the code in, causing the door to open with a whooshing sound.

I held my breath, half expecting the rattle of gunfire, but nothing broke the silence except the furious beating of my heart. Waving me on, Merrington disappeared through the doorway and I had no choice but to follow, wondering what was more likely to kill me first, a bullet or a cardiac arrest.

85

THE DOOR to the server room was solid metal and filled the end of the corridor – an impenetrable barrier protecting the servers within, or so they must have thought when they built it. Tapping the smooth grey surface, the clunking noise told Petr that it was at least three inches thick. The card that the guard – now unconscious on the floor – had provided made the lock flash red, as he'd expected. Only select personnel would have access to the very heart of the American Express empire.

'Explosives,' he said over his shoulder, and a block of C4 was placed in his waiting hand.

Squeezing the block, he split it into three roughly equal parts and shaped them carefully against the hinges, in order to direct the force of the blast inward. If he got it wrong, anyone standing in the corridor would be vaporised. Once the explosive was in place he eased in the detonators and armed them, then moved backwards to where the others waited.

'Cover your ears and open your mouths,' he warned, backing up right to the corner.

Checking everyone had followed his instructions, he realised that the woman couldn't lift her cuffed hands. Shrugging, he pressed the button on the remote and suddenly the corridor was filled with light and sound as the door exploded, the pressure wave washing over them and knocking them backwards.

Picking himself up, Petr grabbed the woman and dragged her towards the gaping hole where the door had been. The woman was screaming, blood trickling from her ruptured ears as he pulled her along, but his men seemed fine – if a little shaken.

He stepped over the body of the guard, the tattered uniform doing nothing to disguise the torn and bleeding flesh beneath. Once inside the room Petr threw the woman into the corner and looked around, waving away the smoke that the air conditioning was struggling to clear.

In the darkness of the emergency lighting, row after row of black, state of the art racks held thousands of terabytes worth of information. Green and red lights blinked at him out of the gloom, and he felt a grin spread slowly across his face.

Motioning to his men to spread out and start placing charges, he turned and took up a firing position by the door, ready to shoot down anyone who tried to stop them.

86

THE EXPLOSION sent me stumbling into Merrington who almost lost his footing and sent us both tumbling down the stairs. We were only saved by the agent's quick reactions as he grabbed the banister with one hand and caught me in the crook of his other arm.

'We're too late. They've blown the damn servers!' He said angrily.

I shook my head. 'If they'd blown the servers I don't think the building would still be here. They were probably forcing an entry.'

The air was swirling with smoke and dust as the air-con pushed it around the narrow corridor. An alarm began to shrill.

'So we go on?' Merrington asked.

I nodded. 'We go on. They've still got Nat. And I'm willing to bet they'll leave her down here once the charges are set. If they even plan to try and escape themselves.'

Merrington opened his mouth to reply. But before he could say anything the sound of booted feet on the stairs behind us made me turn, pistol flying into a firing position seemingly of its own accord.

'Hold your fire!' The voice was muffled, but as the smoke began to clear I saw two of Merrington's black clad teams stacked up on the stairs, rifles pointed towards us, Smith hanging nervously at the back of the group.

'That changes things,' I said to Merrington as he waved them down towards us.

He nodded. 'It does indeed. Cover the corridor while I brief them.'

Before I could reply he was up the stairs, huddled in the middle of the group as they spoke with their heads almost touching. I turned and pointed my pistol down the corridor, feeling under-armed and unprepared for anything that might come out of the smoke. The seconds dragged past but, less than a minute later, a stream of men was moving past me from the stairs and into the smoke, vanishing from sight up the corridor.

Merrington followed, with Smith in tow, moving up to the corner and indicating that we should wait until his team had cleared it. I wasn't going to argue. These men were trained for situations like this, it was their bread and butter and, for the first time in what felt like an age, I felt a surge of hope that we might actually get Nat back alive.

That hope was shattered as gunfire roared down the corridor — a long, scything burst followed by several screams and incoherent shouting. A few moments later, two of the four men who'd entered ran back to our position, appearing out of the smoke and hurling themselves around the corner on top of us in an effort to avoid the rounds that hissed and whined as they spat past.

'What happened?' Merrington demanded as the men got to their feet.

The first one pulled his balaclava off, revealing a surprisingly young face with blond hair and blue eyes. 'They've got the doorway to the server room covered. As soon as we got within sight, they opened up and John and Barry copped it. We're not getting in there without a *lot* more men.'

'What about grenades?' I asked.

He shook his head. 'If they've planted explosives already then a grenade going off could bring the whole place down.' Despite his hurried retreat and the death of his two colleagues, he seemed incredibly calm.

'How long until more men get here?' I asked.

He shrugged. 'We're not getting a radio signal down here, but we're expecting backup in the next few minutes. If we get enough, we'll be able to force an entry but it'll be messy.'

He looked grim, and no wonder. The more we delayed, the greater chance there was that the terrorists would finish what they were doing and bring the building down around our ears.

'Suggestions?' Merrington asked the question quietly, his voice barely audible over the shrilling alarm.

I took a breath to speak, then coughed as the dirty air hit my lungs. It stank of old explosive, smoke and cordite, and the flashing red light strobing through the smoke made me wonder if this was what hell was like. I turned to Smith, who was hovering nervously at the bottom of the stairs.

'Is there another way into that room?' I asked.

He started to shake his head but then paused. 'Uh, maybe.'

'Maybe isn't good enough, yes or no?' I asked, aggression making my voice rough.

He nodded uncertainly. 'Yes.'

'Where?'

He pointed down the corridor that led left from the bottom of the stairs, away from the server room. 'If you go down there, there's a ladder about thirty feet along. It leads down into the maintenance tunnels that run under the server room. The door is code-locked but my card will get you in.'

'Show me.'

He shook his head and shrank back against the wall. 'I'm sorry, I can't.'

'We don't have time for this, lives are at stake!'

He shook his head again, sending droplets of nervous sweat flying in all directions. 'I can't! I'm sorry, I...'

'Forget it.' I spat out the words. 'Where do the tunnels come out in the server room?'

'At the back, behind the last row of servers in the far corner.'

'Right.' I said. 'If I were you I'd get out of here. If you see any more of our boys up there, send them down, eh?'

Smith nodded and turned, hurrying up the stairs and out of sight. Merrington and his men were looking at me expectantly, making me wonder when I'd been put back in charge.

'Right,' I said, 'they know we're here. That means that if we don't put some fire down once in a while they'll get suspicious. One of you needs to stay here and keep them busy while the rest of you come with me. If we take the maintenance tunnel we can get in behind them.'

Merrington nodded. 'Sounds good. What then?'

'When we get in, I'll go for Nat. Merrington, you take out anyone placing charges or hacking into the servers. Third man takes out whoever's guarding the door.'

They all nodded and, as I moved off, Merrington and the officer still wearing his balaclava followed, leaving the blond man behind. As we reached the ladder, a burst of gunfire echoed along the corridor, followed almost immediately by the chatter of an AK-47.

'Well at least that part of the plan's working,' I muttered to myself as I climbed down the ladder into a maintenance tunnel that was just wide enough for Merrington to poke his rifle over my shoulder as I half-crouched, half-walked into the darkness.

It was hot down here and noisy — the whirring of the giant fans interspersed with the sounds of intermittent gunfire. I felt like I was back in the infantry, clearing a stronghold in Helmand, only much higher tech and with a lot more at stake. It wasn't a feeling I enjoyed.

Small emergency lights were spaced at intervals, illuminating the passage just enough that I could see a dozen feet in front of me. As we moved on, the whirring noise of the fans grew louder and the walls seemed to vibrate.

After about thirty feet we took a sharp right hand turn, moving back towards the server room itself, and at the end of the corridor was a short ladder ending in a metal hatch with a code and swipe lock. Moving up to it, I tried to listen for any movement above. But with the fans and the gunfire that still rattled above us, I might as well have been deaf.

Looking at Merrington and his officer I raised my eyebrows, receiving two nods in return. Heart in mouth, I punched in the code and swiped the card before placing a hand on the underside of the hatch and pushing it open.

THE PAIN was incredible. Nat's head felt like it had exploded and been put back together wrong. Her ears were ringing, her brain felt two sizes too big and every sound brought fresh waves of agony crashing into her skull. In the dim light she could see figures stealthily moving through the smoke, setting charges on the server cases, while the bulk of Petr stood a few feet away as he poured rounds down the corridor.

Squirming on to her side, Nat looked around. No-one was paying attention to her. When she'd been cuffed, her keys had been taken but no one had thought to remove her warrant card from her back pocket. Straightening her legs, she stretched her arms down until the tips of her fingers brushed the black leather in her pocket. A few moments of wriggling and she had it in her cuffed hands, fingers slipping in behind the plastic card to grasp the small handcuff key she kept there for emergencies.

She looked up again at Petr but he was concentrating on the corridor, his face fixed in a feral grin as he fired through the door, spent shell casings bouncing off the wall next to him as his smoking Kalashnikov ejected them in a steady stream.

Getting the key into the lock without looking was hard — the small sliver of metal kept trying to slip out of her fingers. But after nearly a minute of trying she got the right cuff free, almost crying in pain as blood rushed back into her hand. Moving slowly, she eased her arms in front of her and undid the other cuff, massaging the deep grooves in her wrists where the metal cuffs had dug into the flesh.

Moving up into a sitting position, she looked around again, hoping to see something that she could use as a weapon. She had no illusions about her chances but she refused to go out without a fight. The cavalry was being held off by Petr, but just one look at the size of him made her think twice about attacking him with her bare hands.

The giant had already been shot once, but the wound seemed to cause him no discomfort and she doubted that her teenage years of street fighting and yearly UDT course would put him down.

Knowing that she had to act sooner rather than later, she pushed away from the wall and scuttled into the darkness, hoping to surprise one of the other men and if she was lucky, disarm him. Gripping the cuffs, her only weapon, she stalked down the rows of servers, eyes scanning right and left for a target.

As the smoke momentarily cleared, she saw a man crouching over the base of a server rack, rifle on the floor next to him as he eased a detonator into a block of plastic explosive. Moving on the balls of her feet, Nat crept up behind him and raised the cuffs over her head with both hands. Teeth gritted with the effort, she brought the cuffs down as hard as she could into the back of the man's head, feeling more than hearing the crack as the metal smashed into his skull.

He slumped forward without a sound, blood oozing from a nasty looking gash in the back of his head. Nat gagged for a moment, bile rising from her stomach as she realised that she might have killed him. Although she was no stranger to fighting, she'd never hurt someone this badly before. Taking a deep breath, she put out a hand to steady herself against the nearest rack as she got herself back under control, realising that if she was going to stop them, she would have to do far worse.

Before she could change her mind, Nat swept up the man's rifle, holding it awkwardly as she turned and made her way back to where Petr held off her allies. The smoke kept her well hidden as she crept back to the corner she'd come from. Petr was still firing down the corridor, empty magazines littering the floor at his feet.

Raising the rifle, Nat tucked the stock into her shoulder and pointed the barrel at him. She'd never fired anything bigger than an air rifle before, but as her left hand slipped the safety off, she knew that she had no choice. If she couldn't stop them, no one could.

The world narrowed — everything but the rifle and her target becoming vague and hazy as she aimed at the back of his head. Gritting her teeth again, she pulled the trigger.

The rifle bucked like a wild animal, fire and heat exploding from the barrel as it kicked in her hands. Rounds sprayed up the wall above Petr's head and sent chips of stone flying in all directions. The big man threw himself flat, arms coming up to cover his head as the world exploded around him, his own rifle forgotten as rounds ricocheted everywhere.

Nat held on grimly, fighting against the recoil to lower the barrel but, before she could get it into position, Petr was up and moving, his shoulder slamming into her stomach and lifting her off her feet to hurl her into a stack of servers.

The rifle flew from her grip as she struck, the wind going out of her as she fell to the ground and gasped for breath. Before she could move, the big man was on her, a wickedly gleaming machete in one hand while the other tangled itself in her hair and pulled her head back, exposing her throat.

'I think you've just outlived your usefulness,' he growled, and as she watched, helpless, the blade rose in an arc and flashed down towards her throat.

WHEN GOOD MEN DO NOTHING

88

THE HATCH swung back on well-oiled hinges, hitting the floor with a clang before I could stop it. I winced, but a split second later there was a long burst of gunfire that covered the noise. Taking the chance while it was offered, I clambered out and took up a kneeling position, pistol pointed out into the darkness between the rows of blinking server lights.

I felt Merrington brush against me as he hauled himself up, then got a tap on the shoulder from the third man whose name I didn't know. *I should have asked*, I thought as I peered into the darkness, *I'd hate to die with someone whose name I didn't even know.* Merrington clapped a hand on my shoulder as he passed, moving towards the main door where the firing was coming from. Our third man stopped next to me.

'You good to go?' he said into my ear to stop from having to shout over the noise.

I nodded but grabbed his arm. 'What's your name?'

'2-9.' He responded from behind the balaclava.

I shook my head. 'No, your real name.'

It wasn't the time to ask but I had a sudden, irrational fear that if I didn't know his name then he'd die, and I'd regret not asking when I had the chance.

'Robert.'

'Another one? We'd better stick with 2-9.' I grinned as I said it and I saw the cloth twitch over his mouth. 'No room for two Rob's, it'd get confusing.'

He nodded and moved off, leaving me alone by the hatch. I considered closing it again to cover our tracks but then decided that the time for secrecy was past. Now we were in we had to move fast.

Gathering myself, I moved to the far wall in a crouching run, making sure to keep as much cover between myself and the doorway as possible. As soon as I hit the wall I turned, checking behind to make sure no one had discovered me yet.

The noise and the smoke, poorly lit by white and red emergency lights, made me feel disorientated. The AK opened up again, this time a long, uncontrolled burst that sent bullets ricocheting around the room. I ducked as one flew over my head before hitting the wall and screaming off in yet another direction.

Guessing that Merrington and 2-9 had started their attack, I began to move again, my pulse racing as I constantly scanned the murky room. All too soon I ran out of cover. The rows of servers stopped twenty feet away from the wall in all directions. To get to where the firing was coming from, I would need to break cover and move into the open space. Steeling myself, I moved around the corner low and fast, only to stop dead in my tracks.

Less than a dozen feet away the huge terrorist was facing me, a massive machete in his hand. His left hand, however, was wrapped in Nat's hair as he pulled the weapon back to hack through her throat. Before I knew what I was doing, I let out a scream of rage which stopped him in his tracks, his head snapping up to look at me in surprise.

I was already moving forwards, pistol raised and pointed at him as I gathered speed. I was beyond rational thinking now, beyond fear or anger. I was in the dark place that I'd been trying to forget since leaving the Army and all I wanted was to do was hurt the man in front of me.

Throwing Nat to one side he ran at me, machete raised over his head. He reached me so fast that I almost crashed into him. Dropping to one knee and almost touching his stomach with the pistol I pulled the trigger twice in quick succession.

The first one hit his hip, folding him over as the second one buried itself in his stomach and dropped him, the machete clattering against the floor. Still scanning the room with the pistol, I ran to Nat and rolled her over. She looked up at me with wide eyes and a slightly bemused expression.

'Are you okay?' I asked stupidly, lifting her by the shoulders and dragging her backwards into the cover of one of the server stacks.

'I can't hear!' she shouted at me as I took up a position in front of her, eyes scanning the darkness for threats.

I nodded just as all hell was unleashed in the room, weapons opening up all around us. I grabbed Nat again and threw us both flat as black clad men poured in through the door and began firing at targets I couldn't see.

Risking a look, I saw that the men were Merrington's, but had clearly been forewarned. They were wearing night-vision goggles that made them look like armed cyclops as they swept through the room. Less than a minute later they were done, and shouts of 'Clear' replaced the gunfire. Sitting up, I looked around in amazement and wondered how we weren't all dead.

Suddenly Merrington came limping out of the smoke with a grin on his face as he saw us huddled on the floor.

'You made it then?' he asked, cradling the rifle in his arms.

'Yeah, I think so,' I said, climbing unsteadily to my feet. 'Is everyone okay?'

He pointed at the body on the floor next to me. 'We are, they're not. All down. The charges are being disarmed as we speak. I don't know about you, but I think we should get out of here.'

I nodded and hauled Nat to her feet. She looked a state, with blood trickling from her ears and her clothing torn and bloodstained, but at least she was alive.

Glancing down at the face of the man I'd killed, I shuddered as I remembered how I'd felt when I'd seen him about to kill Nat. After what had happened back in Afghanistan, I'd always sworn that I'd never kill again. But, when the moment had come I'd reacted, done what needed to be done to save Nat's life. Now I felt sick. As if I'd betrayed a promise to myself.

Pushing the emotions to the back of my mind, I offered up the pistol to Merrington. 'Don't think I'll be needing that anymore.'

He nodded and took it. 'Right. Speaking of which, it might be better if we count him as one of our casualties, if you get my drift?'

I shook my head. 'I just shot a man. Right or wrong, lawful or not, I have to take responsibility.'

Merrington raised an eyebrow. 'You think? The weapon is registered to me. We had men in the room and who knows what might have happened?'

I shook my head again. 'Thanks for the offer, but I *have* to take responsibility.'

'No you don't.' he said forcefully. 'You're a good copper Rob. I'd hate to see you lose your job over something like this. Take the chance I'm offering you.'

I paused, about to protest again when something stopped me. Would it really be so bad to let MI6 take the blame for the shot? The room was full of bodies and as Merrington had said the pistol was registered to him. Providing Nat and I both kept quiet, who would know any different? Finally I nodded. 'That's a pretty big favour I'd owe you.'

'Not really, without you we never would have stopped this from happening. Without both of you. Now get her out of here and let me start clearing up the mess.'

'Thank you.' There wasn't really anything else I could say.

He grinned as I led Nat away from the smoke and the death. She leaned on me heavily, unsteady enough that I suspected she'd ruptured both her eardrums. We didn't speak on the way up, both of us too preoccupied with what had just happened. As we got further from the server room we began passing more and more people, police and MI6 officers in their blacks. As we emerged into the main reception area, it was like some kind of crazy law enforcement festival that had been decorated by someone with a penchant for police tape.

Firemen in full breathing apparatus were hurrying about while paramedics stood by clutching large green bags and oxygen cylinders. As soon as we were spotted, a pair rushed over and took Nat off my hands, leaving me to slump on a brightly coloured sofa for all of about ten seconds before Burke appeared out of the crowd.

'You look like hell.' he said as he reached me.

I glanced up, almost too tired to raise my head now that the adrenaline was gone. 'I feel it.'

'So what happened?'

I shrugged and accepted the bottle of water he offered me. 'Well sir, it's kind of a long story.'

'SO YOU got your killer then?' Burke asked as I finished. We'd walked back to the Nick together and now sat in his office. Or at least I was while he stood with his back to me, looking out over the car park. I'd taken Merrington's offer and kept quiet about my part in the shootings, justifying it with the knowledge that I could do more to atone for it by staying a copper than I would if I lost my job.

'Yes sir, so it seems. Of course it'll come out when the weapons he was carrying get tested for forensics, but he's the only suspect that really makes sense.'

Burke nodded and blew out a long breath. 'You've done some good work here Rob. There were times in the last few days when I thought the city was going to turn into a bloodbath, but you seemed to have pulled it out of your arse, as they say.'

'It was hardly just me sir. Merrington and his lads pretty much saved the day, and my team all played their part. Not to mention all the other officers who worked on it. Even Riley did a good job with the interview plan.'

'Yes, well they'll all be getting commendations, which you'll be writing up as lead sergeant. Except Merrington of course. And incidentally, I've seen the footage of what you did at the hospital and quite frankly I'm amazed you're still with us.'

Something he said tugged at a memory and I sat forward, as I tried to focus on the thought.

'Rob?'

I held up a hand for him to wait. I saw him stiffen slightly but he held his tongue until it hit me. 'Uh, sir, I think we need to look at something.'

'What?' Burke asked.

'CCTV from the rear of Taverner's flat. Something just occurred to me.' I stood quickly and led him down to my office, refusing to say more. I needed his thoughts on the matter and I didn't want to pre-bias him.

Sitting on my desk was an evidence bag with two CDs in it. Pulling one out, I saw that it was the CCTV footage that had been sent up to Sussex House for copying. Sticking it into the PC, I pressed play and the grainy picture of the man coming down the staircase with the bag over his shoulder bloomed to life, clearer and sharper than the original, but not by much.

'This is time-lapse sir, and at first I thought that accounted for the jerky movements. Tell me what you think.'

Watching it again, this time knowing what to look for, I could see that the man on the tape, however poor quality, wasn't the man I'd shot earlier. Burke leaned so close to the screen I thought his nose would touch it.

'Is he limping?' he asked finally.

I nodded. 'I think so sir, and if I'm right then our man from earlier wasn't the killer.'

'Then who was?' Burke asked.

'Give me a lift to custody and I'll show you.'

'THE TIME now is 1754 hours on Saturday 19th August, and we're in an interview room at Sussex House Custody Centre. I'm Detective Sergeant CS462 Steele. Can you tell me your name and date of birth please?'

'You know it already.'

I sighed exasperatedly. 'Just say your full name and date of birth please.'

'Billy Collins, 12/7/74.' came the reply.

'Thank you. Do you agree that there is no-one else present in the room?'

'Yeah.' He grinned, nonchalantly.

'Thank you. You have the right to free and independent legal advice, which you've again declined. Can I ask why?'

'Because you've got shit on me, and you've kept me over twenty-four hours so you're fucked.'

'Thank you for expressing your strong opinions on the matter. That right is ongoing and, if at any time during the interview you feel the need to exercise it, the interview will be stopped until legal advice has been obtained for you.'

'Can we just get on with it?' he yawned.

'Fine.' I tried to keep the satisfaction from my voice as I delivered my next words. 'Billy Collins, I'm arresting you on suspicion of the murder of David Taverner and Reggie Brown. You do not have to say anything, but it may harm your defence if you do not mention, when questioned, something which you later rely on in court. Anything you do say may be given in evidence. Do you understand the caution?'

His eyes went wide. 'Murder? I ain't murdered no one!'

'Well you'll get a chance to explain that after I've asked you a few questions, won't you?'

'I ain't saying shit.'

'Where were you at 1900 hours on Wednesday 16th August?' I pressed.

'With yer mum.' Billy shot back, but there was a raw edge to his voice.

'Funny man. Were you in the area of Oriental Place in Brighton?'

'Never heard of it.'

'It's a road that leads up from the seafront by the West Pier. Nice houses mostly turned into flats. You know, the sort with wrought iron fire escapes at the back.'

Collins' eyes flickered for a second and his breathing quickened before his game face dropped back into place. 'Why do I give a shit about fire exits?'

'Good question. Do you have access to a van, Billy?'

Again the flicker in the eyes. 'No, I've got... had a car, but you lot pinched it.'

'How tall are you Billy?' I asked.

'Eh?' I was breaking all the rules by chopping and changing the questions around, but I wanted to throw him into a spin and so far it was working.

'It's a simple question Billy, how tall are you?'

He paused before answering. 'Six foot.'

'Speaking of foot, I can't help but notice that you've got a problem with your right one. What happened to it?'

'What?' Billy looked perplexed.

'Your foot, or more specifically your right leg. You have a problem with it, don't you?'

He shrugged. 'So?'

'So it makes you walk quite distinctively, doesn't it?'

He shrugged again. 'Dunno, never seen meself walk.'

'I can remedy that.' I pulled a CD from the bag by my feet and held it up. 'I have here exhibit TB/01, a CD working copy of a CCTV tape that shows the rear of David Taverner's flat at the approximate time of his murder.'

Billy was sweating now, his breathing coming in short, fast gasps.

'Maybe this would be a good time to get a solicitor?' I asked, placing the CD in the machine and pressing play.

Collins folded his arms and shook his head. I guessed he was waiting to see what was on the disk before making a decision. To be honest he wouldn't be disappointed – the quality was terrible.

'For the benefit of the tape the CD shows a male matching Mr Collins description walking down the fire escape carrying a large bag over his shoulder.'

'That could be anyone!' Collins interjected, but I could see a glimmer of fear in his eyes.

'It could be, Billy, but it's not anyone, is it?'

'Could be,' he was trying for defiant, but hitting sulky - and fast moving towards desperate.

'We believe that the bag contained a woman named Gemma Hallett. You're a strong lad, aren't you Billy?'

He blinked nervously but tried to sound aggressive. 'I'm getting fed up with this.'

'So have the interview stopped and get a solicitor. I'm sure that'll help you.'

I could see that he wanted to, but he was caught in the trap of thinking that if he asked for one now it would be a sign of guilt. It was almost funny watching the internal argument waging war in his expression.

'Just get on with it,' he spat finally. 'You've got fuck all.'

'So you're saying that you don't want a solicitor?'

'Don't need one.'

'Well, if you're sure. Going back to the CCTV. Even allowing for the time-lapse, I'd say that the person on the tape is walking in a very distinctive manner, wouldn't you?'

He shrugged. 'Dunno.'

'So, going back to the way *you* walk, Billy. Why do you walk the way you do?'

'I got shot in the leg.'

'Sounds painful. Do you have to compensate for that in any way?'

'What?'

'Do you have to compensate. Do you have any special aids that help you walk?'

'My shoe.'

'Yes, your shoe. *This* shoe in fact.'

I held up a white trainer with a built up sole.

'So you're six foot tall exactly?'

He nodded. 'Yeah, they measure me every time I come into custody.'

'With your shoes on or off?' I asked.

'What difference does that make?'

'About the difference between six foot and six foot two I'd guess.'

'Eh?'

'Have you ever heard of firearms positioning forensics, Billy?'

'You what?' He looked confused.

I smiled at him. 'I thought not. It's when you put together a crime scene from bullet holes and angles.'

'What about it?'

'That happens to be my speciality. I've taken all sorts of measurements from the wounds on the two dead men, and you'll never guess what I've discovered.'

'What?' He spat the question defiantly but he knew that I knew and I could see his mind racing with a way to get out of it.

'The shooter was at least six feet two. I'm guessing that that's how tall you are with your built up trainer on. Am I right?'

'That don't mean nothing, there's loads of tall blokes out there.'

'Yes it does Billy, because there was one measurement that was puzzling me slightly until I thought about it long and hard. Normally I can tell the height of a shooter with a tiny margin of error, but this one had me stumped. There might be a lot of tall blokes out there, but how many have links to both the dead men and are only that tall *on one side*?'

He spat on the floor. 'Whatever. I want my solicitor.'

I smiled sweetly at him. 'Of course Billy. The time is now 1802 hours and I'm now switching the machine off.'

I pressed the button on the machine and it clunked loudly. I began to whistle The Girl from Ipanema as I took the tapes out of the machine and began writing on the labels.

'You think you've got me, don't ya?' Billy asked finally, unable to bear the cheerful tune any longer.

I looked up at him and smiled.

'I certainly hope so, for your sake if nothing else.'

'What do you mean?'

I shrugged. 'You remember that MI6 bloke from earlier?'

He nodded. 'Yeah.'

'Well he's hanging around outside and he's desperate to drag you off to Paddington Green custody up in London, where they take all the terrorists.'

'Terrorists? I'm no fucking terrorist!'

'I agree, but the men you were working with were. Turns out they were planning to blow up the American Express building and unless you give our man from London something to work with you'll be tried for assisting in the commission of an act of terrorism.'

'You're just trying to get me to talk.'

'Yes, I am. But I'm doing it because I think that despite everything you've done, you're not a terrorist. I know you killed those men, and I want you to serve time for what you've done, but I also think you've got a chance to redeem yourself in some small way and help us put the final pieces together. If we can work out exactly what happened then we can stop this from happening again.'

'He can't take me away, you've already kept me over twenty four hours!'

I shook my head. 'He can do anything he wants. He's already had MacBride spirited away to God only knows where.' I'd found out about that on the way up to custody, and although I'd been less than happy, I hadn't had time to speak to him about it.

'You what?'

'And you're next. Of course, I can't *make* you talk, but I'll wager by the time MI6 has finished with you you'll be telling them what you had for dinner when you were five. I hear they can be very persuasive. Of course, if you tell me how you were ordered to do it, and why, then that might help...'

Billy swallowed a few times, eyes closed as he came to a decision. When he opened them again they were flat and dull, devoid of their usual arrogance.

'Turn the tape back on.'

'Are you sure?'

'If it'll keep me away from him, yeah, I'll talk.'

My hands were shaking as I put a fresh set of tapes in. I'd just gambled heavily and won. If Collins had picked up even a sniff that I was lying, the whole thing would have fallen apart. I looked up as the door opened to admit a pretty police officer I hadn't seen before, all dark hair and big brown eyes. Rather than the usual tie, she wore a cravat in black and white check over her shirt.

'Sorry Sarge', she said with a smile, 'did your prisoner want water?'

I looked questioningly at Billy. I hadn't asked anyone for water but he nodded and took the proffered cup greedily, draining it in one go. The officer took the cup back and closed the door with a smile. Billy's eyes tracked her as she left the room and I waved to get his attention.

'You ready?' I asked, finger hovering over the play button.

He nodded, drawing in a breath and preparing to tell me everything. I pressed the button and sat back as words began to spill from Billy's lips in a flood that, once started, seemed impossible to stop.

91

NAT SQUEEZED my hand and I looked over at her from the chair next to her hospital bed. She'd been put in a private room with an armed officer on the door - more, I suspected, as a mark of respect than from any fear that she was under threat.

Every firearms officer in the force was on duty and they were struggling to find jobs for them all that didn't involve driving around the city showing a presence.

'So are you going to tell me what happened then?' she asked in a croaky voice.

'Yeah, if you feel up to it.' She'd been asleep when I'd arrived, then woken for a few minutes before drifting off again.

She nodded. 'Can I have some water?'

I passed her a cup and sat back while she drank. When she was done she lay back on the pillows and waved a hand at me.

'Spill it then, before I beat it out of you.'

'Bring it, sicknote. Where do you want me to start?'

'Did Collins admit to killing Brown and Taverner?'

I nodded. 'At MacBride's order.'

'Why?'

'Well it turns out that Merrington was right. They were bringing men into the country illegally, and those men were the ones who we met this afternoon. They knew that the men were being brought in for a particular job, which they were supposed to be part of. As far as I can figure, Taverner got cold feet and decided to turn straight so they got rid of him.'

'But why kill Brown as well?'

'He and Taverner were like father and son. If they'd killed Taverner and not Brown, the old boy probably would have come to us with everything. At least that's what MacBride suspected, so he had him offed as well.'

'What about the boat being blown up?'

'Collins claims he had nothing to do with it, says it must have been the others.'

'Do you believe him?'

'Actually, I do. I've checked his records and he was in the army for about twelve weeks when he was eighteen. He got his marksman immediately and there are notes on his file that say he excelled with pistols to the point that they suspected he'd been handling them since he was a kid, but he's had no explosives training. Whoever put that bomb on the boat knew what they were doing.'

'Did MacBride and Collins know what was going to happen at Amex?'

I shook my head. 'No, they thought they were robbing the place. It seems that a man named Yuri got to know MacBride through the casinos, then came to him asking if he knew any reliable men for a less than legal job. MacBride went for it hook, line and sinker and got straight into bed with the group. If it hadn't been for him, they probably wouldn't have got anywhere near as close to pulling it off.'

'Rob, I saw the kind of firepower they had, they could have just walked in through the front door.'

'No, they couldn't. The plaza in front of the building is totally covered by CCTV. Before they got halfway across it everything would have been locked down and they'd be calling us and screaming for help. For it to work, they had to get inside that loading bay.'

Nat nodded and closed her eyes. I thought she'd drifted off and gathered myself to leave, but her eyes flickered open as I moved.

'Don't you dare; I haven't finished yet.'

I threw a salute and settled back into the chair. 'What next?'

'What about Gemma?'

'She was just an unlucky coincidence. Collins didn't expect her to be at Taverner's flat, and he was only paid for one kill so he knocked her around the head and when he took the gun back to the big chap, Petr, he gave them a present to say thank you for letting him borrow it.'

'He *gave* her to them?'

'Apparently. He was quite clear that he wasn't paid to kill her, I think by telling me he was trying to score brownie points in some fucked up, twisted way. Personally I think he was hoping that they'd use her and then cut her throat so she couldn't identify him, but he got a bit vague when I pressed that point.'

'I'm not surprised. Can she ID him, do you think?'

I shrugged. 'I don't know, but I doubt it. He was wearing a balaclava when he went in. She's still pretty shaken up.'

'Where is she now?'

'On the floor below with three officers keeping the press away from her room. Her daughter's back with her though, and they both seem happy enough.'

'God, I can't imagine what it must have been like for her...' She tailed off and her eyes glazed slightly. I guessed that she was probably remembering how close she'd come to the same fate today and I tried to think of something that would take her mind off the dark memories.

'On the plus side, my sister insists that you come over for dinner as soon as you're out of here.'

'Really? I'd love that, she seems really nice.'

'I agree, her brother's a bit of an arse though.'

'Tell me about it.'

'Thanks. I'll remember that when I'm writing up the commendations. Oh, and we need to have a conversation about a window, apparently, but that can wait until you're better.'

She gave a laugh which tailed off into a hacking cough. I refilled her cup and passed it to her.

'Thanks Rob. What about you? I thought they would have suspended you by now.'

I nodded. 'They would have done if I hadn't taken Merrington's offer. As far as they're concerned all the shooting was done by MI6.'

Nat fixed me with a look. 'Speaking of which, I owe you a huge thank you.'

I waved it away, feeling my cheeks burn. 'You would have done the same.'

'Of course I would, but that's not the point. I would have missed, for one.'

'I'm sure you wouldn't.'

'You didn't see the mess I made of the wall. But seriously, are you okay?'

I opened my mouth to say something funny but nothing came to mind.

Realising that Nat was still looking at me, I shrugged.

'Honestly? I don't know. I suppose time will tell. I promised myself when I left the army that I'd never use a firearm again, but then I wound up working firearms in the police, although thank God I never had to fire my weapon in anger. When I left there, I told myself the same thing but here I am today shooting someone, albeit for a good reason. Who knows, maybe it's like smoking and you can never really give it up.'

She reached out and took my hand.

'I'm sorry you had to do that for me.'

'I'm not. I nearly fell apart when I saw him standing over you...' I tailed off as the image replayed itself in my mind's eye. I shook myself and forced my eyes back up to meet hers. 'Anyway, I haven't finished telling you about what happened. So it turns out that Merrington had his blokes lift MacBride from our custody, and he's started talking. They're exploring the links he's got with organised crime and with this Yuri feller, so I suspect we won't be seeing him again for a while.'

'What about Yuri?'

'Reading between the bullshit, they've got no clue where he is, or if they do then they want him alive and still operating so they can keep tracking him. Either way he's not our problem.'

'So we cracked it then, eh?' she asked with a smile.

'You know, I rather think we did.'

Still smiling, she laid her head back on the pillow and drifted off again, exhausted by the long conversation. Slipping her hand out of mine and resting it on the covers, I eased myself out of the room to find a very tired looking Merrington leaning against the wall outside.

'What are you doing here?' I asked, surprised to see him.

He gave a lopsided grin as he pushed away from the wall.

'Just wanted a chance to say goodbye. I've been recalled to London for a full debrief.'

'Oh. I thought you'd be around for a few days at least.' The thought of him leaving made me surprisingly sad. 'Can you at least stay for a drink?'

He shook his head regretfully.

'Sorry Rob, duty calls.' He stuck his hand out. 'Thanks for everything, and good job on nailing Collins. I honestly thought Petr was our man.'

I shook his hand firmly. 'So did I until I actually had time to think. Is your job always this high octane?'

He shook his head. 'God no. This last week has been about a year's worth of running around. Turns out I might be back down this way soon though. A few seconds before the timers were due to go off someone hacked into the Amex computers and shifted an awful lot of money through several servers to a Swiss bank account. We would never have discovered it if the servers had been destroyed.'

'So it wasn't a terrorist attack after all?'

He shrugged. 'Truthfully? We don't know. It might be that the money was taken for terrorism, it might just be that the whole thing was a cover for a robbery on a massive scale. We're investigating, but we'll probably never find out for sure. Whoever planned this was thorough in covering their tracks. Even with the data from the servers, they've barely left a trace of their movements.'

'Well let me know if I can help.'

'I will do, but I was thinking that maybe next time I come down you can show me the city properly, maybe without being blown up?'

'I'd love to. Just promise me you'll leave the guns at home this time.'

He laughed and walked away, disappearing down the corridor with a wave over his shoulder.

Suddenly I felt terribly alone. Merrington was gone, Nat was going to be in hospital for days and Karl was at home recovering. We'd won, but the cost had been high and I'd nearly lost two people I cared about deeply and an unexpected new friend.

The armed officer standing outside the door gave me a smile and I returned it as I walked away, my mind already chewing over the cases I'd left hanging during the investigation. We might have cleared the streets of MacBride and his gang, but there were a hundred other people fighting to take his place. Nature abhors a vacuum, as does the criminal underworld. By Monday morning there would be a fresh batch of stabbings, shootings and robberies to contend with, and so very few of us to stop it from happening.

Running a hand over my face and rubbing at gritty eyes, I headed home, secure in the knowledge that no matter how bad it got, for at least a few of those responsible for the crime that plagued our streets, justice had been served.

SCREAMING ECHOED through the custody centre, long, drawn out wails of agony that brought every officer within earshot running. Inspector Pruitt, the officer in charge of the Centre overnight, got to the door first with a speed that belied his fifty-one years. He hammered the code into the lock and swiped his card, wrenching open the door to see the prisoner convulsing, his face contorted into a rictus of pain and terror. Green froth dripped from his mouth and stained his chin as he screamed again, his voice hoarse.

Before the Inspector could so much as drop to his knees next to the prisoner, the man on the floor shook as if caught in an earthquake, his eyes bulging out so far that they appeared about to dislodge themselves. With a final drawn out scream, he died in agony, his eyes rolling up into his head as his body stilled.

'Fuck!' Pruitt swore as he looked up at the ring of horrified faces in the doorway. 'Get some medics in here now!'

A Custody Assistant ran off to make a call while an officer came into the room with a hand covering her mouth. Pruitt looked up at her.

'I've only just come on duty, I don't even know his name', he said as his questing fingers checked for a pulse.

'Collins', she said, unable to tear her eyes away from the corpse, 'his name was Billy Collins'.

93

DANNY MACBRIDE paced in his cell, trying to ignore the cat calls and shouting from the other occupants of Paddington Green Custody Centre. He'd been there for hours and no one had so much as given him a cup of tea.

'Oy, I'm dying in here!' he yelled at the door, and nearly jumped out of his skin when the hatch opened to reveal a pretty, dark-haired police officer wearing a smart cravat and holding a polystyrene cup.

'Sorry for the delay love', she said with a smile and an accent that MacBride couldn't quite place. 'It's been a hell of a day. I thought you might like some water.'

94

FIVE MINUTES later she stepped out of Paddington Green Custody Centre and walked three streets over to where she'd parked her car, ripping off her cravat and dark wig and dumping them in a bin on the way.

Tying her blonde hair up into a ponytail, she unlocked the car and grabbed a dark sweatshirt off the back seat, pulling it over her police shirt before getting in. Thus disguised she knew that no one would recognise her now, from the officer she'd fooled into letting her into the custody centre to the sergeant she'd convinced to let her into the cells themselves.

She smiled to herself with the satisfaction of a job well done as she pulled away, losing herself in the anonymity of the heavy London traffic without a trace.

57246326R00265

Made in the USA
Charleston, SC
08 June 2016